The Sidewalk Shadow Disengages Gravity

By Christopher Wright

With Illustrations by Evan Shelley

Lafayette, CA

THE SIDEWALK SHADOW DISENGAGES GRAVITY

Library of Congress Control Number: 2013918086

ISBN: 978-0-9827930-2-2

Printed in the United States of America

This book is dedicated to dinosaurs.

They died so that we might live.

Previously

There was me, Victor, and this cabin in the woods that was apparently the nexus of realities. Somehow the doors got opened, and all the wildest shit you've only ever imagined started popping up everywhere all at once.

Lots of people died.

Fortunately, I didn't know lots of people. And the ones that I did know I've mostly forgotten about. They were alright, I guess, but I've met way better people since.

Like Emma.

Emma isn't her real name, but she never liked her real name anyway. We met right when the world got awesome. So naturally we embarked on a really confusing road trip. In my defense I was probably very dehydrated and going a little crazy. Also, I didn't really care that much what happened. But hey, on our trip we met Jimmy! Emma shot his brother in the face and we've all been friends ever since. He kind of sucks though. Eventually this obnoxious, prophetic robot told us we had to go to the cabin to fix everything or whatever. And then there were these paper superheroes and villains, and Jimmy died, and sprites or fairies or something showed up, and Jimmy came back kind of evil but not all that evil because we're still buddies, and maybe dino-pirates were involved too, and blah blah blah…

Long story short, I burned that cabin down. Mostly to get away from these two other versions of me I encountered inside. They were driving me insane. Both figuratively and literally.

After that, we'd earned some rest and relaxation. Emma and I got nice and cozy, and I'm sure the rest of our weird crew of misfits did stuff too. But I tried to avoid them as much as possible. Just when things were getting perfectly sexy and boring, I got abducted by inter-galactic slave traders. It was pretty much just like summer camp in that it was for chumps and losers. I did get to lead a slave revolt, though, and that was pretty fun. All the other slaves died, but they were dicks. All that really matters is that it led me to meeting Captain Valiant. He was the Bill Murray of the ship, if you envision the ship as the movie Meatballs and bother remembering that thing I just said about summer camp. Other than that he's not really like Bill Murray at all.

Valiant and his lieutenant, Sera, ended up teaming up with my ragtag crew on a journey to Candy Island. Like most places I visit, the island ended up exploding, and pretty much all its citizens died. Except for the ruler of Candy Island, Candy Princess, and a large candy heart I like to call Chalk.

A lot of other stuff happened after that, like Chalk and me winning a dance contest and Emma being murdered by Candy Princess and then me having to go to Hell and kick the Devil's ass to save her. Unfortunately, outside of Hell Emma is all incorporeal and invisible. Not the greatest qualities for a girlfriend to have. It's alright, though, the Devil has a decent set up and is a total pussy.

Anyway, we ended up thwarting Candy Princess's attempt to turn the universe into a candy paradise. In hindsight that may have been a mistake, but Emma deserved some sort of revenge. Besides, candy seems to have an odd penchant for eating humans. It'd be kind of a hassle to be on the run from flesh eating gummy bears all the time.

After the battle wound down, I grabbed a bunch of colorful pills spilled on the street and swallowed them hardcore in order to rejoin Emma down in Hell and probably have ghost sex. Which brings us to…

Currently

I'm pretty much just lying on the ground waiting to die—because that pill thing just happened—and thinking about what ghost sex will be like. I'm guessing tingly.

"What are you doing?!" Jimmy is yelling at me as if he hasn't been here the entire time.

"I'm not repeating myself," I tell him. "If you didn't listen the first time it just means you're a terrible friend."

Captain Valiant appears over me with Sera in tow. "What's all this commotion?"

"Victor just swallowed a bunch of pills," Jimmy is pretty much panicking.

"What kind of pills?" Sera asks, though she doesn't seem too concerned. Jimmy just kind of motions around the ground. Who knew he was so worthless in stressful situations? Me. I knew. But it's still disappointing.

Valiant takes a knee and picks up one of the pills scattered about the street. He examines it closely before putting it in his mouth. He appears to probe it with his tongue for a moment before biting down. "Mmmm. Chocolate."

"Huh?" I say as I pick up another pill and eat it. "Oh hey! M&Ms! Awesome!"

"Y-you tried to kill yourself with M&Ms?" Jimmy asks, probably still trying to get a grasp on the situation. I'd say he's not the sharpest knife in the drawer, but in a world full of knives, Jimmy is a life jacket. Useful in certain situations, but mostly worthless and a complete fashion faux pas.

"No, I tried to kill myself with mystery pills. It just turns out that the mystery was that they were chocolate. Now if someone would kindly shoot me…"

"How did you not notice the M's on each of them?"

"Are you still on that whole M&M thing? Jimmy, that was like so many seconds ago I can't even be bothered to count. They were delicious. End of story. Now somebody please kill me!"

Valiant laughs heartily. "You have your entire life to die, Victor. We just won a *valiant* battle. Now is the time for celebration."

"That's exactly what I'm trying to do," I say, "I need to get back to Emma."

Understanding dawns upon his face. "Ah, victory sex. The fourth most satisfying of all possible love making endeavors."

"You do remember that we know how to get to Hell without, you know, dying, right?" Sera says.

"Yeah," I say, "but I've already made that trek like a thousand times today."

"It was twice," says Jimmy.

"Twice there *and* back," I correct him.

"So four times," he says.

"I'm getting really fed up with your attention to detail, Jimmy. And all I'm saying is that dying would be so much faster than all that walking."

"It would certainly be the most efficient way," Valiant agrees. "Although it's often the journey on which we find *adventure*." Goddamn his impeccable logic. "Besides, the Devil's little playground will make a fitting venue for our victory parade, and I'm sure the Lieutenant would like to see Emma again."

"I would," Sera affirms.

"Fine," I say. "Let's just get this over with." After Valiant gets a few more pictures for his scrapbooks amongst the rubble, we head off towards the Adventure Galley. "You know, Jimmy, a real friend would have killed me when I asked them to."

Jimmy shakes his head as Sera says, "Next time you ask to be shot I'll gladly do it."

"See," I tell Jimmy, "that's real friendship."

KILLING TIME

Prologue

Her trips through time are one too many and her robotic heart is failing; she will persist. Seventeen centuries have passed since she last slept and Panik knows that she only has three more before chronothetics set in. No matter. She can bear it one last time. After dining with the clockwork godheads of the 42nd Century, chronothetics is a blue-shaded dream of the 18th renaissance of physical bliss. The clockwork godheads touch is ecstasy; their kisses madness. She indulged in both copiously and without abandon. Her mind hasn't been the same since. She sees in terrifying, indescribable colors that only get brighter in the dark. But she had accomplished her mission. She recovered the piece.

Panik had been there at the 7th Age of Vicious Enlightenment when it achieved totality and, in that moment, crystallized in murderous perfection. Without hesitation it shattered into 9,080 shards of chaotic desire. Several thousand of which were hurled into the continuum, sending violent ripples every direction in time. Over 6,000 were recovered. Panik kept three for herself.

Before the clockwork godheads, she had battled the demon spawn of the 68th Century's fourth reckoning. They bled fear and fed off unhappy memories, but Panik bested them with her superior knowledge of the Twelve Hundred and Twelve Tantric Sorrows. Dreams bloomed in diamond shaped flower petals wherever they wept. But that was millennia ago. She can hardly believe she's almost finished.

Panik lets out a dissatisfied cough. She feels her skin starting to loosen as her fingernails begin to grow inward. There's an excruciating arousal seeping from her spleen, while a few bloodstained tears run down her left cheek. Her teeth throb to the melody of Venus's

Unparalleled Symphony. Chronothetics is imminent within one and a half centuries. Panik grabs for one of her three personal shards of the 7th Age of Vicious Enlightenment, a serpentine shade that twinkles whenever she half-smiles or is sexually satisfied. Neither is a common occurrence. The serpentine calms her bloodstream, allowing her heart to function in moments of great stress. She slices her forearm twice. Once shallow, once deep. The effect is instantaneous. Her eyes go soft and crimson. The arousal in her spleen expands; grows ice cold. Panik allows it to spread to the rest of her organs. The osmosis of arousal is something she has never gotten used to, but at least she knows her heart can take it now.

She watches the blood drip from her fingertips to the floor. It's completely transparent now. Copper coats her tongue as she cries blood into her mouth. Bleeding her tears onto her shoes, Panik sighs lackadaisically. The arousal has breached her heart. She jabs the serpentine stone into her scarred bicep and holds it there to be safe. Chronothetics is only decades away. She almost waited too long. A few moments more and her heart could have been lost. Whether she requires it or not is unimportant.

She will never give her heart to Time.

1

"How's this one look?" Emma asks, checking herself out in a mirror. "It looks about my size, right?"

"Pretty much," I say. She's trying out different bodies for a day out on the surface.

"Yeah, this one's close," she says. "The ass looks kind of big, though. It didn't look this big on the outside. Do you think the ass is too big?"

"It looks fine. It's a nice ass."

Emma turns to me sharply. "Nicer than mine?"

"No," I tell her. She glares a moment longer, but she's only teasing.

"I'm pretty sure the ass is bigger. The boobs are definitely bigger. Do you ever wish I had bigger boobs?"

"Not really."

"Oh," she says. And then quietly, mostly to herself, "*I* wish my boobs were bigger."

"That's because you're crazy."

"Says the guy who talks to himself."

"I've haven't done that at all since that first time you were, you know, inside me."

She crumples up her nose and frowns. "You make everything sound so filthy." She gives the mirror one last look. "I guess this body is good enough. Let's go before it really starts rotting."

We head to the shuttle that Captain Valiant left for us. We don't use it too much. Fuel is impossible to come by unless Valiant and everyone else come to visit. Besides, Emma and I don't leave Hell often. For obvious reasons.

I watch her walk, ready to support her if she stumbles, but she doesn't. "You're getting a lot better."

She looks at me, unsure what I mean.

"The body," I say. "Walking and all that stuff."

"You mean I no longer look like a paraplegic in an epileptic fit," she says.

"That's not exactly how I would've put it."

"Really, because that *is* exactly how you put it."

"Oh yeah! You looked hilarious."

"Just get in the shuttle," she says, practically shoving me in.

"Why do you care if that body is close to your actual body shape anyway?" I ask as the shuttle lifts into the sky.

"Because I want to go shopping so I can look nice."

"Sexy nice?"

"Just nice."

"What's the occasion?"

"Um," she stalls. "I'd rather not say. I want to make sure you actually come back down to Hell with me first."

"Why, what's happening? Is it bad? OH MY GOD YOU'RE BREAKING UP WITH ME!"

"What?"

"I can change," I plead. "I can try to change. Or pretend to change. I can totally put on the illusion that I have changed to make you like me again."

"I'm not breaking up with you," she reassures. "Why would I want you to come back to Hell just to break up? That makes no sense."

I think about it for a second. "Maybe you were going for some sort of literal metaphor of, uh…feelings?"

"I wasn't…I wouldn't…That makes even less sense than most things you say."

"So what's actually happening then?"

"Well, it's just that," she stops, looking around nervously, "my parents kind of want to meet you."

"Um," I say.

"They kind of died in that whole apocalypse thing."

"Um."

"And I kind of found them down in Hell the other day."

"Uh."

"And I told them about you and they really wanted to get together and I said okay so they're coming over," she says. "Tonight."

"I ssseeeeeeee," I say.

"Please don't be weird about this."

"Okaaaaaaay."

"Because you're being kind of weird right now."

"Well," I take a deep breath, "can you maybe also get some sexy nice clothes?"

Emma half sighs, half laughs and says, "Sure."

* * *

"So do you think they'll like me?" I ask Emma. We've both been ready for her parents to arrive for a while now and have nothing left to do but wait.

"The truth," she says.

"I guess," I say, though I'm hesitant now.

"Probably not."

"W-why would you tell me that?!"

"They're just a bit judgmental sometimes. Don't freak out about it, okay."

"Me freak out? Nah, it's cool, baby." By the time there's a knock on the door, I'm completely freaking out. Emma let's her parents in and greets them while I stand around awkwardly, hoping that maybe they won't notice me at all. But no such luck. They both approach me with wary smiles. Emma's mom looks a little like how I would have imagined Emma in 25 years or so if she'd, you know, lived that long. Her dad looks a bit like Jeremy Irons. If Jeremy Irons had no soul. Which is weird since I think all he is *is* soul at this point.

I shake their hands and I think I say hello? Oh crap! What if I didn't say hello? Too late, the moment has passed. There's no going back now.

"It's a pleasure to meet you, Victor," Emma's mom says with the vaguest hint of an accent.

I nod vigorously. I try to tone back the vigor, but it just won't stop. Why is my head filled with so much vigor?!

"So this is where you live now, Gisela?" Her father asks, also with a slight accent, as he looks around.

Emma's mom joins him and I take the opportunity to pull Emma aside and whisper, "I think these people might be spies."

"Nope," she says. "Just my parents."

"But they have accents, Emma. *Foreign* accents."

"That's because they're German, sweetie."

"Oh," I say, "Wait! Are your parents Nazis?"

"No, Victor."

"Pretty sure you're lying."

Emma sighs. "Why would I do that?"

"One," I explain, "to protect them. Hell probably doesn't like Nazis, and two, you're a compulsive liar."

"Sweetie, we've been over this. I only told you I was a compulsive liar to sound a little, I don't know, dangerous. Because I didn't know who I was dealing with."

"And I've told you, that sounds suspiciously like a lie.

Because it's ridiculous."

Emma's face goes all squinty. "Fine. Now will you come with me and help show them around?"

"Okay, but one more thing. Should I be calling you Gisela?"

"Uh, yeah probably. That won't be a problem, will it?"

"Psh, no," I lie.

Suddenly, Emma's dad is in front of me. "And how do you find yourself liking this Hell, Victor?"

"I uh," I start to panic as I feel everyone staring holes straight through me. What am I supposed to say? What do they want from me?! "I…I. I'VE TOUCHED YOUR DAUGHTER'S NAKED BODY!" Emma's jaw drops, but I can't even begin to read her parents' expression. Do they…maybe they…they must be expecting details? "Uh a-a lot," I say. "I've enjoyed it."

Silence.

And I'm fairly certain that silence is tantamount to consent, so this is actually going way better than expected.

"Alright," I say, "let's do this thing!" And I head off into the dining room. I'm sure everyone else will follow eventually.

* * *

Things have remained mostly quiet at the dining room table. Everyone is still consenting pretty hard over my previous outburst, forcing me to fill the silence all on my own.

"And then he just looks at him, filled with the rage and anguish of the illusion of his heart's desire being stripped away, and says 'Burn.'. Not even an exclamation point there. Just a period."

Then I hear Emma's mom—I really wish I'd bother to learn her name—whisper, "What's he been going on about?"

And Emma whispers back, “Superman, I think?”

“I’m sorry,” I say, “was that not clear?”

“Why don’t we talk about you instead, Victor?” Emma’s dad says. “We’d like to get to know you better, though we’ve already been told quite a bit.”

“You have? It wasn’t from a flock of blue jays was it? Because they are racist liars!”

Emma shakes her head. “I told them about you.”

“Ahh, well what do you want to know?”

“What about your family, dear,” Emma’s mom asks, “did they perish at the end of the world as well?”

I shrug. “I don’t know about my sister, but I think I saw my parents when I was first down here trying to rescue Emma.”

“You have a sister?” Emma asks.

“Allegedly,” I say.

“Emma?” Emma’s mom says.

“What’s that even *mean*?” Emma asks.

“Emma?” Emma’s mom says again

“Yes,” says Emma.

“What?” says her mom.

“Huh?” says someone else. It could have even been me. I’m having a hard time following the conversation.

“You said Emma,” Emma’s mom says. “Who’s Emma?”

“Who said Emma?” I ask.

“You did.”

“No I didn’t. I said, uh…Ella? Which is what I call your daughter whose name is clearly Gisela and not Emma.”

“I distinctly heard Emma,” says mom.

“As did I,” says dad.

“Well, Emma and Ella are pretty similar,” I explain.

"They don't sound all that similar," says dad.

"But they're alphabetically very close so—"

"Are you cheating on my daughter?"

"Dad!" Emma or Ella or whatever I'm supposed to call her says.

"Well," I tell him, "there was this time that I was drugged by a princess and—"

"Why would you bring that up?!" Emma yells.

"Because I have no conversational filter!" I yell back. "You know that."

She eyes me intently for a brief moment before saying, "Good point."

All-in-all, it's still going better than I expected.

* * *

After an intense POW style interrogation in which I reveal things I wish I could forget, Emma and her parents retire to the living room while I do the dishes. Eventually Emma joins me.

"Good night, huh?" she says.

"Does that mean your parents like me?" I ask, hopeful.

"Oh god no," she laughs.

"It's because I'm Jewish, isn't it?"

She grabs a towel and starts drying. "You aren't Jewish."

"But they don't know that."

"And they aren't Nazis," she says.

"If you say so." I pause as I finish the last of the dishes. "You know what we should do?"

Emma shakes her head.

"We should go hang out with Captain Valiant again!"

"You know that I'm dead, right?" she says.

"Sure, but you can always hitch a ride in me or some corpse."

"I happen to find both those options at least mildly disturbing."

"Oh."

"But we should definitely invite them back down here. It'd be nice to see them all again."

"I guess," I sigh.

"It's not like we're going to have to spend every night with my parents."

"That's good."

She smacks me a little for that one.

"Thanks for actually showing up tonight, anyway," she says and kisses my cheek.

Behind us, someone clears their throat. It's Emma's mom.

"We're going to be going now, Gisela," she says.

Emma hugs her mother. "It was good to see you."

"So we'll see you tomorrow," says Mrs. Emma as she heads out the door.

"Come again?" Emma says.

"Yes, dear. Tomorrow."

"Um," says Emma.

"Your father and I figured we might as well move in here. It's such a nice place compared to the rest of Hell. It will be just like when you were little."

"That sounds so…" Emma looks to me for help.

I lean in and whisper, "The word you're looking for is terrible."

"…terrific!" she says. I guess that's almost what I said.

"Until tomorrow then."

"Bye mom," Emma barely manages before her mom disappears, and with the slamming of the front door indicating her parents' departure she turns to me and says, "So *when* did you want to leave?"

* * *

The answer to that question, of course, was immediately. Especially after the Devil showed up at our door wanting to watch The Battle For Endor. I convinced him to postpone until tomorrow, and as soon as he was out of sight, Emma and I started running.

The journey out of Hell isn't all that bad, but it is tedious climbing out of the circles, and there is always the chance that you might run into someone you used to know. We're almost to the river crossing, however, so it looks like we're home free on that front.

"OMG! Victor!!!"

Or maybe not.

"Victor, is that you!"

"Let's just keep walking," I tell Emma.

"Not a chance," she twirls around, somehow forcing me to do the same.

"It totally is you!" shrieks my very own ghost of Christmas past.

"It *totally* is," Emma gleefully returns.

I try to smile. "Hi Teddy."

"I knew you'd remember your little Teddy Bear," the ghost chirps.

"Aw, she's your little teddy bear?" Emma mocks.

"His most cuddly-wuddly teddy bear ever!""

Emma offers her hand to Teddy. "I'm Emma and it is such a pleasure to meet you."

"OMG! How rude am I? I'm Teddy and you. Are so. Beautiful! I can't pull off this pale dead look at all, but you are, like, totally glowing. I *hate* you!"

"Right back atcha," I say.

"Ohhhhh, you and your crazy sense of humor," Teddy laughs.

"Well, I'm leaving now," I inform everyone.

"Waaait! You can't leave before you sing me that teddy bear song you used to sing to me!"

"There's a song?!" Emma asks.

"I have no idea what she's talking about." I really don't.

"Don't be modest, we're all dead here. And you have a wonderful voice!"

"None of that is in question," I say. "I mean, except the me being dead thing. But I still never used to sing to you."

"Of course you did," Teddy says. "There was you and someone else. You'd sing to me every night and…uh-oh! That might have just been an episode of Full House! I totally love that show! In any case we still need to catch up a bunch before you—" her eyes dart sharply to the left, spying another ghost in the distance. "Jonathan? OMG! Jonathan is that you!!"

And as quickly as she came, Teddy vanishes into the fray of spirits. Even for Hell that was a pretty uncomfortable encounter.

"So, ex-girlfriend, huh?" Emma asks.

I don't say anything.

"Looks like I've joined some pretty special company."

I remain quiet.

"Pretty. Hyper. Constantly happy and excited," Emma says. "Kind of reminds me of someone else you slept with."

Guess it's time to break my silence. "Just a couple of points. First, you actually liked Candy Princess before she murdered you."

"And I never said I didn't like Miss Teddy Bear. I'd probably cuddle the fuck out of her if she ever shut up."

"Second," I continue, "I only slept with Candy because I was sad and drugged. No matter how awesome it may have felt, I was still a victim of something."

"You might want to consider excising the last part from point two," Emma offers.

"Noted. And thirdly," I finish, "Teddy had one quality I quite admire in a woman."

"The willingness to have sex with you?"

"All the time," I say.

Interlude

He casts a long, dark shadow on the sidewalk pavement. Long like the day. Dark like the night. Day and night encompass all time, so perhaps his shadow holds within it all time. But that's philosophy and philosophy is for schools and ancient Greeks. Both of which are dead now. Dead like they tried to make him. But they failed, and through fire and immense perversion he prevailed. Because he's a winner.

In the months since the fire, he's killed, maimed, and tortured. All in the name of vengeance. And preparation. Because ultimately a victor must be a master of preparation. And he's always prepared. A lot of people have called him crazy. They're all dead now. Except for two. But he'll show them he's not crazy. Everything else is crazy. He's just trying to fix it all. That all starts right here.

His dark shadow caressing the sidewalk of a place he once knew, he begins the ritual with a single drop of blood.

He can already feel the disconnection.

And then the blood will really flow.

1.5

(How long before they get here?) It's been 10 minutes, Emma. (I'm just anxious to see everyone again.) Uh-huh, you just want to get inside Sera. (Could you please not make it sound so dirty?) No.

Having your girlfriend's spirit inside you can take some getting used to. At least I'm somewhat accustomed to having the company in my head due to a somewhat fractured psyche, but then I never much cared what I thought of myself the way I do with Emma. I'm still not entirely sure if she can hear all my inner thoughts.

(I can.)

That's awkward.

(Not just for you.)

I try to occupy my mind with the most innocuous things possible. Simply taking in the scenery seems harmless enough. The gate to Hell is apparently located in a pretty average suburb. Not some Stepford wife, homeowners's association community, though. The houses—or at least the ones still standing—look to have their own distinct personalities. It's not too different from where I grew up. I realize this might be the first time I've thought about my family, however tangentially, since all this madness began. Well, aside from actively avoiding my parents' ghosts in Hell.

(why don't you ever talk about them?)

They're boring and crazy.

(oh?)

Hey, I have a question: what happened to the clothes you were wearing?

(what?)

The clothes you got for the dinner with your parents. They were very tangible before we brought them into Hell. But then you slipped inside me and…are you naked now?

(I don't feel naked.)

That's weird, right? Because I

Zzzoooooooooop!!!!

Huh, I've never heard that noise before. Emma turns us around.

I hate it when you do that.

(whoa…)

What? I don't…oh!

About 100 feet in front of us, where our little house to Hell used to be, sits a sleek, ellipsoid capsule. Steam or smoke—I can't be sure which; possibly both—tendril from an apparent flawless surface. Then, somehow, it opens and she emerges. Hair matted, her bronze skin flushed, dripping a mixture of sweat and blood. She's stunning. Her eyes, a swirling, vibrant violent, lock onto mine. And she collapses.

"You. Quickly," she pants. "I need sex."

* * *

"My friends!" Captain Valiant proclaims as he marches from his bedchamber wearing only his remarkable smile. "The task is complete. Yet another life has been saved by my *valiant* love making prowess!" Our mystery woman emerges shortly thereafter. Her expression is unreadable, but she certainly looks healthier.

"It was sufficient," she says. "Captain, I would like to bathe before we dine, but I'm having some difficulty working your facilities."

"My apologies. Lieutenant, would you please assist the Lady Panik." Sera groans, but complies without further complaint. And at least I know Miss Mystery's name. I think. Panik doesn't make much sense as a name. Valiant joins me on the sofa in his quarters. "I must beg your pardon for not giving you a proper greeting earlier, but the lady's needs took precedence." I nod my assurance. "I must say that I've missed your company, Victor. You never fail to attract the most enticing *adventures*."

Normally I'd take this opportunity to heap more praise upon myself, but Captain Valiant is the one person who just might be more amazing than me, so another simple nod seems sufficient enough.

"I would go into some of the more erotic details," Valiant continues, "but I wouldn't want to offend your better half."

"Huh?" I reply. "You mean Emma? She's in Sera now. She's more comfortable inside women."

"Naturally. I can hardly think of a place I'd rather be. It appears I should dress myself for our forthcoming meal, but while I do let me regale you with the sensual tale of how I saved a beautiful young lady's life with my manhood alone. The date was this very day. The time: 27 minutes prior to right now. The Lieutenant had set a course for Earth, for we were to be rendezvousing with you and, within you, Emma. My man-bot, The Robot With No Name, busily prepared a most *valiant* feast. The Lieutenant's current lover and my resident spaceboy, Jimmy, was assisting in this matter."

I snicker at the idea of spaceboy Jimmy, assistant cook to the lamest robot this side of the Roboracle.

"Punctuality being one of the 13 keys to lasting friendship, we reached the specified meeting point posthaste, only to find a situation most dire! A striking woman struggling to cling to life! The throes of passion the lone means to stave off the throes of death. With you unable to perform due to the ghost of your lover living within, I, Captain Valiant prepared to embark on one of mankind's greatest *adventures*. Sexual intercourse! Could I rise to the challenge?

Absolutely.

"With barely enough time to situate the young maiden in my bedchambers, we exchanged names—as is the proper thing to do before exchanging bodily fluids—and with a *Valiant* Thrust, I entered her vaginal canal. I should explain, Victor, that the *Valiant* Thrust is a trademarked lovemaking technique I invented for just such situations as these. It has a success rate of 87%, I'm proud to say.

"And so it was that for the next 17 minutes and 37 seconds, utilizing the most calculated sexual procedures taught to me at the Brothel of Infinite Sadness, that I did save the life of the mystifying Panik. You may applaud as it pleases you."

And do I clap? Damn right I do. I don't stop until the Sera-Emma hybrid re-enter the room.

"Ah Lieutenant, I take it our guest is now properly acquainted with the ins and outs of our restrooms?"

"Yes sir," Sera says.

"Very good, why don't you and Victor head to the dining hall. I'll remain behind to escort the Lady when she feels suitably refreshed."

Sera/Emma nod and leave with me following close behind. Making our way down the corridors I decide to broach a sensitive subject. "Emma, I think it's time we had the talk."

"The talk?" she says with Sera's mouth. I can tell it's Emma because she's speaking with a poor accent. I think it's British, but who can really tell. She figured it would be the easiest way to differentiate between her and whomever she's tagging along with, which would be fine if it weren't so terrible.

"Should I let you two be alone for this?" Sera asks.

"Don't worry about it," I say. "We're best friends."

"Well, I'm *Emma's* friend."

"Same thing."

"Not really."

"Let's not get sidetracked," I say. "What we really need to talk about is threesomes."

Sera/Emma burst into laughter.

"I am not having sex with you!" Sera yells.

"Your words say no, but your laughter is arousing."

"That's Emma laughing," Sera blurts out between fits of giggles. "And it's really weird, by the way!"

"Whatever the case may be, I wasn't talking about a threesome with you. I was referring to the Panik situation."

The laughter dies down and Emma, in her awful cockney accent says, "Sweetie, you know I love having these pointless conversations with you."

"Naturally."

"But instead of continuing this, Sera and I are going to, um, not…" And with that they pick up their pace, making a beeline for the dining hall.

"You know I'm just going to bring this up at dinner, right?"

Neither Emma nor Sera acknowledge me.

"A woman almost died today, Emma. What kind of hero does that make me?"

"A hero's life is hardship," she says back. "Deal with it."

I take my time getting to the dining hall, stopping in my old quarters to change into something nicer. When I finally arrive, Jimmy has the audacity to greet me. "Hey, Vic."

"Shouldn't you be in the kitchen, spaceboy?" I ask.

"Nice to see you too," he smiles. "So what did you say to the girls to get them so worked up?"

"Who knows, I was just trying to talk to them about

threesomes."

As usual, Jimmy overreacts. "You can't have sex with Sera!"

"Damn it, Jimmy, I'm not trying to. And even if I was, I don't see what the big deal is. I'm awesome at it and I've already seen her naked."

"Dude, that's my girlfriend you're talking about."

I glare at Jimmy, annoyed. "Why is it that every time I see you, you have to remind me that she's your girlfriend? We all know, Jimmy!"

"Well why do you always have to remind me that you've seen her naked?"

I sigh. "Because it's haunts me, Jimmy. Like a lake that lies on the horizon listlessly; lifeless. The winds from an afternoon storm having just died down. It was gradually at first. For a time that breeze gasped in short gusts, stirring the lake's placid veneer. And then nothing. Shortly thereafter the sun dips below the water. Slipping, sinking beneath the surface. The brief light of day finally extinguished. And the lake reflects what it's left behind. Only the dark, Jimmy. Only the dark." He stares at me, speechless. "Also, she has rockin' boobs."

"Hey!" Emma/Sera yell from across the room.

"I'm sorry," I correct myself, "that was rude. She has rockin' *breasts*." I offer them two thumbs up to show that my error in decorum has been properly resolved.

Moments later Valiant and Panik arrive and we all seat ourselves, ready for a hearty meal. But before we can be served our new guest decides to formally—and bluntly—introduce herself:

"I am Panik, an applied Chronologist from the distant future. I've been led here by an important artifact I'm looking to recover. Have any of you seen something that looks like these?" Panik asks, her attention mostly focused on me, as she lays out three nearly identical items.

"Rocks," I say. "Yeah, I've seen rocks before."

"They look more like broken glass," Jimmy notes.

"Well, I've also broken tons of glass too," I mention. "Sometimes even with rocks."

"These are neither rocks nor glass," Panik corrects. "They are fragments of the 7th Age of Vicious Enlightenment."

"And that would be?" I ask.

"It's an Abstraction so pure it had no option but to manifest into physical form, its perfection then causing it to explode with beautiful agony."

"Of course..."

"Most of the pieces were easily recovered, but the sheer force of its destruction did allow several shards to rip through space-time. And I have recovered all but one of those. My time pod tracked the final piece to this era. And to that hillside on which I arrived. Yet its Terra Scan came up 100% negative upon arrival, with a 1.33% positive reading. There are only two possibilities to explain this anomaly, one of which is a distinct impossibility. So I ask you all again, have you seen, or do you have in your possession, something like these?"

We all say no in one way or another.

"Then space-time must have skipped a beat."

"Huh?" Sera and/or Emma say.

"At the tail-end of my travels I was experiencing the onset of chronothetics, a common affliction when traveling between space-time for too long. I was too weary to be sure in that moment, but I thought I detected an imperceptible jolt. Chronologic Arrhythmia is rare and dangerous. It means that I am exactly where I should be, for I must be, but where I should be is not where I am all at once."

"That makes total sense," I say.

“I've done my best to devolve my thought processes in order to communicate in this era, but some thoughts still cannot be adequately expressed. I can only say that I am in the correct space-time and not, all at the same time.”

“Whatever,” I say.

“Um, Miss Panik,” Jimmy interjects.

“Yes, masked boy?”

“Oh, well I was just wondering what happens if you don't find this thing. Like, what's it do?”

“The Abstraction will permeate through this space-time in cruel, bloodthirsty undulations. This era will drown in an unebbing tide of fury until it is no more.”

“Wait,” Emma says, “is this shard what caused the apocalypse? Will recovering it fix things?”

“No,” Panik says. “This is The First Reckoning of the 21st Century, an epoch infected by a very different Abstraction. Lovesickness. Pubescent it may be, but potent as well. However, Abstractions attract one another and are prone to paradox. In any case, removing the fragment would only keep this time-space from being overwritten. This era is not conducive to retroactive time corrections.”

“That all sounds mildly serious and very confusing,” I interrupt, “but I have an even more serious question: We are going to eat soon, right?”

* * *

We did eventually eat. My meal was incredibly unhealthy. Filled with grease, fat, and sugar. Best meal I’ve had in ages. Down in Hell there just isn’t enough variety. Unless you like freshly grown vegetables. The Devil has a spectacular vegetable garden. But I didn’t survive the end of the world to start eating healthy. Afterwards, we went back down to Earth and are currently sifting through the remains of the Hell House. Panik wants to make sure all her future tech stuff is running properly. Or improperly…I didn't really follow anything she said after showing off those glass rocks. I've already delivered at least a dozen rocks to her and plenty of broken glass, but none of it seems good enough for her.

"Why do you keep placing these at my feet?" she finally asks.

"Because you went on and on about how much you like rocks and broken glass," I say. "Now you have a bunch to choose from."

"That's not what I said."

I shrug and wander up the hillside. Valiant decided to remain on the Galley, still needing to rest from his earlier heroic exploits. Emma and Sera are still avoiding me, and I'm always doing my best to avoid Jimmy and The Robot With No Name, so I go on alone. A little sunshine and relaxation will be nice, but, gazing out across the land, I realize there will be no rest for me.

"Everybody get up here!" I yell.

After everyone scampers up the hill Jimmy says, "What is it?"

"Can't you see?" I ask.

"All I see is grass and some cows," Sera says.

"Exactly!" I exclaim.

"Oh bloody hell," Emma says, most ridiculously.

"You called us up here to look at grass?" Jimmy says.

"Grass, Jimmy? Don't be stupid. Cows!!"

"Looking at cows is less stupid than grass?"

"I don't know, can you make kick-ass leather jackets out of grass? Damn, get your head out of your ass, Jimmy. And No Name?"

"Yes sir," says No Name.

"Contact the captain and tell him we've got some cow killing to do."

"Right away, sir."

"Don't do that," says Sera.

"Yes, ma'am."

"Wait, what?" I say.

"The Lieutenant outranks you, sir."

"Well, what's my rank?"

"You're a civilian, sir. You have no rank."

I grumble a bit while Sera smirks too much. Her satisfaction is irritating. Still, I try to make my case. "I think Valiant would be on board with this, though. I mean, leather jackets are *cool.*" I would have made a great lawyer, no doubt, with such irrefutable reasoning.

Sera shakes her head. Apparently she also went to imaginary law school.

I up my game by calling a new witness. "I bet in the future all the cool people still wear leather jackets. Right Panik?"

"I've worn the skins of many different creatures," she says. "Including humans."

"Your witness," I say.

"What?" Sera asks.

"Case closed," I inform.

Sera and Emma walk away without another word. Jimmy and No Name follow, leaving Panik and me alone atop the hill.

"So, uh, I guess I should probably apologize for, you know, not giving you 'the sex' when you asked for it earlier."

Panik stares, but doesn't speak.

"It's just that my girlfriend, Emma—"

"The spirit currently residing within the star child," Panik states flatly.

"Yeah…wait how'd you know that?

"Which part?"

"Either."

"Through my studies I acquired the ability to see clearly a person's soul. Yours is erratic and hard to define."

"Oh."

"We also exchanged introductions as they instructed me in the functions of Captain Valiant's facilities."

Realizing I never introduced myself I say, "I'm Victor, by the way."

"I know," she says. What a waste of time that was. "As for Sera, she's not the first star child I've encountered throughout the years. Their souls are brighter and more potent, and their touch is warmer. More pure. Although I've never joined with one physically."

"Okay," I say, having already lost interest in whatever question I'd asked. "All I really wanted to say was that I'm sorry Emma wouldn't let me save your life with my penis."

"Monogamy is Love's most difficult discipline. But the greater the difficulty, the greater the reward. I've never practiced it myself."

Despite having no clue what she's talking about, I nod. I don't want to continue down this road. Little more than silence passes between us for the next few moments. Panik periodically shifts her gaze from me to the cows and back again.

I finally break our quiet. "Can I ask you a question?"

Panik doesn't respond, but neither does she object.

"How exactly does the whole sexual healing thing work?"

"I explained this as we waited for our meal earlier."

"You mean that conversation continued after I stopped paying attention?" I say to myself.

Panik looks at me without understanding.

"So you aren't going to explain it to me?" I ask.

"No."

In my disappointment, I kick some rocks. Quickly realizing my blunder, I gather up as many of those rocks as I can and offer them to Panik. She just turns and walks back towards the others.

"I do not get her," I say to no one at all. With nothing else to do, I turn back to the cows. "I will wear your skin, cows," I whisper. "Someday."

* * *

"I don't know, it was pretty confusing," Jimmy explains. We are all, once again, gathered on the bridge of The Adventure Galley having finished surveying whatever it was that Panik was surveying. The Emma/Sera entity still aren't interested in my company, and Valiant is dictating something to The Robot with No Name, so I'm stuck with Jimmy. "She said that because of the stresses of time travel she had her organs replaced with some synthetic/organic hybrid versions of organs. And those are somehow powered by tantric energies. Like through osmosis, or something. I kind of got lost with how it all works."

"I don't ask for much, Jimmy," I say, "yet you always manage to let me down anyway."

"Hey," Jimmy objects.

"I'm just messing with you, buddy. I know you can't help the way you were born." I leave Jimmy behind as I head over to Valiant, who has finished with No Name and is now discussing something with Panik.

"Victor," he greets me, "the Lady Panik was just informing me that she retrieved some excellent data down at her crash site and hopes to have a much better idea of where to begin our *adventures* in a matter of days."

"Perhaps sooner," Panik adds.

"Now, my friend," Valiant starts, "I hear there was an incident down on Earth involving cows."

"Yeah," I tell him, "I was really hoping we might get ourselves some nice leather jackets, but no one was willing to contact you."

"Certainly you agree that ice cream is too delicious a commodity for us to go committing bovinacide," Valiant reminds me. "But worry not, one day we will come across a *valiant* cow who has tragically died during some epic *adventure* and we shall have our leather jackets. And from that day forth we will traverse the galaxies side by side, the envy of all the universe. Until that day, however, we must be patient, for patience is—"

"One of **Valiant's Virtues**," I finish, feeling foolish that I've once again shown such weakness to this magnificent specimen of a man.

"Right you are, my friend," Valiant grins.

"Captain," Sera interrupts. "We have an incoming message from the headquarters of the Inter-Galactic Legislative Omnipresent Operative."

"Ah, IGLOO HQ," Valiant affirms. "Patch it through, Lieutenant." Without another word, the oversized viewing port on the bridge is filled with a very large, very familiar, very smiling face. Sera and Emma groan and grumble.

"Captain Valiant, isn't it just the most lovely afternoon," Candy Princess beams all over the screen. "My friends here wanted me to—OH GOLLY! Is that Victor I see?!"

"Sup," I say.

"I've missed you. So. Much! Have you missed me too?"

"Um," I think. "Maybe a little?"

Sera's head snaps my direction, and I'm pretty sure I can

actually see Emma shooting anger beams at me.

"Hooray!" Candy Princess cheers. "The council asked me to pretty please ask Captain Valiant to come to the embassies to finalize some of his statements in the whole Dread Space Pirate incident in New York. And I said I would love to and since they also said pretty please how could I ever resist? But they also expressed interest in speaking with you, Victor, so I told them I would see what I could do and here you are. It's just so perfectly perfect, isn't it?"

"We would be happy to oblige the counsel, Princess," Valiant responds. "Let them know they can expect us on the morrow."

"I'm so excited I'm practically bouncing out of my dress!" Candy exclaims.

"I bet you are," Sera's voice mumbles, but so lowly that I can't figure if it was Sera or Emma saying it.

"Hi Sera!" Candy answers back. "Are you still mad at me? It's okay if you are, but I. Still. Like. You!" She punctuates the statement with a very pronounced shimmy. Sera immediately hits some button and Candy Princess disappears.

"Set our course, Lieutenant," Valiant orders.

"Yes sir," she complies. Moments later her body turns on me. "You miss her?" Emma asks with a false calmness.

"I said that *maybe* I do a *little*, and I inflected it into a question so as to pose doubt."

"You miss her?" Emma spits, less calmly.

"I didn't want to be rude," I say.

"You miss her!"

"To be fair she smells like sugar and spice and freshly baked chocolate chip cookies. It's intoxicating, Emma. It's intoxicating!"

"After all she's done?" Emma serves.

"Everyone makes mistakes," I softly return.

"She kidnapped Sera! She *killed* me!"

"You're still upset about that? Come on, Em, you killed Jimmy's brother. And Jimmy kidnapped you. In fact, I'm pretty sure I maybe kidnapped you when we first met. Also, we might have kidnapped Jimmy after that brother killing incident. Honestly, there's been a disproportionate amount of kidnapping between us and I'm still really confused about that whole time period and how we all became friends."

"He's got a point," Jimmy says.

"Shut up, Jimmy!" I actually think I could hear both Emma and Sera on that one. But at any rate:

"Hey, no one tells Jimmy to shut up but me. Isn't that right, Jimmy?"

"Um, I guess?" he affirms.

"We're going to bed. Don't follow!"

"Okay," I say, "but you're going to regret that decision."

With an angry grunt and a very crude gesture, they exit from view.

"All I meant was that it's only three in the afternoon. They're going to get pretty bored."

"You probably should have just apologized," Jimmy says.

"And you definitely shouldn't have sided with me," I tell him. "You live, you learn, James."

"James?" Jimmy mutters.

"And by the way, no you can't sleep in my room tonight."

"I wasn't going to ask."

"Sure you weren't l'il buddy." I walk off the bridge, heading nowhere in particular, with a smile on my face, wishing I'd just apologized. I don't like sleeping alone.

* * *

The rest of day passes far too slowly. And the night even slower than that. Sleeping without Emma is an empty feeling. I don't sleep well at all. Thankfully we reach the headquarters of IGLOO bright and early. Though out in space bright and early often doesn't mean too much, which is why I'm taken off guard when I step off the Adventure Galley into actual sunshine. I've been on a few space adventures since meeting Captain Valiant, but oddly we rarely visit other planets. When all of our adventures aren't leading us directly back to Earth—for some reason—we've only really visited big asteroids or space stations. I'm not sure what my expectations were. I've seen tons of sci-fi movies, and I used to eat Eskimo Pies all the time, but I see no signs of futuristic igloos anywhere. It's actually a very low key place. Reminds me of a small Dutch town—not that I've ever seen one of those—or the candy village back on Candy Island. Before it exploded. Candy Princess must like it here. Surprisingly, she's not here to greet us. All things considered, that's probably for the best. The escorts that do greet us are a creature with the head of an ugly bird and a lizard faced dude who might be the same guy who tried to arrest me back in New York. I can't really tell so I don't bother saying anything. I don't want to sound like a racist, after all.

Valiant orders Sera and No Name to stay with the ship, because apparently this place is a hotbed for thievery. It seems like everywhere we go is a hotbed for crime. But I guess that's what makes it so adventurous. Neither Sera nor Emma complain. They're still clearly angry with Jimmy and me. I'd be worried about it, if it didn't happen all the time. Besides, I did manage to drag Jimmy down with me. And that makes me happy. Panik also stays behind since she had no involvement in the New York incident and still has data analysis to do. I think.

Valiant, Jimmy, and I follow our chaperons to a cozy little waiting room. Valiant is immediately called in to give his statement, leaving just Jimmy and me. Again. Instead of paying any attention to him, I choose to focus entirely on a table littered with vaguely familiar looking food. I grab what I'm going to assume is a donut and pour myself a cup of some hot, steaming drink, hoping for coffee or hot cocoa. What I get instead is a piping hot, creamy substance of forest green. But the green slowly shifts into a mocha and then to white. Rhapsberry Cream!

I've only had this stuff once before, back on Candy Island, after I successfully saved some candy folk from a little self-sacrificing. They were going to jump into a volcano in order to keep it from erupting. I stopped them with an impassioned anti-sacrifice speech. No big deal, it's what I do. Naturally, Candy Princess threw us a party to honor my heroics, and there was Rainbow Rhapsberry Cream everywhere. Of course, that volcano did end up erupting and destroying Candy Island. But the party was amazing.

This Rhapsberry Cream is a bit different, however. Not nearly as bright and energetic looking. More rustic in tone. I sip gingerly, not wanting to scald my mouth, and am instantly transported to a small cabin in the forest. The place where Emma and I settled after the apocalypse calmed down. Fresh pine needles and maple syrup infuse the air with electric breakfast delight as Emma quietly chews a bite of pancake and I pretend to read a three week old newspaper. Basically, I'm in a Folger's commercial.

The memory is so strong it's like being punched in the face by a duckling riding a kitten. Soft and adorable. It's fucking relaxing. Floating in this fluffy reverie, I barely notice Sera enter the room.

"I thought you were supposed to stay with the ship," Jimmy

says.

"I am," Sera responds. "I just wanted to see you. I miss you." She embraces him gently. Normally this level of cuteness involving Jimmy would make me uncomfortable, or at least irk me slightly, but I'm flying way too high right now. Still, I never like being ignored when I'm in a room.

"What's with the time machine?" I ask.

"What?" Jimmy and Sera say together.

I motion to Sera's wrist. "You're wearing the time machine."

Sera looks at it uncomfortably. "Oh, um, Panik wanted to see it. She called it a 'cute toy'. Guess I forgot I still had it."

"Does this mean you're done being mad at me?" Jimmy asks.

"That's…complicated," she tells him. "Let's just say I'm taking a time out from being angry."

"So you're still going to be mad after this?"

"Yeah. Sorry."

"Sera, this is ridiculous."

"Humor me this time," she nuzzles up against Jimmy. "I just want to sit here with you for a minute."

"What about me, Emma?" I ask. Sera jumps slightly and looks around the room, but I get no answer. "The silent treatment it is, then." I go back to sipping on my Rhapsberry Cream, content to soak in my delicious memories.

"I should go," Sera says.

"I'll see you in a couple of hours, I guess," Jimmy says back.

Sera stands and Jimmy mimics her. She kisses him tenderly. "Next time you see me tell me this," and she whispers in his ear something I can't hear, but I think I see Jimmy blush. Walking over to the door she says, "Goodbye, Jimmy. I love you." Finally she turns to me, a weak smile tracing her lips beneath a pair of over-moist eyes.

"See you later, Vic."

And then she's gone.

"That was weird," says Jimmy.

"I'm pretty sure she's on her period, or something," I say.

"You always say that."

"And how often am I wrong?"

"Every time," he says. "You're wrong 100% of the time."

"It's either that or you're a terrible boyfriend. Because I'm pretty sure she was about to cry."

"Really? Do you think I should go after her?"

"Jimmy, I say this with the utmost sincerity. I couldn't care less."

"Well, at least my girlfriend is talking to me," Jimmy mutters.

"Emma and I aren't children. We don't take 'timeouts'. We let these things play out naturally. You know, let the anger build and build until it transforms into this hot sexual tension and—"

"Dude, she doesn't even have a body."

"So we just find other healthy ways to let out our anger. Like we kick the Devil in the balls or, I don't know, shoot your brother in the face. And then she gives me a hand job."

"That's what you consider healthy?"

"It's called being an adult, Jimmy. And it's only mildly disappointing."

Jimmy shakes his head just as Valiant makes a grand re-entrance into the room. Which means, thankfully; I don't have to continue this conversation.

"And that's the tale of the last I ever saw of Soul Destroyer: The Destroyer of Souls." Valiant is recounting to our former escorts. The lizard looking one starts to clap. And I think he might be weeping. It's pretty gross, but understandable. Captain Valiant's stories are enthralling.

"It's truly an honor, Captain," the lizard finally manages to spit out.

"It is, isn't it, Agent Klyzzzzt" Valiant replies. The bird faced agent keeps quiet and seems completely uninterested. What a dick.

"Victor, they'd like to speak with you next," Valiant informs me.

"Cool," I say and head off to be interviewed.

* * *

"Please take a seat," the bird thing says. "I'm Agent Twutternut, and you met Agent Klyzzzt during the New York incident."

I nod.

"First things first, why weren't you present at the first set of interviews immediately following the New York incident?"

"I was in Hell," I tell them.

"Meaning?"

"The place people go when they die."

Both Agents scan me up and down. "You don't look very dead to me, what about you Klyzzzzt?"

"Looks and smells alive to me."

"I was down there visiting my dead girlfriend."

"That's a convenient story," says Twutternut.

"Okay."

"And this girlfriend of yours, does she have a name?"

"Emma. Or Gisela, I guess. But mostly Emma."

"Buddy, your story is already showing more holes than Swiss whores."

"What?" I ask, in case I misheard.

Beak-face taps his throat. “Is there a problem with my translator? That’s a common Earth expression.”

“No it’s not.”

“Irrelevant. We’re here to talk about what happened in New York, not your love life. Sick as it may be.”

“You guys brought it up!”

“Just tell us what happened with the Dread Space Pirate Robots.”

“Wait, do you want to hear about New York or the pirate?”

“Is there a difference?”

“Honestly, I’m still trying to figure out the Swiss whores thing. I mean, do they wear less, thus revealing more or do they have some sort of genetic abnormality where they actually have more holes.”

“It was just an expression.”

“Bullshit, sir! BULLSHIT!”

Twutternut sighs. “We just need to hear about Robots’s in relation to what happened in New York.”

“Well…he didn’t have that much to do with it,” I say.

Klyzzzzt hisses and hauls me into a corner. “What are you doing? Didn’t Captain Valiant fill you in?”

“I don’t know. I listen to pretty much everything he says. But sometimes he has the robot or Jimmy tell me things, and I definitely do not pay attention to them.”

“Look, after I took the pirate into custody in New York, I had to tell the counsel that he was responsible for everything in New York in order to get the charges to stick. So just say he’s responsible for everything, alright?”

“So you’ll get in a lot of trouble if the truth comes out?”

“Well, no. I’ll just have a lot of paper work to fill out.”

“Say no more! I’ve got your back.” I march back over to the

interview table. “Ask away, birdman or woman!”

“The Dread Space Pirate Robots—”

“Is responsible for everything! He kidnapped my girlfriend—before she was dead—and then kind of took her on a date where she ended up being murdered! Which was really uncool on so many accounts! Then at some point he burned Candy Princess with some sort of pirate trick or something! He also planned on blowing up New York and blaming it on a bunch of monkeys! And I’m certain he molested Jimmy! I think sodomy might have been involved!

“But don’t bother asking Jimmy, he’ll only deny it. Out of shame. Whether that shame is from being sexually assaulted or because he enjoyed it, we will never know.”

Klyzzzzt hesitates before saying, “That’s close enough to what Captain Valiant said, right?”

The bird-cop shakes its head. “Fine, just bring in the next one so we can get this over with.” Klyzzzzt shows me out the door and summons Jimmy.

Before Jimmy can make a move, I do my best to muster up all of my sincerity. “It’s okay, Jimmy. You don’t have to be ashamed anymore. That room is a safe place.” He doesn’t respond, but he does look scared as he enters the room.

Klyzzzzt hangs back for a minute to grab some Rhapsberry Cream, leaving me to make small talk. “So how long is Robots in for?”

Klyzzzzt sips on his drink. “Huh? Oh, he escaped a few weeks back.”

“Well, what’s all this been about then?!”

“Standard procedure. The council wants a proper report so they can decide whether it’s worth expending resources to try and recapture him. Not likely, though. They’ve already had their trial, and that’s generally all they care about. Those things…freaky. By the way, the pirate left this behind for you." Klyzzzzt hands me a note.

Dear Victor,

It was a pleasure making your acquaintance at the Brothel, and our little duel of wits is one I will truly remember for a lifetime. Thus it is with great regret and a heavy heart that my reputation as a villain requires me to kill you. Just know that it is nothing personal. I'm certain you'll understand.

Until we meet again,

The Dread Space Pirate Robots

After reading it over a few times, one thing stands out. "He has impeccable handwriting." Klyzzzzt nods in agreement. I crumple the note up and toss it into some random corner. "So when you say that trials here are freaky, does that mean, like, sexually?"

"Big time," says the lizard man.

"Nice," I say.

* * *

I'm not really sure if I'm supposed to wait for Jimmy to be done or go back to the Galley, but as there's not much to do on the ship with Emma still mad at me—and also a ghost—I decide to hang out in the waiting room and drink entirely too much Rhaspberry Cream. As it turns out, there's no such thing as too much Rhaspberry Cream. I relive every quaint and quiet moment my life has to offer. If this is what dying is like then I'm ready to joyously slit my wrists and paint a masterpiece with my life…okay, so maybe there is such a thing as too much Rhapsberry Cream. But that doesn't mean I'm going to stop drinking it!

I've no idea how long this goes on for, because it kind of feels like my entire life is happening simultaneously. And there's a decent chance I'm either asleep, having a severely awesome drug trip, or bleeding to death. I'm feeling pretty good. All at once, both doors to the the room open. Jimmy and Twutternut emerging from one, and Sera from the other. Unexpected, traumatic flashbacks of Sera dripping blue and nothing else, Jimmy washing away in a wave of yellow, and Emma suffocated by a pool of her own red penetrate my personal space. Primary memories spanning a spectrum of visible emotion. The colors start to merge as a voice says, "Look who we ran into". It's Sera's voice, but whether it's her voice of memory or present remains unclear until the colors of my friends merge into one giant bright, white heart.

Cue slow motion!

"CHAAAAAAALK!" I scream with more enthusiasm than this room can bear.

The big heart adds a pink word to his face. VIIIIICTOR! it reads. At some point Twutternut attempts to step in front of me, so naturally I trip him. Chalk, seeing his opening, launches himself off the fallen birdman, soaring gloriously through the air, cartoonish hand extended. And we give this little planet the greatest high five it's ever seen.

"Hey," I say.

HEY reads Chalk.

And I go back to sipping on my Rhapsberry Cream.

* * *

After a while, Chalk convinces me to stop drinking and we get to catching up while Sera/Emma are being interviewed. Jimmy, being Valiant's spaceboy, went back to the ship to do spaceboy things.

According to my little candy friend, Candy Princess is in meetings all day, but has invited us all to dinner at the Candy Embassies. Knowing Captain Valiant as well as I do, declining isn't an option. More than likely he's already accepted for everyone, which is unlikely to improve my situation with Emma. My best chance is to get a few cups of the Rainbow stuff into Sera and hope that ghosts can still get high off whatever their host is ingesting.

Chalk says that he doesn't really enjoy the whole politics thing. According to him everyone here is a PUSSY ASS COCKSHAKE. I don't even know what that is, nor do I know if my little buddy was always such a foul-faced piece of candy, but I like to believe that I've had a big influence on him. He also tells me that Candy Princess has really cut back on her ingestion of human/human-like flesh, though she occasionally falls off the wagon. In turn, I tell him about meeting Emma's Nazi parents and Panik, and how I was this close to finally getting a leather jacket. I also make up a story about how I made the Devil cry by removing one of his Jar Jar Binks action figures from its original packaging. Mostly because I want to make sure Chalk still thinks I'm cool.

By the time Sera and Emma reenter the room, I'm rolling on the floor with laughter as Chalk jumps up and down clapping. I briefly feel Sera's hand on my shoulder as Emma deftly slips into my skin.

(What's so funny?) He just gets me, Emma. Are you done being angry? (I was prepared to continue raging for several more hours, but that thing with you and Chalk earlier was too fucking cute.)

Chalk and I go with a no-look high five.

(I did think knocking down Twutternut was a little rude, but he was a total dick during the interview so I changed my mind.) Sweet. (Besides, I really needed to get out of Sera. She and Jimmy need some privacy.) Gross.

"You know I'm still standing right here," Sera says, clearly irritated.

"Hey, we all know that you can't keep your thoughts to yourself when you have a ghost inside you," I reply.

"Emma and I do it all the time," Sera claims.

(It's true.) What?! (I think you might have some brain damage, actually.) Aww.

Sera laughs.

"Whatever, Twinkle," using her real name usually gets Sera's attention. The laughter dies and her eyes go all dark and scary. I'm going to take that as a good sign and breach a personal subject. "So what exactly did you tell Jimmy to tell you that made him blush so hard?"

Sera tries to blow me off. "I have no idea what you're talking about."

(I think that might be the Rhapsberry Cream talking, Vic.)

"I know what I saw. Probably! Look, you don't even have to tell me what you said, but on a scale of 1 to 10 how dirty was it?"

Sera socks me hard in the stomach. "Sorry about that, Emma." Emma uses my thumb to give her a thumbs up as she storms away.

I take a second to catch my breath. "That felt like an 8. Sera, you know that Jimmy can't handle anything higher than a 4. You're going to damage him!"

(Oh, leave her alone.) Fine, Em, but when Jimmy becomes some disgusting sexual deviant who spends all of his time at the Smile Factory in the Brothel of Infinite Sadness doing God knows what with Thor knows who, we'll look back on this day and know we could have prevented it. (When that day comes, I'll be sure to give you a prize.) That's all I ask. By the way, I think we might have to have dinner with

Candy tonight. (I know, Sera and I were still on board when the call came through.) Maybe we could blow it off. (Nah, Valiant insists Sera be there. I can't make her go through that alone. I'll probably hang out in her so we can grumble about it together. Hey, let's not go back to the ship just yet. I want to sightsee.) Captain Valiant says this place is full of crime. (We've got Chalk with us. I'm sure he'll protect us.)

Chalk's face reads I'LL FUCK'EM UP

We spend the next couple of hours wandering around, Chalk skipping beside us, stopping every now and again as he points out places of interest. None are all that interesting, but the sun is shining and the air is breathable so it's still pretty nice. After a while Chalk informs us that he has to return to the Candy Embassies to help prepare for dinner and, with a few goodbyes, he skips away.

(You know what would be fun?) I'm listening. (We should go out into the woods and get freaky.) Emma, if we got caught just imagine how I would come off. I'd look like a degenerate and a pervert! (Which is fine because you are both of those things.) In private. (That's what makes this fun!) For you, maybe. (Exactly.) Nope, I'm putting my foot down on this one, Em. (That's fine, because I can just pick them up.)

Sure enough, that's exactly what she does. Emma has us scampering through the strange forest like a couple of love sick teenagers who happen to have a single body. Do I fight it? Kind of! Am I turned on? Possibly! Will I continue to deny it? Absolutely!

(This looks like a good spot.) I can actually feel your satisfaction, you know. It's both endearing and nauseating. (I've got no body, a girl's got to get her kicks somehow.) Are you like this with Sera too. (Oh *totally*. It's like some sort of sapphic sorority sleepover when we're together. One fine ass celestial body and two girls who know how to work it…ugh, I feel dirty just thinking that.) This from the girl who has forced me out into the woods in order to violate me. (Don't blame me, blame your hormones. They're crazy out of whack today.) I feel pretty normal. (Trust me when I say they are off the charts. Now shut up and let me work my magic.)

Realizing that resistance is futile, I'm ready to give in when we hear a rustle behind us. Emma snaps my head around.

"Hello," Panik says.

"Oh hi there," Emma says, making me sound like a cockney suffering from severe head trauma.

"Don't let me interrupt your activities. I'm merely admiring the local flora. I find it aesthetically soothing."

"Um…"

"I'd offer to join, but I know how devoted to monogamy you are."

"I'm sure I don't know whut you're talkin' about." Seriously, Emma is making me sound like Michael Caine just got beaten within an inch of his life with a cricket bat.

"There's no need to feign ignorance. I'm very adept at detecting arousal. It's a useful skillset. Besides…" Panik's gaze ventures south, where my hand is clearly still down my pants. Emma slowly removes it, her embarrassment burning so hot that it easily engulfs my own. My face feels like it might melt off. "By the way, I finished my data analysis," Panik says with absolute indifference. "The anomaly is you." Without another word she goes back to admiring the trees and wanders off, leaving us in complete silence.

So much for happy endings.

* * *

Back on the Adventure Galley we all have a great time trying to figure out what Panik meant by saying I was the anomaly. Emma thinks Panik might have been talking about her. I object because she doesn't get to be both the most amazing girl dead or alive and an anomaly. We need to share our accolades. Jimmy follows that by calling me a socialist. I demand he take that back, declaring that if I'm anything it's a usurper of accolades. Once Panik returns to the ship, she confirms that she was talking about me. I do a little victory dance, even though nobody thinks I should be excited about it. Not that we have to time to discuss it anymore, as we all need to get ready for dinner. Emma goes back with Sera and I put on my fancy clothes.

We all meet back up outside the ship. Jimmy and Valiant are already waiting by the time I arrive. Valiant looks, well, valiant in his tuxedo while Jimmy looks uncomfortable, awkward, and in desperate need of a woman to dress him properly. Sera and Emma show up with Sera's body bedecked in a deep purple gown and hair to match. I've never seen Sera dressed so glamorous, it's clearly Emma's doing. Panik is the last to arrive, wearing a mocha dress that appears almost painted on. It's such a close match to her skin tone that I can hardly tell she's clothed at all. I even catch Sera/Emma checking her out a little longer than proper etiquette generally dictates.

Before heading out, Valiant orders No Name to stay with the ship. Presumably to keep an eye out for thieves and stowaways. Not that he'd be of much use, but I'll never argue about an evening without robots.

As it turns out, the Candy Embassy is deep in the forest. Our attire isn't exactly appropriate for the hike. Ironically, I find myself missing No Name, as he could easily carry me through some of the rougher patches. But hey, I do have Jimmy for that. I knock him down the first time I try to jump on his back to avoid scuffing my shoes. After that he gets the message. He's so my bitch. The girls choose to brave the environment. Panik with an unyielding grace, and Sera/Emma with the exact opposite. They have their shoes off and their dress hiked up above Sera's knees. It's uncivilized and completely unladylike, but I suppose we can't all have a Jimmy to piggyback us around.

Finally we arrive at the Embassy, a miniature replica of Candy Princess's Candy Castle back on Candy Island. A realization that makes my stomach ache with all that candy. Damn it, I want some candy! Chalk is at the gate to greet us, bowing deeply to the ladies and Captain Valiant, shaking Jimmy's hand, and giving me a no-look fist bump because we're cool like that. He leads us to the dining hall, where Candy Princess is waiting in a frilly, poufy dress that might be made out of cotton candy. She may be a flesh-eating, borderline psychotic with severe boundary issues who occasionally dabbles in murder and kidnapping, but she's undeniably adorable.

Noticing our arrival, her face morphs from that of a regal diplomat to a sex-crazed teenage girl. Before I can react she's practically flying at me, arms spread wide.

Boundary issues.

Her hug takes the wind out of me as she suffocates me with her delicious, sugary scent. I don't dare look over at Sera. The embrace lingers a bit too long, not that it's unenjoyable. When she finally lets go, Candy greets the Captain with a sweet curtsey, and he kisses her hand. Jimmy gets the same treatment, although his attempts to copy Valiant are pretty clumsy. As Candy approaches Sera and Emma, that sex-crazed face returns and she engulfs the two of them in a wicked snuggle.

Sera's hair flashes a violent, fiery red. "Don't touch us."

"Us? Oh gosh is Emma in there too! I'm so happy everyone came. Now we can all be friends again!" The thing about Candy

Princess is when she's not killing people or drugging them to get in their pants, she happens to be the most sincere person I've ever met. Actually, she's pretty sincere even when she's doing terrible things. Not that that makes Emma/Sera's rage any less palpable, but thankfully the Princess moves on before things get dicey. Finally, Candy Princess and Panik make their introductions to one another.

"Aren't you scrumptious looking," Candy remarks.

"Thank you, Your Eminence."

Candy giggles. "You can call me Candy or Princess. We're all friends here!" Emma or Sera mutter something under their breath that I can't quite hear.

"As you will, Princess," Panik says, "It is my understanding that you partake in the eating of human flesh and blood."

Candy Princess blushes. "I've been trying to cut back recently, isn't that right George." Chalk give her a big thumbs up.

"Be that as it may," Panik continues, "I'd be remiss if I didn't offer you a taste." Panik deftly slices open her right index finger and offers it to Candy.

Sera and Emma scoff. "You can't be serious."

"Golly, I couldn't possibly…" Candy declines.

"As your honored guest I would have to insist," Panik reassures.

"Well, if you insist," Candy gently takes the finger into her mouth and begins to suckle. "Oh dear, you *are* scrumptious aren't you." After that, things get weird. The noises Candy Princess makes in-between wet slurping sounds are usually only found behind closed doors. On the sets of porno movies. Sera and Emma stare on at first, with Sera's mouth agape and a look of disgust crossed with mild shock plastered on her face, before they finally turn away. Jimmy's eyes are firmly on the ground. He's statue still. Valiant, of course, refuses to look away. His valiant grins lights up the whole damn room. Chalk is now giving two big thumbs up. To whom, I have no idea. Panik, for her part, is completely unreadable. As for me, I don't have any clue what I'm supposed to do, so I shift my gaze all around in semi-regular intervals until the show finally concludes—which takes quite a while—but eventually Candy relinquishes Panik's finger. Wiping a tiny dribble of blood from her chin, every inch of her visible skin completely flushed, Candy Princess offers a sanguine smile and shows us to our seats.

* * *

A delicate, if not uncomfortable, reticence hangs over the dinner table for far too long after we've all been seated. Candy and Valiant are the heads of the table with me seated to Candy's right, Sera and Emma to her left, Panik directly next to them, and Jimmy next to me. There's a semi-magnificent fountain in the middle of us all featuring a steady flow of Rainbow Rhapsberry Cream. And not the rustic stuff from this morning, but the incredibly vibrant kind from back on Candy Island. Sera and Emma's only hesitation in gulping it down immediately is in waiting for it to transition to the appropriate color. In this case, a sunny yellow. I follow suit, though I could hardly care less about its color.

Before too long the atmosphere of the room transforms, and by the time Chalk brings out the main course even Sera's face looks content. Although Emma and Sera are still not-so-subtly leaning away from Candy. The Princess spends dinner regaling us with stories of mindless bureaucracy, her cheerful demeanor never faltering. Most everyone participates in a little polite conversation. Valiant goes on about his kitten, Gumdrop, who is currently at an intergalactic animal daycare. He says the daycare is just a cover for a covert animal espionage training center, but Sera shakes her head and mouths no as he says it. I still choose to believe the Captain, however. Because he's a fucking hero and shit. Panik speaks about her time studying the Twelve Hundred and Twelve Tantric Sorrows and something to do with a sinister army of love bunnies.

Jimmy talks about stuff. I don't listen.

When the conversation comes my way I try to keep it brief, so as not to slow down my consumption of Rhapsberry Cream. "You know me, I'm awesome," I say.

Candy Princess nods.

"So naturally that Robots Pirate is out to kill me," I continue.

Candy gasps.

"Also, I guess I'm an anomaly of some sort," I conclude.

Candy claps. "Victor your stories are so wonderful! And an anomaly? I don't know what that is, but is sounds neat!"

"That's what I keep saying." I get the doe eyes from Candy a little longer before she turns to Sera and Emma to ask what they've been up to.

With a look of complete serenity, and that atrocious accent of hers, Emma says, "Sod off."

Candy Princess reaction is, well, pretty standard for her actually. "Ooo, are we role playing now? I LOVE ROLE PLAYING! I've got a closet full of costumes and toys." She's also speaking with an accent, and it's much less embarrassing than Emma's.

Sera and Emma scootch their chair a little further away from her. I figure I might as well be courteous and explain. "Emma just talks like that so everyone can tell when it's her speaking instead of whoever's body she's sharing."

Candy Princess frowns and then immediately turns it upside-down. "We can role play later, I guess! Now I hope you're all ready for dessert, because you're about to taste the sweetest thing in the whole wide universe." And after a pause she coyly adds, "After me, of course."

* * *

As the evening dies down, so does the conversation. Too much Rainbow Rhapsberry Cream mutates my body into a prism of electric emotion and I'm having difficulty sitting still. I also have to pee something fierce. Saying something to that effect, I excuse myself from the table. It's not long before I realize I have no clue as to where the bathroom is, but with such a fantastic buzz I'm content to wander for a while.

The castle might be a miniature version of its predecessor, but it's still large. Passing a lengthy table lined with an assortment of blazing, fragrant candles I slow my pace, taking the time to brush my fingers against the base of each candle and blow them out as I move along. Their smoke smells like a Jolly Rancher tastes, and as I reach the end of the table to admire an ornate lighter, I have to resist the urge to take a bite out of one. I fail without regret. Further along the way I encounter a window draped with silken curtains, the tiniest hint of moonlight peeking through the slit where they meet. I am suddenly and inexplicably aroused and continue on my journey.

Shortly thereafter I find myself in the bathroom, though I hardly remember getting there. It's large and lush and features the most incredible shower I've ever seen. It looks like its very own tropical paradise. Violent flashbacks of my first morning with Emma punch me in the gut. A shower we shared in the midst of the end of the world, a memory that belongs to me but may not be my own. Memories layer on top of memories as I'm simultaneously reminded of

Emma sitting in a stolen car sipping on a can of Coke, Emma's lips glistening in the sunset as she holds a smoking shotgun over Jimmy's brother's corpse, Emma lying in the woods with a gaping wound in her side asking me to kiss her but instead I…I…

I shake my head trying to dispel the images as I drop to my knees, retching. Not because of the images of themselves, but because of the almost painful arousal. I dry heave until a thin layer of sweat breaks out across my body. Catching my breath, I look around the room hoping to regain my bearings. I spy another set of those candy candles. Their flames lick at the fringes of my mind and I can see a cabin burning. I see my old house in flames. Comic books turning to ash becomes a supermarket aisle on fire. A holocaust of tiny paper people dance and flail at 451 degrees. I swear I can feel the heat of it still, and it makes me smile and…and…

And I'm already almost back to the dining room. That's weird. Oh well, time for more Rhapsberry Cream!

"You were gone a while," says Jimmy.

I just laugh.

"Fuckin' Jimmy, right!" I say…well, actually I thought I thought it, but it was followed by Candy Princess gently scolding me for using such uncouth language. So I must have said it. "What are we all talking about anyway?"

Before anyone can answer, however, Chalk comes running into the room, frantically waving his arms in the air. At first I think he's excited and wanting to party. Maybe even recreate our epic dance contest victory. But then I notice his chest.

FIRE! It says.

Naturally I get up to reassure the little guy. "Nah, buddy there's no fire. I was just down that hall and it was perfectly fine." I walk back to the hallway to prove it. "See there's nothing wrong with—HOLY SHIT! BIG FIRE!!—I mean, uh, it's really not bad. Just stay calm and we can evacuate in a nice, orderly manner." And other than some mildly shocked faces, everyone does remain calm. It's nice "Hey guys, remember how I said the fire wasn't that bad? I may have exaggerated that a tad. What I'm trying to say is RUN OR DIE!" And with no intention of dying I run like the damned wind.

Being the first out of a burning building is a harrowing experience. You never know who else is going to make it. Sure I could go back in and check, but what kind of idiot goes back into a burning building? Sera, Emma, Chalk and Panik emerge together with Captain Valiant not too far behind, helping a distraught Candy Princess.

Jimmy is the last out and I march up to him immediately. "What the hell, man?"

"Huh?" he responds as if he doesn't know.

"It's common courtesy for the last person in a burning building to fight the fire, Jimmy."

"No it's not! Besides, there's no way I can put out a fire that big."

"You could at least try," I tell him.

"What kind of idiot goes back into a burning building?"

"Such a selfish attitude, but hey whatever, right? As long as you know that come tomorrow when we're all staring at what used to be a beautiful candy castle, that you could have maybe prevented it." Then I walk away. Passing by Candy Princess, I see the tears pouring down her face and I turn back to Jimmy. "Look what you did!" I point at Candy. "For shame!" Then I pump my fist to the sky. "Now back to the Adventure Galley, Huzzah!"

* * *

On the way back to the ship Sera brushes up against me and Emma jumps back to me. By the time we're inside the ship I can feel Emma purring inside me. In our quarters Emma puts my hand in my right pocket and starts fumbling around. I honestly can't tell if she's trying to do something sexual or not, but shortly thereafter my hand closes around something hard. And metallic. She pulls the item from my pocket. It's the fancy lighter I saw in the castle. I don't remember picking it up, but I have a feeling I did something I shouldn't have.

(I've never seen this before, where'd you get it?) Funny you should ask…what if I were to tell you that I might have maybe possibly set the candy embassy on fire? (Are you serious?) Maybe. I know how you feel about me setting stuff on fire but I didn't—(That is so fucking hot!) It is? (Hell yes, fuck that candy bitch. I've never wanted you so badly.) You know, I think you might be right about my hormones, Em. (So what? It feels great, let's get in bed so I can do nasty things to you.) Can I use the bathroom first? (I thought you did that at the castle.) I guess I never got around to it. (Fine, let's get this over with.)

Outside the bathroom door I notice a few nuts and bolts, but I'm in too much of a hurry to give a crap about that. Unfortunately there's far more of a mess on the other side of the door. The bathroom looks like a warzone of metallic debris, and at the center of it is the most unwelcome sight of all.

"I AM THE ROBORACLE." says the Roboracle.

"I know who you are, what the hell did you do here?"

"THE ROBORACLE DISMANTLED THE ROBOT TOO INSIGNIFICANT TO HAVE A NAME. THE ROBORACLE DEMANDS YOU TAKE THE ROBORACLE TO DONNA NATROIS."

Against my will Emma walks over and picks the Roboracle up.

"We haven't seen her since New York," she tells him.

"THE ROBORACLE WILL WAIT. THE ROBORACLE IS PREPARED FOR TRAVEL. FIVE."

"What are you on about this time?" I ask, not really wanting to know.

"FOUR."

"So it's a countdown, eh?"

"THREE."

"Emma, can't we put him down?"

"TWO."

Suddenly something inside me pops, making me very light-headed. Actually, very light bodied. "This can't be good."

"ONE."

Either the world starts to pull away from me, or I'm pulling away from it. It looks like I'm staring at where I was standing through a long cardboard tube, the opening growing smaller and smaller. Then with sudden force the world comes crashing back. Except it's completely different. Everything is silver and black. Sleek and seamless, outlined with soft blue light.

(What just happened?) Fuck it, I'm just gonna pee right here.

Epilogue

Panik sits in silence watching Time gain momentum second by single second, the sweetness of Candy Princess still glazing her lips.

The Princess had been nearly inconsolable after watching her castle burn. Panik, being no stranger to Grief, offered her services to the Princess. The first kiss was gentle with the Princess caught off guard. The second turned violent as Candy Princess forced their lips together roughly. Panik tasted her own blood only a moment before the Princess's tongue breached her mouth. At the taste of Panik's blood the kisses became ravenous yet restrained. Candy Princess's mouth bled as well. Her blood was a syrup coating the back of Panik's throat with suffocating, sacchariferous dulcitude. It was an unsettling pleasure, but it kept the Princess from more tears.

Panik is accustomed to using her body.

As a tool.

As a weapon.

As a gift.

She had long from now dissected the philosophies, studied the arts, and ultimately applied the science of it with unbending exactitude. It is neither a point of shame nor pride, only a cold necessity of continued existence. The organs she houses within her were developed with the knowledge that the only constant currency throughout countless millennia is sex. Easy to come by. Cheap, if not free. It's an essential for Panik and she's not above using her knowledge to alleviate sadness. Grief, with Time, is a heartless killer.

With the Princess finally sated and sleeping, Panik sought to revel in much desired privacy. She unshackled herself from clothing this era has deemed appropriate for her to wear. Panik sees no vulnerability in nakedness. When your greatest enemy is Time there is no protection. Even your own body will betray you to the enemy eventually. So Panik prefers freedom when freedom is permitted. It's not until she finished storing away her gifted clothing that she notices it. Her Uncertainty Clock had turned itself on and is ticking upward.

And so she sits.

And she waits.

It's all Panik can do in her attempt to kill Time.

The problem with killing Time, however, is that it only ends up slowly killing you in the end.

Second by single second.

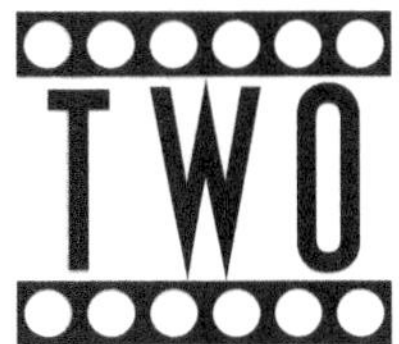

BINARY & BOOMSTICKS

Prologue

Electrical current sparks in the east of Infinite City, waking its inhabitants in simultaneous, silent shock. RoboBot emerges from sleep mode refreshed and revitalized, his circuits relishing in their newfound electric surge. RoboBot goes to work.

RoboBot's occupation is **DETECTIVE**. His primary function is **SOLVING MYSTERIES**, with the main sub-function focusing on **SOLVING CRIMES**. Infinite City has no crime and all knowledge is available and known by all. According to RoboBot's parameters, this means he's doing an exemplary job. This provides RoboBot with a sense of self-satisfaction. RoboBot could not be any better. RoboBot is lonely.

While waiting to be informed of a mystery he knows can never be, RoboBot spends his time printing out complex mathematical equations. He hangs these on his office walls in the hopes that, if he ever has a guest or client, they will secretly admire him for his taste in art and jokes. RoboBot thinks he has a great sense of humor.

As he finishes hanging a particularly amusing equation, RoboBot gets interrupted by a shrill noise.

"Um, hi?"

RoboBot turns towards the disturbance and finds a fleshy, hardly-metallic-at-all thing standing before him. RoboBot cocks his head.

"A-are there any people here?" the noise blurts. RoboBot quickly searches his memory cores and confirms the noise to be a human language. English. RoboBot's interest piques. Having no vocal function, RoboBot decides to send a message via Morse Code. He's not even a single word in when the thing, a human apparently, interrupts.

"Sorry, but I don't speak robot."

RoboBot is confused by this suspected human's lack of understanding of a human invented means of communication. He decides to reassess the situation, opening his never-before-used bio-metric systems. His scans confirm his initial assertion of human. And due to the presence of ovaries and a uterus, RoboBot is able to confirm a female human. Judging from the age range and a quick reference of the literacy rates of English speaking countries, RoboBot takes a calculated gamble and prints out a message for the female.

"Who are you?" it reads. He hands it to her.

"Oh, I'm Lily," she replies, but her response causes RoboBot's circuits to cross. He begins to print.

"A lily is a flowering plant: Genus Lilium. Order Liliales. There are over 100 species of lilies. You are not a flower."

The female human reads and shrugs. "Sometime people name their kids after flowers."

RoboBot ponders this and finds he can create his own joke. He records an image of his guest, placing it alongside a picture of a lily with an equal sign between the two—for mathematics is the only path to comedy—he prints this out and posts it on his wall. RoboBot looks at his guest for a sign of amusement.

"Yeah, that's right," she says, "I'm Lily." She smiles and RoboBot thinks that humans have an odd way of expressing delight. But RoboBot doesn't mind. He respects all cultures. Besides, RoboBot has to concentrate on the matter at hand.

"How did you get here?" He prints.

"I don't know," she says. And RoboBot's prime functions spring to life.

"A mystery!" He prints.

"I guess so," she says.

RoboBot is giddy.

He spends the next several moments re-familiarizing himself with the details of his primary function while simultaneously downloading as many human detective stories as he can find in order to make his former guest, but now client, comfortable. Satisfied, RoboBot continues his duties.

"Take a seat," he prints.

She does.

"You are a very attractive female human," he prints.

"Uh, thanks," she says. Human detectives, RoboBot has found, are very preoccupied with their female clients' bodies. RoboBot worried to learn how often in these stories the detectives had sexual intercourse with their clients. That isn't in any of his system requirements, but RoboBot won't discriminate.

"You have exquisite ovaries," he prints, "and a very fertile uterus."

"Um," she stirs and RoboBot is aware of her heart rate increasing. She is either nervous or aroused.

"Are you nervous or aroused?" he prints.

"C-can we just get back to helping me?"

"Of course," he prints, "that's my primary function."

"But aren't there any *people* here who can help me?"

"Infinite City has never been populated or visited by humans, which is why your presence is a mystery."

"Oh," she says. "And you like mysteries?"

"No, I am a detective. I solve them."

"Well, that's lucky for me then. Do you have a name?"

"I am RoboBot."

"That's kind of cute."

"It's also an accurate representation of what I am."

"A robot."

"Affirmative. Now please tell me the factual circumstances that led you here."

"All I really remember is going to sleep in my bed last night and then waking up outside your door a few minutes ago."

"And how many robots do you know."

"None. Well other than you."

"And that is all the information?"

"Yeah."

"Please wait while I process your information. This may take several minutes. Your patience is appreciated." RoboBot proceeds to dissect each bit of information and cross-reference it with his database of human knowledge. He reaches his conclusion.

"I have solved your mystery," he prints.

Wow, that was fast," she responds. RoboBot can see she's impressed.

"Let me first review the facts," prints RoboBot. "Fact 1: you fell asleep in your own bed. Fact 2: you woke up in Infinite City. Fact 3: you know no robots other than me. Are these facts correct?"

"Yes," she answers.

"Now I will present another fact you may be unaware of. Fact: No human is permitted inside Infinite City without a robot companion. This fact leads me to my first suspect. Suspect 1: RoboBot. He is the only robot you know. However, I am RoboBot and I have never left Infinite City. RoboBot is no longer a suspect. This leads to one conclusion. Cyborgs."

"Cyborgs?"

"Robots made to look human. I have compiled a list of suspects," RoboBot prints out three pictures and hands them to Lily. She looks them over.

"You've got to be kidding me. These are just pictures of Arnold Schwarzenegger, that guy from the Six Million Dollar Man, and some blond woman in a tight red dress."

"My databases say she is a Cylon, a well know race of robot/human hybrids. One of these cyborgs is responsible for you being here. Mystery solved."

Lily looks over RoboBot.

"Oh RoboBot," she says, "no."

2

"Start talking." My bladder empty, I feel like I can finally and calmly deal with trying to get some answers about what the hell is going on here.

"I AM THE ROBORACLE."

Then again, being calm is overrated. "Everyone knows who you are; I want to know *where* the fuck we are!"

"THE ROBORACLE IS UNSURE. WHERE IS DONNA NATRIOS?"

"Why would I know where your crazy girlfriend is? Last time I saw her was in New York." I'd really like to kick something right now, but wherever we happen to be seems pretty devoid of kickable things. It's all very streamlined.

"THE ROBORACLE HEARD FROM THE FATES THAT VICTOR WOULD MEET DONNA NATRIOS AGAIN."

"I thought you cut ties from The Fates," Emma says with my voice.

"THE ROBORACLE CAN STILL HEAR THE FATES. WOULD YOU LIKE TO HEAR STYX?"

"No I don't want to hear Styx!"

"ACE OF BASE THEN." Before I can object, *Dancer in a Daydream* starts bumping from The Roboracle.

(hey, sweetie.) Sup. (for someone who claims to dislike Ace of Base, why do you know the titles of all of their songs?) I just know shit, okay!

The volume of the music increases to an uncomfortable level. "Could you turn that down?"

"THE ROBORACLE DEMANDS YOU DESTROY THE OTHER ROBOTS."

"What other robots? There aren't any—oh sonofabitch!" At least a dozen robots suddenly pour onto what I can only assume is the street, saying things like "Intruder" and "I'm a lame-ass robot" and "Kill all humans". Robots suck so hard. It's a good thing I'm always strapped. As Captain Valiant once wrote in one of his blistering manifestos, "If you're not prepared to kill, prepare to die". Time to get to work.

As much as I hate robots, I admit they are pretty fun to shoot. Although, for all their genocidal smack talk, these robots don't seem very well armed. Some people have an aversion to shooting unarmed opponents, but me, I find I'm much more relaxed without the threat of getting shot looming over my head. The most difficult part of this whole gunfight is Emma using my body to do some wild dancer gymnastics, occasionally causing a stray shot or two. Thankfully she stops before she pulls one of my muscles. And sadly none of the strays hit The Roboracle.

The firefight ends as abruptly as it began. Emma continues to bounce to the beat of the music, but soon that dies off as well, leaving us exactly where we started. Almost. The appearance of a bunch of robots also meant the appearance of a bunch of previously unseen doors. Normally I'd be against going in a door that some murderous robot just came out of, but since these robots seemed especially worthless I figure what the hell. It can't be any worse than waiting out here to be ambushed again. Emma forces me to pick up The Roboracle before we head in. It's not that he can't follow on his own; he's just a self-entitled dick and arguing about it never gets me anywhere. I let Emma take control of things for a while so she can choose which door to enter. If there's one good thing about having your dead girlfriend's ghost inside you, it's that you can be a self-entitled dick too.

* * *

Being a passenger in your own body kicks ass. It's like a fully immersive movie that's mostly boring, but you don't really mind because you never know what's going to happen next. Essentially, with Emma in charge, my body is a never ending surprise party.

(You know I'm not going to do this forever, right?) Don't pretend like you don't love having a body to control again. (But I generally prefer my bodies to not have balls and junk. It makes walking awkward.) Oh, is that why we're walking so slowly, and kind of bowlegged? (I just don't want to smoosh anything, okay!) You didn't seem to have an issue when we were fighting the robots. (Yeah, but I wasn't thinking about it. For some reason, after you handed over control, I became acutely aware that there was a penis between my legs. It's disconcerting…and don't you dare make any jokes about that.) That would be crass, Emma. (Which you are.) Psh, just get back to walking. I tire of these surroundings!

My legs give out and I go crashing to the floor.

O(ow)w! Why'd you do that? (You were being an asshole.) Point taken. But will you please indulge my laziness and walk me around? (Only because you asked nicely, and because the less time spent in this creepy ass place, the better.)

Emma gets my body back on the move. Not that either of us has any clue about where we are, let alone where to go. After a fashion The Roboracle makes himself useful. Sort of. Anytime we happen upon a fork in the hallway, The Roboracle tells us which way to go. I try to convince Emma to do the opposite of what he says, but she won't have it. We spend who knows how long winding our way through endless hallways, and I can't help but zone out every now and then.

Maybe because this place reminds me a bit of my days working in an office, my mind wanders back to the first time I saw Emma. The world had only just gone all apocalypty, my house had burned down—my fault, really—and I'd caught my girlfriend using her genitals to smother a Mexican midget. He didn't seem to be complaining. Looking back, it wasn't much of a surprise. My favorite thing about her had always been her intense sluttiness, and Jesus was a pretty cool guy. Still, it was a pretty ugly scene to walk in on right after you've realized the world might be ending. Figuring my day couldn't get much worse; I decided to go back to work. Sure it looked like the end of days, but if I woke up on Tuesday with everything back to normal I would have had a shit-ton of work to catch up on.

I can't really say how I got from one point to the next—my memory of those of days isn't the most reliable—but I somehow ended up walking into an office building that looked a lot like mine. There was a heap of crazy all around me, though I could hardly care. I just headed straight to where my office would have been if I were in the correct place. Along the way I passed a broken soda machine and grabbed a couple Cokes lying on the ground, but that was the only stop I made. It wasn't until I sat down at not-my-desk that I noticed the girl hiding under it. Shortly thereafter I saw the pictures around the room and realized I was in the wrong place entirely. When I finally grabbed her and dragged her out of there, it wasn't so much that I was trying to be heroic as I was trying to cover my embarrassment of walking into the wrong office. Well, that, and my shame at my initial thoughts when seeing a beautiful girl under my desk. Because they were filthy. I'm talking obscure foreign porno filthy. Like I was picturing Emma on the floor with her—

(Dear Christ!) I'm sorry! (Huh? For what?) For my thoughts. (Oh sweetie, I've managed to block those out for the most part.) You can do that. (If I couldn't, I'd most likely have gone crazy by now.)

Well, then what are you "Dear Christ"ing about? (Use your eyes, Victor.)

Despite an intense desire to not do anything at all, I focus my attention outward and—

"Holy shit!" I say.

(Right?)

I take back control of my body and rush over to the point of focus. "This looks exactly like the wallet I used to have!"

(Wait, what?)

"The resemblance is uncanny, can you believe this?"

(The wallet is seriously what you're taking away from all of this?)

"THE ROBORACLE HAS NO USE FOR WALLETS. A ROBOT'S CURRENCY IS KNOWLEDGE."

"Yeah, I already know that robots sucks."

"THE FATES ARE WHISPERING IN THE DISTANCE. THEY HAVE SAID. "VICTOR SUCKS"."

"That is bullshit and…no, you know what? Even a douchey robot such as you can't bring me down right now. Not when I've got this kick-ass wallet to admire." I pick up the wallet and open it. My spirits take a nose dive. "Ugh, it's all covered in blood."

(Kind of like, I don't know, everywhere around it.) Huh, I guess so, but who cares about that? Another perfectly good wallet has been ruined. (But what about—)

"THE ROBORACLE IS BORED NOW."

It's rare that I agree with The Roboracle. "Me too."

(But the wallet—)

"Is ruined, Em. We have to move on. " I toss the wallet over my shoulder. "Let's go."

* * *

"TURN LEFT." The Roboracle commands. He's been directing us ever since the whole wallet tragedy. My instinct being to do the opposite of what he said caused Emma to take back control. I would have argued, but, you know…effort. I'm being a little bit more attentive now, however, because who knows what wonderful trinkets might be hidden in this incredibly monotonous labyrinth.

Emma, for her part, has been trying to hold a conversation with The Roboracle. A maddening prospect, even at the best of times. "So Roboracle—"

"I AM THE ROBORACLE."

"Right, but what's Donna doing here anyway?"

"DONNA NATRIOS IS NOT HERE. LEFT."

"Um, you mean she's not with us, but she's somewhere in this place, right?"

"NO."

You've got to be kidding me!

Apparently I said that out loud because The Roboracle responds with another "NO".

"Then," Emma says, "why did you bring us here?"

"THE ROBORACLE DID NOT. VICTOR DID. RIGHT."

"No that is not right!" I say.

(I think he means turn right.) I don't care what he means. It's not like I mind taking credit for fucking up. Assuming I can't blame it on anyone else. And do I enjoy stealing credit for things that turn out awesome? Of course! But I don't even know where here is. That robot is just a lying pile of plastic.

"ROBOTS ARE MADE OF METAL."

"So what does that make you?" I yell in frustration.

"I AM THE ROBORACLE. NOW. STOP." I try to keep going, but Emma doesn't relinquish control so easily. "FACE EAST."

"We're indoors," I say. "How in the hell are we supposed to know which way is east?"

"USE A COMPASS." I'm prepared to throw The Roboracle down the hall, but Emma uses my feet to turn in some random direction so that we're now facing one of the walls. "THE OTHER EAST." Emma turns to face the other wall. "GOOD."

"Now what?" Emma asks far more politely than she should. Because what she should have said was "I'm going to kick you" except instead of saying that she should have just kicked him. It's what I would have done.

"KNOCK." says The Roboracle.

And Emma knocks.

* * *

Nothing happens. At least not right away. We just kind of stand around awkwardly and wait. I'm wondering how long we're supposed to do this when the wall opens. Well, not the wall, but rather a door. Looking around now, I can see other vague door outlines around the hall. Something I would have noticed earlier if I cared.

With the door open, there's still nothing. At eye level. I can't really be bothered to look around. Maybe I should be more on guard, but I trust Emma to protect my sexy body. And if she fails, Hell's not so bad a place. Emma, however, does look around. And sure enough, right around my knees, is another damn robot. I reach for my gun, but instead Emma says, "Hello." It's a poor killing tactic, but she's always preferred diplomacy to violence. Since killing Jimmy's brother, at any rate.

The robot doesn't answer back, which is pretty rude. Typical robot arrogance. Instead it prints out a piece of paper and hands it to us. It dawns on me that this smarmy bastard expects me to read something. My urge to kill intensifies. I go for my gun and unleash all of my spectacular wit. "Die robot!" But Emma keeps me from squeezing the trigger just long enough for someone to jump out from behind a desk.

"No don't!" she yells. "He's not a bad robot he's—Victor?"

"Lily?" I say now that I can fully see the girl.

(Great, is this another ex-girlfriend.) Ew, gross!

"Huh?" Lily looks confused. "You think RoboBot is my ex-girlfriend? I've always identified him as guy robot…or wait, you must have meant I'm his ex-girlfriend? That makes more sense. At least as far as nonsensical statements go."

"What the hell are you talking about, Lily? RoboBot?"

(So she's not an old girlfriend?)

"Oh," Lily starts, "are you talking to *your* robot?"

"I AM THE ROBORACLE."

"Uh, hi," Lily says, "but I'm not any robot's girlfriend, ex or otherwise."

"Lily, please," I say, "I'm trying to have a conversation here."

"With your robot?"

"With my girlfriend."

"You're dating the robot?" Lily wonders, "It sounded kind of…male. I mean, as far as robot voices go."

"My girlfriend's name is Emma," I explain.

"Emma the Roboracle?"

"Just Emma! She's not a robot."

(I'm really confused.)

"You're confused? I'm still trying to figure out what you're talking about, Vic."

"That wasn't me," I try to tell her. "It was Emma."

"What was Emma?"

"The person who said 'I'm really confused.'"

"Pretty sure that was you."

"That's just because she wasn't talking with her terrible accent."

(It's not that terrible…)

"Yes it is, Em."

Lily gawks until she's hit with some sort of understanding. "Ohhh, I get it. Emma is your imaginary British girlfriend! Vic, that was kind of cute when you were six, but it's just creepy now."

"Whoa! Let's just get some things straight," I demand. "First, Jem was not imaginary. She was a real life cartoon character who happened to be a rock star and also fought crime."

"Just because you didn't imagine her up doesn't make her less imaginary," Lily interrupts, grating my nerves. "And she didn't fight crime, either."

"She did in my mind, okay! She was awesome. Also, Emma is not British. She's American. Although her parents are probably Nazis."

(They are not!)

"Em, you have to face facts. They're German. Also, Emma is not imaginary. She's a ghost who is currently inside me because she can't take corporeal form outside of Hell."

"You met you're imaginary girlfriend in Hell?" Lily says all judgmentally, "That's weird even for you, bro."

"I did not meet her in Hell, *Lily*! I met her before she died. I just hang out with her in Hell now. By the way, I think I saw mom and dad down there."

(Mom and dad?)

Lily stops with a jolt. "Dude…mom and dad are dead?"

"Probably."

"And this is how you tell me?"

"Yes."

(Mom and dad?)

"What about that is bothering you, Em?"

(She's your sister?)

"Twin sister."

"Allegedly," Lily corrects.

"Exactly. Please try to keep up, Emma."

(I think maybe I shouldn't even bother.)

"How'd they die?" Lily asks.

"How'd who die?" I ask back.

"Mom and dad, jackass!"

"You're still on that? Damn, Lily I don't know. Did you actually expect me to talk to them?"

"That's a good point," she says.

(Wow, your parents must be awful.)

"I wouldn't say awful," I say. "Just overbearing."

"Mildly so. Mostly they're pretty alright, and could you please stop pretending to talk to your non-existent girlfriend?" Lily pleads. "It's weirding me out."

"She's very existent," I counter. "I can prove it too."

"Really," she mocks.

"As long as you're cool having a ghost passenger."

She rolls her eyes. "Sure, why not." I take a few steps forward and grab Lily's arm, immediately feeling Emma slip away. It takes my sister a few seconds to process it all. "Okay, so what now? Am I supposed to—oh! That's, um...Hi." Lily's face contorts into all sorts of goofy expressions as she gets used to her new guest, but she's ominously silent. Then she laughs.

"What's so funny?" I ask.

Lily is almost too distracted to answer. "Huh…oh I'm just getting to know your girlfriend. She's funny."

"But I want to know the joke," I demand.

Lily just shrugs, like she doesn't even care what I want. Inconceivable! The annoyance levels I'm experiencing are pretty severe when I feel something tap my thigh. I look down to see that other robot I'd completely—and happily—forgotten was here. It hands me another slip of paper.

"Anyone else want to read this?" I ask hopefully.

"No," says either Emma or Lily. And they giggle again.

That's when the horror of the situation dawns on me. My girlfriend is sharing a body with my sister, and, perhaps worse than that, they're going to make me read.

* * *

I stare at the piece of paper in my hand, refusing to focus on it. "Are you sure I can't just shoot it?"

"Leave RoboBot alone," Lily says. "He's been helping me out."

"RoboBot is a pretty stupid name," I tell RoboBot. He responds by printing out something else and handing it to me. I refuse to take it. "I haven't even read the other five slips you handed me." RoboBot continues to print. "Seriously, I don't want to read this shit."

"Oh just read it," Emma says with Lily's voice. Or at least I think that's what she said. Like some sort of vocal cancer, her accent just gets worse and worse. I'm a little worried it might kill her, and that makes me laugh because she's already dead. Either Lily or Emma looks at me funny. I shake my head with the universal sign of 'don't worry about it'.

When it becomes absolutely clear that no one else is going to read all of RoboBot's stupid papers—I even ask The Roboracle to do it, but he just sits in the corner eying RoboBot and muttering nonsense about the fates and death—I give in and do it myself. They say things like "Hello, my name is RoboBot" and "it's nice to make your acquaintance" and "I'm a lame-ass robot detective". I might be paraphrasing on that last one, but the point I'm trying to make is that all that reading was completely worthless.

"You're worthless," I inform him. "You don't even write like a proper detective."

RoboBot hands me another piece of paper that reads "I tried emulating popular human detectives, but it made Lily uncomfortable/aroused. This was counter-productive to solving the mystery at hand."

"Hold up," I turn back to Lily. "The robot says you're the reason he doesn't act like a real detective. Is that true?"

"By 'real detective' do you mean creepy and womanizing?"

"I might."

"Then yes. I didn't like it."

"That's very selfish of you," I say, but Lily does this thing she always does whenever I'm around. She ignores me. So I turn my attention back to RoboBot. "Look, if you're going to be a detective, you need to act like one. It might make people uncomfortable, but those people suck." Lily, who is now lounging in RoboBot's desk chair, gives me the finger. "Clearly you already have the cool desk and chair, but you're probably going to want to put your name on the door out there. 'RoboBot PI' it should say. You should consider growing a mustache too."

RoboBot hands me another message. "Robots can't grow mustaches."

"What, are you going to print me out a list of everything robots can't do?" I chide.

RoboBot prints his response. It takes a while. I start reading before it's even finished printing. "Grow mustaches. Sneeze. Defecate. Digest dairy. Smile. Beat other robots at tic tac toe. Wink. Sing Reggae music."

I have to stop there. "What the hell is this?"

RoboBot seems confused momentarily before printing, "A list of everything robots can't do."

"What kind of can do attitude it that? A terrible one is the correct answer. But let's move on. Tell me about this mystery you're trying to solve. I'm a great hero," Lily scoffs, but I can ignore her just as hard as she ignores me. We've got lots of practice at it. "I might be able to help."

"There are humans in Infinite City," RoboBot's paper informs me.

"And Infinite City is…?"

"This city," RoboBot prints.

"Right, and these humans are where exactly?"

"Here, you jackass," Lily says. "RoboBot is talking about us."

"I knew that," I say. "I was just trying to help RoboBot through the process of mystery solving. It's the Socratic Method or something."

"Sure," she says.

"Anyway, what's so mysterious about humans being here? I go places all the time. It's never caused a mystery before."

"According to RoboBot, there had never been a human in Infinite City before I showed up."

"Gotcha," I say. "So it's clearly all your fault. Mystery solved. Now how do we get out of here, Lily? I've got space adventures to get back to."

"Christ, I forgot how much of a pain in the ass you can be," she says, avoiding my question. Typical Lily. "I don't know how I got here, let alone how to leave. Also, Emma was telling me you found a bunch of blood in one of the halls."

"Yeah, so?"

"So maybe we should investigate that," Lily says. "What do you think, RoboBot?"

"Excellent," he prints. "Our first lead."

* * *

It's a good thing for all of us that Emma remembers how to get back to the blood, because I certainly don't, and, as usual, The Roboracle is no help whatsoever. He seems more intent on keeping his distance from RoboBot. In fact, he's been actively ignoring all of RoboBot's attempts to talk with him. At least, I think that's what all those beeps from RoboBot are about. Not that it's much of a surprise; The Roboracle has never liked other robots. It's the only thing we have in common. For my part, I do my best to instruct RoboBot in the fine art of being a detective, if only because Lily and Emma keep conversing via thought and leaving me out.

"First things first," I say, "we should probably get you a cool hat. Where's the robot hat store around here?"

"Robots don't wear hats," RoboBot informs me.

I shake my head. "That's an unfortunate set back, but we can probably work around it. What's important to realize, is that since my sister is your client it's almost inevitable that you'll end up nailing her."

Lily shoots me an icy stare that chills me to the bone. I say that because it sounds pulpy, and I need to get in the proper mindset to really help out.

In the meantime, RoboBot is busy printing something. It turns out to be a picture of RoboBot alongside a picture of a nail being hammered alongside a picture of Lily with a question mark at the end. It's wonderful.

My laughter gets Lily's and Emma's attention and they grab the picture. "Ah what the hell?! Vic, I don't like you teaching RoboBot this shit. He's a nice robot."

"They don't call them dicks, for nothing," I say. "They're hard men who play dangerously with loose women. And bang them in order to solve mysteries. It disgusts me too, but we've got to play by the rules."

"Have you ever read a detective novel?" Lily asks.

"I've read *of* them," I say, putting the whole thing to bed like my mom used to put me to bed in the vacant dark of night. She put Lily to bed too. We were only kids then, not knowing the seductive, sinister paths our futures had in store. Vivacious ghostly girlfriends and robot sex. The stuff of dreams and nightmares. No, we were innocent and sweet—and in Lily's case, really annoying—all we knew was that night was black and we were sleepy.

"Yo, Vic," Lily snaps her fingers in my face.

"What?" I say

"You spaced out there."

"That's because I was trying to get the feel for the whole detective scenario. Thanks for interrupting." Now where was I? Something about putting myself to bed noirishly…damn it, never mind. "Anyway RoboBot, it's vital to know that because Lily is your client and the dame you're most likely to bang in nauseating fashion—unless we come across another broad soon—she's also probably connected to the entire mystery. She might even be behind the whole thing."

"You're such a douche," she says. Emma laughs. It's weird how Emma's laugh always sounds the same no matter whose body she's in.

Arriving back at the scene of the crime, assuming bleeding is a crime in Infinite City, I decide it might make sense for me to take in the surroundings this time around. It's not usually my style. When you spend year after year in one classroom or another, and follow that up with a couple different office jobs, you just stop giving a shit. It's all the same. Sure there might have been a teacher or two who thought it was progressive to put the desks in a circle instead of rows, and that was fine until the hottest girl in class caught you staring for too long, but shockingly she asks you to the prom only to dump pig's blood all over your nice new dress! And sure, most of that happened in Carrie, which is the entire point: If you don't spice those classroom memories up, they blend into a monotonous montage of who gives a fuck. Even Hell was a disappointment once I realized it was nothing but a lot of barren land filled with dead people trying their best to piss you off.

This is different, though. Detective work. And detectives pay attention to everything. At least that's what they claim. I'm instantly suspicious because, staring at the bloody wall and floor, I'm totally bored already.

The hall is nothing special. It's a fucking hall. A little more simplified than a typical office building, but still a hall. The doors are harder to make out, but once you've seen one open their little camouflage trick loses its effect. As for the blood, there's a lot of it. I think. Can't say I'm much of an expert on bleeding, I've always tried to keep mine to myself. I'm not entirely sure, but it looks darker, browner than when we first passed. However, the only real thing of note is the robot intently scrubbing away at the mess. It's about the same size as both the Roboracle and RoboBot. Probably comes up to my knees. It looks pretty harmless.

I draw my gun to take it down. RoboBot raise his arm, stopping me. He works his way over to the other robot and they exchange a series of beeps, like a dial-up modem. Afterwards, the other robot scoots away, disappearing into a doggy-door sized compartment in one of the walls.

RoboBot returns with a slip of paper already in hand. "That was a CleanerBot," it says. "Just doing his job. But I convinced him to take a break while I examine the scene."

Emma asks a question, but I can't even understand her with that damn accent anymore. I'm pretty embarrassed for her. Lily ends up clarifying. "Emma was wondering if the CleanerBot saw anything."

"Negative," RoboBot prints. "He heard a scuffle and what sounded like one voice arguing with itself. But that's all."

"That was probably us," Emma says, now with an exaggerated southern drawl. It's still bad, but no longer cringe worthy. And we can understand her. "Although I don't know about the scuffle."

"Did I kick The Roboracle at any point?" I ask. "Because I usually want to."

"No," Emma says, "you just threw that wallet down the hall."

"What wallet?" RoboBot prints.

"A really nice one," I say. "But it was completely covered in blood. Totally useless."

"Where did you throw it?" RoboBot prints.

I point down the hall, and RoboBot scuttles off to look. Lily and Emma follow, but The Roboracle and I just hang around the patch of blood. Something about it makes the hair on my arms stand at attention. I crouch down, touch it, and get slapped in the face with a dizzy stick. There's a feeling that you get when something's on the tip of your tongue, but you can't quite spit it out. Except I don't have the vaguest idea of what I'm trying to think of. Probably I'm just coming down from my Rhapsberry Cream high. I drank a crap ton of that stuff.

The dizzy spell fades as quickly as it set in, and RoboBot and the girl[s] are already back. They didn't find anything. RoboBot assumes the CleanerBot already disposed of the wallet, which according to RoboBot means it would have been incinerated. Another wallet lost to fire. So sad.

RoboBot doesn't concern himself with the lost potential clue for long, he gets right to work examining the blood stain from all angles. The rest of us can't do anything but wait.

"Hey, Vic," Lily says to quell the silence. "What's the deal with you always trying to shoot robots, anyway?"

"They suck, is the deal," I say. "Besides, when we showed up here we got attacked by a bunch of inept robots. Don't want to take the chance of that happening again."

RoboBot's head snaps back to look at me like it is spring-loaded, which it might be. He lets out a series of urgent bleeps before handing one of his printouts to Lily.

"He's asking if you're sure about the KillBots," she says.

I shrug and Lily takes another message from RoboBot.

"He says that KillBots are against Infinite City's Prime Directive and that we need to get back to his office immediately."

RoboBot is halfway down the hall by the time Lily finishes reading his words. We rush to catch up. It's not hard; robots rarely seem to be fast. Once we're back on pace, Lily grabs me with a hug.

"It's good to see you, bro."

"Yeah," is all I say. But it's enough to make her smile.

* * *

Back in RoboBot's office there's not much to do. RoboBot asked not to be bothered while he calculates something, or maybe reads more detective novels. Who knows? But his immediacy in getting back here doesn't line up well with his current state. I use the time to look around the office. It doesn't take long; the office is barely bigger than a janitor's closet. There's a plain metal desk and a plain metal chair. Everything in Infinite City appears to be made of metal—and maybe some fiber glass—and it strikes me as mildly morbid. Like if New York or San Francisco were made of human bones and flesh. That might be fine for Backwater, Alabama, but for a major city it's just weird. Or at the very least, impractical. Human bones and flesh just aren't sturdy enough for a city. They've tried it in Hell, and that city is in constant need of repair. At least metal is sturdier that skin.

The one thing that stands out in the office is the collage of insane math equations—most of them faded from the harsh light of the room—plastered on the walls. Math was one of my stronger subjects, but the stuff on RoboBot's walls is like calculus on acid. Staring at this stuff long enough would probably be enough to give you post-traumatic stress.

Lily comes up beside me. "RoboBot insists these are all hilarious jokes."

I look them over again, trying my best to find the humor. "Even that one about you?" I motion to a picture of Lily and a lily. She goes red for a second, but only shrugs. "So he likes math jokes," I say mostly to myself. "Hey RoboBot, you forgot one."

RoboBot doesn't have facial expressions to rely on, but he cocks his head in a way that conveys a decent amount of annoyance. No one was supposed to interrupt him. But I'm sure this is important. I clear my throat. "Seven eight nine."

He tilts his head further to the side, no longer looking annoyed. "7 8 9?" He prints.

I check my pocket for a pen, but don't have one on me. Lily understands what I'm looking for—she usually does—and generates one of her own. Just below RoboBot's "7 8 9" I write "sounds like 7 ate 9". RoboBot take the paper back and scans it. His eye lights grow so large they're in danger of blowing a fuse.

"Human mathematical humor?" He prints.

"Yeah, it's hilarious," I lie. Lily and Emma are busy shaking Lily's head at me, but when they notice RoboBot turn to them for reassurance, the head shaking sharply cuts into a nod of reassurance. RoboBot does a 360 turn and rushes to the wall, plastering the new joke right next to the picture of Lily's lily.

"You're mean," Lily whispers, failing to force the smile off her face.

"You're just jealous that I've got a joke on his wall," I say.

The Roboracle, who has been mercifully silent all this time, waddles over to examine the new joke. He gazes at it for a long moment. "THE ROBORACLE'S MOTHER. THE ODOMETER. TOLD THIS JOKE OFTEN." There's static in his voice when he says it, something I've never heard before. Maybe it means his batteries are dying. Fingers crossed.

* * *

RoboBot went immediately back to his quiet contemplation, and The

Roboracle went back to his quiet condemnation, so Lily and I decided to do some catching up. Thanks to Emma, Lily had already heard most of what I've been up to, which means she does most of the talking. She took the whole apocalypse thing in stride, viewing it as something that would work itself out in the long run. "I was overdue a nice vacation," she says. "I did considering checking to see if you were doing okay, but, you know…effort." Then she says, "Oh my god. You two are exactly the same,"

"Uh," I say. Because that didn't make sense.

"That was Emma."

"You forgot your awful accent," I tell her. "And we're not that similar."

"Yes you are," Emma says, this time in full Southern mode. "Trust me; I've been inside you both."

"Ew," Lily and I say simultaneously.

"See! Exactly the same."

"That's not fair," I say. "You said something gross."

But Emma doesn't seem to be listening; she's on a roll and won't be deterred. "Yet you guys are always like 'Us related? Psh! Allegedly.' What the fuck does that even mean? I mean, like, seriously what does it mean?!"

"Well," I start, "like I said, our parents could be kind of overbearing"

"But they had this weird mix of fascist dictator and hippy," Lily continues.

"Mostly it wasn't a big deal," I say.

"Because they were also really unobservant a lot of the time," Lily says.

"A complete and confusing contradiction at every turn, it was impossible to keep up with them"

"So we both figured we couldn't actually be related to them"

"But she looks a lot like mom"

"And he looks a lot like dad"

"So clearly [s]he's the one related to them," we say together once again.

Emma's response is simple. To giggle wildly. "Okay, I'm sorry I asked." The laughter doesn't stop there, though, and Lily's face is one of distorted fear and hysterics. If you've never had someone else laughing wildly inside you, it's pretty surreal and terrifying. Seeing it happen to someone else, though, that's hilarious. It's not long before I'm laughing right alongside them. It only gets worse from there.

I'm lying on the floor, trying to catch my breath, when RoboBot taps me on the shoulder and gives me a piece of paper. I read it to myself before noticing that Lily and Emma, having mostly composed themselves, are waiting to hear what it says.

"Uh, apparently RoboBot has decided he needs to interface with the main hub of the city, or something, to get a better idea of what's going on. I don't know why we needed to know, but whatever."

RoboBot is already well on the way to doing the whole interface thing. A slot opens in the wall farthest from me, and RoboBot backs into it. The Roboracle cautiously scampers over to examine the situation. All RoboBot's lights grow brighter as he plugs in. Everything is fine. For about 3 seconds. That's when RoboBot unleashes a deafening screech. I can barely manage to cover my ears, let alone do anything else.. The Roboracle, however, doesn't hesitate, zapping the interface port and freeing RoboBot, putting an end to the ear piercing howl.

I check my ears to make sure they aren't bleeding, before following Lily and Emma to check on RoboBot. His lights are completely out. Normally I wouldn't be too upset about a robot shutting down, but RoboBot is probably our best bet at getting out of this city, and, well, I kind of like the little bastard. He is by far the least horrible robot I've met so far. Before I can get too down about the whole situation, The Roboracle zaps RoboBot much like he had the interface port, and RoboBot sparks back into operation.

RoboBot scans the room wildly, his body shaking and his eyes blinking with an epileptic fury. Gradually he calms down, beeping something to The Roboracle. It's not the first time RoboBot has tried communicating with my worthless little robot companion, but the result is the same. The Roboracle ignores him and goes back into his corner.

Lily approaches RoboBot gently. "What just happened?"

RoboBot hesitates before printing a response. Lily takes it and reads it to herself.

"There's a virus in the system?" Lily asks.

RoboBot shakes his head and hands her another slip.

"What's he saying?" I ask.

"Oh, sorry," Lily says. "He said there's something like an error in the city's interface. Something dark and black."

"That's kind of redundant."

"Just let me finish. Apparently it's not a virus. Or at least he doesn't think it is, but he made a point of clarifying that he's no doctor—well he says DoctorBot—but it doesn't feel like a corruption of the software. He says it's more comparable to a degenerative disease. A corruption of the whole form. From shell all the way to the circuits."

"So it's bad," I say. RoboBot nods and gives Lily another printout. "He says we need to go to the control center of Infinite City," Lily stops abruptly, looking down at RoboBot. RoboBot doesn't meet her gaze. His eyes are small. Lily looks back to me. "And if we can't fix the corruption we have to destroy Infinite City."

Interlude

He watches his shadow hum with the soft pulse of the control panels behind him. The muffled sounds from his prisoner merge with the lights, forming a mesmerizing cacophony of pain. Luck had been with him so far, he never imagined finding one of them so quickly. These things take time, he knew that. Patience is a virtue. And who is more virtuous than he? But he'd already been so patient, and the universe rewarded him.

The initial arrival had been disorienting, and this new world appeared mostly harmless. That will change, he thought. He could feel it with each hallway traversed, spreading his darkness wherever there was light. He would cast his shadow across the entire city if need be. Step by step. But then he found him.

Or rather they ran into each other. At first he saw relief in the other's eyes. It was brief. What followed was fear. And pain. And blood.

His plan all along had been to kill the other, but he likes the throb in his fists after the beating. He likes sounds of agony. Mostly he likes the blood. Not just the redness of it, but the smell. Despite all the planning, all the waiting, he's in no rush to end it.

Besides, he still has one other to find, and perhaps this one could be useful to that end. He's nothing if not practical.

2.5

The idea of blowing up an entire robot city has its appeal, I can't lie, but it sounds like a lot of work and, I mean, what's the worst that could happen?

So I ask.

According to RoboBot, we could be looking at a full blown robot invasion, which still doesn't sound too troubling. The robots here are less intimidating than The Robot With No Name. After I tell RoboBot that, he prints, "There is a reason this city is named Infinite City. The robots will never stop coming. And they will learn. Not stopping until all organic life is gone."

"How can you be sure?" Emma asks.

"I felt it as I interfaced," RoboBot prints. "The urge to destroy. To kill. It was optimal. Almost…desirable."

"Oh," she says.

Even with the destruction of his city looming, I can't help but notice RoboBot is sort of cheery. As if reading my mind he prints out, "This is the greatest mystery in the history of Infinite City. ☺"

Normally the first thing I do before one of my famous hero quests is stock up on supplies. Infinite City, however, is lacking in the heroic supply department, so when RoboBot tells us to follow him there's really nothing left for us to do but follow.

As usual, The Roboracle demands to be carried. Lily and Emma oblige for some reason, but I can't complain. It means I don't have to do it. No one is really talking, so I do something I know I'm going to regret. "Hey Roboracle."

"I AM THE ROBORACLE."

"What's RoboBot keep trying to say to you?" I ask.

"LIES."

"About what?" Emma asks. But The Roboracle doesn't respond.

As we pass our old friend, the blood stain, RoboBot stops us.

"I want to question the CleanerBot again," he prints and knocks on the compartment the janitor robot had scurried into. The door opens and the CleanerBot emerges. Everything is fine until he sees Lily and me. The little bastard goes berserk, screaming "Kill human!" in just about every language known to man. Before I can react, he's on top of me…scrubbing my feet. To his credit, he's scrubbing pretty hard.

"It's probably okay if you shoot this one," Lily says. RoboBot affirms with a nod. But I hold off. "What are you waiting for?"

"He's doing a pretty good job shining my shoes," I say.

"We don't have all day, bro. Plus, I'm starting to get hungry and I don't think Infinite City has lots of food."

It's a pretty good point. I shoot the CleanerBot in the eye and shove his carcass out of my way, cutting my hand as I do it.

"Stupid dead robot," I mutter.

"You're bleeding," Emma says. RoboBot turns to see. Scanning my injury briefly, faintly humming like a dishwasher.

"You'll live," he prints and wanders over to the blood stain again, buzzing a little louder. And then he's on the move again, handing more messages back to us. "The corruption is spreading quickly, but hostilities only seem directed at humans."

"Maybe we should wait in your office while you go to the control center," Lily says.

"Negative. If the core cannot be fixed you'll be more effective at destroying it."

"Sounds fun," I say.

"There also may be a clue as to how you got here," RoboBot prints. "And how to get you home. You won't want to be here if we have to explode the city."

I'd forgotten about that part, but the reminder makes it easy to keep following.

* * *

We weave our way through the maze of hallways for far too long. Times like these make me miss Emma doing all the work for me. Also, I'm getting hungry. I can't have been in Infinite City that long, but the dinner at the Candy Embassy seems like ages ago. It doesn't help that my metabolism is amazing and I burn calories like a simile for things that burn really fucking fast. Damn my Olympian like physique!

No one has said much of anything since I murdered the crap out of the CleanerBot. Occasionally Lily or Emma will giggle, letting me know that I'm being left out of a conversation that I could surely add my trademarked wit to. But whatever. Their loss. And it gives me time to reflect on some things that have been gnawing at me.

Ever since arriving in Infinite City I've had this feeling that I can't quite place. It could just be low blood sugar, but I don't think that's it. There's something familiar about it. But I can't quite put my finger on the when or where or why of it, just that my instincts are telling me it's important somehow. And Captain Valiant always says that a hero's most important tool is their instinct. Well, aside from their genitalia… I wish I knew what mine was trying to tell me—my instinct, not my penis—and I wish the Captain was here. RoboBot is fine, hell as far as robots go he's James fuckin' Bond, but no one can lead an adventure quest like Captain Valiant. He's universally renowned for adventure, after all.

Then again, so am I. (yeah right.)

I jolt to a stop. Emma and Lily do too.

"Did you just talk to yourself?" Emma asks.

"I…did I?"

"You haven't done that in a long time," Emma says.

"I'm confused," Lily says. "What's going on?"

"I'll explain later," Emma says. Lily's eyes are full of worry. "Maybe I should rejoin you."

"I'm totally fine," I wave off her offer, hoping I sound convincing. "Let's keep going." Emma's restlessness lingers behind Lily's gaze, but she relents and keeps walking.

That was really weird.

* * *

The trek to wherever we're going grows more disquieting by the step. Emma and Lily look my way from time to time, their unease palpable. I smile at them when I happen to notice, but it does little to dispel their concern. My concern keeps growing too. Not because of my issue, but because it's so damn quiet. Cities are supposed to be full of life and noise and activity. Infinite City feels dead. Or worse yet, haunted. The thought of robot ghosts makes me shudder as I imagine The Roboracle haunting me throughout eternity. Finally I have to break the silence.

"Where are all the robots?"

"I don't know," RoboBot prints. "They should be out doing their jobs, like me. The corruption must have reached full saturation during mid-day interface. The faster we reach the control center the better."

"Where exactly is the command center?" Lily asks.

"Underground, but the entrance is outside in Perfect Square, which isn't far from here," RoboBot prints. As if on cue, RoboBot taps the wall and a door opens leading to the street. Not far from us is a scattering of robot parts. This is where Emma and I teleported in, or whatever you'd call how we got here. I'm about to tell RoboBot, but Emma beats me to it.

Excited by the news, RoboBot inspects the area with robotic enthusiasm. I have my gun at the ready in case we have to sit through a sequel of Robots Attack. Emma and Lily wander over to the scene of the robot massacre and dig through the debris, eventually coming up with what looks like an arm or leg. I look at them quizzically.

They shrug. "It's better than no weapon."

All the while, RoboBot zooms around the block searching relentlessly for clues of any sort. Finally he makes his way back over to us, printout already in hand.

"There is a thin point in the atmosphere, growing stronger," it reads, "along with trace amounts of weapon discharge and urine."

"Jesus, Victor," Lily says.

I shrug. A guy's got to pee when a guy's got to pee. "What do you mean by a thin point in the atmosphere?"

"I'm uncertain. There was a similar occurrence in the location Lily first appeared. I wrote it off as sporadic ionic dispersion since I couldn't make sense of it, but to find the same anomaly here can't be coincidence. Because a detective doesn't believe in coincidence. I will keep analyzing as we continue on our way."

Before following, I head back over to where we first arrived. I'm light-headed again like I'm disconnected from myself and everything around me. But it's brief. Emma and Lily wait for me to say something, their whole body might as well be a question mark. I just shake my head because I have no answers.

Outside is even more disconcerting than the inside. Infinite City is already cold and unwelcoming enough for a human, but the emptiness makes it a sci-fi horror movie waiting to happen. And sci-fi and horror are two genres that rarely mix well together. I try to imagine what this place might be like on a normal day. All I can come up with is RoboBot, The Roboracle, and No Name standing around laughing at Chalk, who has 7 8 9 bold on his chest. Infinite City transforms into the bridge of the Adventure Galley as I lose myself in a daydream. Captain Valiant lectures Jimmy about what it means to be a spaceboy. Sera sits in the Captain's chair. She pulls a lever and a wave of Phoenix Solution covers her from head to toe. Candy Princess kneels beside her, licking the goo from Sera's arm as Panik sits naked and cross-legged reciting tantric instructions. And I can feel Emma next to me, full bodied. Her lips only inches from me. Her breath hot on my neck. She whispers something that might be indecent even for the bedroom. I grin.

"What's that goofy smile for?" Lily asks, shattering my far too vivid imaginings.

"Uh," I say.

"He's probably thinking about sex," Emma says. Hearing it come out of my sister's mouth makes me a little queasy.

Lily isn't nearly as bothered. She usually isn't. She only shrugs and says, "That sounds about right." I really wish Emma would get out of there. Who knows what they might be thinking about me.

* * *

Eventually we come to Perfect Square. It's hard to miss due to the mammoth robot statue protruding from the center. If Infinite City had better lighting, we most likely could have seen it from much farther away. The statue is pretty unnerving. Not because it looks so realistic—it does, but that's beside the point—what's really awful is that it's identical to The Roboracle. If there's one thing that terrifies me, it's a giant version of The Roboracle blasting Ace of Base and still demanding to be carried everywhere. I'm not kidding when I say I've had nightmares about it.

Before we enter the square, RoboBot approaches The Roboracle, once again trying to communicate through a series of beeps and tones. I expect The Roboracle to ignore them, as usual, but this time he answers. Although the volume of his voice is much lower than usual and his eyes remain trained on the statue looming in the distance.

"LIES. I AM THE ROBORACLE."

RoboBot looks to me or Lily for guidance, his eyes large like a starving puppy. It's strangely effective, but neither of us has any clue as to what's going on, let alone what to do about it. And if the expectation is that I help The Roboracle, well fuck that. He sucks.

Perfect Square is exactly that, a large perfect square. Robots are very literal about everything. It's one of the things I hate about them. Other things include: they are demanding, worthless, loud, they have limited music libraries, they can't transform into cars or jets, and when you say "Go go Kill-Bot net!" no net go-gos. I'm also going to add Perfect Square into my dislike category. It literally has nothing other than the Roboracle-esque statue.

As we get closer, I can see an open door at the base of the statue. That's probably not a good sign. It's obvious that's the door leading down to the command center, and either someone or something has gone down there already, or they just came out. Here's hoping for the latter. Smashing robots is fun, but I don't have an endless supply of ammo, and, quite frankly, I'm just tired. It's been a long day of pointless interviews, fancy feasts, fires, and mysteries. Too much more and I'm likely to pass out from being too awesome.

The Roboracle starts trembling as we close in on the entrance.

"STOP." When we don't, he shakes free of Lily and Emma and backs away, repulsed. As if he and the statue share the same magnetic polarity. Who knows, maybe they do. Robots and magnets don't mix. I've tested that theory.

Still, we don't have time for this mechanical brand of nonsense. "What the hell is wrong with you?" I go to grab him, but Lily's voice stops me.

"Vic, you might want to see this."

I join Lily and Emma while RoboBot hangs back with The Roboracle. Lily is looking at a plaque near the base of the statue that reads:

Here stands the shell of The Roboracle

He foresaw the rise of Infinite City

And gave his circuits for us all to live

"Let me get this straight," I say as I rejoin RoboBot and The Roboracle, "You're not actually The Roboracle?"

RoboBot offers me another printout. "I tried to tell him that he was a copy, but he wouldn't listen."

The Roboracle shifts his gaze between the statue, me, and RoboBot. "I AM THE…FAUXBORACLE?"

"Ha!" I say.

Lily and/or Emma smack me in the arm. For some reason they're concerned and think I should be too. I disagree, but don't bother saying so. It'll only lead to a boring argument where Emma will badger me about my "lack of compassion" and Lily will probably bring up that time I killed her virtual pet and blah blah blah. There really is no good that comes from having your sister and girlfriend share a body. Even at its best, it causes mild nausea.

I make a silent promise not to laugh, though. At least I can do that much.

* * *

Turns out I was wrong. My self-control is incredibly lacking. I should have known that, but I try to believe the best of myself. When I realize I'm about to bust up, I take a little walk around the square. Like I said, there's not much to see. There aren't even benches to sit on. Robots must not need to sit down, which makes me wonder why RoboBot has a chair in his office. Not that it really matters, but I'll have to ask him about it later.

I do my best not to lose myself in my thoughts as I wander around. They've been increasingly sexual lately, and the last thing you want to see when emerging from one of those fantasies is your sister's face. And the rare times my mind doesn't get all sexy, well, it just gets disturbing. Not just because of the violent imagery, but because it feels…natural. It's easier when Emma is with me. I can get lost in her thoughts instead. She keeps me grounded. She keeps me together. Since she's been with Lily I've been woozy. And not just out of disgust that she's inside my sister. It's worse than that, somehow.

Since there's nowhere to sit, I lie down in the middle of the street, or whatever you might call this. And I'm hit with a sudden wave of déjà-vu. I just can't figure out what vu I'm déjà-ing.

(I could tell you.) Fuck, not this again. (you just don't want to hear what I have to say.) You're damn right I don't; I'm done talking to myself. There's nothing you can tell me that I don't already know. (which is why you should probably listen.)

"Uh, Victor," Lily's voice calls out. Great, they probably heard me talking to myself again. Heading back to the other side of the square, I freeze. There are about a dozen robots between me and the others. No worries! There's more than one way around this square. I calmly make my way around the other side. Same situation. Unfortunately, there are not more than two ways around. Squares are such stupid shapes.

I lock eyes with Lily and Emma. They're only a few feet from the entrance to the control center, but the robots are closing in on them. I mouth for them to go. Lily shakes her head, mouthing for me to get over there, so I mouth that I can't get over there because of all the robots, causing her to mouth back "what". We don't really have time for these shenanigans, so I take matters into my own hands.

"Hey robots!" I yell, and two dozen glowing eyes shoot my direction. The robots start towards me, which I'm pretty sure is what I wanted, but I've forgotten why. "Uh…um…" I turn and run.

"What are you doing?" Emma screams. I love that even in a crisis situation she has the wherewithal to use her dumb accents.

I flip around into a backwards run. The robots are all concentrated on me. That's good. "You guys go! I'll meet up with you once I've dealt with this!"

They hesitate, but I wave my arms in the universal "get the hell on with it" sign. That gets them going. Albeit reluctantly. With them safely off, I can focus on the important things in life. Like trying not to die. The problem is, Infinite City sucks nuts and there's nowhere on the street that offers any cover. Looking around, I can't find a single good place to make a stand, but what I do see pisses me off. The robots are a good ways back—they aren't very fast, apparently—and have started back towards Perfect Square.

"Hey," I shout. They don't pay attention.

"Goddammit, you've got to be kidding me," I mutter and run back towards the robot mob. Approaching them, I tap the nearest on what I take to be its shoulder.

It pivots and scans me. "Kill all humans?"

"Kill this," I say as I put a bullet in its face. That does the trick, the chase is back on.

It's not a very exciting chase, though. I'm power walking—at best—to make sure they can keep up with me. The plus side is that none of them seem to have weapons, so they're really not much of a threat one-on-one. Still wouldn't want to get surrounded by them, of course. A couple dozen metal arms beating on you can't feel good. I fire off a few more rounds to take out the robots closest to me. Noticing I still have plenty of time, I yank one of their arms off. No need to waste ammo on these losers. I skip away casually, making my way towards one of those faint door outlines. It opens and I duck inside—well halfway inside, I still need to make sure the robots follow me in here—and I'm back in one of Infinite City's famous hallways. A perfect choke point for inept KillBots.

(so are you ready to talk?) I'm kind of busy here. (but you have to know what this means.) Shut. UP!

I force myself to keep from cracking up, finding the tiny fissure in my mind and pushing. There's a sudden flash of…me. And I'm filled with pure, blinding hate.

It's hot.

It's angry.

It's amazing.

The first robot steps inside and I unleash the fury.

I'm not sure how long it lasts, but the moments that follow are a poorly constructed collage of metal against metal. The robots get a few shots in, but I hardly feel a thing. I'm flying on unadulterated adrenaline and rage. At some point I drop my robot arm and go hand-to-hand, grabbing the robots by their heads and ripping them clean off while I scream obscenities that would make Candy Princess swoon.

There's oil everywhere. My hands are black with it, my clothes drenched. I can taste it. It's a massacre. Finally, it ends.

I slump against the wall. Heart pounding. Out of breath. Dripping with oil and sweat. I haven't felt this alive in weeks. I slide into a sitting position as I survey the carnage, and I start to laugh. That turns out to be a big mistake.

Every door in the hallway opens so suddenly that I get an intense feeling of vertigo and worry that I'm about to be sucked into some sort of black hole. No such luck. Instead I'm faced with a hallway lined with fifty or so robots, all glaring at me with malicious intent.

"Oh fuck," I say, slipping on all the oil as I struggle to get to my feet and run.

The robot nearest me must be a CleanerBot, because it is simultaneously slapping me with one hand and picking up robot debris from the battle with the other. Pushing it away, I manage to crawl out of the hallway and back onto my feet. I can still see The Roboracle statue in Perfect Square. I sprint towards it, this time not bothering to look back to see if the robots are keeping up.

* * *

I slip more than once on my way back to Perfect Square. All that oil is making it a real bitch to get traction. It doesn't help that the street is practically a frictionless surface. I can hear the robots behind me chanting "Kill, kill, kill". Stupid murderous robot mob always trying to kill me! Is it so much to ask that just one of my adventures doesn't involve suck ass robots? As much as RoboBot is sort of okayish, I'm really warming to the idea of blowing this whole city to high hell. Let the Devil deal with these dicks. I'm sure he'd appreciate having all the droids for his Star Wars re-enactments. Although I doubt robots have souls.

When I slip for the 40th time or so, I pause for a few seconds to wipe the soles of my shoes with my shirt. It's not as effective as I'd like, since my shirt is also soaked, but it does enough to get me a little more grip, and I manage to make it back to Perfect Square without falling again.

At the door I see that the robot horde is pretty far back. Enough to hope that they might give up the chase. Out of sight, out of mind is the best case scenario. Fingers crossed. I duck into the entrance to Infinite City's control center.

After a few steps the room jolts to life, causing me to jump before I realize I'm in an elevator. The good news being there's no way all of those robots can fit in here at once, so if they are following they'll need to break up into waves. Maybe I should wait at the bottom and deal with them as they come. Of course I don't know if there are others down there, and finding Emma and Lily should be my first priority. It'll be easier to fight with at least one extra able body.

The elevator reaches the bottom and opens with a whoosh. The first thing that hits me is the heat. My entire body is blasted with a gust of hot air. If I wasn't already sweating, I would be now. It's disconcerting because the rest of Infinite City is so cool. It's so well air conditioned that it's just shy of sitting in giant refrigerator. But it's near boiling down here; feverish. The walls are lined with giant computer servers that whir gently. Except the whir sounds more like a groan, and every light down here flickers to the rhythm of an exhausted heart. A dying heart. RoboBot said that whatever is wrong with Infinite City is worse than a virus, and that may be true, but this whole place definitely feels sick. Terminal even.

Worse still, I have no idea where to go. I'd expected a straight shot to wherever it is we were going, but the path breaks off in three directions: right, left, and straight. I look down each and they all branch off into even more pathways. If the command center is the heart of Infinite City, then I'm expected to navigate its arteries and veins. The good news, if I'm right, all paths would lead where I want to go. The bad news? They also lead away. So I better choose the right direction. Making matters worse, I have no idea which way the others went, but I have to trust that RoboBot knows where to go. I choose the straight path because…well, it's the one right in front of me. And my philosophy will always be to take the path of least resistance.

Aside from the sweltering heat, the acoustics down here are completely insane. I hear footfalls everywhere. They could be Lily's or my own. I haven't the slightest clue. And there are whispers. And shrieks. Some I'm sure are the machines, others I can't tell. If I thought the quiet in the streets was unsettling, this is far worse. I can't even tell if all those bots have followed me down here. I keep my gun holstered. It's too tense down here for firepower. Last thing I want to do is shoot my sister in the face because she sneaks up and startles me.

I call out for Emma and Lily a couple of times, but the echoes are so distorted that it's pointless. At best it will just lead unwanted visitors my direction. So I walk and listen to the horror movie sounds surrounding me. Hoping I'm heading in the right direction, and not wandering to a slow death of dehydration or a robot mauling.

* * *

Going straight isn't always an option, sometimes the paths only go left or right. In those cases my plan is simple; a right followed by the first left I can take. Seems like that should keep me close to the straight path I prefer. The good news is that I haven't hit a dead end yet. At least, I think that's good news. It could just mean I'm getting farther from where I'm supposed to be going.

It hasn't cooled off any, and I think the oil covering me is trapping in most of my body heat. This must be how those birds I used to see on the news after a big oil spill felt. Which is to say, kind of miffed. I want to take a shower and sleep. I want an ice cold Coke and Emma's head resting on my chest. Or, since that's not possible, I want her spirit snuggled up next to mine. I want to take these oil soaked socks off. And I absolutely do *not* want to walk anymore. If I have to take another step I might scream. I take another step. And I hear a scream that could have been my own. I think. I don't remember screaming, but I did just warn myself I might do it. Then again, I also realize there's a good chance I'm suffering from heat stroke, dehydration, and/or general paranoia.

Whatever the case may be, I'm still walking and I'm still alone. My mind is frustratingly blank. If there was ever a time I could do with an inappropriate hallucination, it would be now. But no, I'm stuck here, grounded in an endless jumble of flashing lights and creepy noises that's likely to serve as my tomb. I always knew, somewhere deep inside, that stupid robots would be my demise. From the moment I first met The Roboracle in that supermarket, there's always been a voice nearby, whispering about my death. Granted, most of the time it was The Roboracle's voice—he's a real asshole—but occasionally it was my own voice telling me all about how that asshole The Roboracle is going to get me killed.

So this is my reality now. Sore feet, eerie noises, flashing lights, and a never-ending maze of awful. I consider sitting down and waiting for the end, but Emma would probably be disappointed in me. And I know Captain Valiant would find it unacceptable. This isn't even the first time I've dealt with a maze. The last time was at The

Brothel of Infinite Sadness. Emma was in trouble. I didn't think. I just ran. I guess I could view this similarly. Emma *may* be in danger. Although she's already dead, so how much danger could she really get into? Lily's still alive, though, and if she's in trouble I would love to save her life so I could rub it in her face. I am sick of her gloating about beating me in the 2nd grade spelling bee. Spelling is such a worthless skill. This may finally be my chance to one-up her. For the first time ever, I wish The Roboracle was with me, because I could use some music to fire me up. Fuck it, I'll sing it myself. And this time I won't be stuck with Ace of Base or Styx. I can go with the greatest motivational song of all time. Wake Me Up Before You Go-Go. And as soon as I've put the boom boom into my heart, I'm burning through the corridors like a marginally concerning house fire. I'm motivated, but I'm not that fast.

I don't think and I don't stop moving. I do my best work when I'm not thinking. Barreling around turn after turn, I'm making good time, either to the Command Center or my eventual grave. Whatever. Progress is progress. And progress makes me feel good. It makes me feel accomplished. Without realizing it, my sprint turns into a skip, which is a good thing, because right around the next corner I plow into something.

It's Lily. We're both sprawled on the floor. There's relief plastered all over her face. And something behind her eyes that elicits panic in me. I know that look. It should never come from my sister.

It happens too fast. Exhausted and out of breath, I'm helpless to stop the horror as Lily kisses me.

On the mouth.

Passionately.

There's a terrible moment where it all…lingers. Then Lily pops to her feet like a jack out of a box. "What the fuck, Emma!"

"Sorry," Emma tries to apologize.

"Sorry?"

"I was just so relieved, I forgot where I was."

Lily paces erratically up and down the hall. "Do you have any idea how…oh god I think I'm gonna be sick."

"Jesus, it was just a kiss."

"Just a ki—no, it was gross. So gross."

I've managed to finally, carefully get to my feet. Still too stunned to speak.

"Come on," Emma says. "Look on the bright side. Now you guys have had a little Star Wars moment."

"What?" Lily responds, clearly exacerbated.

"I bet the Devil would love to hear about this," Emma giggles.

And I've had enough. "NO! No one will ever speak of this ever! Do you understand?!"

Emma rolls Lily's eyes. "Whatever. You guys need to lighten up."

"Maybe you should go back with my brother," Lily says. "No offense."

"Yeah yeah, I get it. But you do realize you'll have to touch each other for that to happen," Emma teases.

I scowl.

Lily grabs my arm only long enough for Emma to make it back to me.

(Heeeey.) I'm not ready to talk to you. (Come on, I was worried about you. We thought we heard you screaming somewhere.) I thought I heard that too. (Huh?) But that's no excuse to kiss me with my sister's mouth. (At least your sister is hot.) Hey, I don't want to hear that coming out of my mouth!

"Uh," Lily shuffles around uncomfortably, "can you guys have this conversation later. Like when I'm not around."

I nod.

Lily turns away from us, her voice becoming almost a whisper "But thanks for saying I'm hot."

I hate everything about today.

It's only after the whole incident is over that I notice the two robots were watching the whole thing. RoboBot hands me a slip. "My lips are sealed. Both literately and figuratively."

"Uh, thanks," I say.

"NOT THE ROBORACLE'S," says The Roboracle.

I hate him so much.

* * *

With things settled down, everyone fills me in on what I've missed. The bottom line: not much. Essentially it's the same weird noises and dreadful walking I've experienced. Then I tell them about my robot slaughter and how there might be another army somewhere behind us. RoboBot doesn't think we need to worry since we're almost to the core, and if we can't fix the problem there we're all mostly fucked anyway. That's me paraphrasing. I don't think RoboBot even knows how to swear.

I'm pretty bummed that I'm expected to keep walking, but at least I've got company again. Although I am giving Emma the silent treatment. And she's being kind enough to humor me with it, despite being able to hear my thoughts whenever she chooses to listen. Aside from "The Incident" she's practically perfect. I have to be mad at her a little while longer, however. To prove a point. Not that I'm entirely sure what the point is, but that's never stopped me before and I'll be damned if it's going to stop me now.

Another wave of horror movie sounds ripples past us. None of us flinch—of course half of us are robots—but Lily is visibly irritated. "What is this, the Phantom of the Operating System?"

I shake my head, hoping my disgust in her pun transfers. "Seriously, Lily?"

"What?"

"That was pretty lame."

"You're just mad that you didn't think of it first."

"Psh!"

"Exactly, you're jealous," she says.

"Hardly! If I'm upset it's only because I know I would have delivered it better."

"Uh-huh."

"I'm just saying, if I'd made the joke no one would have complained."

"Because you're the only one complaining," she argues.

"So we're in agreement," I say.

"Sure, if we're willing to ignore reality."

"Reality is overrated."

"Because it has a natural Lily bias," Lily says, and I'm sure I see an added skip in her step now.

"You better not be talking about the 2nd grade spelling bee," I say.

"You're damn right I am."

"We were eight!"

"And I was already clearly better than you."

"Spelling is a worthless skill," I say. "No one needs that crap."

Lily scoffs. Like, right in my face!

I pick up my pace so I can get right in *her* face. This is the most important argument ever. "Height was a bullshit word and you know it! It doesn't follow any of the proper spelling and phonetic rules."

Lily smiles, filled with smuggy smugness. "You lost, bro. Except it."

"I before E, except after C. Where's the C, Lily? Where's the fucking C?!"

"Justify it however you want—"

"And it doesn't sound like neighbor or motherfucking weigh. It was a 3rd grade word, at least!"

"Uh-huh."

"I got jobbed," I say.

"Right," she says.

"Because Mr. Donaldson had the hots for you," I explain.

"We were eight!" she says, as if I didn't already use that argument.

"That one didn't work for me, it sure won't work for you," I tell her. "Besides, he was a pedophile."

Lily pauses. "He did go to prison for molesting kids, didn't he."

"Like 2 years later," I say.

"Okay, but I'm better than you at everything," she says.

"Like what?" I demand to know.

"Uh, like soccer."

"Soccer sucks, Lily. It's a bunch of people running up and down a field, kicking a ball instead of just picking it up. I can't just pretend I don't have hands, damn it!"

"That's how the game works," she explains.

"I don't need your condescension. I know the rules. They're crap. And no one ever scores because of them."

"It's a challenging sport," she argues.

"It's boring. In what universe is 0-0 a good game? And who cares if you were good at soccer? Name something practical that you're better at."

"Well, you just ended a sentence on a preposition. So grammar."

"I said *practical*. No one cares about grammar."

Lily comes to a full stop, looking me dead in the eye. "You really want to go there?"

I have no idea what she means by that, but The Roboracle and RoboBot are looking on with intense interest—well, with The Roboracle it's probably disinterest, but RoboBot seems to be studying the situation like it's a whole new mystery to solve—so I can't back down now. "I really do!"

"Callie Simms," she says. Callie was my first serious girlfriend. She's the girl that finally absconded with my virginity after years of me trying to give it away. She was 17 and she was amazing. Mostly because she wanted to get into my pants as much as I wanted to get into hers. Callie used and abused me like an employee discount on high grade pharmaceuticals. It was a fun six weeks.

"What about her?" I wonder.

"She said I was better than you. Biblically."

I cock my head ever so slightly to the left. "By that you better mean she thought you were better at forming intriguing, if not crude allegories in order to explain the universe."

"I do not mean that," Lily smirks. "And neither did Callie."

(Wait, you're gay, Lily.)

"Please stay out of this Emma," I say.

"Don't talk to your girlfriend like that," Lily says.

"What? I said please!"

"I'm not gay," Lily clarifies. "But I do sometimes enjoy the company of women."

I groan. Not because I hate the idea of her with women—I hate the idea of her with anyone—but her rejection of labels is nearly as obnoxious as The Roboracle's…well, everything.

"And one of those women happened to be Callie Simms," she taunts.

"Shut your filthy mouth! This is the grossest conversation ever."

Lily is no longer addressing me alone; she's making a speech to the whole room. Sure, that's not much more than me, but she's still making a show out of the whole thing. "She said I was better than Victor." Then she pauses and looks me straight in the eye. "At everything."

"Aaahhhh," I scream. "That's totally unfair! I mean she was the first girl I ever…and you are a girl so you probably have…there are things you have in common that I was unfamiliar with and you had practice probably. I bet I could have given your boyfriends better hand jobs but why are you making me think these things?!" I'm hyperventilating a little.

"Are you crying?" Lily laughs.

"If I am, it's only because of the nausea, I assure you."

I'm not in much of a laughing mood, but Emma is so I don't have much of a choice.

Lily drapes her arm around my shoulders. "Don't get too worked up. Everyone knew Callie was a bit of a ho. And I always put my bro before ho's."

"After you've banged them, apparently," I say.

"Well, yeah. Besides, the week before, we had those big oral essay presentations in English. You remember those? You presented the day before I was scheduled to go. And you stole my essay."

"I got an A," I tell everybody.

"And I had to spend all night writing a new one, which got a B minus. I needed to get you back somehow."

"Nice," I say. "You should have rubbed that in way back then."

Lily shrugs. "I felt kind of bad afterwards. Especially when she went on and on about how much she got off with me. You know, compared to you."

"I think you made that very clear already," I say. "The point is, you're weak. You could have exploited that years ago. Really emasculated me. Probably would have meant years of therapy and erectile dysfunction."

"Ew."

"But now I've got a hot girl inside me—"

"Interesting choice of words."

"And I'm happy and awesome. All because you couldn't go for the jugular," I say.

There's a long pause, and suddenly RoboBot claps and jitters, handing Lily a message. "He says 'that was almost as riveting as metamathmatics'. Whatever that means."

"I never really bother trying to make sense of robots," I say. RoboBot is on the move again, and Lily and I are only a step or two behind. Surprisingly, The Roboracle is rolling around on his own, keeping pace well enough.

Lily leans toward me. "Just so we're clear, I won that argument."

"Fine," I concede. "If you're so desperate to base your argument on 'facts' and 'reality'."

"Why wouldn't I?" she asks.

"Look around, Lil. Reality went out the window months ago."

* * *

The closer we get to our destination, the clearer a lot of the noises become. Less muffled, at least. I can almost make out a word or two, but mostly it's still a lot of groaning. The acoustics have improved to the point that it's nearly possible to tell which direction each sound originates from. Everything sounds closer. Including sounds that I'm certain are behind us and that I have little doubt belong to the robot army that chased me down here. With any luck they're far enough away that we can do what we're here to do and get out before there's a confrontation. It doesn't help that I don't actually know what the plan is, or that the robots would be blocking our exit. But all that will sort itself out in time. Or it won't and we'll all die. Worrying about stuff like life and death is a waste of time. I'm pretty sure Captain Valiant told me that. Or maybe I read it in Sun Tzu's <u>Art of War</u>. The point is, I hate plans.

On the bright side, the heat has let up. With each step the temperature seems to drop by a full degree.

"AIR CONDITIONING." The Roborocle voices his approval.

I wonder if maybe Infinite City has dispelled the corruption on its own, but RoboBot explains that is unlikely. Odds are that all cooling systems have been rerouted to the central server to keep it from overheating. All that really matters to me is that I'm no longer hot.

That relief is short lived, however, because my sweat mixed with the rapidly dropping temperature has me shivering. Emma crosses my arms, rubbing them with my hands, hoping that any kind of friction helps. It doesn't, but not much else can be done. I doubt I'd be in this situation if I'd been allowed to kill those cows for leather jackets.

Suddenly my head shoots with pain. The sharpness of it morphs into a throb. I shake it off and sniffle. Instinctively, I wipe my nose, half expecting to find blood. But there's nothing. The drastic swing in temperature is really taking its toll on my body, for some reason. I glance at Lily, wondering if she's having a similar experience. But if she is she's hiding it well. Another step and I double over, like I've been hit in the stomach with a sack of hammers.

There's a horrible moment where I can't breathe and my eyes feel as if they're straining to escape their sockets. Lily grabs me as I stumble. Her lips are moving, but my ears are full of cotton. I want to tell her I don't understand. Or at least shake my head. I don't think I manage either. Emma is frantic inside me. But I can't make out a single one of her thoughts. She's never felt so far away. I'm almost grateful. Maybe she isn't feeling what I am.

Agony.

Desperation.

Fear.

Anger.

Arousal.

Joy.

I can't make sense of any of it. Maybe I don't want to. The throb in my temple pierces my skull. Then comes that feeling of disconnect, like I'm no longer tied to the world. It's pulling away from me, or I from it. My own scream echoes down the corridor, racing towards me. And when we crash into each other I answer it in equal measure. Eyesight blurring, I'm only vaguely aware of something dripping on the floor in front of me. Oil? No, that's dry. I lick my upper lip and tastes pennies. Then, with a single dry heave, it stops.

The first thing I do is wipe my face, but there's nothing there except cold sweat. Looking back at the ground, there's also nothing. Tentatively, I test the strength of my legs. Everything's fine. Lily helps me to my feet, but I don't really need it. All that pain is gone.

Like it happened to another person entirely. I feel fine.

(What the hell was that about?) I don't know...are you okay? (Yeah, I only felt a little bit of all that. But you—) I'm fine. Seriously.

Lily looks me over, not believing me. "Are you sure? That was...freaky."

"I'm just dehydrated, probably," I say. It might even be true. I mean, I'm definitely thirsty. "Come on, we've got a city to save. Or destroy. Right RoboBot?"

RoboBot doesn't respond immediately. It's obvious he's canvassing me like he would a crime scene. Eventually he does nod. I hope that closes the topic.

A few minutes later, RoboBot prints something for us. "The central server is approximately 800 meters down the next access strip. It's not usually guarded, but we should prepare for all possible outcomes."

"I figured I'd just smash everything," I say.

"That's Plan B," RoboBot prints.

"Cool."

"Plan A is connecting to the central server to see if I can clean the corruption."

"Isn't that kind of dangerous?" Lily asks.

"Danger is a detective's life, Lily."

"That's not reassuring" she says. "Especially after the last time you hooked up into the city."

"I know what to look out for this time. I should be able to avoid corruption for potentially several minutes. It's also my best shot of solving the mystery of how you and Victor arrived here."

"I guess," Lily allows.

"Trust me, baby doll," RoboBot prints.

Lily squirms. "I really wish you wouldn't say things like that."

RoboBot turns the corner and we all follow. I can't quite make out what's at the end of the corridor yet, but the growl of the machines grows more urgent and the pulse of the lights speeds up with nervous energy. My own pulse responds in kind, though I'm not sure why. Soon the pulse morphs into a strobe and I feel like I'm at a silent rave where the ecstasy has been laced with amphetamines and an escaped killer is lurking somewhere in the shadows, starving for blood.

The room whispers, but this time it's not the machines. "There you are."

Somehow I know the voice, but the cold and the lights have me so disoriented that my mind refuses to place it. All I know is the sound of it fills me with hate. Beautiful, all-encompassing fury. Before I realize it, my gun is in hand and I'm sprinting. Lily is yelling at me from behind, and Emma is frantic in my head, but I'm not listening. I want to hurt something. I want to find that voice and whisper sweet, murderous nothings in its ear as I choke the life out of it. I want to kill.

There's a laugh that may or may not be my own. Who the fuck cares. Then, without warning, a cry of frustration. And I can see a figure in the distance. And something else. Something huddled at the figures feet. Through the space and flashing lights I can't make out much, but I'm sure that something at the mystery voice's feet is shaking. And there's one other thing of which I'm certain. I can't see it, but I know the thing at the end of the hall is grinning like a madman. Because so am I.

As I close in, something strange happens. The figure begins to pull away without moving. It fades and shrinks and diminishes in a dozen other ways that don't make sense. Aiming the gun, I prepare to fire. Emma stops me. Even though she feels far away inside me, I can just make out the why of it. She doesn't want me to damage the central server. And I miss my shot. Because by the time I reach the room, the figure is gone—along with the thing curled up at its feet—leaving nothing but its shadow dancing in time with the beat of a silent song. Flickering inversely with the dying lights of Infinite City.

* * *

The Command Center of Infinite City isn't large. It's a modest sized, circular room with lots of machinery and three corridors branching from it. Lily and the robots aren't far behind me. The rush of blood to my head has subsided—along with most of my murderous urges—and I can finally hear Lily scolding me. Or rather cussing me out. She's got quite the mouth on her.

Catching up—and her breath—she pushes me into one of the main control panels. "What the fuck, Vic? I mean, seriously, what the fuck?!"

"What's the big deal?" I wonder.

"I don't know, bro," she says. "You start running and screaming and laughing and whispering strange shit with a loaded gun in your hand and it's kind of disturbing."

"Huh," I say. "Well, I missed my chance, so whatever."

(And why were you trying to push me out?)

"What are you talking about?" I ask.

(It felt like you were trying to kick me out of your body. I was doing all I could to hold on and keep you from destroying everything down here.)

"Sorry," I say, trying to hide my concern, which is pretty pointless when the person you're trying to hide from can read your thoughts and feelings. "But hey! It's over now. It's all good. Probably."

While Lily and Emma lecture me, RoboBot is busy probing the

scene. As it turns out, a lingering shadow wasn't the only thing left behind. There's blood too. Again.

"There's a thinness here," RoboBot prints. "It's much stronger. Fresher. This could be your exit."

"Um," Lily, Emma, and I say at the same time.

"I don't really see an exit here, RoboBot," Lily looks around, confused.

RoboBot ignores us. "I'm going to plug into the city now. I'll keep communications open as best I can." He doesn't wait for a response before jacking into the system. Then all we can do is wait. RoboBot keeps his word. A steady stream of paper flows from him, mostly saying nothing. When it finally has a message worth reading, it's not good.

"There are robots approaching from each pathway. At least three score. They will arrive momentarily."

Reading the message brings one important question to mind. "Three score? Who talks like that?"

(Does that mean three score in total, or in each direction?)

"And shouldn't we be able to see them already?" Lily wonders.

Just on cue, the lights settle and blare brightly. And we can see them all. They really blend in with the scenery quite well.

"Feel better?" I ask Lily.

"Nope," she answers. They're a few hundred feet away, marching in rows of six. How many rows, I can't tell, but ten would be a reasonable guess after what RoboBot told us.

"They're easy to kill, at least," I reassure.

"That's good. So…you take the right, I take the left, and we meet in the middle."

"Sure. Hey Roboracle, how about some fighting montage music?"

"I AM THE FAUXBORACLE."

"So is that a no?"

"THE FAUXBORACLE IS NOT WORTHY OF THE GLORY OF STYX. OR ACE OF BASE."

"What the hell are you good for, then? Will you at least do that shock thing you can do. You know, help us fight?"

"FIGHT FOR YOU? NO."

(What about Donna? I thought you wanted to see her again. Isn't that why you're here?)

Even Emma sounds pissed at The Roboracle—and that's rare—but it actually gets The Roboracle in gear. "FOR DONNA NATRIOS. THE FAUXBORACLE WILL DO ANYTHING." He moves between Lily and me. "THE FAUXBORACLE WILL TAKE THE MIDDLE."

"Gee, thanks." I say. "Dick." Then everything goes epileptic and the party really starts.

For all my complaints about The Roboracle—and I truly do loathe him—he does really fire me up for some robot smashing. Considering all my recent experience with dismantling robots, I hand my gun to Lily. She might need it more than I do. I urge Emma to go along too. I know she has plenty of experience with guns and kicking ass. Can't say the same for Lily. Emma doesn't argue.

That settled, I don't bother waiting for the robots to get any closer. If I let them get into this room, they'll be able to spread out and surround us. Time to take the fight to them. I bulrush like a badass, grabbing one of the bots from the middle of the first row while trying my damnedest to rip the bastard's head off. Then one of his buddies to my right reaches out and shocks me.

"What the fuck?" I scream.

There's a pause in the gunfire behind me. "What's wrong?"

"One of them shocked me," I grab the arm responsible and attempt to wrench it off. "They never did that before."

"RoboBot did say they would adapt."

"It's a pretty sorry excuse for evolution, then. Severe static shock isn't exactly life threatening."

"Then stop complaining."

"It's just annoying, is all," I mutter to myself as I finally free the shock arm from its user. A few more robots have started shocking me too, but I manage to kick them back pretty effectively.

More gunshots pound my eardrums before Lily and Emma yell, "We're out of ammo." I risk a glance back and can see Emma has already started in on her interpretive dance of death. They'll be fine. Turning back, the one armed robot grabs for his former arm, and I slap him with it. To my surprise it fries the hell out of him. Awesome. I smack the entire front row and they start smoking like a future cancer patient. Their corpses provide a slight road block, but it won't last for long. I use the shock arm some more, but it has lost most of its juice. I need to find a way to slow them even more. Then I see one of the disabled bots spurting oil from its neck joint and it gives me an idea. It might not work, but it's worth a shot. Taking the spent shock arm, I use it like a baseball bat to knock off the robot's head. Warm oil erupts towards the ceiling, and I push the robot over so all the oil gushes towards his friends. Their traction is instantly disrupted, buying me time to catch my breath and maybe find another makeshift cattle prod.

Suddenly, a series of beeps ring through my ears. "THE ROBOT-BOT REQUESTS THE FAUXBORACLE INFORM YOU THAT HE HAS LOCATED THE SOURCE OF THE CORRUPTION. THE FAUXBORACLE HAS COMPLIED."

I glance back to see The Roboracle resting idly next to RoboBot. "What the hell, Roboracle? You're supposed to be helping us fight."

"THE FAUXBORACLE HAS ALREADY WON. THE FAUXBORACLE ONLY WISHES HE COULD PLAY STYX IN CELEBRATION."

I take a bit of a gamble—not much of one, the oil really has my group of bots floundering—and rush back to check on the center corridor. It's littered with scrap metal.

"How the…" I scratch my head and look towards Lily and Emma. They've built up a nice barricade of corpses, but that can't hold forever. "Well you could help the rest of us."

"THE FAUXBORACLE WAS CHARGED WITH THE CENTER."

"A few tips would be nice, at least," I say, knowing it's pointless.

"YES. THEY WOULD BE." Like I said, pointless. He exchanges a few more beeps with RoboBot. "THE ROBOT-BOT IS CURRENTLY ENGAGED IN BINARY BATTLE WITH THE GREAT DARK CORRUPTION. THE FAUXBORACLE FORSEES FIERY DEATH."

"Yeah, well you're a fraud," I say.

"THE RO…" The Roboralce stops short, a hint a static blaring from his speakers. "I AM THE FAUXBORACLE."

I've already wasted too much time with this crap. My attention needs to be on crushing some robots. Only there's a problem. The robots are no longer trying to advance. They're smashing the walls around them. If I thought the noises emanating from this place were horrible before, they're nothing compared to now. Infinite city is shrieking.

"Uh, this is bad isn't it?" Lily says from somewhere behind me.

Without realizing it, RoboBot has crept up behind me, print out in hand. "The corruption is too deeply imbedded, but it has shifted its parameters. It's no longer concerned with destroying all of humanity."

"That's good, right," Lily say, reading over my shoulder.

"No. It now views you as the much bigger threat. It's activated Infinite City's Implosion Initiative. Every robot in Infinite City has been charged with destroying core systems to keep anyone from deactivating it."

"You're telling me that we've turned an entire city into a suicide bomber?" I say.

We wait for RoboBot to print his response. It ends up being a simple "Yes."

"So what do we do?" Emma asks.

"You leave," RoboBot prints.

"How?" We all ask simultaneously.

"Presumably the same way the others left," RoboBot answers.

I keep a close eye on all the robots surrounding our most obvious exits. "Which is?"

"A mystery. ☺"

"That's helpful," I say.

"I suggest you stand right here, where the thinness is strongest."

"And then what?"

"I understand humans have many gods that they pray to in times of distress."

"Seriously," I say.

"What about you?" Lily asks. "What are you going to do?"

RoboBot already has his printouts ready. "Use the debris to attempt to build a protective barrier, and run through the events of the day in order to solve this mystery." Before trotting off towards the chaos, RoboBot stuffs a piece of paper into Lily's pocket.

To his credit, RoboBot works fast and effectively, arranging the multitude of rubble with mathematical precision. Maybe it's even funny to him.

"We should help," Lily says. Emma concurs, and even I'm inclined to agree. But something keeps me quiet and holds me in place.

"THE FAUXBORACLE WOULD NOT RECOMMEND IT."

Lily starts toward RoboBot. Instinctively I grab her, shaking my head. Infinite City growls and quakes with a frightening ferocity. And we're at the epicenter. Lily squeezes my hand, and Emma slips back to me.

(Hey guys, don't worry. Being dead isn't so awful.)

Emma tries to laugh inside me, but it's not very convincing.

"Why do you sound so worried, then?" Lily wonders.

(Well, the whole dying part kind of sucks.)

"That's comforting," Lily says. The quaking intensifies as the panels surrounding us blow their fuses. Sparks fly past us causing Lily to flinch. She's pretty easily startled. It's kind of embarrassing.

A chunk of ceiling crashes down beside us, barely managing to miss The Roboracle. I curse his luck. More and more debris falls, particularly in RoboBot's vicinity. Lily tenses with each piece. RoboBot isn't fazed. He deftly dodges every potential disaster, picking up whatever hits the ground and adding it to his defensive barrier. For a minute or two I actually think this might work out okay. Then Infinite City roars, and I know we're about to die.

The hallways are long enough that we can see the approach. Fire rushes towards us, a tangerine torrent intent on washing the flesh from our bones. RoboBot looks at us before pushing up against the sturdiest portion of his wall. He beeps something. Something that sounds painfully human. Something that sounds like goodbye.

That's when the flames swallow him.

I glance at Lily, her grip tightens and I notice her other hand clutching inside her pocket. Tears frame the corners of her eyes as she squeezes them shut. Emma is trying to tell me something, but I can't hear her. I can't hear anything but the flood of fire. Everything feels oddly disconnected when the heat finally reaches me. Sweat trickles down by forehead, stinging my eyes, seconds before the inferno reaches us. I don't blink. I want to see this. Then the fire kisses us. Hard. We're shoved back with terrible force. I expect to feel my spine snap when I hit the console behind me.

But it doesn't.

Because I never hit the console.

I don't hit anything at all.

The flames that threatened to engulf us are frozen, far away, and getting farther with each breath. Until they're gone. There's only darkness. Lily's hand is still in mine, I can feel it, but I can't see her or anything else. I wonder if maybe this is dying. If it is, Emma was lying. This is peaceful. I count to five. And somewhere before six, we crash back to the world. Not Infinite City, though. It's my bathroom on the Adventure Galley.

We're home.

* * *

Lily opens her eyes with a sharp breath, and coughs. It takes her a minute to grasp the change of scenery. "Where are we?" Her voice is dry, probably from the last blast of heat in Infinite City.

"The Adventure Galley," I tell her. "More specifically, my bathroom." I notice, much to my disappointment, that The Roboracle made the trip with us.

Lily notices something else. She sees the disassembled robot parts all over the floor. Her hands go to her mouth. "Is that RoboBot?"

"Uh," I say.

She drops to her knees and begins gathering up the pieces, hope splashing over her every movement. "Maybe we can put him back together."

"That's actually The Robot With No Name," I explain.

She bites her lip. "So…"

"I don't think RoboBot made it."

"Oh," Lily drops the scrap metal and slumps against the bathroom wall, crying quietly. Her hand goes back to her pocket and she pulls out the paper RoboBot placed in there before…well before everything went all explodey. She sniffles and wipes the tears from her face. Then her expression contorts. "Goddamnit." She turns her attention to me. "This is your fault, you know."

"Huh?"

Lily pushes herself back onto her feet and tosses me RoboBot's final message. It says: "Sorry we never got around to the intercourse, sweetcheeks."

"Aww," I can't help but smile. "That's pretty classy."

"Shut up," Lily says, but her mouth twitches like she trying really hard not to smile too.

I read the message one more time. RoboBot was pretty fucking cool. You know, for a robot.

Epilogue

A lone CleanerBot suverys the charred wreckage that was once Infinite City. Appalled, it begins to sweep at the debris. Lying motionless in the rubble that powered the great city is RoboBot. Scorched and partially melted, electric impulses misfire weakly throughout his system. All power within RoboBot reroutes to preserve his primary function. RoboBot meticulously reviews all data pertaining to the first, and greatest, mystery he's ever encountered. He reevaluates Lily's story and Victor's appearance. He checks the data regarding the strange atmospheric disturbances that accompanied their arrival. He studies the data he pulled from the corruption within Infinite City. But mostly, like any good detective, he focuses on all the blood. Despite a draining power source RoboBot's review is absolute. Minutes pass in an endless hum of computation. And in a flash he sees it all.

RoboBot solves his mystery.

RoboBot prints out a single name for his new human friends to read. His auditory and ocular sensors too damaged for him to realize he's alone, his injuries so massive he doesn't even notice the CleanerBot snatch up the piece of paper and incinerate it. RoboBot is blissfully ignorant.

Satisfied with a job well done, RoboBot awaits full system shutdown. RoboBot wants nothing more than to die with a smile on his face.

Of course, robots can't smile.

A CRISIS IN RETROACTIVE CONTINUITY

HERR DOKTOR MUSIKSPIELER

R.P.

STEEL CANYON

10c

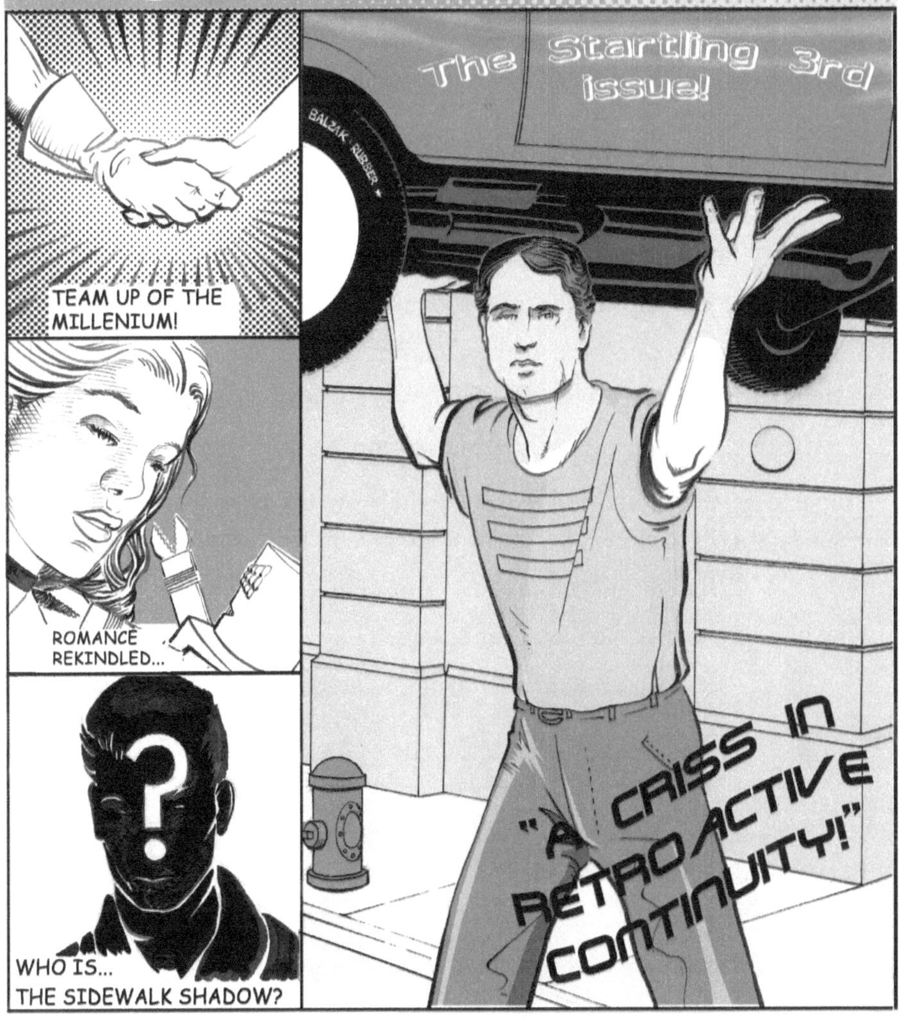

3

Lily wants to shower. I don't blame her. I see myself in the bathroom mirror and it's a pretty nasty sight. Much worse than Lily, really, but I know she needs the privacy more than I do right now. I show her how to work everything in the bathroom and then get out of her way. I'm ready to pass out. I'm so exhausted, in fact, that I plop down on my bed before I even notice I'm not alone. Sitting cross-legged, right next to my head, is a very naked Panik.

"There you are," she says.

"Uh, hi," I say.

(Damn it, is she gonna try to have sex with you again?)

"No, I'm just waiting and meditating."

"So why are you naked?" I ask.

"Clothing restricts the flow of tantric meditative energies."

(See, that still makes it sound like you're here for sex.)

"I have no need for sex, currently," Panik says. "However, if you wish to engage physically with your partner at any time, Emma, I will be content to allow you possession of my body for the act. It would be mutually beneficial for all parties."

(Uh, thanks…) That is pretty nice of her. (Shut up.)

"But I would ask that we wait until after we've spoken of your whereabouts this evening," Panik says.

"Could we maybe do this in the morning?" I ask. "I really just want sleep."

"Hey, Vic," Lily emerges from the bathroom dressed only in a towel, "do you have any clothes I could bor—hello gorgeous naked woman." She shuffles uncomfortably, ducking back into the bathroom ever so slightly.

"Hello pretty toweled girl," Panik says.

"Why is there a naked woman in your bed, bro?"

"Apparently clothing is restrictive to meditation," I tell her, still lying on the bed, my eyes closing against my will. Not that I fight too hard. I have a feeling Lily might start flirting with Panik soon and I don't want to see that at all. "If you two are gonna get weird, just do it somewhere else. And then never tell me about it."

"Victor," Panik says. "It's important we speak—"

I'm already drifting off. "Tomorrow."

"I'm not that tired yet," Lily says. "I could feel you in on some of it…um, I mean fill you in."

"Either would be adequate," Panik says.

"Not here," I mumble.

"My quarters will suffice," Panik says. Those are the last words I hear.

* * *

Panik and Lily are making out in front of me and it's really pissing me off. Not just because I'm jealous that Lily has her hands full of one of the most perfect asses I've ever seen, but because PDA is only appropriate when Captain Valiant does it. With him it's a master class in bargaining and seduction. Without him it's just my so-called sister one upping me again.

Even from across the room I can hear Panik's whispers. She's telling Lily how she just went back in time and taught Lily all of her thirty-seven erogenous zones. Lily says she remembers and Panik moans. When Candy Princess joins them I know in my heart this is the worst place in all of time to be. Lily sticks her tongue out at me as I leave. Panik bites it. Candy sucks on the blood. Lily's always been too desperate to please everyone.

Outside, Jimmy stares up at the stars. I approach him tentatively. The moon is bright and alien and lonely in the sky despite the plethora of stars surrounding it.

"The Opal Moon is nearly full," Jimmy says. "And it's all alone." There's desperation in his voice that makes him seem younger than he is.

The Roboracle appears next to Jimmy. Or maybe he was there all along. "IT MEANS DEATH. FOR YOU MORE THAN ANYONE."

Jimmy nods, still transfixed by the glowing moon. Sera approaches from behind, covering Jimmy's eyes with her hands.

"Don't worry," she whispers. "With our powers combined we can form him."

"Captain Valiant," Jimmy says.

"I'm already quite formed," says Valiant from nowhere. "Just ask the lovely Lily."

"Did you hear that, baby? We did it!" Sera celebrates.

"DEATH."

Jimmy and Sera giggle.

"Let's go screw Victor's sister," Sera demands.

"And then choke the life out of her?" Jimmy asks like a kid in a candy store.

"Anything for my baby," Sera says.

"THE ROBORACLE WILL WATCH. AND RECORD. THE FATES LOVE SNUFF FILMS."

They disappear.

Something tickles my neck. It's Emma. Just as I remember her from the very first time I saw her.

"Everyone else is with Lily," I say.

"I know," she says.

"But you're here."

"I've already been inside her. She's warmer than you."

I don't argue.

Emma unzips her pants. "Let's go find a place to fuck."

I follow her through a door that wasn't there and we're back in the bathroom. Emma tears off her clothes and I feel an immense sadness. She always looked amazing in that shirt. Now it's ruined. She tries to kiss my sorrow away, but the remains of her shirt lying lifeless on the floor tug at my heartstrings.

Emma slaps me and I forget about the shirt. She grins. "You like that don't you, you little bitch!"

She slaps me again. Harder. "All that pain makes you feel like a real man, doesn't it? I'll show you real pain." Emma drops to her knees, leaving me with only my reflection.

I see myself.

A handprint and lipstick on my face.

A shift.

Bloodied and bruised.

A shift.

Oil stained and ragged.

A shift.

A murderous smirk.

Everything changes, but never me.

"Hello, sir," a voice interrupts. I look down, past what Emma is doing, and see the disembodied head of The Robot With No Name.

"Look at this mess," he says. His voice as chipper as ever.

"We've really fallen apart, haven't we," he says to me.

And Emma bites down.

* * *

I wake to an empty bed. Nothing unusual about that. But I also wake to an empty body. Or emptier than when I went to sleep. Emma's not here with me. There's a brief moment of panic, until I notice the note next to the bed letting me know that Emma jumped into Lily to help explain about last night's little excursion. Sometimes I forget that, being dead, Emma doesn't really get tired the same way I do. Can't say I'm not a little relieved that she wasn't inside me during that dream. I'm never sure exactly how much of my dreams she perceives, but there's really nothing about the latest one that I'd care to share. I'd be happy enough to forget it myself.

First things first, I need a shower because something smells awful and I'm pretty it's me. The hot water feels wonderful, although I do miss Emma. She's a great shower buddy. Even dead. Besides, I know how much she misses the little things in life. Emma never complains about being dead, but I can feel her exhilaration whenever we shower. Or eat. Or get frisky with my sexy body…which she's been really into lately for some reason. Feeling someone else's feelings is an incredibly intimate experience. Emma never lets me get upset about what happened to her, but since she's not here right now I can't help but feel sorry knowing that she never gets any private moments anymore.

In the midst of my minor wallow fest, the bathroom door opens. I freak out a little and almost fall.

"Victor," Captain Valiant says. "I hear you had quite the *adventure* last night."

"Uh," I say.

"I must say I'm disappointed. You should have invited me along," Valiant reprimands.

"I, um, I didn't have much choice, Captain. I'm so sorry!"

The Captain chuckles. "No apologies necessary, my friend.

Adventure is a fickle lover. When she calls, you must abide immediately, lest you suffer her wrath."

"Right," Thank god he's not upset.

"Enjoy the rest of your shower, Victor. You've earned it. But do hurry. Breakfast is waiting for us, and we have much to discuss."

I rush through the rest of my shower, because keeping Captain Valiant waiting isn't an option. No big deal, I was getting bored with all the scrubbing. Some of the oil refuses to come off, so I'm still splotchy, but who cares. I dress and head to the mess hall. Jimmy is the first to see me and he waves like an idiot. Sera is next to him, naturally. Her hair is a blinding canary yellow this morning, and her eyes a magnificent purple. It's jarring at first, but she pulls it off as usual. Lily is on her other side chatting up Panik, who manages to feign interest. At least I imagine she's faking it, Lily isn't that interesting. Captain Valiant is seated next to Panik, admiring his own reflection in a spoon.

It looks like I'm the last to arrive. I curse silently. I just hope Captain Valiant won't hold my tardiness against me.

"Gooood morning," Candy Princess sings from behind me.

I swivel around. "Oh, uh, you're here," I guess I wasn't the last to show up. That's a weight off.

"Of course, silly," she says. "My house burned down." Candy frowns in her own patented exaggerated fashion as she hits the word down, but it only last about a second. "But now I get to spend more time with you!" She pokes my nose.

"Well, every cloud has its silver lining," I say.

"Oh golly! That's so beautiful! You're so poetic."

"Yeah, I know." I notice Sera glaring at me in a very Emma-like way. "I should probably go."

"Wait! Who's the new girl," she whispers like a shy kid at a birthday party.

I sigh. "I guess I might as well introduce you." We make our way over to the table, Sera is still burning a hole through me and Candy. There's no doubt that Emma is somewhere behind those eyes. I flash a smile. "Candy, this is Lily. My sister. Allegedly." Lily says that last part with me, causing everyone to give us curious looks of curiosity. Jimmy even says, "Huh?"

Emma, in her cute southern accent, deals with him so that I don't have to. "It's just some weird sibling quirk of theirs."

I ignore them and continue with the introductions. "Lily, this is Candy Princess."

Lily stands, making like she's going to shake Candy's hand. "You're *the* Candy Princess?"

"You've heard of me?" Candy glows.

"Oh, I've heard of you." Without another word Lily punches Candy square in the face. Candy plops down to the ground like a toddler just learning to walk. Chalk chooses this moment to walk in, his blank expression instantly replaced with a giant exclamation point as his hands shoot comically in the air.

"Nice," Sera says, stuffing a piece of pancake in her mouth.

"What was that about?" I ask.

Lily scowls at me in sheer disbelief. "She killed Emma!"

Candy's face is painted with similar disbelief, her lower lip quivering and voice quavering. "Only once, though."

"And I only punched you once," Lily says. "You'll live. For now."

Captain Valiant glides over to Candy Princess, helping her back to her feet. "Now, Miss Lily, that's no way to treat a guest on our ship." He flashes that valiant smile of his and I fully expect Lily to swoon in 3, 2—

"And you are?" she has the audacity to ask!

"The fuck, Lily?" I say.

"What?"

"That's Captain Valiant! Captian. Motherfucking. Valiant! This is his ship. How do you not know that? You were sitting, like, five feet from him."

"Excuse me," she gets all sassy now, "but I'd only been sitting there for about thirty seconds and he'd spent the entire time staring at his spoon."

"He wasn't staring at his spoon, Lily. He was staring at himself *in* that spoon. Because look at him, he's dazzling!"

"Now, now, Victor," Captain Valiant interrupts. Not that anything he says is ever an interruption. "It's my fault for not introducing myself earlier. It was very uncouth and in direct violation of my own *valiant* guidelines. I sincerely apologize for my lack of civility, Lily. Not only are you a guest on my ship, you are my dear friend's sister and utterly stunning." The Captain kisses Lily's hand and winks. "I hope you can forgive me."

"Um," Lily's voice trembles as she blushes ever so slightly, "okay. But I won't apologize to her." She waves off-handedly at Candy.

"That's okay," Candy says. "I already forgive you." You really can't kill the chipper inside her.

"Excellent," Captain Valiant proclaims. "With all that settled, let us eat so that we may discuss last night's grand *adventure*."

* * *

Breakfast is delicious, as usual, and I'm more than a little pleased that Lily and Emma relayed last night's escapades to Panik quite thoroughly. They also fill in everyone else on the whole affair. Lily still has trouble discussing RoboBot without getting misty-eyed. Although I think she's milking it to get some sexual healing from Panik. One of my favorite things about Lily is her willingness to exploit a person emotionally for sexual gain. She'll act like she's above that kind of thing, but really she's just a politician who endlessly panders to all her more physical special interests. And I applaud her for it. As long as I never have to hear about it. Of course, she's kind of wasting her time with Panik. That woman will sex-up anything with a pulse—probably several things without a pulse too—but I have to appreciate Lily's commitment to her craft. I give her a thumbs up to let her know it. She shakes her head like she doesn't know that I know that she knows that I know what she's up to. But we both know that's just not the case.

As the story continues, occasionally I interject something between bites of sausage. Like how I fought nearly 1000 robots single-handedly and saved everyone's lives. But mostly I don't have much to do other than keep eating. Eventually Panik gets around to asking about that shard thing that she has an unhealthy obsession with. we're all still just as clueless about that, though.

"But you have been near it," Panik says.

"Not that I know of," I say after swallowing a particularly fluffy piece of pancake.

"It wasn't a question," she says. "The test results from last night show a spike in your blood pressure, adrenaline, and a very specific neurotoxin found only in rare Abstractions or very emotionally repressed demon spawn that won't be born for another eight centuries."

"Tests? What tests?" I ask.

Panik sips on a green drink I've never seen before. "The ones I performed while you slept."

"That's creepy."

"Lily also showed similar, albeit less violent, spikes during her tests."

"Bleh, I don't want to hear about you testing Lily. Or any spikes that may have occurred."

"Oh grow up, bro," Lily says.

"You grow up," I counter, brilliantly.

Lily's only response is her stare. And I know it's on.

"Oh my stars!" Emma says. This accent thing is really having an odd effect on her.

"What?" Jimmy wonders.

"Why I do believe they are having a staring contest. I've never seen anyone do this with him voluntarily." Staring contests have always been the go to competition for Lily and me. They're the perfect balance between determination and zero effort expended. "I can't look away."

"I wish you didn't have to use my eyes for this," Sera says.

"Calm down," Emma says. "It's not like I'm making you watch Astralporn."

Astralporn? Why don't I know what that is?

"At least that has action, and an actual climax," Sera complains.

I bark a laugh and offer my hand for a high five, but no one answers the call. I can't worry about that, though, I've got staring to do. Winning this is the most important thing ever.

There's a thud on the table, and seconds later something scalds my lap. I jump out of my chair wiping at my legs, trying to avoid significant burns.

"Ha! I win," Lily proclaims.

"A *valiant* showing," Captain Valiant claps.

That's when I see the overturned cup on the table, a stream of hot chocolate flowing directly from it to me. "Damn it, Jimmy!"

"I didn't do it," he says. "It was Sera."

Sera nods.

"Don't blame Sera," I tell him.

"I uh—"

"You what? Was that your cup?"

"Well, yeah but—"

"But what?! If you'd managed to drink your hot chocolate like a man, Sera wouldn't have had anything to knock over! Fuck, Jimmy! FUCK!!!"

I storm out of the room, not wanting to face Lily's gloating. I hate her victory face so much. Almost as much as I hate Jimmy's normal face. Also, my pants are wet and need to be change.

Fuck Jimmy.

* * *

Back in my room I'm still reeling from my defeat, but at least I have dry pants again. There's really nothing else to do in here. Still, I can't rejoin the group just yet. My shame is too fresh. They will never accept me back into the fold so soon. So I do the best thing I can: I lie in bed grumbling indignantly at the ceiling. Someday I'll get Lily back. We'll have a rematch. The when and where are a mystery, but it will happen. And when it does I'll enter unflinchingly into the fold. Because that's how staring contests work. I'll stare so hard I'll make her eyes bleed. Then with those bloody tears streaking down her face, I'll pounce on her and rip her stupid eyes from her stupid head. Then I'll crush her eyes under my foot and laugh. And when everyone else looks at me like I'm a madman I'll say "Can't you see the vitreous humor in it?" That will most likely be accompanied with silence, so I'll explain that vitreous humor is the goo in a person's eye, thus making my previous comment a multi-layered pun worthy of songs and epic poems…then I'll burn everyone to the ground! Hahaha…

…

…

…

I shake my head violently. That little revenge fantasy sure got out of control quickly. Not really sure where it came from, but whatever. I'm still going to avenge that loss. Just, you know, minus the maiming and junk.

There's a knock at my door.

"Enter," I command.

It's Jimmy.

Lame.

"Hey, Vic," he says. "Just wanted to apologize for the whole hot cocoa thing."

"Obviously," I say, not moving from the bed.

"So we're cool?"

"I'm cool. You, on the other hand…"

"Come on, man!"

I finally sit up. "Look, Jimmy. I want to forgive you, I really do, but an apology won't erase that loss from the record books."

"It was just a staring contest, dude."

"And I *lost*," I say. "In front of everyone. In front of Captain Valiant, Jimmy!"

"The captain doesn't care."

"Tsk, tsk. So naïve."

"Nah, man, he still thinks you're cool," Jimmy says.

"You think?" I wonder. "Yeah, yeah you're right. I am pretty great. I mean, if there's anyone he's disappointed with, it's got to be you. How long's it take to drink hot chocolate, anyway? And then coming in here calling it hot cocoa. That's just weird."

I expect Jimmy to leave now. I'm pretty sure our conversation reached its natural conclusion. When he continues to hang around I say, "By the way, No Name is still in pieces in the bathroom. How about you clean that up for me?"

"Um," he says.

"Fix him up, bury him, toss him in the trash, I don't care. I'm gonna let you decide. I think you've earned it."

"Um," he says.

I hop off the bed and clap Jimmy on the shoulder. "Thanks, buddy! You're a real pal." I skip out the door, leaving Jimmy behind, off to find Emma and Sera, or Captain Valiant—anyone, really— and whistling as I go.

I run into Chalk as I wander the halls. It's hard to tell with him, but he seems a little blue.

"What's up?" I say.

Chalk shuffles his feet for a few seconds before his face reads, U DIDN'T TAKE ME WITH U and then in a blink, I WANTED 2 SMASH ROBOTS 2. He follows that up by plastering on a sad face emoticon.

"Aw, man. I didn't even want to go. I would have asked you to come along if I'd known I was going."

YEAH? his face reads.

"Totally," I tell him.

Panik appears around the corner, business as usual. "I need a minute of your time."

"Me?" I ask, knowing the answer but hoping I'm wrong.

She nods and beckons me to follow her. I tell Chalk I'll catch up with him later before jogging after Panik. Back at her quarters, Lily is waiting for us.

"What's this all about?" I ask.

"I want to do some additional tests with you and your sister," Panik says.

"No way am I getting freaky with you two. Maybe that's all copacetic in the future, lady, but right here and now it's super gross."

"Jesus, Vic," Lily says. "You're embarrassing."

"Don't tell me you're okay with this!"

Lily rolls her eyes, but it's Panik who speaks. "This isn't about sex. Test means test. I have no need for playful euphemisms. I have a working hypothesis regarding why/how you ended up in this Infinite City."

"Oh," I sit down next to Lily. "That's cool. Let's get on with it." Panik pulls out some strange devices. A few I've seen before when she did earlier tests, a few I haven't. Then she does some science-y stuff. Or maybe it's sexual. I don't know because I stop paying attention pretty early on in the whole process. My mind wants to wander, but I keep it on a leash. The places it goes these days are not acceptable for any company.

Surprisingly, Panik remains fully clothed. Which is a good thing. On our 18th birthday, Lily dragged me unwittingly to a strip club. Apparently she thought it would be funny to watch me squirm as I was surrounded by seedy naked women and my sister. The plan worked on her end, she laughed about it for weeks. I hated her for slightly longer. I don't really need a repeat of that situation. Last night was close enough, but I was too tired to be bothered. Besides, it would look pretty bad if Emma and Sera walked in on that kind of scene. For several reasons.

Finally Panik says, "Finished."

"Um, okay," I say. "Does that mean I can go?"

"If you wish."

I do wish, so I go to leave. But Lily's question stops me halfway out the door. "What do you think the problem is?"

I probably should have asked that by now, but the thing is, like with most things, I don't really care that much. Sure, randomly popping into a city of robots all hell-bent on killing you is a hassle, but so is being used as a science experiment.

Panik's attention is focused on a bunch of doodads instead of either of us. "The theory I'm playing with is that you've become un-tethered from gravity."

"Does that mean I'm going to be able to fly?" I ask, doing a terrible job of containing my excitement.

"Not that kind of gravity," Panik says. And my world sucks all over again. "Transdimensional gravity. It's the theoretical force that holds you to a specific plane of reality, as well as holding said planes together in the first place."

"Uh-huh," Lily and I say together. I kind of hate when we do that.

Panik pays no mind, however. "Even where I'm from it is more myth than science. But in my travels I've seen many myths realized. I've learned that magic, myth, and science will eventually find a point of intersection. Time is vast, after all. It doesn't dismiss possibilities, or even impossibilities. So I don't either."

I lean against the door frame. "Let's say you're right, what happens now?"

"Popular theory says that you'll form your own anti-gravitational field—that's what I'm testing for, albeit crudely—which will grow exponentially. Dimension skipping will continue, possibly at an increasingly accelerated rate. After a short while, entropic annihilation will commence. Depending on which scientific prophecy you subscribe to, this will lead to reality either exploding, imploding, flash freezing, or simply disintegrating."

"That sucks," I say, "but what makes you think all this gravity mumbo-jumbo is happening to me?"

"To us," Lily corrects.

"Science and intuition," Panik says. "In my search for the last remaining shard of the 7th Age of Vicious Enlightenment, my Time Pod lead me to you, Victor. Seemingly erroneously. But my Time Pod doesn't make mistakes. You've already been established as an anomaly—"

"You have?" Lily says.

"Obviously," I say. Lily really needs to keep up.

"And as I've explained," Panik continues. "An Abstraction left to its own devices outside its proper time/space designation will act as a full system wipe and/or reboot to the current time-stream. Which is exactly what an anti-dimensional gravity field would accomplish. It's simple deductive reasoning. More likely than not, you are a symptom of an ancient future Abstraction."

"Make sense to me," I say. Even if it doesn't. "So what do we do next?"

Panik swivels her chair towards me. "First I will let my tests finish their calculations. While they do that, your sister and I will most likely engage sexually. Orgasmic energies, through osmosis, are a great benefit to the accuracy of science." Lily blushes, whereas I just try to forget hearing it. "Assuming my hypothesis is correct, the next step is to figure out how to stop it before the fall of reality. Failing that, we treat the symptom instead."

"Meaning," I say, desperately hoping it doesn't involve more sex talk about Lily.

"Meaning, we kill you," Panik says.

"Oh. Neat."

"Or messy. Death comes in all forms." Panik studies her instruments one last time. "The tests need one last push." She starts undressing while addressing me. "Things will be getting sweaty. You may stay if you'd like."

"Uh, no he can't!" Lily blurts out. Not that I needed her to say anything. I'm already gone. The future must be a really fucked up place.

* * *

I don't know how long I roam The Adventure Galley trying to shake the appalling thoughts Panik and Lily implanted into my brain. The hate I feel for them boils. It's giving me a headache. Before I know it, I find myself on the bridge. Captain Valiant and Sera—and therefore Emma—look like they're preparing for departure.

Valiant notices my arrival first. "Ah, Victor. Just in time for takeoff."

"We're leaving already?" I ask.

"Indeed we are," Valiant says. "Our business here is complete, and there is no doubt *adventure* out there waiting for us to unsheathe it and stab away our boredom."

"Do I have time to say goodbye to Chalk?"

"No need. Chalk and the Princess will be joining us."

Sera and Emma grumble something at that.

"Now Lieutenant, the Princess is our guest and she's lost her home once again. She's assured me there will be no more murder or kidnapping this time around." It's apparent that Sera and/or Emma would like to protest, but they keep quiet, realizing it's pointless.

"Where's Jimmy?" Sera asks instead.

"I don't know," I tell her. "Cleaning or something, like a good spaceboy."

She rolls her eyes and says, "You're such an ass." Then she flips some switches and the ship hums to life. Emma takes over her voice. "Lily and Panik were looking for you. Did they find you?"

"They did," I say. "Unfortunately." Emma cocks Sera's head, mildly perplexed, I suppose. "Don't ask."

Even with Emma controlling some of her basic functions, Sera never misses a beat with her takeoff preparation. The way she and Emma can coexist in one body is impressive. Sitting down next to them, I get a surprise visitor: Captain Valiant's kitten, Gumdrop.

Gumdrop hops into my lap, curls up, and purrs. "I thought you were in daycare."

Gumdrop mews.

"She finished her training this morning," Valiant beams. I'm not really clear on the extent of her training, but I can totally believe Gumdrop is a spycat now. Her purr is so soothing. Perfect for lulling a target to sleep and then spycatting the crap out of them.

"The Galley's ready for takeoff, sir," Sera informs.

"Uh, before we get space bound, maybe I should tell you about a few things," I say. And as much as it pains me, I recount my little rerun as a science experiment for Panik. I gloss over all the icky sex stuff, still hoping I can erase those memories from existence.

When I'm finished, no one seems worried in the slightest. Sera pats me on the shoulder, which is undoubtedly Emma's doing, while Valiant chuckles.

"This is why I love having you onboard, Victor. You always bring the *Adventure* to the Galley. Now if you'll excuse me, I must make a brief address." The captain goes to his captain's chair and presses a button. "Attention esteemed guests, our time at IGLOO Headquarters is at its end and we are moments away from liftoff. But worry not, the Lieutenant is a fabulous pilot, you won't feel a thing. I'm happy to say that our occupancy has nearly doubled since our arrival, and as we leave one world behind knowing that many more await us in the future. Our destination today, as always, is *adventure* and our demeanor shall forever be *valiant*. Have a glorious remainder to your morning. We shall convene again for lunch in a few hours. Captain Valiant out." Valiant points to Sera who, in turn, does her pilot thing. And we're airborne.

As Sera works her mojo, Valiant beckons me to his chair. After carefully moving the sleeping Gumdrop off my lap, I heed his call.

"Victor," I love it when he says my name, "we were discussing the predicament you and your sister find yourselves in, and it got me thinking about my own predicament." Valiant pauses valiantly. "Lily is very attractive. She arouses me. So you see my problem."

"Um," I say.

"You are my friend and Lily is your sister. While the blood relation might be alleged, I must ere on the side of caution. Certainly the hero's code is clear. You love as fiercely and as often as you fight. But there is a subsection that pertains to relations of your *adventuring* partners. Thus I must be blunt: Victor, I wish to sleep with Lily. But only after we've exhausted ourselves physically. Sexually."

"Uh-huh," I say.

"Victor, I can't cut any corners here. I need to be perfectly clear that I am speaking of joining my genitals with Lily's."

"I get it," I say, trying to figure out why I have to be so involved in my sister's incredibly active sex life. "While I'd be personally honored to have you do absolutely anything you want to any member of my family, Captain, I'm not sure you're exactly Lily's type. She kind of prefers people more…anatomically similar to herself." Despite the way she flaunts it, Lily's usually very coy about her sexuality. She's never identified herself as a lesbian, but I've haven't seen her with a boyfriend since high school.

Valiant takes the news in stride. "I could never fault someone for preferring the gentle caress of a beautiful woman. But I've also found that my physique, charm, and sexual prowess can overcome almost any obstacle. So I must ask your permission to investigate the matter to its end, and, hopefully, to your sister's vagina."

I groan involuntarily, but I give Captain Valiant whatever permission he requires, asking only that he keeps the details to himself. Something I never thought I'd find myself asking.

I rejoin Emma and Sera. One look at me has Emma asking what's wrong. "You're pretty pale," she says. "What were you and the captain talking about?"

"Lily's vagina," I say.

"What?"

I wave the question off, but Emma and Sera's interest won't be brushed aside. "I swear, this happens whenever she's around. All my friends ever want to talk about is banging my sister."

"I'm sorry, sweetie," Emma says through both a mock frown and Sera's laughter.

* * *

After about half an hour off spacing around, Jimmy and The Roboracle make an appearance on the bridge. "That was a real mess to clean up. No idea how long it'll take to fix up RW. I've been trying to get The Roboracle to tell me what happened, exactly."

"I AM THE FAUXBORACLE."

"Is he ever going to stop saying that?" Jimmy asks.

"Probably not," I say. If The Roboracle goes by his general MO, he'll take something that's mildly amusing at first, make it as annoying as possible as quickly as possible, and then really saturate everybody with it until they want to jab pencils into their ears, realizing deafness is a sweet release compared to one more word from the god awful Roboracle. Or maybe that's just me.

"Anyone want to play some cards?" Jimmy pulls out a deck. And since there's nothing better to do, I sit down and let Jimmy deal. Since space is pretty empty, Sera and Emma are able to join in while Valiant keeps an eye on everything else.

I lose every game because they decide to play some wonky version of rummy that makes no damn sense. Of course, they claim it's just regular rummy, but that's bullshit and doesn't explain why I keep losing. At some point during all this, Candy Princess and Chalk skip into the room like a couple of cutesy cartoon characters. Except Candy's mouth and teeth are bloodstained. She gets visibly excited when she sees us playing games.

"I love games! I bet Victor is winning."

"You'd lose that bet, bitch," Sera says.

Candy gasps. "Sera, language!"

"Fuck your language."

Candy giggles. Same old, same old.

By the time Panik and Lily show up I'm long past sick of this stupid game. Panik is once again wearing her skintight body suit that's capable of making almost anybody blush. Her demeanor is as blasé as ever. She's the picture of perfection. Lily, on the other hand, looks something of a mess. Her hair is ruffled, her clothes eschew, her face painted with satisfaction. It's disgusting.

"Cover your shame!" I demand. Lily's response is an obscene gesture. Typical.

Candy Princess scooches closer to me. "What's her shame?"

"The copious amount of sex she's been tossing around."

The blood staining Candy's mouth appears to spread across her entire face. "Oh."

It's not embarrassment I hear, though, or at least not entirely embarrassment. There's something else contorting Candy's face. I've seen that look a time or two before. I groan. "Please don't kill my sister, Candy."

Her face manages to brighten, and her voice is soft as cotton candy. "I already promised the captain that I wouldn't kill anyone…but because you asked so nicely, I'll promise twice!" I still don't like the way she's looking at Lily, but I'm sure it'll be fine.

Lily joins us a minute or two later. Candy is nothing if not friendly. "Hi, Lily! You look so lovely." Lily mumbles something slightly less friendly, but Candy either doesn't hear or doesn't care. "And Panik, doesn't that outfit just make you want to eat her up?"

"Uh," is what Lily manages.

"You smell like her," Candy grins. Now things are getting weird. "She let me taste her, you know. A lot."

"Whatever," Lily says with no attempt at hiding her disgust. Candy excuses herself, singing a song as she goes to snuggle with Gumdrop.

"How do you deal with her?" Lily asks.

"Aside from the cannibalism and murder, she's alright," I say.

"Don't forget the kidnapping," Sera says before her voice slips into Emma's southern drawl, "and the serial date rape."

"That's a little overblown," I say. "I'd classify it more as 'occasional date rape'." That gets a groan from everybody. "I guess I just don't see the need to be rude, because, guys, I believe in rehabilitation over punishment. It's one of the things that makes me so special." I'll let them suck on that moral superiority.

"If by special," Lily says, "you mean completely retarded, I think we can all agree."

Sera doesn't just laugh, she snorts. "Why can't you be more like her?"

The smugness oozing from Lily is nearly as vulgar as her sex hair. But it just rolls off me like rain off a nicely weather treated deck. Yep, that's me, emotionally weatherproof…bunch of jerks.

Emma, Lily, and Sera engage in mindless small talk while I sulk. Jimmy, in the meantime, has been beckoned by Captain Valiant, and they're both chatting with Panik about something, Panik's eyes intermittently shifting from them to me.

After a bit, Sera goes back to her ship flying duties, leaving me and Lily alone. Despite still being irritated by her, I decide to give her a head's up regarding Captain Valiant's intentions. Her response: "Cool."

"That's it?" I say.

"Um, cool…beans? What do you want me to say? He's attractive, and word is he might have saved Panik's life with his, uh, manhood. That's impressive."

"Yeah it is," I say.

"How would you feel about it?" she asks.

"I try not to feel anything about your sex life."

"Exactly. So, cool. Granted, I'd rather get with Sera. But I'm not sure Jimmy could handle that."

I gasp. "Don't talk about Jimmy like that. Obviously he couldn't handle that. He's like twelve. Just thinking it has got to be illegal, Lily."

"Psh, he's not twelve. He's plenty old enough. Besides, someone's got to teach the boy."

"Would you stop with that kind of talk! Jimmy will learn like any other self-respecting man. Trial and error. Just stick with Panik, how about that?"

"Yeah, she's nice," Lily says. "There's this thing she can do with her tongue—"

"I don't want details."

Not that Lily listens. "And last night we did a little roleplaying." I cover my ears but can still hear everything. Note to self: find a way to soundproof hands immediately. "She was Catherine Zeta Jones naked and wanting it, and I was me, giving it to her hard."

"Wait, what?" I make the mistake of lowering my worthless hands.

"Wait what for what?"

"What?"

"That's what I'm asking?"

"You said something that reminded me of something," I explain.

"That's helpful. Was it when I said I was giving it to her hard? Because that reminded me of the time I gave it to Callie hard."

My hands shoot back to my ears but are as porous as ever.

"Or was it the thing about the tongue?" I shake my head with violent force. If I can't block the sound maybe I can scramble my brain enough to forget this conversation. But Lily won't even allow me this luxury as she pulls my hands down. "She's really, really good."

"I hate you," I say.

"But she's a little too easy and to the point. A girl could use a little challenge. Don't get me wrong, she's great for a fling, and maybe a little beyond that but…it might be fun to get my flirt on with the captain."

At this point I have no choice but to get very serious with her. "Lily, you will not lead Captain Valiant on. If you start down that path, I don't care if you're gay, straight, bisexual, asexual, pansexual, objectum-sexual—"

"Objectum-sexual?"

"Don't interrupt. What I'm saying is that I don't care what you're into. If you even flirt a little with the Captain, you will put out!"

"If you say so," Lily says.

"I'm serious, Lily. Don't fuck this up for me!"

"You need to chill, bro," she says before continuing to jabber on about some such nonsense. I do my best to zone out. In part because I've spent years talking with Lily, so how much could she say that I haven't already heard, but also because I'm more than a little worried she'll start talking about Panik's tongue again. That's not a risk I'm willing to take.

Bored by pretending to listen to Lily, I yell across the bridge, "Hey are those tests results back yet?"

Panik shifts her attention my direction. "They're still gestating within the miasma of sexual force Lily and I left behind." Even Lily can't help but make a disgusted noise at that. And somewhere behind me Candy Princess exhales an exaggerated hurumph.

"Sorry I asked," I say. That'll teach me about feigning interesting in anything ever again.

* * *

Chalk hops over and sits himself between Lily and me, so the two of us decide to teach him some card games. He picks them up quickly and is destroying both of us by the third game. When the fourth game is underway my thoughts fog up like **a** bathroo**m** mirror during a shower. A weary pressure seeps into **the air** I **breath.** I yawn to alleviate it. It doesn't work. Invisible **walls push inward** with delicate, rigid force. Chalk's face reads **What's Wrong?** in sweet salmon certainty. I shake my entire bo**dy, but the** air shakes back, pulling my skin tighter and tigh**ter un**til my bones threaten a mutinty. My brain freezes **in** a satin heatwave as I try to speak. I only cough half-heartedly.

The world contracts slightly; slowly.
And my gums ache as my sinuses
hammer a four inch spike
directly into my nasal
cavity. I sneeze.
And I see my
words fade
into

A
tear
drop that
echoes imperfectly
down my left cheek
A drip or drop of
perfect clarity
splashing

A
tear
drop that
echoes perfectly
down my right cheek
A drip or drop of
imperfect clarity
splashing

A
tear
drop that
echoes imperfectly
down my left cheek
A drip or drop of
perfect clarity
p a h n
s l s i g

to the floor. I blink harder than should be possible. Everything is dark. Imagining the Adventure Galley in the flat vacuum of space, I force myself to open…

...MY EYES
DOES ANYONE ELSE FEEL WEIRD?
HEY, HOW'D I GET OVER HERE?
VALIANTLY, MY FRIEND.
NICE! BUT STILL...
I'VE GOT A BAD FEELING ABOUT THIS.
-POOF!-
LOOK OUT!!!
BEEYOOP! BEEYOOP!
ERT ! PROXIM
ERT !
OXIMIT
OH NO.
SHREEE!!
AHHHHHHHHH HHHHHHHH HHHHHH!!!!

WE'RE GONNA DIE!!
AH, DEATH. THE FINAL ADVENTURE.
WAIT. WE'RE SLOWING DOWN!
IT'S A MOUSE... NO! A JET SKI... NO, WAIT...
ENTHEUS!
CATCH!

ONBOARD
WE NEED TO HELP ENTHEUS!
WHO'S THE NAKED CHICK?
CENSORED
NAKED?!
I'M NAKED!! I MEAN... LOOK I HAVE MY BODY!!
UM, MAYBE STOP LOOKING NOW...
GUMDROP SAYS
MEOW
GUMDROP IS RIGHT. WE CAN'T OGLE EMMA FOREVER. A CRAPPY SUPERHERO NEEDS OUR HELP. THIS LOOKS LIKE A JOB FOR CAPTAIN VALIANT AND HIS PARTNER
AWESOME VICTORY
WHOA, THAT ACTUALLY WORKED.

MEANWHILE, IN THE SECRET LAIR OF THE SIDEWALK SHADOW...
WHY DON'T YOU JUST KILL ME?
IN DUE TIME. AFTER YOU'VE HELPED ME KILL THE OTHER. BUT WHERE IS HE? WE'VE BEEN HERE FOR WEEKS!
...WHICH WAS BRIEFLY THE SECRET LAIR FOR THE TRAGIC VILLIAN, SOUL DESTROYER: DESTROYER OF SOULS.
TIME MUST MOVE MORE SWIFTLY HERE. YES. YES, THAT'S IT! I CAN'T FEEL IT. CAN'T YOU?
I CAN'T FEEL ANYTHING DUE TO LACK OF CIRCULATION. LOOK, IF THIS IS ABOUT WHAT THAT DEMON DID TO YOU...
I SAID NEVER TO SPEAK OF IT!
I'LL NEVER FORGET THE HORROR OF THAT DAY! BUT THIS SOUL-DESTROYER, WHOEVER HE WAS, HAS MANY TOOLS...
TOOLS ARE NORMALLY USED FOR BUILDING. bUT ALSO DESTRUCTION. I WILL USE THEM FOR BOTH. TO DESTROY MY ENEMIES THUS BUILDING A PATH TO VICTORY.
AND TO THE VICTOR, GOES THE SPOILS.
I GET SPOILS?!
I SAID VICTOR, NOT VICTORS!
AW...

BACK ON THE GALLEY
I FEEL LIKE I MISSED SOMETHING IMPORTANT.
STILL DON'T KNOW WHY I DIDN'T GET A COOL SUPERSUIT.
YOU GOT YOUR BIRTHDAY SUIT.
VERY FUNNY.
I JUST HOPE SERA GETS THE DOOR OPENED SOON SO I CAN KICK SOMETHING.
HEY, I'VE SEEN YOUR GIRLFRIEND NAKED NOW!
JIMMY, DON'T MAKE ME PUNCH YOU IN THE $#%&@!
HMMM...
@!#$ AND (#$%^$ AND %$##% YOU MOTHER ^%$$%^%^ *# $#~ $%^ $##%@! WITH #$%^&*(#$%^ %^&* AND YOUR $%^%^&&*&^%$#~ @!#$%^~MAKES ME WANT TO *(#$% AND A CHOCOLATE COVERED^%$#~ *%$^&*#$) WITH A CHERRY ON TOP!!
TEE-HEE!
GOT IT!!
I CAN BE OF BETTER USE ON THE SHIP USING TANTRIC MEDITATION.
UH, YEA I'LL STAY BACK TOO.
WHOOSH
GROSS, LILY... TIME TO PUNCH MY DISGUST AWAY!

BEFORE I JOIN THE FIGHT I SHOULD FIGURE OUT WHAT SUPERPOWER ACCOMPANIES THIS AWESOME SUIT. THERE HAS TO BE ONE.
POW!
FLIGHT MAYBE?
OOOOF!!!
NOPE.
WHUUD
INVISIBILITY?
HEY, HEY GUYS! CAN YOU STILL SEE ME?
YES, YOU MORON!
THANKS SERA!
TELEKINESIS? NO. HMMM...
SERA, ARE YOU THINKING ABOUT THAT TIME I SAW YOU NAKED?
GO #%*& YOURSELF!
THOOM!
NOT TELEPATHY EITHER.
SHOOT, THIS IS HARD.
WE COULD REALLY USE SOME HELP, SWEETIE!
CHOC!
JUST A SEC!
SEVERAL MINUTES LATER...
SO IT'S NOT FLIGHT, HEAT VISION, SUPER SPEED, SUPER BREATH, X-RAY VISION, TELEPATHY OR SHAPE-SHIFTING. WHICH MEANS IT HAS TO BE...
SUPER STRENGTH!!!
YOU OVER THERE! PREPARE TO EAT MY ...VICTORY FIST!

RRRRAAAAAA
AAAAAA
AAAERIAL FIST-SLAM
PUNCH
OUCH

3.5

I wake to a familiar face and I know I'm either dreaming or dead. My mouth is too dry to speak, so I only manage a croak as Emma leans over and brushes her lips against mine. They're soft and warm with her breath. Not dead. And the pain is too tangible for a dream.

"Welcome back to the land of the living, Mr. Superhero," Emma says. And I feel her breath on my face.

"You're alive," I finally manage, sitting up.

"You don't remember seeing me before the fight?" she asks.

"It's all pretty fuzzy," I say.

"I wish that were the case for everyone else. So embarrassing."

"Wait…were you naked?" I ask.

"Great, now you can relive my humiliation too."

I smirk. "You looked great. You *look* great."

Emma glances at the ground and tucks a loose strand of hair behind her ear. "It's nice having my own body again. Everything feels so much more real, you know." I shake my head. "I guess you wouldn't. But trust me. How's your head?"

"Feels like I got punched in the face," I say. I finally take a second to scan my surroundings. We aren't on the Galley. I don't know where we are, but I don't see anyone else in the room. "So what's it going to take to get a re-enactment of your embarrassment?"

"Guess you're not feeling too awful," Emma says. I pull her to me. "Everyone is just outside."

"I don't care," I say. And she doesn't fight it.

Then the door opens.

"Oh #$%! you, Jimmy!" I scream.

"Uh," Jimmy stammers like a #&%ing moron. "I'm sorry! It's just that…hey you're awake."

"Very astute," I say.

"We were worried that maybe you fractured your skull or something."

"Why are you still here?"

"Well, Panik says your test results aren't fully matured—or something like that—and Entheus is worried about Anexia, but he won't tell us why without you. He says it wouldn't be right to begin a team-up while one of the heroes is incapacitated."

Damn it, that's true. "Fine, I'll be out in a minute."

Jimmy scuttles away.

Emma offers me her hand. "Come on, let's go mister."

"Aw, can't we keep them waiting for a few minutes more."

"Well get to that later, sweetie," Emma says. "Promise."

"Fine," I pout. "So Anexia, huh?"

"Yeah, it's kind of weird to be here and see Entheus, you know, in person. Donna too."

"Donna's here?" I wonder, and Emma nods. "Where is here, anyway? I mean, more specifically than just Anexia."

"This is Entheus's Satellite of Illumination. At least I think that's what he called it."

"Let's get this over with, then." Emma leads the way, and I follow dutifully. How could I do anything else with the outfit she's wearing. She may not have been gifted a snazzy—albeit ultimately worthless—superhero getup to begin with, but she's certainly got one now. Short purple skirt with matching knee high boots. The top looks like it was one of Entheus's that got shrunk while doing the laundry, so she's even got a nice "E" type symbol on her chest. And she's covered in glitter for some reason. She kind of looks like a Supergirl rip-off, but there's nothing wrong with that.

Stepping out of my little hospice room, I get a jolt. I'd been expecting to see something along the lines of a Fortress of Solitude knock-off. You know, to keep the trend going. Instead I find myself standing on the whitest sand I've ever seen. I bend down to run my fingers through it. It's like powered silk, and I realize this, not glitter, is what's making Emma sparkle. Off in the distance is a tranquil sea—or maybe ocean, I don't know how these things are classified—that glows in the warmth of an yellow-orange sun.

"Holy $#*!"

"Pretty awe-inspiring, huh," Emma says.

Jimmy pops up out of nowhere, once again ruining the moment. "This is the legendary diamond sands beach of Anexia."

"Diamond?" %*&# this outfit for not having pockets! "And what's so legendary about it? Other than, you know, all of this." I motion to pretty much everything.

"Didn't you ever read any of those STEEL CANYON comics?"

"#$&* no, Jimmy! They looked terrible."

"They were kind of neat," he says with very little conviction. "Poorly structured, sometimes hard to tell what's going on from panel to panel, but pretty fun…anyway, this isn't actually Anexia. It's the Diamond Moon of Anexia, Entheus's home. And it's legendary because this is where Inspiration was born."

"Sounds pretty stupid."

Jimmy laughs as if I'm joking. Because he's also pretty stupid. But hey, you can't choose your friends. I think that's a saying, at least. It definitely applies to Jimmy.

We find everyone else lounging about like they don't have a care in the world. Kind of strange considering the chaos that surrounded our arrival, but I'll almost always choose lounging over doing stuff. Our little posse has expanded quite radically in the last couple of days. First Panik, then Candy and Chalk, The Roboracle and

Lily, and now Entheus and The Donnanatrix. It's getting overwhelming. And Emma's right, it's $#@%ed up seeing Entheus and Donna as actual full sized, fleshy people.

Entheus appears to be having a heroic pose-off with Captain Valiant, while Donna sits with The Roboracle in her lap. She doesn't seem happy to see me, which I don't get. I've kind of, sort of always liked Donna slightly. She's quite a bit sexier in person than in paper, and that makes the way she caresses The Roboracle all the more shudder inducing.

I seat myself beside Lily, and Entheus finally takes notice. "Ah, Victor has joined us! Welcome to my home."

"Sup," I say.

"I wish we had more time for pleasantries," Entheus smile falters, "but Anexia is in dire peril and we've already wasted too much time."

"Because you wouldn't tell us anything without Mr. Awful Victory over there," Sera mutters.

"What was that, Lieutenant?" Valiant asks.

"Nothing, sir."

"It's Awesome Victory," I whisper to her. She ignores me. "So what's this dire situation, anyway?"

"A great shadow has fallen over Anexia," Entheus announces, "and I fear its darkness may swallow us all."

* * *

"After our heroic battle in your metropolis of New York, I spent months trying to find a passage back to Anexia. My journeys lead me, not surprisingly, back to one Miss Donna Natrios and The Brothel of Infinite Sadness."

"The Brothel is a place of many secrets," Donna says. "Of course, Entheus wanted to go home, but I was trying to escape it. See, I had recently gone back to, well, here—much to my sweet Roboracle's dismay."

"I AM THE FAUXBORACLE."

Donna frowns, but continues. "I was looking for a little old-fashioned immorality, the kind you can't get at the brothel, and I was missing my more three dimensional form. Things were great at first. The old gang and I had a real blast, corrupting teenagers with rock & roll and some of the more exotic drugs I'd grown accustomed to at the brothel. And with Entheus gone, there wasn't much to keep us in check. Sure there are other heroes, but they lacked the inspiration to oppose us without their figurehead. Teen pregnancy rates skyrocketed. It was glorious! Mwhahahahaha!!!" Donna clears her throat. "Um, but then something strange happened. The Opal Moon rose alone in the sky one night a few weeks ago. A dark portent, you might remember."

Emma nods. Sera looks to Jimmy for answers, but he shrugs. Most likely because he was off pretending to be dead and cutting pieces of himself off to raise nasty zombie things when Entheus first told us that story.

"Way to drop the ball, Jimmy," I say.

"What?" he says. Typical, clueless Jimmy.

Donna is undeterred by our little interruption. "That's when things got bad. The Immoral Many were no longer satisfied with casual vices. They got violent. Now I'm all for a good superhero vs. supervillain showdown or the occasional S&M session, but they were blood thirsty. They weren't just talking about murder. Not even genocide. They wanted to commit terracide. So I ran. I ran back to my Roboracle. But he was gone. Instead I ran straight into Entheus. Literally."

"It took a heroic amount of convincing," Entheus says, "but after an hour or so, Miss Natrois relented and lead me back home."

"It was strange, though," Donna continues. "I'd only been gone for an hour—two at most—but days had passed and things were worse than ever. The streets of the Steel Canyon ran red with blood, and…and I wanted to join in."

"More troublesome than that," Entheus says. "All the cries for help. The screams of torment,. The despair. I wanted to turn my back on it all—or a small part of me did—and once again the Opal moon shone bleakly in the sky. Only this night it wasn't alone. From all the ashes, bones, and destruction on Anexia, the Ashen Moon is reforming. Death hangs its unforgiving shadow over Anexia, my friends, and it grows larger by the day."

"Is that all," I say, fairly unimpressed.

Donna sneers. "No. The specter of death and darkness isn't content with merely infecting the present with its horrors. It's seeping into our past and rewriting it."

Panik sits more alert as Emma asks, "How can you know that?"

"Because, my dear," Entheus smiles weakly, "we can feel our memories fogging and shifting. The Diamond Moon is a place of light, inspiration, and serenity. It's shielded us, but not entirely. The shadow of the Ashen Moon is far-reaching and unrelenting, and we can't stay here while every moment Anexia wails in agony. Yet each trip back weakens our memories, replacing them with newer, darker thoughts. Miss Natrois and I do our best to hold on to our pasts. We regale one another with tales of our former battles, but it's become more and more difficult. I've become increasingly…disenfranchised." Entheus gazes to the sky. "I can no longer remember my origin." He shakes his head solemnly, and when he looks back at us a smile has returned to his face. "With your arrival, however, hope springs anew. Whatever is responsible for the reformation of the Ashen Moon is a threat that can only be defeated by a team-up of the Multiverse's most renowned heroes."

Sera snorts. "Victor is one of the Multiverse's greatest heores?"

"Why, of course, star child," Entheus replies. "Have you not bared witness to his ability to join together the forces of good and evil for a common cause? He made allies of me and Donnanatrix, two sworn enemies. And the very evil we fought together sits here, beside you, completely reformed." Jimmy squirms. "Then there was our most recent battle together. Was it not a fight against the deceptively named Candy Princess? And is she, too, not here now, an ally?"

"I wouldn't call her an ally," Sera says, "but she is here, unfortunately."

"Don't listen to Sera, Mr. Entheus," Candy says. "Sera's just a grumpy puss. We're all best of friends now!"

"Naturally," Entheus says. "Nothing less could be expected when the great Victor is involved. So I ask now, can we count on your help?"

"We live for *adventure*." Valiant declares.

"Then victory is all but assured," Entheus beams.

"So where do we start?" I ask.

"I would like to perform some tests on Miss Natrois and Entheus," Panik answers.

"Of course you would," I say.

"Whatever the lady wants, I will comply," Entheus says. "Though I must say I've always found a good punch to be a more effective approach than science."

"Me too," Donna agrees.

Panik doesn't appear to care. "Punching is more effective

when you know what you're meant to be punching. Otherwise you're just expending valuable Time and energy. Energy can be replenished, but never Time." I'm not sure anyone knows what she's talking about. "My equipment in still on the Adventure Galley, if you would care to join me." Entheus and Donna follow, although Donna isn't too pleased about leaving The Roboracle behind. "And Lily, I might need your assistance." I grumble, wishing I didn't keep hearing this stuff.

Candy leaps to her feet. "Can I come too?"

"If you wish," Panik says. Lily doesn't like that, but she goes along anyway.

I stand up too, and shake off the diamond sand. "So, looks like we have some free time…what's there to do here?"

* * *

Jimmy, Sera, and Valiant decide to inspect the Galley and make sure it wasn't badly damaged during the crash, while Emma, Chalk, and I walk along the beach. Chalk doesn't hang around long; instead he splashes immediately into the ocean, his face saying WARM as he hits the water. Removing our boots, Emma and I wade in, and even with Chalk's declaration, I'm still taken aback by how inviting it is. Emma moans slightly, and gets embarrassed when she realizes it.

"The water feels really nice," she says, almost shyly. Neither of us speaks again for a long while. It's one of those moments where words are more likely to ruin things. Still, silence never lasts forever. "Are you worried about what's going on here?"

"Nah," I say.

"Oh," she frowns.

"Why, are you?"

"Maybe a little," she says, biting her bottom lip. "It's just that since we've been here I've been having some weird memories too. Ones that I didn't have before and couldn't have happened."

"Like what?"

She hesitates. "Never mind, it's not important."

"If it's bothering you…"

Emma takes a deep breath. "Well, it's just, do you remember that night after Jimmy was, uh, swept away and The Roboracle was malfunctioning and Entheus and Donna had just told that weird Opal Moon story?"

"Sure," I half-lie. Most of that trip is a mangled mess of memories.

"We ended up falling asleep and then Jimmy kind of kidnapped me because he was pissed off at you." I nod. It sounds right enough. "Now I'm kind of remembering it differently. I remember you, um…killing me."

"Oh."

"I know it's crazy, but it's so vivid. And there's this other memory that's even worse. It's back when we were fighting Jimmy at the cabin in the woods, and suddenly I remember being skewered by a tree branch. That's not even the worst part. It's what you do afterwards. You…ugh, I can't even say it."

"That's okay," I say. "I know."

"You do? You're having the same memories? I'm not gonna end up dead am I?"

"Em, you're already dead. Or you were."

"Oh yeah…but still, what if our whole history is wiped out and rewritten to match these new memories?"

"I don't think that's going to happen."

"But we're having the same crazy memory glitches."

"No we aren't. I've had those memories since they happened."

"Huh?"

"Remember how I kept trying to tell you about those two other versions of me I met in that stupid cabin?"

Emma nods. "I kind of thought you were making most of that up. None of what you said made much sense."

"Most of it doesn't make sense to me either, but I wasn't making it up. And those memories you're having are memories of what those two did to their version of you."

"Oh…what the #%&$?! That's totally #$%&ed up! But why am I remembering this stuff now?"

I shrug. "I don't know. Not really. Except, I've been feeling sort of similar to the way I did back then. Lots of weird, violent, sexual urges. Or at least weirder than usual."

"I've noticed. Is that why you started talking to yourself again in Infinite City?"

"Maybe."

"Still, why now?"

"I guess we could ask Panik, but that'll probably lead to an awkward naked moment and talk of Lily doing things I never want to hear about Lily doing. It might just be that this whole dimensional gravity junk is similar to that whole Tripleverse Bleed stuff that was going on when we first met. Although, do you think maybe it's possible—"

"Hey guys, mind if I join you," Lily says, walking up behind us.

"That was quick," Emma says.

Lily sits down next to her, already barefoot. "Yeah, well Panik explained what she wanted to do. I'm pretty open-minded, but I have my limits."

Emma scrunches her face. It's a look I've missed desperately.

"What'd she want you to do?"

"Please don't answer that," I say.

"Don't worry, bro. I don't even want to think about it." Lily lies back, putting her hands behind her head. "It's so peaceful here. It's hard to believe all that death and $#*! is going on up there." She points towards Anexia, looming ominously in the sky. "I kind of wish we could just stay here. #$%^ everything else, you know. But that would probably be wrong, right?"

"Probably," Emma says without much confidence.

"Oh hey," Lily sits upright. "I just realized I've never properly introduced myself to you, Emma."

"Don't be ridiculous," Emma says. "I've been inside of you."

Lily laughs. "Awesome."

"Wow," Emma smirks. "I still can't believe you two try to convince people you aren't related. So what? Are we supposed to shake hands or something?"

"I think a hug would be more appropriate," Lily says. So that's what they do. "It's nice to finally meet you, but I hope you don't mind me saying you're far too pretty for my brother."

"I don't mind, but I love him anyway."

"We all have our faults," Lily says.

"You guys are both #@*$," I say. And like the #@*$ they are, they laugh at me.

* * *

Night falls swiftly on the Diamond Moon of Anexia. Valiant, Jimmy, and Sera finish up their inspection of the Galley, and Entheus and Donna eventually rejoin us too. Panik and Candy, however, remain absent. Lily doesn't show any overt signs that it bothers her, but the way her eyes occasionally shift towards the Adventure Galley makes me think it does. If only a little. She doesn't let it keep her down, at any rate, and allows herself to get swept away in both Valiant's and Entheus's tales of adventure and heroism. The two of them are becoming fast friends. And I'm incredibly jealous. Not that I'd let it show. Jealousy is not one of Valiant's Virtues. Instead I manage to enjoy the stories.

"So what's the strangest adventure you guys have ever been on?" Lily asks during a rare break in the oral action.

"Besides my exploits with Victor," Entheus says, "it would have to my lone encounter with the saddest villain I ever did meet. Soul Destroyer: Destroyer of Souls, he was called."

"Wait just a moment," Valiant interrupts, "you've battled the Destroyer of Souls?"

"You know him?" Great, another thing they have in common.

"Indeed. He destroyed the soul of my beloved cat, Lolipop." Gumdrop chooses that moment to jump into Valiant's lap.

"I'm very sorry to hear that, Captain. I too know what it is to lose a pet in battle. Express, the Mega Turtle."

"I miss that turtle," Donna says. "Plantera cried for a week after he accidentally killed him."

"May he, and all our lost loved ones, rest in peace," Valiant says. We drink a solemn toast to the fallen. "But please, do tell about your fight with Soul Destroyer. He vanished after what happened to Lolipop, and I worried for his wellbeing. He was an animal lover, after all, and never really seemed cut out for the villain life style."

"I got much the same impression, Captain," Entheus explains. "Which is why it was such a strange skirmish. This Soul Destroyer came out of nowhere to build a most elaborate secret liar, yet he didn't try very hard to keep it a secret. He practically begged any hero to come and stop him. Being the dutiful hero, naturally I complied. His heart never was in the fight. In fact, he spent most of it apologizing profusely for all his crimes. And while he had all kinds of weapons to employ, he fired them only at the walls. As if he was compelled to fire, but was terrified of actually hitting someone."

Valiant surprises all of us by laughing. "Ah, classic Soul Destroyer. So what happened to the poor fellow?"

"I defeated him soundly and took him into custody, where he vanished as mysteriously as he appeared. The strangest part is that I never could remember where that secret lair of his was."

The stories continue on like this for quite some time, and it seems that with every tale a new jeweled moon appears in the night sky. I think Entheus once mentioned there being sixteen of them. There are at least a dozen decorating this evening. Sapphire, Ruby, Emerald, Amethyst, a flashing yellow moon—and so many others—for which I have no name.

After a while everyone separates, retiring for the night, until only Emma and I remain. The air is cool, but far from cold, and an intermitted breeze blankets us with chilling warmth. The many moons of Anexia reflect in stunning prisms off the diamond sands, creating a hundred thousand tiny rainbows at our feet.

I ask Emma if she's tired. She shakes her head. Then she closes her eyes and inhales deeply before taking my hand. "Let's go down to the water." I don't object. The water is as warm as it was earlier; warmer even than the air is now.

"I've missed this," Emma says. "Water. The feel of air rushing over my skin Breathing," She puts my hand to her chest. "My heartbeat." Her heart is steady and strong. "When I'm inside other people I can feel all of this stuff, but it's so…disconnected. Like I'm feeling it through a giant wool coat." For the first time in a long time I see Emma cry. Not giant sobs and sniffles, just a few tears that sparkle with the light of a dozen moons. I wipe them away as best I can, but some escape. Emma rubs her cheek against her shoulder with a half-smile, extinguishing the fugitive tears. She wades out further into the ocean. "Come on." I look around, unsure. "You aren't afraid of getting a little wet, are you?" She teases. Then she pulls off her shirt, covering herself haphazardly, and tossing the shirt onto the sand.

"What about everyone else?" I say thinking more of her inhibitions than my own.

She grins a wicked grin. "They aren't invited." That's when her skirt flies past me. Any arguments I might have had vanish as Emma splashes deeper into the Diamond Sea. We're nearly chest deep when I finally catch her. Our foreheads graze one another. And she kisses me. Not softly like when I first woke up here, not even all that friendly. It's greedy and it's hard. The water shifts as we do, with a starved grace. Despite the multitude of moons, the current is weak. Emma, however, is not. The ebb and flow of her body is a reckless torrent, and with it comes the tide.

After, we stand motionless, Emma's head resting on my shoulder. Whether or not the warmth there is because of the lapping sea or because she's crying again doesn't seem important. Neither of us care to move. Or speak.

I concentrate on the thin layer of water separating us.

The brief rush of air that flows between us.

The way her chest brushes against mine with each breath.

The softening throb of both our hearts.

I've missed it all too.

* * *

The morning comes too soon. We spent the night on the beach. At some point we dressed, but it didn't keep our every orifice from getting caked in sand. We sneak back onboard the Adventure Galley like two drunken teenagers who've missed curfew. I hop in the shower and Emma joins me half a second later. Part of me expects a repeat of last night. But instead Emma shuts her eyes and lets the hot water wash over her. Watching her transform from a diamond statue to a real flesh and bone girl is almost magical. Without ever opening her eyes, Emma slumps down on the shower floor. I decide to give her some privacy. It's been a long while since Emma had any time to herself. While getting dressed, I'm happy to find a spare costume. I didn't really want to have to wear a sand covered outfit all day, but I also wasn't ready to abandon the superhero look. Today feels like a day for fighting, and one of Valiant's most important rules is that a hero must always look the part. When Emma finishes her shower she finds she isn't so lucky.

Being as dead as she was, there's not much for her to wear. Meaning she's stuck with her grossly over-bejeweled costume. "At least some of my underwear is still here. Having to wear sandy underwear would not have been fun. Speaking of which, why is my underwear still here and none of my other clothes?"

"Don't ask me," I say. "I kept all of your clothes. I think Valiant's spaceboy was charged with cleaning our quarters after I joined you in Hell."

"Okay, so why did Jimmy keep only my underwear?" she says, clearly not believing me.

"I don't know, Em. It's Jimmy. He probably got to your underwear drawer and had a panic attack."

"Aww, he probably did. Cute," Emma goes back to sorting through her currently oft-mentioned unmetionables. "I don't know how anyone is expected to fight in this outfit. Any kicking, swift movement, or gust of wind and my panties are on full display."

"So make sure to wear something pretty," I say.

"Gee, thanks." Emma pulls out a pair that look like very short shorts and are covered in tiny skulls & crossbones. "I guess these will have to do."

"Where'd you get those?"

"The Brothel of Infinite Sadness. Like most of the rest. Which is why they're almost all incredibly inappropriate, you know, unless I want to be flashing my @$$ to everyone all day long."

"No one would complain," I say. Emma rolls her eyes as she finishes dressing.

We meet up with everyone else in the Dining Hall. Emma doesn't hesitate; she's shoveling food down her throat like a pelican on speed. She takes a brief moment to smile up at me and say, "Sooo good," before getting back to work. The rest of us are more reserved in our eating habits.

Panik doesn't bother waiting for us to finish eating before delivering her science report. "After a detailed inspection of both Entheus and Donna Natrios, I can say with 98.2% certainty that the retroactive memory confusion they're experiencing is due to the missing shard of the 7th Age of Vicious Enlightenment. A retroactive time correction is not unusual when dealing with rogue Abstractions.

"Furthermore, my theory regarding the anti-dimensional gravitational fields has proven correct. Both Victor and Lily were engulfed by one. However, Lily's was smaller and showed a slower rate of growth. This required further investigation. I continued observing Lily in a manner we'd become accustomed, while also running a few diagnostics on Victor. Both after he was knocked unconscious during the battle of super-people," I really wish she'd stop doing things to me while I'm unconscious, "and immediately after he and Emma had finished their aquatic anacreontic activities."

Emma's face glows brighter than the Ruby Moon of Anexia. "I thought everyone was asleep," she says mostly to herself, stunned.

"Um," Sera says, "no one was really asleep." The look of sheer horror painted on Emma is perhaps one of the most adorable things I've ever seen. I know that shouldn't be my first thought, but I really have missed her face.

"I was asleep," Jimmy says. Of course he was. "What's anacreontic mean?"

Valiant is the first to answer the call. "It means, my young spaceboy, that Victor and Emma proffered their supple flesh to the heavens and earth in an impassioned, fervent play that would make even the gods blush in joyful pride." Emma buries her face in her hands and groans.

"Um," Jimmy says.

"They got it on in the ocean," Lily says.

"Oh," Jimmy offers me a nervous thumbs-up, while Chalk leaps onto the table to give me a high five. It would be rude to ignore the gesture. Then, to my astonishment, Lily also reaches across the table and high fives me.

Lily shrugs. "I wish I didn't see what I sort of saw, but Emma's hot." It might be the biggest compliment she's ever given me.

"Oh my god," Emma says, still hiding behind her hands, "can we just let Panik finish."

Panik waits a beat before continuing. "As I was saying, I kept a close eye on Lily and Victor and something unexpected has occurred. Victor's anti-grav field has increased at such a rate that it manage to snuff out Lily's."

"Ha! Suck on that, Lily!" I exclaim.

"Yes, it's an incredibly exciting development," Panik says.

"Now if we're unable to counteract and ultimately negate the field, we'll only have to kill Victor."

"Yep, suck on that, bro," Lily counters.

"Damn it."

"Worry not, Victor," Entheus says. "We have the greatest team of heroes ever assembled. We will crush whatever evil holds your life in the balance, as well as saving Anexia from the shadow of doom."

"Have we any leads on the whereabouts of your shard?" Valiant asks.

"Perhaps. Judging by what Lily, Victor, and Emma reported about their time in Infinite City, I believe the shard must be in the care of the individual—or individuals—they briefly gleamed. The working theory, considering the way they vanished, is that this person—or persons—is also under the influence of an anti-gravitational field. If that's the case, it should be simple enough to track."

"Excellent news!" Valiant proclaims.

Suddenly Sera slaps something from Jimmy's hand. Jimmy stares at her, glassy-eyed. "What?" He slurs as he speaks.

"You were cutting yourself," Sera says while she wraps a napkin around Jimmy's hand.

Jimmy looks down, dumbfounded. "I was?"

Donna hisses. "We should have anticipated this. The boy is already under the thrall of the Opal and Ashen Moon. Mwhahahahaha!"

"Miss Natrios is correct," Entheus says. "I commend your rehabilitation, Jimmy, and have even forgiven you for my untimely death, but it might be best for you to sit out this fight."

"I recommend restraints," Donna says.

"I don't want to be tied up," Jimmy complains.

"That's what they all say, but secretly everyone likes a little bondage. Mwhahahaha!"

Jimmy begs for anyone to back him up.

"Uh, she might be right," Sera says. "I mean, your face has only just healed."

"Wait," I interrupt. "What do you mean his face has healed?"

"Oh, well," Jimmy explains, "it turns out if I don't keep cutting the flesh off it, it heals up pretty well."

"So why are you still wearing that mask?"

"Because you said it was cool."

"I said no such thing. I said your skeleton face was cool and that the mask made you look like a cheap knock-off of a dude who sidekicks around with a bunch of mutated reptiles. Minus the hockey stick that made him intimidating."

"So Casey Jones isn't cool?"

"Not without the hockey stick, Jimmy. And now you're telling me your skeletal face is gone?" I turn to Sera. "Can't we let him cut his face up a bit?"

Jimmy offers her his best doe-eyed, bunny rabbit, give-me-what-I-want-because-I'm-%*&#ing-cute-look. It's an complete failure.

"Absolutely not," Sera says.

"Looks like you're mine, boy," The Donnanatrix smirks. "Don't worry. It'll only hurt a little. No matter how much you beg. Mwaha!"

"We have to do this now?" Jimmy asks.

Sera takes his hand. "Might as well get it over with, right?"

I don't want to miss whatever Donna might do to Jimmy, but Emma hangs back to speak with Entheus, so I linger too.

"Entheus, may I ask you something?"

"Of course, m'lady," Entheus says.

"Is…is it common for people to come back from the dead

here?"

Entheus's expression is momentarily unreadable. "The phrase 'Heroes never die' is not uncommon on Anexia." Emma waits, maybe expecting Entheus to say more, but he doesn't.

"Thanks." Emma says, though she doesn't sound all that reassured.

"What was that all about?" I ask.

"While you were unconscious Panik might have implied that my body could just be a side-effect of this place. Maybe I could lose it next time we jump."

"Oh."

"Don't worry about it. Being dead isn't the worst thing," she grabs my hand, "but maybe hold on to me just in case."

* * *

"Ow," Jimmy whines as Donna tightens the restraints on his wrists. She slaps him for his outburst.

"Hey!" Sera says. "This isn't some S&M deal."

Donna dismisses her. "He's enjoying it."

Jimmy shakes his head.

"Just tie him up, nothing else." Sera orders.

Donna scowls. "The else is the fun part."

"Don't worry," I say. "I'm sure Lily will let you tie her up later."

"Excuse me," Lily objects.

"What?" I say. "You were thinking it."

"Obviously, but I wanted to *say* it too. You know, like seductively and stuff."

"And I didn't want to hear it."

"Fair enough. But it's still true." Lily winks at Donna. And maybe at Sera too. Whatever. They both smile to some degree. I don't get how she does it. Those two usually give me dirty looks. Not the good kind.

As Donna finishes the binding of Jimmy, I lobby pretty hard for a gag as well. Donna is pretty keen on the idea, but Sera flashes me one of those aforementioned dirty looks. In the end, I don't get my way. Donna and I both sulk. It doesn't last long, however, as Panik starts in on another of her nonsensical diatribes. This time about how to track down our mysterious foe using blah blah blah. I tried paying attention at first, but quickly realized I didn't want to. Anything important, Emma can fill me in on later.

At some point Emma says, "What about The Roboracle? He might be able to give us some clues about what to do next."

Donna looks directly at me. "He's…unresponsive lately."

"Well we certainly can't sit here waiting while Anexia suffers," Entheus says.

"Absolutely not," Valiant agrees. "There's far too much *adventure* to be had and lives to be saved. We can follow you down to Anexia, Entheus, and join you in battle while we allow Panik the proper time to lock on to our target."

"What are we waiting for then? The Steel Canyon awaits!" Entheus flies off, preparing to guide us back to wherever this Steel Canyon is.

It's a short flight and we manage to avoid crashing this time, so things are looking good thus far. Valiant directs Sera to land the Galley on top of the highest building in the city, so our first course of action is to strap on the jet packs we have lying around the armory. I haven't used these since Candy Island exploded.

Before we're able to exit the ship, Sera salutes Valiant.

"Captain, requesting permission to remain with the Galley, sir."

"An excellent idea, Lieutenant. It would be unwise to leave the ship and the lady Panik alone until we've surveyed the surroundings. Permission granted. In fact, it might be prudent for only a few of us to venture forth. Victor, Emma, and I will join Entheus and The Donnanatrix on the ground."

Candy Princess chooses that moment to burst into the room, out of breath. "I'm ready!"

"I'm afraid you'll have to sit this one out, Princess," Valiant says.

Candy's eyes go full puppy dog and her lower lip juts out to form her patented pout-face. "But I altered one of my dresses so I could play superhero too. See." Sure enough she's shortened her dress even shorter than Emma's skirt, and she's really amped her cleavage up to an impressive level. Also she has a cape with a cupcake on it.

"I'm sorry, Princess, but we need people here in case we become incapacitated. You'll have to help Panik locate her artifact if we're unable to do so. Can you do that for me?"

"Of course, Captain! But you'll make it back in time. You've got Victor with you." She bats her eyelashes at me. Then Emma slaps the $#*! out of her.

Candy's eyes water a bit, but she never stops smiling. "I'm so happy you got your body back Emma! Now it's like I never did anything bad at all and you're so pretty and you hit really well! Way better than Lily." She sticks her tongue out at Lily. Then tackles Emma with a hug.

Emma pushes her off and storms out in a huff, while Lily looks like she's ready to practice her punching. Valiant and I leave them all to their own devices. I'm not entirely sure they'll all be alive when we get back, but the ship *has* been a little over crowded.

Chalk catches up to us as we exit to the roof of the skyscraper. Apparently I'd been too distracted by Candy Princess's outfit to notice him earlier.

CAN I COME 2? Chalk's face reads.

Valiant shrugs, leaving the decision to me. "I'd love to have you along, little buddy, but I think these girls might need a chaperone to keep them from maiming one another. Can I count on you to keep the bloodshed to a minimum?"

CAN I SEDATE THEM?

"Only as a last resort."

U GOT IT! His face says, and he sprints back on board.

Emma is waiting for us on the roof, jetpack ready. "Glad to see you could pull yourself away from Candy's @$$ long enough to join me. Do I look that skanky in this thing?"

"You look way better," I tell her.

She ignores me. "I look ridiculous. I might as well be naked."

"I agree," I say. In response, Emma jumps off the building. Valiant follows suit, and I have no choice but to do the same. Entheus and Donna are already on the street, Entheus helping a young boy to his feet. The kid stares at him, awestruck, and then runs across the street and inside a battered building. Other than that, everything is quiet. Not that I expect that to last for long.

The streets themselves are littered with debris. Entheus sifts through the worst of it in search of survivors, the rest of us follow his lead. At best, all we find is more wreckage. At worst, body parts. But nothing living. The quiet is broken after Donna recovers a very tiny limb:

"Well if it isn't the prodigal daughter and Anexia's favorite son," a gruff voice says from behind us.

"You animals!" Donna spits, twisting around so quickly my

mind has difficulty making sense of it. "You're doing this to children?!"

"It's Animauler, baby, you know that. And it turns out babies aren't as tasty as they look." Animauler isn't alone, though. He's got the entire Immoral Many with him. "I suppose this means you haven't seen the dark, and won't be joining us. It's only a matter of time, you know. The Ashen Moon grows every night. Soon its pull will be too strong for any to resist. Until then I guess we'll just have to enjoy hurting you and your friends."

"I call dibs on Entheus's little girly sidekick," says a three-eyed beast I recognize as Triclops. "You remember me, girl? I'm not so little now, am I? I'm going to enjoy #%&$ing and killing you. Not necessarily in that order."

Entheus shakes, anger lacing his words. "You dare speak to a lady like that?"

A pale woman I've never seen before smirks and says, "Go on. Give in. The rush of anger. The release…it's euphoric."

"You can't goad me, Zombirella."

"We'll see. Don't you wonder whatever happened to that other little sidekick you had? What was her name…Lucy?"

The color drains from Entheus. "Lucky." It's barely a whisper.

"Ah, of course. Inspiration and Luck combined for an unstoppable heroic force. And where is she now, Mr. Superhero?"

"I…I don't remember. Did she go to college?"

"It's delightful watching you struggle. Think very hard and maybe you'll remember. Or would you just rather we take you to her grave?"

"That's a lie…a trick of the Ashen Moon's shadow."

"You don't sound so certain. Come on, it won't take long to see. We left her face mostly intact. The things we did to her body, though…"

In a flash, Entheus has Zombirella by the throat. "LIES!" he roars.

Zombirella cackles. "Yes! Do it! Inspire this whole retched planet with your rage." She leans in as if to kiss him. "Kill me."

For a moment I actually believe he might, but Captain Valiant intervenes. "Kill you? Now where's the *adventure* in that?" His voice somehow breaks the hold Zombirella has over Entheus. Not surprising, he has that effect on everyone.

"The Captain is right," Entheus says, calmer now. "We will settle this like gentlemen and…whatever you are. In the grand tradition of superhero and villain we shall battle."

"So we're finally gonna fight?" Emma says. "Because three eyes over there needs to find out what it actually feels like to #*!% with me."

Donna laughs. "Mwhahahahaha!"

"Wait! Hold up," I say before things get too fighty, and I point to some leafy mother%$#*er. "You're Plantera, right?"

"Yeah," he says. "So what?"

I check the surroundings. Lots of metal and concrete, but no dirt and definitely no green $#*! "I'll take him." No one does anything. "Um, we can fight now." And just like that, it's on!

Donna charges into battle, whips in hand, headed straight for Animauler. Emma—elegant like a flower, vicious like the same flower anthropomorphized and instilled with severe anger issues—dodges a Tri-Optic Blast with impeccable elegance, picking up two pieces of rebar as she somersaults out of the way. Valiant, on the other hand, calmly waits for the fight to come to him. I can't really concentrate on what happens to everyone else for very long because I find myself locked in an epic stare down with the douchebag known as Plantera.

"You know what I hate most about superheroes," he says. "All the synthetic clothing. Whatever happened to a simple cotton blend?"

"So your plan was what? To squeeze me to death with my clothes?" I ask.

"Well, yeah. But I've got other tricks too." Plantera's face scrunches up with horrible effort until sweat trickles down his brow. "What the #$%*? Don't you eat vegetables?"

"Ha! Do I strike you as the kind of guy looking to live a long and healthy life? I say the more processed the better! Vegetables can go %#*$ themselves."

That really gets under the plant-man's skin. He quite literally vibrates with anger. "You think you're a funny guy, huh? Well let's see how funny you find this!" Suddenly a yellow cloud bursts from Plantera, covering me nearly head to toe.

I sneeze a few times. "Dude, did you just try to pollinate me? That's so not cool, man!"

"Yeah, what're you gonna do about it?"

I didn't want to have to resort to this, not right away, but this sick #$*! leaves me no choice. I draw my gun. "It's time for your stamen to meet my pistol, %*!$#." Then I shoot him in the crotch. "Pollinate that."

As Plantera writhes around like a fish out of water, totally clashing with his whole plant theme, I rush over to help Emma. Turns out she doesn't need it. Triclops is more of a Cyclops now that Emma has jammed that rebar into two of his eyes. Donna is whipping the $#*! out of Animauler, while Valiant stands valiantly over a couple of fallen Immoral Many. I don't think he even broke a sweat. The rest are fleeing from Entheus.

"We'll meet again, heroes," declares Zombirella. "The shadow of the Ashen Moon isn't the only shadow you need to worry about."

"Shouldn't we follow them?" Emma asks as they escape.

Entheus considers the options. "Normally I'd say yes, but they are not our top priority. Besides, they'll be licking their wounds for a short while, at least, and they're never too difficult to find."

"We should return to the Galley," says Valiant. "Panik may have news for us. If not, we should hydrate. Who knows when we'll get another chance."

"A sensible plan, Captain," Entheus concurs. "Go back to your ship. I'll aid with clean-up here. Just call when you're ready to move out. It won't take much more than a whisper for me to hear."

* * *

Back at the Galley, Chalk is waiting for our return. "Status report?" Valiant asks.

IT'S ALL GOOD Chalks face reads.

"Excellent!" We follow the captain to Sera and Jimmy's quarters, where Jimmy is still complaining about being tied up. "Anything to report, Lieutenant?"

"No, sir. It's all quiet. Other than Jimmy," Sera says.

"Now that you guys are back, does that mean you're going to untie me?" Jimmy asks.

"That's a negative, spaceboy," Valiant says. "Things are no less dangerous than they were before." Jimmy whines some more, but it doesn't change his situation. Even Sera isn't interested in listening to him anymore.

"How were things down there?" she wonders.

"Dire," says Valiant. "Many dead, many more suffering."

"We did have a nice little scuffle," Emma says. "I got to gouge out two of Triclops's eyes."

"Sweet. And what happened to you?" Sera asks me.

"Plantera tried to pollinate me," I say quietly.

Everyone laughs.

Even Jimmy.

%*&#ers.

Lily, probably hearing everyone revel in my humiliation, appears in the doorway. "What's so funny?" It takes a good long while for anyone to get the explanation out through their howls, but Lily gets the gist of it sooner than I hoped. Because I was hoping for never. "So a plant man %#$* on you?" I don't say a word, but my expression is enough. "I think this is my favorite day ever."

"%*# all of you!" I stomp off towards my own room so that I can clean this $#*! off me. When I'm almost to my room I nearly trip over The Roboracle.

"Oh, hey," I say.

"I AM THE FAUXBORACLE."

"Yeah, I've heard."

Without warning I'm slammed against the wall, The Donnanatrix inches from my face. "What did you do to him?"

"Huh?"

"My Roboracle was fine when I left him. Now he's filled with doubt."

"THE FATES TAUNT THE FAUXBORACLE WITH THEIR WHISPERS. DEATH IS RISING." Once again static intrudes The Roboracle's ramblings. "ONLY DEATH CAN STOP IT."

"See," Donna tightens her grip on me, "all this because you took him to that awful city!"

"He doesn't seem that different to me. And it's not like I wanted to take him. He showed up looking for you."

Donna relaxes slightly. "You're lucky I like you and Emma so much."

"You do?"

"If I didn't I wouldn't have bothered talking first," she picks up The Roboracle and continues down the hall. "But Victor better watch his back, for the wrath of The Donnanatrix will be sated somehow, Mwhahahaha!"

"You do realize that theatrical asides only work in plays, right?" I yell after her, but she's already gone.

Back in my room, I look myself over in the mirror. It's ridiculous, yellow is not my color. But before I can turn on the shower to wash away my shame, Emma ambushes me with a flurry of kisses. "That fight got me so hot." I try to say that I can tell, but it gets muffled by her tongue in my mouth. Then she sneezes. A lot. "Whoa…sneezing is awesome!" She nuzzles against my face and breathes in as deeply as she can, sparking another sneezing fit. It's so endearing that I can't bring myself to remind her where the pollen came from, but I think she remembers anyway. "Uh, maybe we should clean you up."

She grabs a wash cloth and does the work for me. As she does she whispers something so filthy my mind can't even process it, which is probably for the best because someone knocks on the door. Emma answers it, leaving me to finish washing up. I hear Sera's voice, but can't really make out what she's saying. Can't say I care all that much right about now. Her stay is brief, but it did give me enough time to get mostly clean. I head back to the bedroom, noticing Emma dropped a little something earlier. Emma doesn't even let me get out of the bathroom, she crushes my dreams right where I stand. "Captain Valiant wants to have another briefing." I sigh and pick up what Emma dropped.

"You'll probably want these then?" I say as I enter the room.

"Uh, thanks," she says and puts her panties back on.

* * *

Paying attention to one of Valiant's briefings usually isn't a problem, as long as he's the one talking. But, of course, like any self-respecting man in a leadership role, he's letting everyone else do the talking for him. Couple that with Emma's silent flirting and I'd be hard pressed to even describe the chair I'm sitting in, and that's considering I've sat in this chair dozens of times. About all I'm capable of doing is nodding whenever I think I hear my name, which may or may not be appropriate. I do manage to gather that Panik is having difficulty locking down a second anti-gravitation field. Or rather she's reading faint traces of mine all over the place. Valiant no longer seems content waiting around and wants to follow any lead, no matter how faint or seemingly irrelevant. Once he gets the taste of adventure he's insatiable.

No one objects to Valiant's plans of going on the offensive, who could ever disagree with him. "As we're all in agreement, I suggest everyone brush their teeth now. We could be in for a long day."

Panik follows us on the way back to our room. "Is there something we can do for you?" Emma asks.

"Not particularly," Panik says. "Your tantric aura is fascinating, however. I've never studied the sex drive of the recently resurrected. It's quite powerful."

"Is that your way of asking to join us?" Emma wonders. "Because at this point I'm willing to do just about anything if it means I get to take my clothes off."

"Wait, what?" I say.

Emma smiles in such a way that I have no idea if she's being serious.

"The captain was adamant that we spend this time on oral hygiene," Panik says. "But you're free to do with my body as you please while I do so."

I have no idea what's going on, but I do know that Lily comes along and destroys it. "Hey, what's up?"

"You're ruining my life!" I tell her calmly.

"Uh, okay…so is the captain serious about the teeth brushing thing? Because I don't get it."

"Proper oral care is important, Lily!!"

"I'd like to get some proper oral care," Emma mutters so that only I can hear.

"Am I missing something here?" Lily wonders.

"Emma is suffering from a post-rebirth supra-phenomenon," Panik explains, "that's most likely being compounded by my own atomic pheromones."

"What?" we all ask simultaneously.

"My pheromones are intelligently designed to advance the mating process in a more rapid fashion."

"Are you saying you manipulate people into having sex with you?" Lily says.

"I don't," Panik says. "My pheromones do. Just like yours, except more efficiently and radioactively."

"Am I going to get cancer from banging you?!"

"The radiation is mostly harmless, and my orgasms have natural healing auras. You'll be fine. All of this is necessary for my survival. Often I can't waste time trying to persuade sexual interactions. So my pheromones take your natural desires and bring them to the surface more quickly. And in closed quarters like these they can have the added side effect of boosting every living libido."

Then she addresses Emma. "Now, as I was saying, if you don't mind me multi-tasking while we copulate I'm more than willing to join in."

"Um, maybe next time…" Emma says.

"Very well, you know where to find me."

Lily lingers for a while.

"What?" I finally say.

"You were going to do it with Panik?"

"I have no idea what I was going to do, and thanks to you I'll never know."

"I realize that Panik will get it on with anything that moves, but there should be boundaries, bro."

"What about Callie Simms?"

"Oh my god! When are you going to get over that?!"

"I found out like two days ago."

"Exactly!"

"I'm gonna go brush my teeth," Emma says, leaving me and Lily to argue. After a while we forget why we even started fighting and go our separate ways.

I end up walking in on Emma brushing her teeth. I join her, but the look she gives me makes it clear I'm unwelcome. Not due to anger, but more like I interrupted a very private moment. I finish up and back out cautiously, unsure if I even want to know what's going on with that toothbrush. In any case, I'm left with no other choice than to do the unthinkable. I go hang out with Jimmy.

"Hey, Vic," he says.

"Um," I say.

"Are you here to untie me?"

"Um."

"Didn't think so. So what's up?"

"Um."

"Hey, who do you think would win in a fight: Superman or Entheus?"

"#*&$ this $#*!, I can't do it! That is literally the dumbest question anyone has ever asked me!"

"Really?"

"And that's number two, Jimmy. You gonna go for the trifecta?"

"Uh, I don't think so..?"

"Gah!" I can't even last another second in this hell, so I bolt. During my escape, Candy Princess grabs me and pulls me into her room.

"Victor, I have the most important question ever!"

"Okay," I say.

"Am I supposed to wear underwear with this outfit? And if so, which pair?" She holds up two pairs of panties. One with rainbows and unicorns all over them and another that says "Eat Me".

"Candy Princess, this is not an appropriate conversation for us to be having."

"Why not?"

"First, because everyone should wear underwear unless they're living in porno-world."

"Oooh, where's that?"

"It's fictional, Candy. And second, Emma still isn't over the whole murdering her to steal me thing you did. I'm still kind of miffed about it too."

"But I've said sorry sooooo many times!"

"Sorry doesn't usually work for murder and date rape."

"Do presents?"

"Maybe."

"Then I'll make you both the best presents ever! And Sera too!

Hooray for friendship!" Then her glee fades into a cartoonish severity. "Now which pair do I wear? If you don't tell me, I won't wear any."

* * *

Not that having Candy Princess attempting to get me to visit her candy playground is a new occurrence, but she's usually a bit more subtle than just flashing her naughty bits every chance she gets. Mostly she comes off pretty naïve and follows it up with something moderately dirty. I can only assume this, too, is down to Panik's super radioactive pheromones floating around the Adventure Galley. In fact, now that I know about that, everything is clearer. Candy's more overt come-ons, Valiant's pursuit of Lily, Lily humoring those pursuits, every single thing Emma has done recently…even the noises emanating from Donna's room make a sick sort of sense. It's almost a relief, really, because I was worried all my crazy urges had some deeper meaning, but it seems like it might just be some psycho-sexual feedback from Panik the sexbot. Which isn't to say it's still not mildly disturbing. I know things are past their saturation point when I find myself back on the bridge and Sera—her hair a faded pink—looks at me and says, "You know, you actually look pretty good in that suit."

So I respond the only sensible way. "We have to get off this ship before an orgy breaks out!"

Sera studies me, trying to figure out if I'm serious. I indicate with exaggerated arm movements that I am. "Just because I said one nice thing about you doesn't mean I want to #*$% you."

"That's what you think, but all the while you're sitting here stewing in an airy cocktail of radioactive sex-fumes that, given enough time, will make your libido go full Hulk and you won't be able to resist smashing your celestial, perfectly formed lady bits into my sexy bones.

They're so sexy!"

Sera politely waits to make sure I'm finished. "Please leave now."

"That's a good idea," I say. "For the sake of our friendship."

I go to my room and sit perfectly still on the bed. Every noise is a potential sexual predator. I must be ever vigilant. My only worry is that Emma is out there roaming the halls. One wrong turn could lead her to sexual disaster. She might even be caressing Sera's hot body as we speak. And I'm missing it…I mean, and I'm not there to protect her from such a folly. Such a fleshy, filthy folly. Then again, everyone makes mistakes. In fact, we learn from those mistakes. If I don't allow Emma and myself to make every erotic error I've ever thought of…well doesn't that mean I'm keeping us from learning very valuable life lessons? I'm on the verge of rushing out the door, intent on erring on the side of awesome, when Captain Valiant shows up and saves the day by saying it's time to move out.

* * *

Our first stop is uneventful. Lots of destruction, but the cause of it is long gone. The next stop is more of the same. I'm not exactly sure how Panik is choosing which sites to go to first; she mentioned something about a complex chorno-algorithm, but I'm too worried about her aphrodisiatic presence to pay attention to anything else. I have to keep my eyes on her, and it has nothing to do with the form fitting outfit she's always wearing or the form to which it's fitting. Nope, nothing at all. By the time we get to our third stop, I'm getting kind of bored.

"This is the old warehouse district," Entheus tells us as we exit the Galley. "It's a maze of villain hideouts. Mostly abandoned."

"We all thought choosing a place where everything looks almost identical would be a great advantage when the occasional cop or hero came snooping around, but a lot of villains would lose track of their own lair," Donna adds. "My friends weren't exactly the brightest bulbs in the box."

"Miss Natrios and I will scout ahead. We'll be back before you know it," Entheus says. That leaves the rest of us—minus Jimmy who is still bound, but sadly still not gagged—to sit around and do jack all. I continue my watch on all my inappropriately dressed female colleagues with their tight shirts and short skirts and smooth skin. It's a danger zone for promiscuity. I can hold back, but the way that Emma and Sera are chatting, the proximity of their supple bodies…it's too much! I insert myself between them.

"Ugh," Sera says.

"It's for your own good," I explain.

The two continue their conversation. It seems innocent on the surface, but any keen observer could hear how it's laced with spicy tension.

"You're hair looks great today," Emma says.

"Thanks," Sera says.

So much tension!

The rusted metal around us creaks, reminding me of the Infinite City underground., if Infinite City were a dilapidated, twisted mess. The next creak is more like a groan.

"Hey, it's like the return of the Phantom of Opera," I say, basking in my cleverness.

"Don't you mean Phantom of *the* Opera?" Sera says.

"No, see Opera was a slightly obscure web browser," I say.

Lily swivels my direction, a full on gawk across her face. "I can't believe you're trying to sequelize me."

"If by sequelize you mean taking something you did and doing it way better, then yeah."

"No, I mean taking my pun and bastardizing it, like almost every sequel ever."

"Um, excuse me. Sequels are awesome. There's X2, Star Trek: The Wrath of Khan, Dawn of the Dead, The Empire Strikes Back, The Godfather Part 2."

"The Godfather Part 2 is, at best, as good as The Godfather. And don't even think of saying Superman II, because you know that's bull$#*!"

"I still have no idea what either of you is talking about," Sera says.

"Okay, let me explain Victor's idiocy," Lily says. "Back in Infinite City I made some throwaway comment about there being a 'Phantom of the Operating System'."

"That's cute," Sera says.

"I know, and this guy got jealous that he didn't think of it first so now he's trying to steal it. Which doesn't even make sense because NO ONE ELSE WAS THERE for your sequel pun to hit the mark. Also, it was terrible."

"Terrible? Yours was so on the nose it was trite, Lily! Mine was much more high-brow."

"We were literally in a city's operating system. What does a stupid web browser have to do with that or this rundown warehouse we're in?"

"Jimmy would have gotten it," I say. "He'd be on my side. I can't believe Jimmy's ruining things when he's not around too!"

"Don't blame Jimmy for your shortcomings," Lily says.

"I'll blame whoever I want!"

"Why can't you be more like your sister?" Sera asks.

"And stop always stealing my friends!"

"We're not really that close," Sera says.

"Ahem, I hate to interrupt," Entheus says. I have no idea when he got back. "But I believe Miss Natrois and I may have found something."

* * *

As daylight rapidly fades, Sera and Chalk are again charged to remain with the ship while the rest of us follow Donna and Entheus through the twists and turns of abandoned warehouses. When we reach our destination I can't say it looks very special or unique. Just another abandoned, worn down building.

"This way," Donna says. She leads us through another door, but instead of the expected concrete floor, we find ourselves standing on dirt. Lumpy, lumpy dirt.

"I guess dirt indoors is kind of weird," I say. "Though I'm not sure it was worth the walk."

Emma studies the room, runs her fingers over the dirt. "Sweetie, I don't think it's just dirt indoors. I think…I think this is a graveyard."

Panik rubs some dirt between the balls of her thumb and index finger. Then she sniffs it. "There is death here. Slow death. The decomposition process is negligible."

"You can tell that just from smelling the dirt?" Lily asks.

"Of course," Panik says like it's no big thing. I tend to agree, seems like a worthless talent. "That's not all. There's some sort of spatial anomaly here. Or there was one. It's absence sings vibrantly."

"Which means?" I ask.

"Just a point of interest. Captain, Entheus, does anything here look familiar?"

"Why do you ask?" Valiant wonders.

"During a post and pre-coital moment, Lily chronicled the encounters both you and Entheus had with a certain Soul Destroyer, and the tales indicated that he had a mysteriously vanishing base of operations. The music of this time/space fits the profile of a sporadic mobile construction. And you learn when dealing with Abstractions and increasing Uncertainty, that coincidence is fiction."

"I'll have a looksee, then," Captain Valiant declares. Entheus, however, is white as a sheet, his gaze never wavering from the mounds of disturbed earth. Emma doesn't look much better.

"I think I need a little fresh air," she says and walks back outside.

Lily, who is currently trying to reenact Panik's dirt trick, offers to go make sure Emma is okay, but I'd rather do it myself.

I find her sitting against the building, staring up at the sky. "You okay?"

"Yeah, just a little nauseated. I forgot what that felt like too. Can't say I missed it too much." She looks at me, almost embarrassed. "You'd think someone who's spent so much time in Hell wouldn't be bothered by a little mass grave."

I sit down next to her. "Is that all that's bothering you?"

"Not really. Those conflicting memories are getting, I don't know, more potent or something. Plus I'm still adjusting to having a body again. Is this how you felt when we first met? Because I feel like I'm falling apart."

"You'll be fine," I try to assure her. "It doesn't get much worse than some mild discombobulation here and there." I glance upward, expecting to see a jeweled sky shining down on us, but I only see a single pale moon and something dark near it, like a phantom moon. Or a shadow. “Where are the rest of the moons?”

“Huh?” Emma follows my gaze. “I hadn’t even noticed, I guess I was…oh.” Emma leaps to her feet.

“What?”

“The Opal Moon,” she says. “It’s bad, remember.”

“Sure, all that junk about life and death and the dead rising and…oh $#*!!!” We rush back into the warehouse. “Guys, we might want to leave. Like right now.”

“Why?” Lily asks, still crouched in the dirt. Her attention on us, she doesn’t notice the ground squirm beside her, and I don’t have time to warn her before a hand bursts from the ground, grabbing her wrist. She screams.

“That’s why,” I say. At least a dozen corpses rise from the ground, surrounding Lily.

To everyone’s surprise, it’s Candy Princess who is the first to act. “I’ll save you!” She jumps directly into the fray, her skirt flying up unceremoniously as she does. Then she punches the zombie looking to make a snack out of Lily right in the nose. I’m not sure if it’s the punch or the sound of Candy’s giggles that causes the thing to release its grip, but Lily is freed nonetheless. Lily scrambles towards us—and the exit—while Candy continues to punch, kick, and laugh joyfully.

Emma watches in disbelief. “Does her underwear say EAT ME?” I pretend not to know. “Fingers crossed that it’s a sign of things to come.” Finally Donna and Valiant join the fight. Although it’s more about stopping Candy than actually fighting.

Valiant manages to pull her from the mob after a few seconds. “Time to get back to the Galley, Princess. That goes for everyone.” Candy pouts, but complies.

Everyone falls back, save for Entheus. He’s locked on to a shambling corpse that looks to have once been a young girl. It’s hard to tell through all the dirt, but she appears to be dressed nearly identical to Emma. The acoustics of the warehouse make his whisper audible.

"Lucky," he says.

"Entheus," Captain Valiant tries to shake him to his senses, "we really have to go."

"I'll meet you at the ship," Entheus says softly.

"Entheus…" Donna starts.

Entheus turns to her sharply, his eyes burning white. "Go."

Donna hesitates only briefly. "You heard the man, go!"

We run without looking back. The noises tell us that there's probably nothing back there we want to see. Piercing shrieks of pain blend with the rush of blood to my head, creating a surreal cacophony of torture beating against my body. And somewhere, somehow, I kind of like it.

If not for Donna, we most likely would have been lost in a network of worn out buildings. Without a hitch, she guides us back to the Adventure Galley where Chalk is waving frantically. The dark makes it hard to read his face until we're nearly on top of him.

JIMMY IS FREAKING THE %&$* OUT is what he's trying to tell us. Of course he is. %#$^ing Jimmy. Tucked away comfortably in bed and he's still a &*$$^. We find Sera pacing up and down the halls, her relief when she sees us is almost tangible.

"Chalk says Jimmy is freaking the %&$* out," I say.

"That's an understatement," Sera says. "He's alternating between thrashing around and making god awful noises. Occasionally he does both. Please tell me we're getting out of here."

"We have to wait for Entheus," Captain Valiant tells her, "but I'd recommend preparing the Galley for take-off."

"Yes, sir."

Donna peeks outside. "I don't want to tell you how to run your ship, but Entheus can fly. He doesn't need us to wait for him."

"Be that as it may, I never leave a member of my crew behind."

"Suit yourself. Little does he know that a hoard of the undead are converging upon us as we speak. Mwhahahaha!"

Emma, Lily, and I rush to the exit. It's not a pretty sight. Every single warehouse in this place must have had bodies stashed somewhere inside.

"Chalk, I think it's time to come inside," Emma says.

He turns to us. His face says I GOT THIS

Candy Princess pops up beside me, bouncing with excitement. "Yay, more superheroing!" She bounds toward the door, but Lily pulls her back.

"You helped me back there. This is me returning the favor."

"But—"

"But nothing, Princess," Lily says.

Candy looks from Lily to me. I do my best to tell her that Lily is right. "Okay, fine." She sulks off down the hall.

Chalk, meanwhile, is laying waste to the zombies. But they keep coming. Emma finally runs out and grabs him. He kicks about in protest. "You'll thank me for this later. Captain, we really need to get out of here."

"We wait," is all Valiant says.

"Can we at least close all the doors?" Lily asks, but Valiant remains silent. "I guess we fight then."

Just as the first group of corpses reaches the loading bay of the Galley, bodies begin to fly in the distance. It spreads like a shockwave, tossing the undead in all directions before finally knocking those closest to us into the dark of night. With a whoosh, Entheus is standing before us with someone whipping around in his arms.

"I suggest we go now, Captain."

"Lieutenant!" Valiant bellows. That's all it takes for the loading door to snap shut, and before we know it we're airborne.

The girl in Entheus's arms struggles heroically, but he shows no sign of even the slightest effort expended. "We need to go back to the Diamond Moon. Lucky is…she's very sick."

"I hate to be the one to tell you," I say, "but I'm pretty sure she's—" Emma and Lily smack me together, shaking their heads.

"She's what?" Entheus's eyes have just a smidge of instability dancing behind them.

"Uh, she's wearing the same outfit as Emma…that's got to be pretty embarrassing for her."

Entheus chuckles. "Don't you worry about that. Lucky has never been overly concerned with fashion. And she'll have no problem with Emma borrowing her clothes. She's a very amiable girl. You'll see." Lucky snaps at Entheus's face. "And playful too! Even through sickness she's such a joker."

None of us know what to say as we watch Lucky continue to claw and bite at Entheus. The only thing that seems clear is that keeping quiet is definitely in our best interest.

From down the hall, Jimmy's voice echoes. He sounds giddy. "Who's here?"

"Um, everyone!" I yell back.

"Not you," he dismisses me. It doesn't hurt my feelings, though. I don't even care what Jimmy thinks. "The new girl. Bring her to me."

Upon hearing Jimmy, Lucky calms, albeit only slightly. Still, Entheus is hesitant. While he may have forgiven Jimmy for getting him killed that one time, Entheus obviously doesn't fully trust him. It takes some coaxing—and more than a little pleading from Jimmy—but Entheus finally relents.

The moment Lucky is dragged into Jimmy's room she relaxes. Jimmy sings one of his nasty songs, while Lucky sways to the non-existent beat of it. Or maybe she's about to fall down. Zombies aren't exactly known for their motor skills.

"Well aren't you a pretty girl," Jimmy says, the way most people talk to kittens or puppies or any sort of baby, really.

Entheus doesn't appear amused. "She's not a child, Jimmy,"

"Sorry, she's just so beautiful."

Beautiful is perhaps the last word I'd use to describe Lucky. I mean, it's obvious that she used to be quite the looker, but death hasn't been kind to her. What I'm trying to say is Jimmy is one twisted #^*%. Watching Jimmy and Lucky interact is, I think, the most disturbing thing I've ever witnessed. And this is coming from someone who has reenacted Return of the Jedi with the Devil. It's one of those things that make you sick to your stomach, yet for some reason you're compelled to keep watching. So I'm quite thankful when Sera's voice blares out of the intercom.

"Uh, Captain you might want to see this. I think we have a problem."

Whatever the problem is, it can't be more unnerving than what Jimmy and Lucky are doing, so it's no surprise that we all follow Valiant to the bridge.

"What is it, Lieutenant? What am I meant to see?"

Sera motions to the windows. "That."

"I don't see anything."

"That's the point. The Diamond Moon should be right here. But it's just…gone."

Entheus stares, his face twisted in confusion. "That…that can't be. Lucky needs to go there. It was her favorite place in the entire galaxy. The Diamond Moon can't be gone."

The Donnanatrix, having just arrived with The Roboracle, says, "What's the Diamond Moon?"

That's probably not a great sign.

"Miss Natrios, surely you jest? The Diamond Moon is my home. We spent the better part of the last week there together," Entheus says.

Donna's expression remains blank.

"This can't be happening. Nothing is as it should be." Entheus's frantic body language makes me think he's on the verge of a mental breakdown. That's something I'd rather not be around for.

"What now, Captain?" Sera asks.

"We continue on our course," Valiant says. "Panik, have you a next destination in mind?"

"With my Uncertainty Clock ticking into uncharted territory, and a morphing terrain, I might need more time," Panik says.

"Time is a luxury we can't afford, I'm afraid."

"Time is never a luxury, Captain."

Their conversation continues, but I find it harder and harder to concentrate on it as my head fills with a terrible buzz. It's a sound and frequency that could cancel a heartbeat. A song with absolutely no beat. And it's all around me. I've heard it before.

"Would someone tell Jimmy to stop it," I say.

"Stop what?" Emma wonders.

"No one else hears that?" But I don't need them to answer, it's clear they don't. "I, um, I think I know where we should go."

* * *

I do my best to explain, but it's obvious everyone is skeptical. I don't have much to go on, just wild intuition. In the end, though, no one offers any better plans of action, so we set a course for the Opal Moon. It shouldn't take long to get there, but we have a few minutes to prepare. Not that anyone knows what to prepare for. Although The Roboracle isn't too pleased with our destination.

"THE FAUXBORACLE DEMANDS WE TURN AROUND. DONNA NATRIOS AND THE FAUXBORACLE DO NOT WISH TO GO WITH YOU."

That's news to Donna. "This is my home, my sweet. You know I must go. I cannot sit back and watch it die."

"DONNA NATROIS SHOULD LISTEN TO THE FAUXBORACLE."

"Donna Natrois will not be told what to do. Especially by a self-proclaimed fake!"

"I AM…" The Roboracle pauses and his speakers fill with static. "I AM THE FAUXBORACLE."

"Oh darling, I'm sorry. You know I can't always control my temper."

This is where I have to stop paying attention. Their relationship makes my skin crawl. I don't even understand the mechanics of how it works. Even though I've seen some of the actual mechanics of how it works. And thinking about that puts images in my head that will cause scars that last long after I die.

While I desperately try to block out both Donna and The Roboracle, Panik taps my shoulder. "May we speak privately?"

"Um, I guess. But no funny business," I say. Panik doesn't speak; instead she leads me out into the hall. "So what's this about?"

"I've found that people are often more compliant when separated from groups."

"What exactly am I meant to comply to?"

"Since my arrival you have been at the center of nearly every phenomenon that's occurred. Every bit of chonologic says you hold the key to the shard I'm searching for, yet you clearly aren't in possession of it. Now you suddenly know where we should go without even the slightest bit of tantric sciences to back your conclusions. How is that?"

"I don't know," I say. "It's a hunch."

"You do know," Panik says. "And to make matters worse, my Uncertainly clock has hit 18:00. The highest I've ever seen it is 20:20."

"Okay, hold up just a second. What exactly is this Uncertainty Clock?"

"A clock that measures the level of uncertainty."

"And if it goes past 20:20?"

"That remains an uncertainty. But it's beside the point. What aren't you telling me?"

"I don't know."

Panik blinks twice. "If you'd only let me share minds with you we could dispense with this wasteful chatter."

"Would sharing minds involve sharing bodies?"

"Of course, how could you share thoughts without a proper interface. And bodily fluids are the best telepathic conductors in this era."

"Well you could ask Emma, but…"

"Believe me, I will if I run out of other options. While I might be fond of your sister and the rest of the crew, if you think that your death—or the death of this era—matters to me…you cannot begin to fathom how much I've lost. But I will not lose this shard and I will not lose to Time. Never again." With that, Panik marches back onto the bridge.

Emma is waiting with a question or two on her lips when I walk back in. "What was that about? She didn't molest you, did she?"

“Unfortunately she just lectured me about who knows what. It was only mildly erotic.”

Emma smiles, but it’s strained. “I’m worried about Entheus. All of these horrible things, I don’t think he’s seen much like it before.”

“He spent some time in Hell,” I try to reassure her.

“Yeah, but Hell isn’t so bad. Watching your world slowly fall apart, though, seeing that girl Lucky dead, his home disappearing…I don’t think he can handle it. Should I talk to him?”

“Whatever you want, Em,” I say.

She takes my hand. “Come on.”

“Oh, I have to come too?”

Entheus is busy staring out into space, back towards where the Diamond Moon used to be. “Hey, Entheus.”

“Why hello, m’lady,” Entheus says. “Have I told you how fetching you look in that outfit?” He tries to grin that classic grin of his, but he ends up looking more pained than ever.

“Does it bother you that I’m wearing this?”

“Of course not, why would it?” Entheus’s eyes never leave the window. “In truth, it reminds me of happier times. When Lucky and I traversed the galaxy without a care in the world, never the slightest worry that we might lose to whatever evil we faced.”

“We won’t lose today, either,” Emma says.

“As you say.” There’s no conviction in his voice.

“Would you like to talk about her?”

“I,” Entheus pauses and swallows hard, like he’s choking on his own thoughts. “Lucky was a very special girl. The accident that gave her powers also took the life of her parents. But she never lost her love for life. If anything she had more than anyone I’d ever met. Or have met since. Despite having no home, she never used her gifts for personal gain. Instead she protected those who had fallen through the cracks of society. That's how I met her. The Immoral Many were taunting some of the orphan children as they are wont to do, and I was between intergalactic adventures so I naturally went to shoo the Many on their way. But there was this one brave girl standing nose to nose with Animauler—and anyone who's been close to him knows that's dicey for the smell alone—and she was saying 'why don't you jerks take a hike!' Then she did the unthinkable, she punched him right smack in the kisser. And Animauler ran off crying." The old Entheus is almost recognizable as he wades through his own personal pool of nostalgia.

"Oh hey," Donna says, having made her way over to join us. "I think I remember that. Yeah, yeah! Animauler pouted for at least a week after that. And I remember…I remember thinking how much that girl reminded me of myself. I was jealous when you took her under your wing too. Wondered why no one ever did that for me."

Entheus's shoulders slump as he deflates all over again. "I'm sorry I failed you, Miss Natrios."

"It's okay," Donna pats him on the back awkwardly. "I would have made a horrible hero. Too much morality. Not enough whips and chains."

"It's kind of you to try, but it seems I fail everyone in the end."

"Hey, that's no way for the Inspiration of Anexia to talk," Donna scolds. "The only way you're gonna fail anyone is with that attitude, mister!"

"But Lucky, she's…she's…"

"A hero. Because of you. And what's that saying you hero-lovers are so fond of? Heroes never?"

"Never die. But that's just—"

"I know very well what it's just. And I also know that if we are to have any hope of saving Anexia, we need you to inspire us. The way you inspired Lucky. Mwhahahaha!"

"I…thank you Miss Natrios," Entheus says and stands a little taller.

"Please, it's Donna."

"Of course, Donna. I should go check on Lucky and Jimmy while I still have time."

"That was really nice, Donna," Emma says.

"Ugh, don't remind me," Donna sticks out her tongue in mock disgust. "We need that big galoot in top form if we want to save our hides is all."

"Okay," Emma says, but I don't think she's buying it.

"Hey Donna," I say before she can walk away. "What's your origin anyway?"

She thinks about it for a while, long enough that I'm sure she's not going to answer at all. But then she looks down at The Roboracle and starts: "There was this guy I had a thing for. I was working at the local library at the time, and he'd come in every week to check out a book or two. He didn't pay much attention to me, so I got it in my head to start reading whatever he was checking out. That way I could strike up a conversation with him and he might finally notice me. But it took me weeks to finally muster up the courage to say a word.

"I finally managed it one day, though. I haven't the faintest idea what I said; I only know that it was monumentally embarrassing. Still, he smiled. And the next time he came in he actually walked right up and talked to me. Me! Mousy little Donna Natrios. He even started asking me for book recommendations! I was in heaven. Then…then he, one day he asked me out on a date. I was so excited I nearly swooned right then and there.

"Later that week I dressed in my fanciest get up—which wasn't very fancy, I was just a librarian—and he took me to the hippest restaurant in the entire Canyon. I ate foods I couldn't even pronounce and I laughed at all of his jokes. Even the stupid ones. Especially those. I just wanted to make a good impression. And when he invited me back to his place I knew I had.

"He lived in the biggest house I'd ever seen, and when he showed me his own personal library I couldn't help but ask why he bothered coming to our silly public one. He looked at me shyly and told me he was lonely and looking for someone to share his interests with. That he was waiting for the courage to talk to me. A fella like that nervous to speak to me? It was wild!

"He offered to get us both a drink, and naturally I accepted. I'd never had any alcohol before that night, but I had a swell buzz going from dinner and I didn't want him to suspect how unsophisticated I truly was. While I waited, I browsed his book collection and I was shocked to find so much of it focused on bondage. On torture.

"When he returned to find me looking through his books, well he had this twinkle in his eye. This hunger that I'd never seen. At least not directed at me. He explained that the subject fascinated him and wondered if it fascinated me as well. I lied because I didn't want to offend him. Because I was a little bit drunk. Because I wanted him to like me.

"I didn't even know what bondage was. Not really. He told me that we could do all sorts of things together. Things I didn't understand. But I didn't want to disappoint him. He was so beautiful and kind. Or he seemed to be. So when he asked me to spend the night, I didn't even know how to refuse.

"The thing is, I'd only ever even kissed a boy once before, so as he ripped my clothes off and tied me to his bed I thought maybe this is normal. Maybe this is what married couples do behind closed doors. Even as he had his way with me—even through the pain—I never protested. Because the way he looked at me. The passion in his eyes…I liked it. But when it was over, he didn't untie me. He kept me. For days. Whipping me. Experimenting on me. Violating me with needles. With his...everything. In the end, however, he did me a favor. One of those concoctions he injected me with made me stronger and faster. Allowed me to fly. I broke free one day while he was out, but I didn't flee. Instead I waited for his return, and upon it I gave him back every gift he gave me. And I loved every second of it.

"At one point I did ask what he'd given me to make me so strong, but of course I'd already ripped out his tongue by then. Mwhahahaha!"

"THE FAUXBORACLE WISHES TO KILL THAT MAN."

"Oh darling, that's sweet. But he's long dead. In the end he begged for death. Or at least I think that's what he was doing. It really isn't easy making sense of a tongue-less man."

"Sorry I asked," I mutter.

"Donna, that's awful," Emma says.

Donna shrugs. "I think it used to be cuter. Safer. But I can't remember that anymore. All I know is right now I want to tie someone up, straddle them, wrap my hands around their throat, and inhale their last breath with a kiss."

"Well that's fucked up," Lily says.

"Wait," I say, "did you just say 'fucked up'?"

"Sounds like we both did, bro."

"Any chance this is a good sign?" I wonder. "You know, as opposed to a portent of terrible and painful things."

"Probably not," Sera says.

"But worry not, Victor," Valiant says. "For out of pain and terror often comes the most rewarding *adventure*."

* * *

Not long after, the Opal Moon comes into full view. Sera flips a few switches here and there—none of which I have any idea what they do because apparently I'm not to be trusted around sensitive equipment—and the Adventure Galley slows its approach.

"What now?" Sera asks.

"We follow the flow of death," Panik answers.

"That sounds like a bad idea…whatever it means," Sera says.

"Would you mind elaborating?" Valiant asks.

"Can't you see it? The color of death is an umbilical cord connecting the two satellites," Panik says in her typical absurd fashion. I doubt anyone has any clue what she's talking about.

"Do you mean that path of debris between the moons?" Except for Lily. I doubt anyone has any clue what she's talking about except for Lily is absolutely where my last thought would have naturally concluded if Lily's voice hadn't so rudely interrupted them.

"I still don't see anything," Emma says.

"Lily's senses have most likely been enhanced by our physical relationship," Panik says, much to my intense dissatisfaction.

"Cool," Lily says.

"I can guide the ship if you'd like," Panik says. "I've piloted much more complex than this."

"Um," Sera looks to Captain Valiant for an answer.

And answer he does. "An excellent idea! That will allow the Lieutenant and the rest of us to prepare for our landing. I suspect we won't be welcome visitors."

"Really, we're just going to leave her here to pilot the ship without supervision, sir?"

"You worry too much, Lieutenant. Just relax and have faith,"

Valiant says. "And that's an order."

Sera complies and everyone, except for Panik, heads down to the armory. Candy skips alongside the captain, humming some foreign tune. "Do I get to come again?"

Valiant smiles at her. "You proved yourself a *valiant* fighter earlier, Princess. If you wish to come, you'd be most welcome."

"Yayay! I love coming!"

Emma and Sera offer a grunt of disgust, while Lily snorts out something that might be a laugh.

"Does she always say stuff like that?" Lily whispers to me.

"Sometimes," I say.

"Because she's a whore," Emma adds. "Captain, you're not really going to let Candy have a weapon, are you? She's not exactly trustworthy. Hell, almost all this craziness started happening right around the time she showed up again. For all we know she's behind everything."

"That's an excellent point," Sera says.

"Oh you two," Candy laughs. "I'll earn your trust. With the best presents ever!"

"Is it going to be another cup of poison?" Emma asks. "Because I don't want it."

"No, silly. It's a surprise and you'll love it so much forever and ever! Once I figure out what it is… And to show you how so very sorry I really am, the only weapons I'll take will be my fists. I'm gonna punch so many bad guys for you!"

"Well I'm going to take a big weapon," Emma says. "I hope you don't accidentally walk in front of it while it's firing."

"Awww, you really do care!" Candy goes back to humming her unknown song while Emma grumbles her well-known grumble.

* * *

The great thing about the armory on the Adventure Galley is there are weapons for every situation imaginable. Of course you've got your guns and knives and throwing stars. But you also have musical instruments, sexy outfits, and doggy chew toys. I'm not entirely sure what most of those are for. Not that it matters. Captain Valiant says everything in this room has its purpose and I don't ever doubt Captain Valiant.

Donna spends her time checking out the wide assortment of whips and gags. The Roboracle has tapped into some fuel supply, presumably for his flamethrowers that he doesn't use nearly often enough. Sera is stocking up on knives and throwing stars. Emma grabs some of those too, but she also lives up to her promise of finding the biggest weapon she can carry. I have no idea what it is, but it looks intimidating. Candy finds a punching bag and dances around it, lackadaisically throwing punches and kicks as she does, showing enough skin to make a stripper blush. I catch Lily stealing a few glances. But when she notices me noticing her she mumbles something about pheromones and goes back to browsing Valiant's collection of guns and swords. Me, I dig through the more unconventional weapons. There's a bottle of bubble bath, something that looks like a Rubik's Cube, a few scented candles, a book in a language I've never even seen, and a slew of other stuff that I can't even being to understand. But eventually I find what I'm looking for: a big spray canister loaded with weed killer. I strap it to my back and am finally ready. That Plantera douche is in for it now!

Once everyone is properly weaponized, Valiant marches back to the bridge to check on Panik. He returns only a minute or two later to brief us on the situation. "It appears as though Panik is in the process of setting us down about half a mile west of the debris line. If we've been spotted, our enemies aren't letting it be known. We'll have to be cautious. But the element of surprise may still be on our side. This may very well be our greatest *adventure* to date.

"I have one of our long distance communicators and Panik will remain at the helm. We'll remain in touch should we need a sudden evacuation."

"Panik?" Sera interrupts. "What about me?"

"You're more valuable in the field, Lieutenant."

"But Jimmy—"

"Will be fine."

"Yeah, he's got his new friend to keep him company," I assure her.

"New friend?"

"Entheus's old sidekick, Lucky."

"She's here? With Jimmy? Is…is she cute?"

"She looks like she used to be cute."

"What's that mean?"

"It means she's dead."

Sera frowns. "Emma's dead—or was—and she's still cute."

"Thanks," Emma smiles.

"And Jimmy loves dead things," Sera says. "That sounded better in my head."

"I don't know how," I say.

"Look, I'm just curious if you think Jimmy thinks she's cute."

"You know what's cute," I tell her. "That you're jealous of a dead girl."

"What? No I'm not! Shut up!"

"Don't worry," Lily says. "You're way sexier than her. Alive or dead."

"Oh, um…thanks." Sera says, unable to meet Lily's eyes.

"No, thank you," Lily whispers. I'm pretty sure I'm the only one who hears it and I give her my most unbelieving look, which means it's full of squints and face-crinkling, and maybe a little head-shaking. "What?"

"I'm the only one that's allowed to make Sera uncomfortable like that."

Lily claps me on the shoulder. "Deal with it, bro."

* * *

Entheus is already waiting for us outside of Jimmy's room. It's clear he's uneasy about leaving Lucky, but around Jimmy she's hardly more than a piece of furniture. A horribly mangled and rotting piece of furniture. But she seems harmless enough. Almost happy. And Jimmy is content too. He's no longer complaining about his restraints and he's humming one of his freaky songs. I guess it's his way of communicating with Lucky. I don't really care; I'm ready to commit a little herbicide. This is just a useless stop along the way. Once Sera lets Jimmy know she'll be off fighting with us, we're finally allowed to get going.

The surface of the Opal Moon is hard, smooth, and shimmers just slightly as we walk. Like a chameleon, Sera changes her hair to match the ground. I'm not sure if it's even a conscious choice or some natural instinct she has. Not that it matters. Our destination is clearly visible, but from down here that faint path of debris is much more imposing. A thick, dirty vortex that flows upward into space and roars fiercely. Panik landed the Galley behind a small hill, most likely as cover—which, looking around, is no easy task, the Opal Moon doesn't offer much of it—so we can't see where the whirlwind begins. But we'll get there soon enough. Probably sooner than I'd like.

Going over the hill would be the quickest way, but it would also leave us very much in the open. More so than now, at least. So we opt to skirt around it. Entheus and Donna also stay grounded. Sticking together seems the most sensible option since we still don't know what we're up against.

Coming around the bend we get a much better view. The base of the vortex dances arhythmically with flames. From here we can see a few people shambling around it. Some tossing things into the fire, others flat-out walking into it. I guess it makes sense. The path stretches all the way to the Ashen Moon, of course it would need ashes to reform. Beside the giant ash tornado, there's only one other structure of significance anywhere in sight. About a quarter mile away from the fire pit is what looks like a small observatory.

The closer we get, the clearer the scene becomes. There's nothing living anywhere to be seen. Only corpses that haven't enough good sense to realize that being dead means you can lay down your burdens and stop with all the menial labor. As for what they're throwing into the fire when they aren't busy throwing themselves in, that's simple enough. It's the body parts from their fellow zombies that are too decomposed to have the decency to remain in one piece. Or babies that are unable to crawl themselves into the flames. I think everyone else is horrified—except maybe Donna and The Roboracle—but I'm just glad they aren't attacking us.

"We have to stop this monstrosity," Entheus says, keeping his voice as low as possible.

"You could try," someone says behind us.

Entheus doesn't bother turning. "Zombirella."

"And friends," a gruffer voice adds. Must be Animauler

We all turn to attack, but they're too close and too fast. The

Immoral Many even manage to get the jump on Donna. Entheus, however, eludes them momentarily and charges. But as soon as he's in punching distance he pulls up; pain coursing through his muscles.

Zombirella holds up a very ugly rock. "That's right, the Opal Moon happens to be quite rich in Apathite. Not feeling too inspirational now, are you?"

"Wait, hold up," I say. "Apathite? Why not just call it Indiffentanium?"

"D-don't even joke about Indiffentanium," Entheus says, struggling for breath.

"Seriously, that's a thing too? You know, if I ever meet the people who wrote your comic I'm going to kick them square in the balls."

"Vic, this really isn't the time," Lily says.

"Why not? These guys suck and someone needs to tell them."

Sera sighs. "Yep, we're gonna die."

"We're going to die *faster*, Sera. Trust me; I'm doing us all a favor. Unless you actually want to sit through more of this. And who would want that?"

Sera and Lily groan.

"Now ladies," Valiant says. "Death is nothing to groan about. Just look at our lovely captor here. Zombirella is it?"

"Y-yes," Zombirella answers.

"Such an exotic name. Your parents should be commended." Valiant smiles his valiant smile, and you can almost see Zombirella melt.

"Oh, well that's only my villain name," she tells him.

"Bravo," Valiant says. "But might I ask what your birth name is?"

"I don't normally tell my enemies my real name," Zombirella

says as she twirls her hair between her fingers. "It's just so personal."

"We were prepared to engage in mortal combat, what's more intimate than that?"

"I don't know."

"Please."

Zombirella bites her lip. "Jane. Jane Doe."

"Simply exquisite," Valiant says. "Did you know that the first girl I ever loved was named Jane. You remind me so much of her."

"Really?" Over the course of a brief conversation, Zombirella has transformed from intimidating villainess to your typical Captain Valiant groupie.

"She taught me everything I know about being a lover." Zombirella's eyes widen to the point that one falls loose from its socket. "Everything." With that, Captain Valiant does the impossible. He makes a dead girl blush.

That's when I see an opening. Chalk is kneeling next to me. He, like the rest of us, was disarmed earlier. But I notice he was able to hide a tiny blade. Where he hid it I've no idea, but who cares. I subtly get his attention and make a stabbing gesture to the tank still strapped to my back. Chalk makes no indication he understands, but I know he does.

"Hey Plantera," I say.

"What?" he says.

"Nothing, just making sure you were still behind me."

"Huh?"

My only response is a nod to Chalk, who leaps to his feet and stabs brutally into the tank of herbicide. There's a sharp hiss as a thick cloud of poison spreads around me and, more importantly, Plantera. He screams through wet gasps. All attention turns to us. Only for a few seconds. But that's all the time everyone else needs.

Valiant wastes no time, bulrushing Zombirella, knocking the Apathite from her grasp. "I do believe under different circumstances we could have taught each other much," Valiant tells her while Donna uses a whip to toss the Apathite far from Entheus. That's the last thing I notice before I feel Plantera's hands wrap around my throat. That'll teach me to get lost in other people's moments. I throw an elbow back. It hits Plantera with a sickening squish. He's trying to say something, but it's garbled, like he speaking with a mouth full of marshmallows. I rips at the hands around my neck and to my shock a couple of the fingers tear right off. It's possible that I squeal in disgust, but thankfully everyone else is too busy to notice. I swivel around, punching Plantera in the chest. I don't know if he has a rib cage or not, but if he does it collapses. He falls to the ground struggling for breath.

This is my moment to finish him. All I need is a pithy one-liner. Let's see, he's a plant...what's interesting about plants? Shit, I think he's about to die. Gotta speed this up. "Um, I, uh...SOMETHING ABOUT CHLOROPHYLL!" I stomp his face before he can die on his own. Damn, I can't believe I choked so hard. Oh well, no one was paying attention. I'll come up with something later for when I recount the story to everyone.

Amped from my utter ownage of Plantera, I'm ready to help out the rest of the team. But apparently things are under control. Emma's completely blinded Tri-clops now. Sera and Lily are kicking an Immoral Many dude whose name I never bothered learning. He's begging them to stop. They don't. Donna is cackling—as she's wont to do—while The Roboracle sets stuff on fire. Entheus is in an aerial battle with Animauler. Candy Princess is punch dancing all over the place with Chalk cheering her on, and Captain Valiant is finishing up with Zombirella when, suddenly, she shoves him away.

"Enough!" she screams. Then she begins to whistle; softly, but sharply. The notes bore into my skull; delicate, but insistent. And for the briefest moment I understand the beauty of death…that is, until a rotting corpse tries to bite me. Mesmerized by Zombirella's song, I failed to notice the horde of zombies marching on us. "Prepare to feel the power of the only child of the Opal Moon!"

We brace for the fight, but we're already surrounded. Even that jackass Plantera has the audacity to un-die. Such bullshit. To make matters worse Entheus is visibly drained from Apathite exposure, and he was our best hope. Things aren't looking good for us, when a voice calls out from a top the hill.

"The only child?" It's Jimmy, with a knife in his hand and Lucky by his side. "I beg to differ. Now let's see who the favorite is." He slices his hand open and starts in on one of his grating songs of death, or whatever it is he does.

"Damn it, Jimmy," Sera says while Jimmy gleefully sprays his own blood all over the place. And at least half of the zombie swarm turns on the rest.

"This can't be," Zombirella howls. But my attention is drawn in the opposite direction. Out of the corner of my eye I catch the back of a hooded figure entering the small observatory. Without another thought I sprint in that direction, evading a bunch of handsy corpses as I go.

It's an uneventful run, which suits me fine. I'm pretty tired of everything I do being so full of events. Sure there are plenty of zombies staggering around, but zombies have a terrible center of gravity. It's like they all have an inner ear infection.

I run. They fall. I run some more. The observatory is only a few yards away now. I don't slow as I approach the door. I don't hesitate. I just bust right in, slightly out of breath. The hooded figure stands at the far end of the room, facing away from me. The lighting is such that the figure casts an exaggerated shadow across the wall.

"I was worried you wouldn't make it," he says. "I do hate when people are late." He turns toward me, lowering his hood. "I'm sure you do too." And there I am, staring right back at me.

* * *

"Sorry," I say. "I feel like you're waiting for me to say something."

"That's quite alright," the other me says. "This must come as quite a shock."

"Um," I say. "Not really. I recognized my voice as soon as you started speaking. And we've met before, although I'm not sure which one you are."

"Well," the mystery me seems to be taken off guard, "you must have some questions, yes?"

"I do, actually. Did you set up the lighting to make that crazy menacing shadow, or what that just a happy accident?"

"The shadow sets the atmosphere. Atmosphere is important. It sets a mood. Without that, people might mistake your motives. And if no one knows your motives, how will they ever take you seriously?"

"Ah, Victor3 it is," I say. "You know, a simple yes would have sufficed, but that's cool. So how have you been?"

"How have I…you just…" Before Victor3 can finish whatever that was, Lily barges in.

"Hey, why'd you just ditch us out there?" she says, initially addressing Victor3. "Wait, there's two of you. Why are there two of you?"

"Actually there's three," I say from somewhere behind me. It's confusing, but another me, me2, steps out of the shadows and grabs Lily.

"Hello, sister," Victor3 says.

"Seriously, what the fuck is going on?" Lily asks.

"You see, the thing is," I start, but apparently no one is going to be allowed to finish an important sentence because that's the moment Emma shows up.

She looks from me to me to me and then back to me. "Huh, there really are three of you."

"Yep," I say.

"It's nice to see you again Gisela," Victor3 says. Me2 is completely unable to look at Emma.

"Who's Gisela?" Lily wonders.

"Long story," Emma says. "So, uh, what are we doing?" Victor3 is about to answer, but I quiet him with a hand gesture. And it's good that I did, because right on cue Candy Princess twirls into the room. And I mean she literally twirls. I'm actually more interested in why she did that than why I'm face to face to face with me, myself, and I once again, but I don't think anyone else is.

"Are there more monsters to fight in here?" Candy asks. Then her eyes light up. "OH. MY. GOD! Three Victors?! I've had so many naughty dreams that start just like this. Can I keep them?!"

"Who's that?" the two other Victors say.

"I'm Candy Princess. And I could just eat you two up!"

"Can we just keep on track here?" Emma asks.

"Please," Lily says. "Because I still have no idea what's going on."

"Well allow me to explain, sister dear," Victor3 says.

"Hold on," I say. Something just occurred to me and it can't wait. "Can I say something really quickly?" No one objects. "Did you guys see me kill Plantera out there?"

"Um, not really sweetie. Kind of busy," Emma says.

Awesome, I'm in the clear. "That's too bad. Because it was totally badass. He was all begging and shit and I looked him dead in the eye and said 'I've had my chlorophyll of you' and BAM! Face stomp."

"What does that have to do with anything?" Victor3 asks.

"Nothing, it was just cool," I say.

"Can I continue then?"

"Dude, I don't care. I didn't realize I was such a dick."

"I did," Sera says from the doorway. "Great, now there are more of you."

"How many more times is this going to happen?" Victor3 asks.

I—being Victor3—looks to me—who is me—who looks to Sera for clarification. "What?" she says.

Victor3 has a hissy fit. "None of you are taking this seriously! But that's fine. I'll teach you a thing or two about being serious…after I've explained exactly why we're all here!"

"Aw dang," I say quietly.

"What?" Emma whispers.

"I just never thought I'd be the kind of guy who delivers an expository master plan speech. You know, if I was evil and junk. It's disappointing to learn I'm not above those kinds of clichés."

Less disappointing is that I've already missed some of Victor3's diatribe. "…and when I finally came to that cabin in the woods, all my companions were wisely dead. Because there is wisdom is nullifying potential threats before they can become fully realized threats." This guy really is longwinded. "But little did I know that the greatest threat was inside that wooded shack. That threat being him!" Victor3 points right at me.

"Nice," I say.

"Not nice," he says. "The opposite of nice, which is—"

"Mean?" me2 says.

"Hateful?" Lily says.

"Unnice?" I say.

"Dirty!" Candy Princess squeals.

"I'm telling the story, damn it! It just wasn't nice, okay. Because that one," again with the pointing at me, it's getting kind of rude, "hadn't killed any of his companions. Not a single one of them. How is that responsible? They were clear and potential dangers to the mission at hand."

"That's a little unfair," I say. "I mean, Entheus died and so did The Roboracle. I just used one of your Roboracles as a replacement. And I definitely tried to kill Jimmy."

"You did?" Sera says.

"Oh yeah," Jimmy enters the scene. "Ran me through with a sword."

"Uh, that was me, actually," Emma says.

"Was it? Huh, well I pretty much deserved it anyway."

"He really did," I say.

"Well it wasn't enough!" Victor3 yells. What an ass. "And to make matters worse, you deceived me and left me to burn with that one." He motions to me2. "You have no idea what he did to me."

"I have a pretty good idea," I say. "I heard some things on the way out of the cabin. I think it involved sodomy."

All eyes go to me2.

"In my defense," me2 says, "I was possessed by a sex demon at the time so I wasn't in full control of myself…but it's not really rape if you're doing it to yourself, right?"

"I told you never to talk about that," Victor3 says.

"And I told you that you'll never get over your anger issues until you confront it," me2 says. "That was actually advice given to me by the sex demon. Turns out he was pretty nice guy—or demon, whatever—who was just going through a rough patch. We're cool now."

"Sex demons are often misunderstood," That's Panik. She's flanked by the rest of the crew. "So this is what you were hiding from me. Where's the shard?"

"Who are you?" Victor3 asks. "And what are you talking about?"

"I know you have it. I can feel its proximity."

Just let him finish his stupid speech," I say. "He'll probably explain everything. Eventually."

"No, you know what, forget it!" Victor3 is all in a tizzy again. "Still none of you are taking this seriously and I told you I would teach you a very serious lesson about being serious. Now you'll know what suffering is!" He pulls out a gun and fires. Before I can even react, me2 dives in front of Emma. The blast from the gun makes the funniest sound as it smashes into me2's chest. Kind of like a cat meowing into a kazoo.

"That was unexpected." Victor3 says, now kneeling in front of a large something that I assumed was part of the observatory. He appears to be entering some sort of code. Entheus charges him while Valiant and I shoot our own guns. Everything passes through him as he vanishes. Giving a sly wave as he goes.

Meanwhile, Emma is crouched beside the other Victor, and he's not looking too swell. He's saying something to Emma. All I can make out is: "Sorry for what I did to you..." He keeps trying to speak, but his words dim and his whole body flickers until he's just gone.

There's no time to mourn or do whatever we should do in this situation, because Sera is over studying that thing Victor3 was tinkering with. Her news isn't great. "Uh guys, I think this might be a bomb."

Naturally everyone gathers around it to check it out. Because that's the sensible thing to do with bombs.

"Damn it, Draid," Donna says.

"What's a Draid?" Lily asks.

"One of the Immoral Many. Bomb aficionado. Although he used to be content with small bombs that would blow up children's birthday cakes. This, though…this is a Planet Destroyer."

"How do you know that?" Jimmy asks.

"It says so right here," Donna points to the bomb, where it quite clearly reads PLANET DESTROYER. Say what you want about super-villains, but their complete lack of subtlety can be refreshing.

"Don't fret," Entheus smiles. "I'll handle this." He lifts the bomb, but only about 3 feet off the ground. His muscles tremble, and he nearly drops it.

"Entheus, stop!" Donna demands. "It's made with an Apathite alkali. Put it down before you drop it and blow us all to smithereens!"

Entheus grunts, but complies. "I'm sorry everyone."

"Nonsense," Valiant says. "What about this Draid? Is he here? Can we persuade him to disarm it?"

"Well, um," Donna says. "The thing is…The Roboracle kind of set him on fire. There's not much left of him."

"THE FAUXBORACLE IS SORRY. DONNA NATRIOS." His voice is laced with static again.

"Don't be, darling. It was beautiful."

"Lieutenant, spaceboy, can you disarm it?" Valiant asks.

"I've never seen anything like this before," Sera says. Jimmy is equally perplexed.

"Panik?" Valiant asks.

"Bombs have never been my expertise. Given enough time I could do it. But six minutes is not enough time."

"That's not even enough time for us to get back to the Galley and get off the moon," Sera says.

I shake my head. "Some days you just can't get rid of a bomb." I've always wanted to say that.

"Well put, Victor. I'll have to put that in my next book," Valiant grins. "If we manage not to die, of course."

"Then it's settled," Entheus says. "I'll do it."

"But we just saw you—" I try to say.

"I'll do it." And through great struggle Entheus hoists up the bomb and carries it outside. "This vortex should help me carry it away."

"Maybe the vortex can carry it away on its own," Emma says.

"I fear not, my dear. And if there's one thing I've learned, it's that bombs and fire don't mix. I'll have to carry it myself."

Donna stops him short of the vortex. "No. It will kill you." She pauses, her eyes follow the vortex upward. "I'll do it."

"It will kill you too, Donna."

"Anexia needs you, Entheus. The world needs its Inspiration. Me? I'm just an Immoral girl."

"DONNA NATIOS MUST NOT GO."

Donna bends and kisses The Roboracle. "This darkness that's infiltrated me, my past…Donna Natrios must go." She takes the Planet Destroyer from Entheus. She struggles with the weight of it, but she bears it nonetheless. Still, Entheus helps guide her into the whirlwind of ash.

"WAIT. THE FAUXBORACLE HAS SOMETHING TO TELL EVERYONE." Donna looks to the timer on the bomb, apparently there's enough time to hear him out. "BACK IN INFINITE CITY. VICTOR KISSED HIS SISTER. ON THE MOUTH." Everyone turns to Lily and me.

"You're so dead, robot," I say.

Donna only smiles. "Goodbye, my love." She begins to rise.

"Donna," Entheus calls after her. "You're more than just an immoral girl. You're a hero. And you know what they say, heroes—"

"Never die," she finishes. "I know. For all the good that'll do me." The speed of her assent increases. "Now it's time for the Ashen Moon to meet the Mistress of Pleasure and Pain. The Beauty of Bondage. Man's deadliest desire…The Donnanatrix! Mwhahahaha!"

The echo of her maniacal laughter lingers long after she vanishes into the void of space. Then there's no sound at all, only a brilliant flash that illuminates the dark skies of the Opal Moon as the Ashen Moon is torn asunder.

"NOOOOOOOOOOOOO." The Roboracle howls.

Jimmy hunkers down next The Roboracle and tries to console him. "Hey, buddy. It'll be okay."

The Roboracle quiets and then swivels towards me. "THE FAUXBORACLE IS FINE. JIMMY. DID YOU HEAR OF VICTOR'S INCESTUOUS ACT WITH LILY?" Dude, what the fuck? "THE FATES WOULD ALSO LIKE EVERYONE TO KNOW THAT VICTOR HAS INAPPROPRIATE SEX DREAMS INVOLVING LILY."

I feel everyone's eyes on me and Lily says, "Aw, gross."

"Hey," I defend myself. "That first part is a misrepresentation of what happened, and the stuff about my dreams is a flat out lie. What the hell, Roboracle?"

"I AM THE FAUXBORACLE. AND THE FAUXBORACLE THINKS YOU ARE A PUSSY."

"Oh yeah, what would the Fauxboracle think about a bullet to the face?"

"THE FAUXBORACLE WOULD LIKE TO SEE YOU TRY."

"Don't push me," I say, gun in hand.

"THE FAUXBORACLE DOESN'T THINK YOU HAVE THE BALLS. YOU'LL JUST SIT BACK AND WATCH. WHILE EVERYONE ELSE DIES FOR YOU." Again, static infiltrates The Roboracle's speakers, getting more pronounced with each word. I'm reminded of every time his voice has broken up like this and I glance up to where the Ashen Moon once was. "GO ON. PULL THE TRIGGER."

I take a breath and say, "No."

"N-NO? BUT THE FAUXBORACLE HAS BEFOULED YOUR REPUTATION IN FRONT OF EVERYONE. YOU MUST WIN BACK THEIR RESPECT WITH VIOLENCE."

"No."

The static reaches a fever pitch. "THE FATES HAVE FORESEEN THE DEATH OF THE FAUXBORACLE. AT YOUR HANDS. YOU MUST KILL THE FAUXBORACLE. YOU MUST. THE FATES NEVER LIE. THE FAUXBORACLE MUST DIE. PLEASE." By the end, he's almost incomprehensible through all the crackling from his speakers.

"The Fauxboracle is a fake," I say. "Why should anyone listen to him?"

"I-I...MISS DONNA NATRIOS. LIFE WITHOUT HER IS LIFE WITHOUT AIR-CONDITIONING. WITHOUT STYX. UNBEARABLE. WHY COULDN'T THE FAUXBORACLE SAVE HER?"

"Because she had to save us instead. and you know who she probably wanted to save most of all? The Roboracle."

"I AM THE ROBORACLE?"

"If you want to be."

The Roboracle tilts towards the sky and a sound escapes him

that is almost a sigh. “YES. THE ROBORACLE WILL BE THE ROBORACLE. FOR DONNA NATRIOS.” Then after another pause. “THE FATES SAY EVEN THE TINIEST OF BAD HABITS CAN SPELL YOUR DOOM.”

“Yeah, whatever, that’s great,” I say. “Now if you ever piss me off again, I will shoot your face off.”

“JIMMY. WOULD YOU LIKE TO HEAR STYX ONE MORE TIME.”

“Uh, sure man,” Jimmy says, and soon the soothing, if not ominous melody of “Come Sail Away” drifts through the air.

Emma grabs me as I walk away. “That was really sweet.”

I shrug. “I know what is like to watch the girl you love die.” Emma takes my hand and kisses it. Something floats down, coming to a rest on her eyelash. “Hey, is it snowing?”

Emma looks up, puts her hand out and catches a flake. “Actually, I think it’s glittering.”

Everyone turns to the sky to see it filled with the remains of a dead moon, somehow made beautiful. A flake lands on my nose and a memory of Lily and I having a snowball fight when we were kids surges through me. Another brushes my finger tips and I remember Jimmy watching Sera drink Rhapsberry Cream on Candy Island, her hair changing color as fluidly as the drink itself. Each glitter-flake brings with it a renewed memory. Captain Valiant and I fighting through a hoard of space robots. Lily kicking some guy in the balls after he shoved me down on our first day of school. And Emma. Always Emma. The first time she smiled at me. Really smiled. And the second. And the third. I’m losing myself in flurry of reverie. Then an unfamiliar girl’s voice calls out nearby.

“Entheus? Where are we?”

“Lucky?!” Entheus cries out. “You’re alive!”

Sure enough, there Lucky is. Young and pretty and very much not dead.

Lucky laughs as Entheus embraces her. "Why wouldn't I be?"

"No reason," he says.

"Okay, but…" She pauses as she notices Emma. "Hey! Did you replace me?"

"Oh, never," Entheus says. "Emma there just needed to borrow some clothes."

"Good," Lucky says. "Because you know I plan on coming back once I've finished my degree in Moral Studies. Those Immoral Many won't know what's hit'em once I'm back."

"I don't doubt it for a second," Entheus says.

That's when all hell breaks loose.

* * *

"What was that?" Lily yells.

"It sounded like an explosion," Entheus says. "There must have been more bombs planted elsewhere." Another explosion rattles the Opal Moon, this one much closer. "We should evacuate immediately."

"What about all these people?" Lucky asks. Sure enough, she isn't the only zombie who has regained their heartbeat.

"Captain, get your people back to your ship. Lucky and I will evacuate the moon."

"We'll help," someone from across the way says. It's Zombirella, Animauler, and a few other Immoral Many members. "We're sorry for what we did."

"Save your sorrys for the judge, Ms. Doe," Entheus says. "We've got lives to save." Another blast rocks the moon. "Victor,

Captain, back to your ship. Now!"

"You heard the man," Valiant says. "Let's go. That's an order."

We're nearly back to the Adventure Galley when Jimmy says, "Wait, who grabbed The Roboracle?"

"Oh %^&! me," I say.

"We have to go back!"

"Um," I say.

Just then, Lucky whooshes by. "You talkin' about that little robot?"

Jimmy nods.

"Don't worry, I'll grab him. You guys just get outta here."

Sera and Valiant beat the rest of us to the Galley by a long shot, and they waste no time. The ship is already off the ground before the hanger bay doors have closed. Something detonates close by, shaking the Galley. Chalk loses his footing and slides toward the open door, HELP! written across his chest. Candy Princess stabs out, grabbing him just in time. But another blast knocks both her and Chalk out the door. Candy barely manages to grasp the edge of the door. I want to help, but without warning my equilibrium gets all wonky. I can't even walk two steps without falling down.

"I think we're about to jump again," I say.

Emma glances at the hanger doors, which have started to close. Candy is screaming. "Damn it," Emma curses and rushes to their aide. Somehow she's able to pull Candy and Chalk to safety alone, moments before the doors snap shut. My vision blurs right as another jolt slams into the Galley. The force is so severe that Emma is sandwiched between Candy and a very unforgiving wall. The collision is such that, through my wonky sight, I could almost swear that Emma is swallowed up by Candy. Then an even larger explosion hits and I lose myself completely.

When the world comes back, everything is calm. Valiant come on the intercom. “Everyone check into the bridge ASAP.”

Now I’m not one to leave Captain Valiant waiting, but there’s one slight problem. “Um, where’s Emma?”

“What do you mean, I’m right here,” she says, although something isn’t quite right with her voice.

“Where?”

“Here.” And that’s when I see her. Except that I don’t see her at all.

“Oh crap,” I say.

“What?” Emma searches herself tentatively. It’s not hard to pinpoint the moment she realizes she’s no longer herself. “Oh fuck no…”

“Now, Emma,” Candy Princess says. “You’ll have to watch your language while you’re inside me.”

And Candy Princess smiles.

IN MEMORY
DONNA NAT
HALL
HEROES
WHERE H
S NEVER DIE!

TURNING A MAGIC TRICK

Prologue

And they all lived happily ever after.

It's what every young girl of the Summerlands dreams of, and Breen was no different. She would meet her true love during some daring adventure, of that she was certain. Where she differed from her peers was which part she might play. Most every girl of the Fay envisioned herself as the beautiful damsel in distress who would be rescued by a magnificent hero, be he prince or lord or magician's apprentice. Breen dreamed, instead, of being that dashing hero. She couldn't fathom why every girl she knew would fantasize about being captured and rescued. They all knew at least three girls who had been. Yes, they had their true loves now, but the parts before the rescue, according to these girls, were not like in the storybooks.

It wasn't just about being locked away in some faraway tower. The captors molested the girls. One poor thing even had her womanhood…violated. She talked sweetly about her young hero and how madly in love she was, but Breen could see a pain behind her bragging. No, Breen wanted to be loved, but she didn't need to be saved. And so what if every boy she knew was too proud to be rescued by a girl? Breen would be some other beautiful girl's hero if need be. Breen would love whomever destiny chose for her. It might be that the butcher's son was the only person to ever make her heart flutter and her body tingle, but she'd practiced kissing with her girlfriends. They were soft and sweet kisses. Exactly as kisses should be, she wagered. How hard could it be to love a lovely girl? Not hard at all, Breen thought.

Breen's friends all mocked what they called her boyish ambitions, but she didn't care. She'd rather be taunted as a fool than chained up by strangers who might try to befoul her innocence. No charming prince was worth that in Breen's mind. Her mother also laughed at her, but in that gentle way that mothers do.

"Your father never needed to save me," she had told Breen. "Oh he'll claim that he has. He used to try to convince me that he magically healed me from the FairFlux. But that's just his pride talking. If you want to be a hero, my love, be one."

Breen's father was less encouraging. Whenever talk of her future came up he would sulk away, most often to the tavern. Her mother assured Breen that he was merely distraught at the idea of his little girl growing up and having a life and family of her own.

"Men like to put on a brave face for their women," she said with a smile, "but that's only because we're their greatest weakness, you know." Breen wasn't entirely sure she did know, but she never doubted her father's affection. Why it was just two days ago when Breen experienced her great blossoming and her father openly wept. So overcome with emotion was he, that he bid Breen take a stroll down to the spring. Breen thought it was sweet that her father would be so struck by her blossoming. She spent the rest of the afternoon being teased by the winged girls who could tell with a single look that Breen was a woman now. They frolicked around without their petals, causing Breen to blush. That made the teasing worse. The winged girls tried their mightiest to convince Breen to play with them as she used to when she was a babe, but with her blossoming also came shame. The winged girls liked it not one bit, and neither did Breen. Her sense of annoyance, however, was outweighed by the thought of someone chancing upon her bare flesh.

As the day waned Breen bid the winged girls farewell. They told her to return before she bedded another and they would teach her how to properly love. Breen wasn't quite sure what they meant, but still she blushed again and the winged girls giggled.

Upon arriving home, she found her father waiting for her at the dining table. He motioned for her to come sit on his lap, something she hadn't done since she was half as grown. But she was happy to do so. Her father struggled to smile and said, "Now that you have blossomed, love, you'll have to take a little journey."

"A journey?" she asked.

"Yes, but only a short one. Out into the clearing beyond the spring."

"Why, father?"

"To meet your destiny, my sweet."

"My destiny?" Breen whispered, her mind racing with so many possibilities she hardly heard the rest of what he's saying. She didn't, however, miss the sorrow behind his soft smile. His eyes betrayed him on that. So when he finished explaining about what she must do, Breen took her father's hand. "I'm sorry I grew up, daddy."

For the first time, his smile faltered and his whole face told the same sad tale of his eyes. "So am I."

That was last evening. This morning she woke early—though in truth she hardly slept, her excitement was so great—and fixed herself a fine breakfast, for she knew any journey should not be undertaken on an empty stomach. Breen had hoped her parents would be up already, but since they weren't she decided to wake them with breakfast in bed. She wasn't as good a cook as her mother, but she was sure they'd eat it happily. Her smile vanished when she opened her parents' bedroom door to find her father awake and alone, his eyes red and puffy.

"Where's mother?" Breen wondered.

Her father wiped his face. "She…went to the Market. She wanted to make you a special breakfast."

"But the Market is so far away, and I've already eaten. I even made some for you and mother."

"So you did. I'll make sure to save it for when she returns."

"Can't I wait for her?"

"I'm afraid not, love. Now go get dressed. Don't be late."

Breen dressed quicker than she would have liked. She didn't know what was awaiting her out in the clearing beyond the spring. Would she be meeting her true love? Would there be an awful troll or minotaur she'd have to battle. Her father hadn't told her to bring a weapon, not that she had any to bring. In the end she chose her best dress. It was made by one of the winged girls, modeled after what they wear. Her parents couldn't afford one of the flower petal dresses, so they settled for one made from the deep red autumn leaves of the Winter Fade Tree. Her father could hardly speak when he saw her, and Breen didn't ask him to. Breen waited as long as she could for her mother to return, but she never did and her father insisted Breen must leave immediately. She didn't argue, but seeing her father struggle with losing his little girl hurt her heart. She wanted to tell him to not be so silly. That she'd still be his daughter forever and always, but instead she made a silent vow that whatever her destiny should be, she would make her father proud.

So it was that Breen found herself nearing the clearing, her imagination alive with the dreams of her impending destiny. If this was the day she was to meet her true love, she only hoped that she was pretty enough to be loved. That was her thought as she entered the clearing, but to her dismay the clearing was empty. At least it appeared to be. Breen searched all around for any clue as to why she was sent here. Could this all be a prank? No, that was something that her schoolmates might concoct, but not her father. Was she late? Had she missed her destiny all together because she had been too lost in her own daydreams? Breen was on the verge of tears when all her unspoken worries were answered.

"You aren't late, child. You were early."

Breen turned to the sound, and what she saw caused her to let out some odd mixture between a gasp and a sigh. "A unicorn."

"Yes, child. Are you ready for your destiny?"

"I..." Breen hesitated before adorning her brightest smile. "Yes, Mister Unicorn."

"Very good. Remove your clothes, child."

"My clothes?"

"Yes," the unicorn said, "that dress has no place here."

"O-okay." Breen removed her dress, taking great care to fold it properly. Then she laid it in front of her and turned her attention back to the unicorn

The unicorn made no movement, his voice remained even. "All of it, child."

Breen bit her lower lip as she looked about the clearing, worried some passerby might spy her. She saw no one and removed her undergarments, placing them atop her dress.

The unicorn raised his head, his nostrils flared. "You certainly have blossomed." The winged girls had made the same remarks yesterday as they frolicked in the spring and Breen had giggled right along with them when they did, but there was something layered underneath the words when the unicorn spoke them that made her shudder. "Are you cold, my sweet?"

"Yes," she lied.

"This won't take long. I can only assume your father didn't tell you why you've been sent here."

"Only that I would meet my destiny."

"And so you shall." Breen found herself unable to meet the unicorn's stare. Instead she looked anywhere else. And what she saw troubled her more than her nakedness. More, even, than that soft undercurrent in the unicorn's voice. In the whole of her life she'd never known the forest to be so...empty. "But did your father never tell you of his one grand adventure?" Breen shook her head. "Your father once loved a girl so much that when she fell gravely ill he set out in search of the one thing that might cure her." The unicorn bowed his head, accentuating his horn. "In truth, I could have made it easier on him. I do always have a sense when a bargain is near. But then shouldn't love always be a struggle? He found me, of course, after a sort. He pleaded his case quite passionately. This girl had come stricken with the FairFlux."

"My mother had the FairFlux before I was born," Breen managed.

"That must have been her, child. How pleasant to hear they're still together. Your father told me such a harrowing tale. But the wretched thing I am, I was too caught up in my own affairs to truly listen. The poor man was so distraught he was willing to give anything for my horn. But I am a generous creature and only asked one small favor. He didn't hesitate to accept the terms."

Breen momentarily forgot her modesty, replacing it instead with curiosity. "What did he promise you?"

"Only a meal," the unicorn smiled. It's a sight few have ever seen and one Breen wished to never see again. But as her mother used to tell her, "You must take care with what you wish, love."

"But I've brought no meal," Breen told the unicorn.

"Of course you have," the unicorn replied. Then Breen remembered her dress folded neatly on the ground. She picked it up and stepped forward to present the unicorn his gift, but the unicorn cocked his head and said, "Do you really believe a unicorn would debase itself with leaves?"

Breen's lower lip began to tremble. "I have nothing more

Mister Unicorn."

"Don't be silly, my sweet," the unicorn said. "You're everything I need."

"I don't—" But whatever she meant to say was cut off in a pinch. Breen stood there, astounded by her sudden inability to form words. Then she felt the warmth running down her chest. When she looked down to find her chest once again flowing a deep crimson her only thought was "But I took my dress off." The unicorn was now directly in front of her, lapping at her breast. The red melting away to reveal her soft flesh again. She pushed back in both protest and confusion, but weakly. Breen wanted to scream at him, but not a single breath could find her lungs. Breen clawed at her neck trying to force the matter, And she felt her blood rush over her fingers where the unicorn had ripped out her throat. Tears stung her eyes as realization dawned upon her. But it wasn't her life she cried for, it was her dreams. Breen wept soundlessly knowing that she would never know true love. That she would never be anybody's hero.

She couldn't even save herself.

4

"Get me out get me out get me ouuuut!!!" Emma freaks out, causing Candy's body to flail about. Under different circumstance it would be funny, but I somehow doubt Emma would appreciate laughter in this particular situation.

"Relax," I say, grabbing Candy's arm. "Just come here." I wait for Emma to join me, but it doesn't happens.

"I…I can't," Emma says. "I can't get out! Why can't I get out?!"

"Um," I say.

"Ugh, it's so sticky in here," Emma complains.

I pat Emma/Candy on the back. "Uh, there, there?" At least one of them doesn't seem to appreciate it, so naturally I do it more. But faster.

Thankfully, Panik cuts short my expert comforting technique. "Your spirits are intertwined."

"What's that mean?" Emma asks. She has Candy's body hyperventilating at this point.

"It's a phenomenon called Spontaneous Spiritual Siamesism. Your spirits have meshed together indefinitely."

Candy Princess hops up and down. "Emma and I are body buddies?!" Oddly, Candy's voice is so much more high pitched than Emma's that there is no difficulty telling the two of them apart. I always thought her tone was natural, but now it seems maybe not. As long as it keeps Emma from doing accents, I guess it doesn't matter.

"So I'm stuck in here?" Emma says, finally able to compose herself. "Okay, fine," she pulls the gun from my waistband, "meet me in Hell."

Panik moves so swiftly I don't even see her grab Emma and

Candy. "I wouldn't do that. It's not the body you're tied to. Death won't untangle your souls."

Emma's tears well in Candy's eyes. "Then what will?"

"The first recorded Spiritual Siamese separation won't be performed for another eight centuries."

"Meaning?"

"You're stuck for now."

"Wait," Lily says. "How can you tell all of this?" She's asking Panik, but I respond instead. I don't like being quiet for too long.

"She can see the colors of people's souls, or some such nonsense."

"Essentially," Panik says. "Though it's hardly nonsense. It's an ability born from unspeakable trauma."

Suddenly Sera's voice crackles over the ship's intercom. "Uh guys, the captain is still waiting. He's just sort of frozen in one of his heroic stances and refuses to move or speak until you all show up. So anyone who isn't dead, I would appreciate your presence so I know where I'm supposed to fly the damn ship."

"I guess we should go," I say. I attempt to take Emma's—or Candy's—hand, but my hand might as well be a hot stove the way Emma reacts.

All she says is "don't". And me, I don't say anything.

* * *

On the bridge we do, in fact, find Valiant doing one of his trademarked hero poses, but upon seeing us he relaxes. "Ah, there you are. Despite my posturing, I was starting to worry none of you survived."

I apologize as best I can. "Sorry, Captian. There was an incident with Emma that sidetracked us."

"That's quite alright. But where is Emma, she wasn't injured was she?"

"Um," I say.

"Emma is my body buddy now!" Candy Princess squeals.

Sera stares at Candy in disbelief. "What?" is all she can choke out. And all Emma can do is nod Candy's head slightly. All of the color drains out of Sera. Not just her face, but her hair, her eyes…for a moment Sera's entire body loses its light. She goes to hug Emma, but something in Candy's eyes tells Sera it's best to just not do anything.

Candy, however, is jittering with joy. "Emma doesn't feel like talking right now, because she's super sad about losing her body again, but I'm going to make this the best body she's ever had! We're going to dance and sing all day long. My body is so much fun, you'll see, Emma. I'll make you love it soooo hard!" Candy Princess continues to gush excitement with no end in sight.

Captain Valiant, realizing that waiting this celebration out isn't an option, ignores it the best he can. "While I'm interested in learning the details about what exactly is going on with Emma and the Princess, I fear it will have to wait. As you may have noticed, Anexia and its moons are nowhere in sight. Couple that with Emma's disappearing body and I believe it's safe to assume we have made another jump.

"The Lieutenant has cross-referenced our known star charts and it appears we're back in our own dimension. But another jump could come at any time. And if our last trip is any indication, being mid-flight might not be the safest thing. Lieutenant, please chart a course to the nearest planet with a breathable atmosphere."

"Yes, sir," Sera complies.

"In the meantime I'd like to hear as much as possible about these other Victors we encountered."

That's my cue to explain my previous encounter with those

two. Most of it isn't news to Valiant, and I really don't know too much about them other than they are me. Or, at least, they are sort of me. Since one of the other Victors seems to be dead now, I focus on the other one. All I can tell them is that he is perhaps the most pensive fucker alive and has a serious overabundance of violent urges.

"That's a clear symptom of prolonged exposure to a tangible Abstraction," Panik says. "There's no doubt he has the shard I'm looking for."

"Lot of good that does when we don't know where to find him," Sera says.

"We'll jump again," Panik tells her. "Soon probably. And he'll be wherever we end up."

"But why didn't we jump with him back on the moon?" Lily wonders. "I mean, you say this whatever field Victor has is always expanding and that's why we jump when he jumps, right? But we were plenty close to the other Victor when he jumped and we didn't go anywhere."

"Everything involving Trans-Dimensional Gravity is theoretical. I don't believe anyone ever envisioned identical anti-grav fields co-existing in the same space/time. My best hypothesis would be that when multiple identical fields come together, they close in around their host. If our Victor had jumped first we very well may have been left behind with the others, forced to jump with them. Or it could be that we've somehow homogenized with our Victor's field. Of course it's all merely speculation at this point."

There's a bit more back and forth between everyone as they discuss the next course of action, but I'm too worried about Emma to listen much. Candy Princess still hasn't quit buzzing with delight. She's like a hummingbird of happiness fluttering about and beaming outrageously whenever she notices me watching her. Yet somewhere inside all of that, Emma is in her own personal hell. And I don't think this is a hell where I can join her.

All the talk exhausts itself in time, and we close in on some planet that will be suitable enough for us to make camp. Captain Valiant thinks that now would be a good time to get some rest. I still don't know what to do about Emma. Judging by Sera's overall body language, she must be feeling similarly. Eventually she lets go of her apprehension and goes to talk to Candy and Emma. I can't hear what she says, but Emma's reaction is clear enough. She brushes Sera off the same as she did me earlier. For the first time I can recall, Sera looks to me for guidance. All I can do is shake my head. Then Candy and/or Emma shares a brief exchange with Panik before following her somewhere.

I walk over to Lily. "What was that all about?"

"You know Panik, she wants to run tests," Lily tells me.

"Oh."

Lily does her best to comfort me. "Hey, Panik knows tons of crazy shit. Maybe she can do something for Emma."

"Maybe," I say. Not that I believe it.

"So, um, I'm gonna try to get some sleep. Unless you want me to hang around for a while?"

"Nah, I'm cool."

Lily hesitates briefly before wandering off, leaving me with Captain Valiant, Chalk, Jimmy, and Sera. "You all should really get some rest," Valiant says. "Who knows when we might get another chance. *Adeventure* is just around the corner."

"I'm not really tired," I say.

ME NEITHER Chalk's face tells us.

"Yeah, I'm pretty amped up," Jimmy says.

"Really, Jimmy?" I ask.

"Yeah, why?"

"Sera," I say, "have you noticed all the cuts on Jimmy's hands?"

Sera snatches Jimmy's hands and sighs. "Damn it, Jimmy. We need to get these patched up. Come on." She leads him off the bridge, presumably towards the med bay.

"I get the feeling you have something to say, Victor," Valiant says.

"I just, um…what should I do about Emma?"

Valiant paces about the bridge. "I've loved many women in my day, of course."

"Of course," I say.

"But I must admit, it's uncharted territory even for me, my friend. Nearly all of my great loves ended in betrayal. One way or the other. It's my fault as much as anyone's."

"I'm sure that's not true."

"Your faith in me is nothing short of *valiant*. But it is true. My heart has always belonged to the great *adventures*. It's cost me much, to be sure, but I don't regret a thing. Because I followed my heart. It may seem cliché and useless right now, but it's the best advice I can give. Listen to your heart and it will guide you where you need to be in the end."

Chalk throws his hands to the air and his face says BUT I DON'T KNOW WHAT 2 DO!

Valiant chuckles and I tell Chalk not to worry about it, but he won't have it. He tells us he'll figure it out and runs off to find Candy and Emma.

"Now that we're alone," Valiant says. "How about we discuss a more serious matter?"

"Sure," I say.

"What are you sister's turn-ons? I simply must see her naked soon."

Damn it. This conversation is going to get ugly. It almost makes me wish I hadn't gotten Jimmy banished.

Almost.

* * *

I spend the rest of that night—or day; I really don't know what time it is ever—trying to scrub my talk with Valiant from my memory. Sure it would have made more sense to decline to answer Valiant's questions, but denying Valiant anything is so antithetical to basic human instinct that I was compelled to comply. The man is a universal treasure. A little traumatizing on my end is the least I can do to make him happy.

Eventually I do manage some sleep. It's restless, filled with fever dreams I hardly remember. There's something about a pretty bug—a butterfly, maybe—that screams. And there was blood. Lots of it. All-in-all, not nearly as bad as most of my dreams lately.

Even still, I wake up almost refreshed, and I'm anxious to see how Emma is doing. Part of me hoped she'd show up in the middle of the night, but I knew that was unlikely. Maybe she'll have adjusted a little by now. I head to breakfast, expecting to find her and Candy there. But I don't.

"Has anyone seen Emma?" I ask.

Jimmy swallows whatever he's eating. "She came by asking for some of those Steel Canyon comics. Not sure why. Haven't seen her since."

Chalk tugs at my arm. OUTSIDE his face reads. I grab a few pieces of cinnamon toast and head out to find her. Whatever planet we've landed on is scenic enough. The Galley is settled in a large field of faded blue grass. Off in the distance, a stark black mountain rises above a patch of low clouds. The air is brisk, but pleasant. There's a farm girl near the Galley, digging, but I don't see anyone else.

I can't think of a single reason this girl should be here. It's not until I approach her that I realize it is Candy Princess. It occurs to me that this might be the first time I've seen Candy in anything other than a dress. To see her in only jeans and a white shirt, her hair in a ponytail, is incredibly jarring.

"Hey," I say.

Neither Candy nor Emma stop what they're doing, but I do get some acknowledgement. "Hey." It's Emma's lower pitch.

"I brought you some toast."

"Thanks," she says, but keeps on digging. Other than the shovel and a pile of dirt, the only other thing out here is the stack of Steel Canyon comics that Jimmy mentioned.

"So, what's going on?" I ask.

"Donna died and…I don't know. I wanted to say goodbye I guess."

"I can help with the digging."

"I'd rather do it myself. It helps me keep my mind off…everything."

"Okay, but eat." Emma opens her mouth, most likely to protest, but I seize the opportunity and shove some toast in there. She bites down, annoyed and reluctant at first, but if there's one thing Emma can't resist, it's a little cinnamon toast. She devours that first piece in ten seconds or less. "You want me to get you something to drink?"

"Please," she nods. A few crumbs fly from her mouth, and she covers up to keep any more from escaping.

Back in the mess hall, Chalk has already whipped up a batch of piping hot Rhapsberry Cream, so I pour a cup for myself and Emma/Candy. When I tell everyone else what Emma is up to they say a proper memorial sounds like a nice idea and that they'll join us once they've finished their meal.

Outside, I don't hand Emma her drink right away. I just watch her dig. Emma and Candy never looked particularly alike, but every body movement, the way she carries herself now, the way she wipes sweat from her brow, it's all undeniably Emma. I've seen her in a couple other people before, but she always treated those people—their bodies—as if she was a guest. Sure there was always her laugh, or a facial tick here and there, but that was the extent of it. Yet here, watching her dig, I can almost forget Candy Princess exists at all. After a minute, Emma and Candy come over and take the Rhapsberry Cream from me.

They sip delicately and glance back to the freshly dug hole. "I guess that's deep enough. It's not like we're actually burying a body."

"How are you doing?" I ask.

"Bad," she says. "Not as bad as last night, but Panik seems certain that there's nothing any of us can do. And apparently any sort of travel to the future is too dangerous with all the other crap that's going on. The plus side is that Candy is willing to do whatever I say."

"That's good."

"It would be better if she didn't get turned on by being bossed around," she says before her voice jumps up an octave or two. "Emma! That's private!" Emma groans. "I don't know how long I can put up with this." I take her hand, but she gently pulls away. "Sorry, it's just you have no idea the things she thinks when you touch us. I…I can't handle that stuff right now. I should get on with this." She picks the shovel up again.

"Everyone else said they'd like to, um, participate too," I tell her.

"Oh, well that's nice. I guess there's no hurry." She sits down and goes back to sipping her Rhapsberry Cream. I sit with her, but I do my best to keep enough distance so as not to upset her. I try to enjoy my drink, but all I can concentrate on is space between us. It's only a few feet, but I know that right now I could half that space over and over and still never be able to reach her.

* * *

Around ten minutes pass before the rest of the crew join us. Normally I can't get enough alone time with Emma, but seeing everyone right now is a relief. Candy and Emma had been having an argument about proper memorial attire, and Candy tried to drag me into it until Emma told her to shut up. It doesn't help when Captain Valiant shows up in formal wear. Candy says, "See!" which causes Emma to slap Candy's face and only really hurt herself. Everyone else is dressed casually, though, so I don't feel too underdressed. I can only hope Valiant doesn't hold it against me.

Lily shows up carrying a small box. When I ask her about it she says, "I thought…I know most people here didn't know him, but maybe we could also say goodbye to RoboBot while we're doing this? I, uh, put his last message to me in this box. It's all I had of him."

"That's a great idea," Emma says.

It's not all that atypical, as far as these things go, despite us laying to rest a robot detective and a comic book librarian/dominatrix. I guess funerals are pretty much the same no matter who—or what—they're for. Valiant starts the service with a eulogy so moving I can't even begin to describe it. So riveting is his presence that his words roll off my mindspace like water on wax. No one can follow that man.

But, of course, Jimmy tries.

And boy does he bomb. He goes on and on about the first time The Roboracle and Donna met, but good luck making sense of it with all his blubbering. Luckily Lily is much more entertaining, talking about RoboBot's awkward sexual advances. Emma ends up telling everyone about a night she spent with Donna where Emma got really drunk and Donna did her best to teach Emma the finer points of bondage. I remember that night less fondly, because I had to spend it with Jimmy and The Roboracle. Then when Emma and Donna returned, I spent the rest of the night holding Emma's hair back while she puked. Still, I've had worse nights. After that, Emma is in a generous mood and allows Candy to hum a sweet little lullaby. When it comes my turn to speak, I don't really know what to say so I do what I do best. Improvise.

"The Donnanatrix liked to cackle maniacally a lot. RoboBot liked jokes about math. When I first asked Donna about her penchant for theatrical asides, she gave me a paper cut. I never got to ask RoboBot why he loved math jokes because he exploded. Donna liked whips and chains and tying people up and probably Elvis's gyrating hips because that comic she's from is really old and terrible. RoboBot liked mysteries and wall sockets and motor oil. You know, robot things. I think. I didn't really know him that well. But what I do know is that of all the robots and dominatrixes I've met in my life, I liked those two the best. Because they both shared one common trait that I admire more than just about anything. They died to save me. And that's pretty awesome."

Panik finishes the ceremony off with a poem:

"From Time all things all born
And in Time do they all end
With Happiness, Heartache, and Scorn

Time gives and takes yet never bends

Life is fleeting because Time won't stop
With Death, Time murders but commits no crime
And you will be left but one lonely teardrop
If ever you surrender your heart to Time"

* * *

The thing about funerals: they're kind of a downer. So the mood afterwards is sullen and muted and altogether depressing. We bury the comics and the box with RoboBot's final message, but then we're mostly at a loss for what to do. Captain Valiant invites us all back to his quarters to share drinks and more memories. We all go, but there's a lot more drinking than talking. Emma and Candy especially overindulge. They drink like…well like two people sharing a single body. And not just Rhapsberry Cream, but hard liquor. Weird intergalactic alcohol I've only ever seen in Valiant's quarters. I find myself wondering if Candy Princess has ever even had real alcohol before. I try to slow them down, but Emma brushes me off and Candy is just enjoying the buzz.

Sera eventually intervenes and convinces them to go lie down somewhere. As Sera leads them from Valiant's room I hear Emma say, "You smell delicious."

"Uh, let's just get you to bed," Sera says.

The rest of us stick around, but only because there's nothing much else to do. No one says it, but it's clear we're all just waiting until the next time I jump us somewhere.

Unfortunately, Jimmy decides now would be a good time for small talk. "Do you think The Roboracle made it off the moon safely?"

"Man, I don't care," I tell him. "But probably. Even when he's not around, you just know he's gonna pop up again eventually. The Roboracle is just like herpes. You can't ever get rid of him."

Somehow Jimmy finds that to be a relief. I hope Sera comes back soon, but she doesn't. And without Sera, Jimmy is the first to abandon our miserable little party with some excuse about working on putting No Name back together. Can't say I blame him. There's only so much sitting around in one place I can handle. Not that I'm opposed to sitting around doing nothing, but I prefer to change my location from time to time to keep things interesting. That's my excuse for leaving, at least.

Back in my room, I do my very best to enjoy the silence. Because there's not much else to do. Only problem is, I'm monumentally bored, so I decide to take a shower instead. That's not in the cards, though, because as I pull back the shower curtain I find an unexpected visitor, Candy Princess and Emma standing in the shower in nothing but a towel.

"Surprise!" they say. Then I'm being kissed recklessly. Everything about it is sweet and oh-so-wrong. Just like that time at Disneyland when I stole Lily's churro. She punched me in the stomach. I threw up. I wouldn't be shocked if this situation ends like that.

I break the kiss with as much care as I can. "What are you doing?"

"Seducing you," Emma says, her speech slurred. "Seductively."

"And what happened to your clothes?"

"I guess we lost them," Emma attempts to kiss me again. When I don't let her, she shifts her strategy and the towel falls to the floor. "Looks like we just lost our towel too. Whoops!" Candy

Princess giggles.

"You're drunk," I say.

"Aw, look at you noticing things! Did you also notice the naked body in front of you?"

I pick up the towel and wrap it around them, but they only shrug it off. "Maybe we should sit down and talk until you're sober."

"Ugh! Talking is boooring. Sexing is awesome. So just do me, damn it!"

"You don't want that," I say.

"Wrong! It's the only thing I want," Emma says.

"Me too!" Candy agrees.

"See, we finally agree on something," Emma says.

"Well, I'm not so sure it's a good idea," I say.

"Oh really," Emma says. "Then why'd you take your pants off?"

I glance downward to find my pants around my ankles. I don't remember doing that at all. "Just because I have uncanny reflexes in situations like this is not necessarily a sign of consent."

"We disagree. And I think you do too. I know part of you does."

In case I wasn't clear on which part, Emma and Candy make sure there can be no mistake. I remain as still as possible. The grip they have on me…one false move and things are going to hurt. This is definitely going to end up like the churro incident. As Emma drops Candy's body to its knees, I brace for the inevitable. In a life filled with shame, this moment could top it all. Then with nearly all hope lost for getting out of this situation unscathed, I hear a glorious sound. The sound of vomit spewing into the toilet. Like a gentleman, I pull up my pants and make sure none of it gets in their hair. Disaster averted!

* * *

As it turns out, Candy Princess has never thrown up before. So while I dodged one bullet, I now have to deal with a drunken princess freaking-the-holy-fuck-out about how she's dying. Because not only has she never been sick, the only time she's ever seen people throw up is right before they die. Sitting there with Candy panting "I don't wanna die" I flashback to when Emma and I first met. Me driving, Emma in the backseat curled up chanting "I don't want to die", an ice cold Coca-Cola somewhere near the passenger seat just begging to be opened. Sometimes I miss those days.

"You're not going to die," I tell Candy, but she doesn't believe me.

"Emma says we are!"

"Em, could you stop mindfucking Candy?"

"Victor. Please. Language," Candy says, trying to catch her breath between heaves.

"And don't you dare take her side," Emma says.

"I'm just trying to calm her down."

"Fuck her feelings."

"Please stop saying that word!" Tears stream down Candy's face.

"Shut up and die, whore," Emma says.

Part of me wants to run, part of me wants to hold their hair back—not that Emma is allowing that—and part of me really wants a churro. But all I do is say, "I don't know what I'm supposed to do!"

"You're supposed to—" but whatever Emma was going to tell me gets cut off by stream of puke. I doubt it's okay to rub their back, leaving me to sit slumped against the wall, paralyzed with fear of doing the absolute wrong thing.

My paralysis gets broken by a knock at the door. Meaning I'm lucky enough to get to leave the bathroom to answer it. It's a huge relief to be out of there. I open the door to find Sera and Lily staring back at me. They don't look nearly as relieved.

"What the hell is going on?" Sera asks.

"Emma and Candy are puking in the bathroom," I explain.

"How'd they get here? I swear they were passed out when I left them."

"I don't know, but maybe you can calm them down."

Sera marches into the fray. She returns three seconds later. "Why are they naked?!"

I only get as far as opening my mouth before Sera's fist is planted firmly in my gut. By the time I catch my breath enough to say nothing happened, Sera's already back in the bathroom.

"Jeez," I say. "At least someone could have enough decency to give me a churro."

"A churro?" Lily says. "You son of a bitch!"

Then she punches me too.

"What the fuck?!" I say, still struggling for a proper breath.

"You reminded me of the churro incident."

"We were ten!"

"Some scars never fade," she says, and Candy Princess continues to wail through a sea of vomit. It's going to be a long day.

* * *

It takes a couple of hours, but both Candy and Emma exhaust themselves enough to pass out. Sera somehow managed to wrap a robe around them in the middle of their storm of sickness. I carry them to the bed and Sera asks Lily to go find some clothes for them for later.

"I could do that," I say.

"You've done enough," Sera says. Her implications are more than clear.

"But I didn't do anything!"

"Just go," she says. "I'll take care of her. Someone has to." I want to argue at first, but Sera is glowing a deep, terrifying shade of red and I'm worried she might go all Dark Phoenix on me and blast me with some of her ill-defined star powers, which leaves me with no idea of where to go or what to do. Fresh air would be nice, though. Not because of all the puking—Candy's vomit smells disturbingly like vanilla extract—but because all the sexual mojo Panik is pumping into the Galley is really starting to screw with me. Watching Candy & Emma bent over the toilet with the smell of vanilla coating the room…it's best to cut that line of thought so short it'll spend the rest of its life complaining about how it never gets to ride rollercoasters.

I expect to be alone outside, but instead I find Chalk propped against the Galley, a big frown plastered on his chest.

"What's wrong, little buddy?" I ask.

In a blink his chest reads IT'S ALL MY FAULT

"What's your fault?"

EMMA BEING SAD

"That's got nothing to do with you," I tell him.

BUT IF I HADN'T FALLEN…

"Aw, man, you couldn't have known. No one blames you."

R U SURE his face reads.

"Yep, don't worry." Chalk relaxes a little and we just hang out.

Night falls without much warning, but any temperature drop is minimal. The air is sweet with honeysuckle. Or something similar, at least. The lack of artificial light makes the stars pop. So vivid and so low I could almost believe they're dancing in the trees. Wait a second, they are dancing in the trees.

"Chalk, do you see that?"

SEE WHAT? his chest reads. Then I hear a faint, girlish giggle echoing across the fields.

"You didn't hear that? I think there's something out there."

???? is all his chest shows.

"Crap, am I hallucinating?"

I'LL GET THE CAPTAIN! Chalk runs back aboard the ship while I remain as still as possible. Soon the laughter turns to whispers, beckoning me. Towards what, I don't know.

A hand clamps down on my shoulder. "And where do you think you're going?"

"Huh?" I say, turning to see Valiant and the whole crew—even Gumdrop and Candy & Emma are out here. I'm several yards into the grass fields and I don't even remember standing up. "I, uh, I'm pretty sure there's something out there." I point to a line of trees a couple hundred yards away.

Panik comes over and touches my face. "Clammy. A jump could be imminent."

"But over there…" I say.

"Could be a natural thin point between dimensions, they're more common than you'd think."

"Well, what are we waiting for," Valiant says. "*Adventure* is that way."

I shake some of the cobwebs from my mind, then head over to Emma and Candy. "Are you sure you should be out of bed?"

"Candy's body recovers quickly," Emma says.

"And I didn't die!" Candy cheers.

"Congratulations," I say.

"Look," Emma says, unable to meet my eyes, "I'm, um, sorry. For, you know…all that."

"It's cool."

"It's really not."

I don't know what else to say, so I just walk next to her and hope that's enough. Then I notice the oddest thing—or at least the oddest thing in the last minute or two—with each step we take the sky brightens. It could be that night on this little planet it really short, but those whispers I was hearing earlier have returned and now sound like a song. I yawn, causing my ears to pop, and suddenly a sun burns bright in the sky. The grassy fields have transformed into a lush forest that glistens with morning dew. A bird sized bug whooshes by and Jimmy jumps; swatting it away. What a pussy.

More startling than that is when something above us says, "Did you see that, Jaela? That cheeky fella tried to spank you?"

The birdy-bug reappears in front of Jimmy, and it turns out it's not bird or bug at all, but rather a winged girl dressed in rose petals. "This one?" she asks. We all look up, searching for who she's talking to.

She's not hard to spot. "Yep, that's the one."

"Oh, I-I, um, I'm so sorry," Jimmy stammers. Because that's Jimmy's specialty.

"You should be," the one apparently named Jaela says. "You missed." She smiles and winks.

"Uh, what?" Jimmy says.

"Go on," Jaela juts out her backside. "Give it a good one."

"You, uh, you're sprites, right?" Jimmy asks. The rest of us are too busy enjoying his discomfort to speak. Well, that's why I'm keeping quiet.

"Sprites!" Jaela and her nameless friend spit simultaneously.

"Ick! How could you think we're one of those sloppy prudes? Can't you see our beauty? Aren't we simply dazzling? We're fairies, of course!"

Candy's body stiffens like she's just received an electric shock. "Oh. My. Goodness. I love fairies!!"

"Course you do," Jaela says. "Everyone does." Then she turns her attention back to Jimmy. "Now come on, boy. You owe me a spanking. No need to be gentle."

* * *

Jimmy looks to be on the verge of a panic attack before Valiant steps in and saves him more embarrassment. "I must apologize for my spaceboy. He's a little shy."

"I like'em shy," Jaela says. "Isn't that right, Nya?"

Nya flutters down next to Jaela. "I just like it when they can't stop staring at me. Makes me feel pretty. I mean, prettier than I already know I am."

"No doubt your beauty is a wonder to behold," Valiant says.

"Thank you, handsome," Jaela says.

"And thank you for gracing us with your splendor, but I must ask: What is this place?"

"Why it's the Land of Endless Summer," Nya says. "It's Faerie."

At that moment, a smaller winged girl with chestnut hair zooms into view. "Ugh. This ain't Faerie it ain't. Yeh vain trollops always tryin' ta claim everyt'ing as yer own."

"Go away, little sprite," Jaela says. "These people don't want to look at your ratty leaves. We were just about to invite them to come bathe with us in the Topaz River."

"Course yeh were yeh nasty li'l sluts. Ne'er miss a chance to show off yer tittes do yeh."

"Oh, hey! I get it now," I say, my attention fully on Emma and Candy Princess. "This is the accent you were trying to mimic all that time, right?"

"Maybe," Emma mumbles.

"In that case, I apologize. It was pretty good. I mean, the accent itself is awful, but your impression nailed that aspect of it."

"You 'gain," little miss chestnut says. "Why's it always you?"

"Have we met?" I say.

" 'ave we met?! We canna stop meetin'. Yeh burnt down that bleedin' 'ouse instead o' fixin' t'ings. An then yeh show up an I 'aven't seen Crim since!"

"Um," I say. "I have no idea what you just said."

"She's one of the sprites we met at that little cabin in the woods," Emma explains.

"Oh. Nice to see you again!"

"Nice is it? Be a 'ole lot nicer if yeh tol' me where Crim was."

"What's a Crim?"

"She's a pri'ee li'el red 'eaded sprite yeh daft donker!"

"A pretty sprite?" Nya says. "As if."

"Donker?" I say.

Once again Captain Valiant does his best to get things back under control. "I think there might be a mistake Miss…"

"Chessy," the sprite says.

"The thing of it is, Chessy, my friend, Victor, isn't exactly one of a kind. It's likely that the Victor who you met again is not the one you see here today. But odds are that one is somewhere nearby."

"What are they talking about?" Nya asks.

"I wouldn't know," Jaela says. "I stopped listening when they stopped talking about us."

"Shut yer traps, yeh fairy trash," Chessy says. "I jus' wanna find Crim is all."

"Perhaps we can help you find her," Valiant says. "We could use a guide."

"I can guide yeh as far as the Market. But Imma wood sprite I am."

"That would be most appreciated."

"So no one is coming to watch us bathe?" Jaela says.

"I want to play with the pretty fairies," Candy pouts.

"Me too," Lily mutters under her breath.

Valiant addresses the fairies: "If we succeed in our *adventure* we might just join you for a victory celebration."

"A party?" Nya says.

"Oh we love parties," Jaela says. "But if you get bored with this filthy sprite, we'll be at the river. Dripping wet." The two fairies flutter away, but as they pass me, Jaela stops. "Don't I know you from somewhere?"

"I don't think so," I say.

"You didn't play with my petals once?"

"I don't even know what that means."

"Oh, I think you do," she pokes my nose.

"Um," I say.

"Then again, all you mortals look so similar. You all have that same lovestruck look whenever you see me. It's what I admire most about you all." With that, she and Nya disappear into the woods.

Chessy spits in their direction. "Good riddance."

* * *

Before we follow Chessy wherever she's planning to lead us, the Captain and Panik want to check on the Galley, but it seems we were too far away from it when we jumped because it's nowhere to be found. Panik is dissatisfied since she won't have access to all her science-y equipment to help us track me down. Valiant is even more distraught. He hates leaving the Galley unattended. But Gumdrop perches on his shoulder and that calms him.

That leaves us with only the weapons and supplies we happened to have on us, so it's a good thing that Chessy is taking us to some store, or something. Candy is so excited by Chessy's presence that even Emma can't seem to keep her bottled up. She must ask two dozen questions in rapid succession. Chessy answers kindly enough. Or I think she does. I still can't understand most of what she says. What I do pick up is almost exclusively anti-fairy jargon. A few times I think she insults me as well. If I remember correctly—and I often don't—she took the whole cabin burning thing especially hard. Even if that was The Roboracle's doing. When Candy Princess mentions that she's, well, a princess, Chessy perks up. "Yeh should seek out our queen yeh should. I ain't nev'r met 'er or not'in', but I 'ear she's right pleasant she is. Loves guests. 'Specially other royalty."

"Ooooh," Candy claps and addresses the rest of us, "can we?"

"If time is on our side," Valiant says, "then perhaps, Princess."

"Time is never on our side," Panik says. If it wasn't for her super pheromones and wickedly sexy body I don't know how Panik would ever get laid. Because her personality is a total mood killer.

As we continue on our way, I do my best to take in the scenery because listening to the sprite kind of makes my head hurt. It looks eerily similar to the forest surrounding the aforementioned cabin, but somehow off too. First, all the little creatures we pass along the way look right at us. Not in fear, but with curiosity. And instead of scattering some actually follow us. A few squirrels tail us in the trees and catch the eye of Gumdrop, who mews at them. That startles them, but they keep tracking us when they realize Gumdrop has no plans to leave her perch.

Chessy stops abruptly. "This is as far as I cin take yeh. Market's through tha trees. Canna miss it."

"Why can't you come with us?" Sera asks. "We could really use your help finding our way around."

"Imma wood sprite, girly. I ain't got much power out there. And these is dang'rous times they is. Yeh need a guide, yeh'll find one at the Market. Juss look 'round. But don' take not'in' without givin' somet'in' in return, yeh 'ear. And please, find Crim will yeh."

We leave Chessy to her forest and step into the clearing. She was right, there's no way we could have missed the market. It's not just a store; it's a whole damn city teeming with life of all shapes and sizes. Fairies glide from any vendor with a mirror to the next. Rabbits sell produce to all manners of carnivorous creatures without worry of being eaten by them. Something that I can only describe as a goblin shouts to passersby, peddling what he claims are the most beautifully bound and rare books in all the land. The sky sparkles and sizzles. And not just with energy or some other random metaphor, it literally sparkles and sizzles. There's actual, tangible magic in the air. In a lot of ways it's not too dissimilar from the market place at The Brothel of Infinite Sadness. Except it's brighter, cleaner, and much, much happier.

"First things first," Captain Valiant says. "We might need supplies. Lieutenant, you and my spaceboy should seek out the basics along with packs to carry it all. Lily, you can help Panik search out any supplies she might be able to use for tracking. Chalk and I will shake hands, make friends, and learn all we can of this land. Victor, you,

Emma, and the Princess should inquire about the other you, and a few more weapons couldn't hurt. We'll meet back here when we're done. Is everyone clear?"

"Yes, sir," Sera says, and the rest of us nod.

Emma, Candy, and I go straight to the book peddling thing. Mostly because I really want to know what he/she/it is. As we approach, the thing's face twists into what I can only assume is a smile. That or it's trying to intimidate or threaten us. It sniffs the air. "Ah, a mortal and," it sniffs one more time in Candy's direction, "and one of the Confectionaries! We don't get many of your kind—either of your kinds—around here anymore. Is this your first time in the Summerland Markets?"

"Yep," I say.

"Then welcome! I'm Groff and these are my books," the goblin-esque thing makes a sweeping gesture towards the books behind him. "Now what might you be looking for? I have cookbooks and storybooks. Picture books and text books. I have history books and puzzle books and books all about books or books that never even mention other books. There are magic books and horror books. Books that will make you laugh and even books that will laugh back at you."

"So you have a lot books," I say.

"Many and more, my good fellow. My wife can't wait to rid of them all, truth be told." Well, at least that explains the gender question. "Wants to make room for babies and torture racks. Women, huh?"

"Uh, yeah."

"So what'll it be, anything catch your fancy?"

"Actually, I'm kind of wondering if you've seen someone," I say.

"I've seen plenty of someones."

"What about me? Have you seen me?"

"I'm looking at you right now. Seeing you clear as the day is long."

"But I mean before now."

"As in before you showed up here a minute ago?"

"Yeah."

"Nah, can't say I saw you before I first saw you," Groff says. "Sorry I can't be of more help. Sure you don't want some books."

"I don't know," I say. "You have any books with weapons stored in them?"

"Not today, I don't. But I think I've got a book just for you," Groff rummages through a stack of book and comes out with thickest of the lot. "This here will tell you everything you need to know about the Summerlands, and sometimes knowledge can be the best weapon. If that fails, you can always hit someone with it."

"That's really nice, Mr. Groff," Emma says, "but I'm not sure we have any money."

"I'm sure we can work out a trade of some kind. It's what we do here. And since you lot are new to the Summerlands and I like you so much, we can work something out. How about a story?"

"A story?" Emma says.

"Sure, everybody's got stories."

I think about it for a second or two. Everyone is looking at me so I better just say something. "Okay, okay. I got this." Well, no backing out now. Guess I'll just wing it. I clear my throat and get crazy serious. "Once upon a time a prince was born. He was a robust and healthy babe. His cries so thunderous, the whole kingdom could hear them. But being a prince he, even as a baby, had more decorum than to cry needlessly. Yes, he was the baby to end all babies.

"Then on his first birthday, this would be king was struck ill."

"Was it the FairFlux?" Groff interrupts.

“Indeed it was the FairFlux.” Whatever that is.

“That’s rough. Poor kid.”

“And the FairFlux was true to its name, for it treated the young prince no differently than it would a peasant child.”

“Hey, I never thought of it like that,” Groff says. I’m an awesome storyteller.

“The king and queen tried everything to cure their son. No magic potion was left untested. They even tried a newfangled mortal medicine called penicillin, but the FairFlux is a virus and not some bacterial infection so that was a waste of time. And just when things seemed to be at their worst, the prince closed his eyes and never opened them again. The end.”

“Seriously,” Emma says, followed by Candy saying, “But did they all live happily ever after?”

“Nope,” I say. Candy’s lip quivers.

“That,” Groff says, “was a very practical story. You know how many kids die of the FairFlux? Lots. But the way people talk about it, you’d never know it. It’s about time someone spread some social awareness. The book is yours. And you know what?” Groff turns back to one of his book stacks, pulling out a much smaller tome. “This one’s on the house, and if I happen to see you again, I’ll be sure to let you know.”

“Thanks, Groff,” I say and we wander off towards another random stall. “You know, for an ugly monster thing, he was pretty nice.”

“That’s a little racist,” Emma says. “Speciesist? What’s the proper term here?”

“He smelled like frogs,” Candy says. “I don’t like frogs.”

“Nobody asked you,” Emma tells her.

“Oooo,” Candy points to a vendor a few dozen yards away,

"look at the pretty dresses!"

"I swear she has the attention span of a 6 year old. You have no idea what it's like to be stuck in here."

"Can we go look at the dresses, please!"

"We're supposed to be looking for weapons. And me. I don't think we'll find either over there," I say.

"But both Panik and Captain Valiant have said that a woman's body can be a very dangerous weapon," Candy tells me.

"I have heard Captain Valiant say that before," I say.

"You can't be serious," Emma says.

"How often is Captain Valiant wrong, Emma? Never, that's how often."

"Fine, whatever," Emma concedes. "Let's just get this over with."

* * *

The vendor of the dress kiosk is, unsurprisingly, a fairy bedecked in flower petals that appear to be spun from silver. "Finally, a beautiful woman worthy of my beautiful dresses. You have no idea how hard it is to watch my creations befouled by such unsightly beasts."

"That's rude," Emma says.

The fairy keeps on smiling. "Manners are for those not fortunate enough to look like us, honey."

Emma groans while Candy remains enthralled by all the extravagant clothing. "Did you make all these, Miss Fairy?"

"Course I did, honey. And please call me Trilla."

"I'm Candy Princess!"

"*The* Candy Princess?" Trilla the fairy asks.

"You know me?"

“I know *of* you,” Trilla says, “or rather of your people. Everybody does. Some of the other fairies say that the Confectionaries are the sweetest lovers. Tell me true, are the Candy Canes really that big?”

“Oh my god,” Emma mutters.

“I’ll take that as a resounding yes,” Trilla giggles. “You must be here as a guest to our Summer Queen. I’ve been trying to get her to look at my dresses for decades, but she’s so loyal to that cocky little Sprig. A pixie! Can you believe that? They’re only a few steps above sprite.”

“Um,” I say. “We’re actually here looking for someone.”

Trilla eyes me up and down. Mostly down. “Is this your man slave, Princess? He doesn’t look like any Candy Cane.”

“Oh no,” Candy says. “That’s Victor. He’s my body buddies boyfriend.”

“I’m not sure what that means, but it sounds kinky. You royal types sure know how to party. So who is this someone you’re looking for?”

“It’s him,” Candy points to me.

“Looks like your search is over, then.”

“Oh but there’s another him,” Candy clarifies.

“I see. You want twin man-slaves. Can’t say I blame you.”

“No, no! His twin is already with us and she’s a girl.”

“Are you having me on, Princess?”

“I would never!”

The fairy shrugs. “How bout we just get you in some of my dresses and you can worry about your little scavenger hunt later, huh? Let’s have a look at this one.” Trilla hands Candy a pale silver dress that refracts the light around it, making it glow. “I wove it from one of the rarest flowers in all of Faerie. It grows at the bottom of a river and is nurtured only by the loveliest reflections of the most beautiful fairies. I was saving it for the Summer Queen, but I can make an exception for a princess. Let's get it on you."

Candy looks around, but it's Emma who speaks. "There aren't any changing rooms. We aren't expected to get naked out in the open are we?"

Before Trilla can answer, Candy screams "I'll do it!" and starts pulling at the fly of her jeans. Although, it's clear that Emma is fighting her on it.

"You're a little daft, aren't you," Trilla says. "I like it. I've always felt my dresses deserve that kind of enthusiasm. But why struggle with undressing—and really these peasants aren't worthy of your royal nudity—when we can just do this," Trilla taps Candy and Emma on the shoulder and are instantly enveloped in a puff of glitter. That fades to reveal Candy's body, now dress adorned. But that's not all. Candy's hair, previously pony-tailed, now cascades down her bare back with a few flowers woven into small braids. It occurs to me then that at least half the Market is staring directly at her. With the snap of her fingers, Trilla summons a full length mirror. "Now that's how a princess should look."

Candy beams and even Emma lets out a breathless "Wow".

"You must wear this dress to meet the Summer Queen," Trilla says. "Imagine how jealous she'll be."

"But we aren't here for the Queen," Candy reminds Trilla.

"Are you kidding," Trilla says. "Half the eyes of Faerie are glued to you right now. The Queen will seek you out. Trust me."

"Well," I say. "We still don't have a way to pay for it. Unless you want me to tell you a story. I'm sort of a renowned storyteller."

"What do I look like, a common troll?" Trilla says. "Although I can think of plenty of other things you could give me." Her eyes never wander above my waste. I feel so wonderfully cheap. “But I’ve got a better idea,” she turns all her attention back to Candy and Emma, “a kiss. I’ve always wanted to kiss a princess.”

“But you’re so tiny,” Candy says.

“Don’t you worry about that, honey. I’ll do all the work. That is, if we have a deal. The dress for a kiss?”

“Okay!” Candy yelps.

“Don’t I get a say in this?” Emma wonders.

“Please, Emma. Pleeeeeeease!”

“Oh whatever. Just let me know when it’s over.”

Trilla is confused by Candy having to bargain with herself. “Is that a yes then?”

“Mmmhmm,” Candy replies.

“Good,” Trilla says. “Now close your eyes and let the magic happen.” Candy complies and Trilla glides up to Candy’s lips. As she presses her much smaller lips to Candy’s she kind of turns into a nightlight, and before long she glows so brightly I can’t see a damn thing. All I hear is a few muffled mmmmm’s. Then it’s over. “Aren’t you a sweet thing.”

Candy’s face burns strawberry red. “Thank you, Miss Trilla.”

“You are very welcome,” Trilla winks. “Now go on, I’ve got plenty of other customers to deal with. And don’t forget to tell the Queen where you got that dress.” Candy says her goodbyes and we restart our journey through the Market.

“You know,” Emma says after we’re far enough away from Trilla’s boutique, “that was a whole hell of a lot of tongue for such a small girl.” She half-smiles. I think it’s the first time she’s smiled inside Candy—well, the first time sober—but that little half-smile quickly distorts into a grimace. “Goddamn it, Candy!”

“What?” I ask.

"She's thinking about eating Trilla," Emma says.

"I'm sooory," Candy says. "But she tasted like magic!"

Emma sighs. "I was better off dead."

* * *

Emma and Candy continue to bicker—both silently and out loud—which means I only catch snippets every so often as I peruse random stalls for weapons or leads on my whereabouts. I don't have much luck. I attempt to barter with a Minotaur over a sword he claims slew the ancient blight of the Summerlands, a dragon known only as Puff. I offer him a song about Puff the Dragon in exchange, but the song ends up offending him. Apparently his grandfather was killed by Puff. And yeah, maybe I mention that his grandfather was likely a giant pussy for getting killed by a dragon that liked to spend its free time frolicking in mist. But I don't think that gave him the right to call my grandfather a pussy too.

After that little brouhaha, I need a little entertainment to cool off, so I wander over to the produce rabbit. Because it's a *talking* rabbit! Turns out the rabbit—whose name is Remy—isn't a fan of that Minotaur either. We spend the better part of 20 minutes trading insults across the Market square with that bastard. Remy also tells me he might have seen a guy who looked a lot like me a little earlier, but he also admits that most mortal humans look alike to him. He says it so apologetically, though, that it's impossible to be offended. Rabbits have a lot better manners than blue jays, that's for sure. Soon Remy has to get back to peddling his goods, so I leave him to it. I can see another weapons kiosk in the distance, but it's much farther away than the little area where we're supposed to meet back up with everyone else. Naturally, I choose the path of least resistance.

Emma and Candy have either given up their little squabble or they've taken it completely internal. Without thinking, I reach for Emma's hand, forgetting it is Candy's too. For a moment she also forgets. But the lapse in memory ends soon enough and Emma jerks the hand away.

"What are you doing?" Emma says.

"Sorry, reflex," I say.

"Oh, gross!" Emma says.

"That's an overreaction."

"What? No, not you. It's just whenever you touch us, Candy starts thinking about screwing you. Or eating you. Or both."

"Emma!" Candy cries. "That's a secret!"

"You don't get secrets, bitch!"

"Language!"

"Fuck you and fuck your fucking language! Fuck fuck fuck fuck fuck!"

I prop myself against a nearby tree, sigh, and hope the others get back soon. I hate to say it, but even Jimmy will do.

* * *

Emma continues her swear-fest for quite some time. She keeps swearing long after Candy has been reduced to tears. There's something profoundly disturbing about seeing someone with a satisfied smile while tears stream down their face. Meanwhile, I sit and wave at all the passersby giving me the evil eye for not doing anything about the hysterical, beautiful princess who appears to have Tourette Syndrome. When Panik and Lily show up, I couldn't be more grateful. Not that they can quell the two souled beast before us, but at least all the shoppers' disdain can be divvied between the three of us now.

"What exactly is this all about?" Lily asks.

"Candy's cannibalistic urges," I say.

"Oh. You guys find anything useful?"

"We got a couple of books and that dress," I tell her while Panik whispers something to Emma and Candy. Whatever she said quiets them down, even if they're likely keeping it going with their thoughts.

"How'd you score that stuff?" Lily wonders.

"Well, I got the books for a story and Candy got the dress for a kiss."

"Seriously? Everyone we talked to wanted gold. I didn't even think of offering anything else."

"I did," Panik says now that she's quieted the other two, "but I didn't think we had Time for sexual commerce. Besides, those exploits get far more complicated with non-humanoid participants, and most of my protective gear is back on the Adventure Galley. May I see those books?"

"Sure," I hand her both of them.

She studies the smaller volume. "Hmm, a book of magic. Archaic, but potentially useful." Then she gets right to work reading it. It's not long before Jimmy and Sera make their way over to us. I first notice them as they're making some sort of deal with Remy the Rabbit for vegetables. Once that's done, they join us. Along with the produce, they've also acquired a few backpacks.

I take the monstrous book back from Panik and shove it at Jimmy. "Here, you get to carry this."

"Uh, okay," he grabs it from me. "Jeez, it's heavy."

"Man up, Jimmy."

"It's cool, I've got it," he flips through a few pages. "Wow, this must be, like, the whole history of this place."

"Whatever," I say. "Did you guys get anything other than vegetables? You know how I feel about those. It reminds me of Hell."

"Yeah, I know," Jimmy says. "I told Sera, I said 'Victor doesn't want any vegetables, let's go over to that butcher over there'," he points in a direction I can't be bothered to follow, "but, um, I think knowing you didn't want the veggies made Sera really want to get them."

"Could you be any more worthless, Jimmy?"

Jimmy ignores my question—even though it wasn't rhetorical at all, I really think I should know if he can be anymore worthless—and keeps talking, but I zone him out. I'm going to have to eat carrots because of him. It's bullshit. Jimmy is still blathering on when Captain Valiant, Gumdrop, and Chalk return. Valiant tells us of all the valuable connections the three of them made. He's not sure exactly how they might come in handy, but this is Captain Valiant we're talking about. Of course they'll come in handy.

We're trying to figure out our next course of action when someone shows up and makes the decision for us. An armored woman with a spear in her hand approaches us. "Excuse me, are you the monarch of Candy Island?"

"That's me!" Candy says.

"The Summer Queen requests your presence." I guess Trilla was right on about this Summer Queen. "You will follow me when you're done at the Market." And this lady isn't much for small talk.

"Can my friends come too?" Candy asks.

"Your royal guard is always welcome."

"Hooray! Let's go!"

"No time like the present, I suppose," Valiant says.

"All Time is like the present," Paniks corrects. Whatever the hell she ever means. We start following Miss Spear, but I spot that asshole Minotaur again and have to stop everyone abruptly.

"What is it?" Valiant asks.

"You see that Minotaur way over there?" I say. "He kind of hates me—"

"You've already made enemies here?" Sera says.

"It's not my fault. He's a dick. Anyway, he has this cool dragon slaying sword and I think we can bargain it away from him. Lily, go up to him and tell him you'll punch me right in the face for that sword."

"You think he hates you that much?" Lily asks.

"I did call his grandfather a pussy."

"Oh."

"But then he called *our* grandpa a pussy."

"That son of a bitch!"

"Wait," Sera says. "I think it might be more convincing if Lily and I both offer to punch you in the face."

"I like the way you think, Sera," I tell her. "See, Jimmy, that's true friendship."

"Punching you in the face is true friendship?" Jimmy asks.

"No, ripping off an asshole Minotaur for me is true friendship," I can't believe I even have to explain these things. "And you didn't think to help."

"I could punch you now."

"Too late, the girls are already over there."

We all watch as Lily and Sera make their offer. They're too far away for us to hear, but at one point Lily points towards me and the Minotaur nods. Then Sera makes a punching gesture and the Minotaur smirks, at which point Sera and Lily walk back our way. Without a word Sera socks me good. Lily follows up with a punch of her own. I'm considering selling it by dropping to the ground when Sera kicks me in the balls. I don't really have to sell anything anymore. This might not have been my best idea ever.

As I lie on the ground trying to block out the pain Sera says, "He, uh, upped his price."

Lily snickers. "I'll go get the sword now."

It takes a minute, but once the pain dissipates Sera is offering me her hand and I take it. Lily is back with the sword by then and she hands it to me. I glance over to the Minotaur just in time to see his jaw drop. I drape the sword across my back and give the bastard both middle fingers. Then I limp along after the rest of the crew. I bet if Jimmy had been the one to kick me it wouldn't have hurt so much.

"Thanks a lot, Jimmy," I mutter.

* * *

"Where exactly are we going?" I ask after we've been following the Queensguard for a few minutes.

"To the Queen's castle," she says, but I've looked all around and can't see anything that resembles a castle.

"But where is that?"

Our escort points to a faraway mountain. "There."

I groan. "That'll take forever!"

"It's closer than it looks," the guard says. "As long as you know which path to follow. We'll be there in less than fifteen minutes." I look toward the mountain floating on the horizon and can't believe it.

A few more minutes pass and our guide makes a sharp left turn into the forest. The tree cover is too dense to see the mountain anymore. We walk in a straight line for maybe 5 minutes before the guard turn right. We follow her for maybe 20 feet, and then she turns right again. Meaning we have to be walking parallel to the path we were just on. I'm pretty sure this lady is fucking with us. She probably wasn't even sent by the queen. I bet she's in cahoots with that douchey Minotaur. Or maybe she was sent by the other me to mess with the better me, which would be me me.

Judging from everyone else's expressions, they're all as suspicious as I am. I might have to get my slaughter on. I'm about to draw my sword when we emerge from the woods. It's much darker than when we entered, which doesn't make sense. It had to be midday, and that was like ten minutes ago. Looking towards the sky, I realize what's happened. We're standing in the shadow of the mountain.

"Oh," I say.

"Enough gawking," our escort says. "The Queen awaits." She leads us towards a cave at the base of the mountain.

"The castle is in the mountain?" Lily asks.

"No," the guard says. "The mountain *is* the castle." We walk through the cave and somehow emerge in a meadow. "Welcome to Castle Solstice." The air is rich and dense, like after a warm summer rain, and mixed with the scent of freshly cut grass. Sunlight bathes every inch of the meadow.

"It's enchantments," an unknown voice says. It is soft and inviting, and the woman it belongs to is nothing short of stunning. Her dark skin is in direct contrast to her bright, sky blue eyes. She's barefoot and wears something that resembles a toga, though it's far more elegant. I thought her a woman at first glance, but the closer she gets, the younger she appears. She can't be more than seventeen. "I'm Nerissa, Queen of the Summerlands." Candy Princess steps forward as she approaches and curtseys sweetly. "You must be the Confectionary Queen of Candy Island."

"It's Candy Princess, actually, Your Highness," Candy says.

"Please, call me Nerissa," the words are hardly more than a whisper. "And these must be your royal escort." Nerissa knells before Chalk. "Such a lovely heart."

Chalk bows and when he rises again his face reads THANK U, and I could swear the pink of his letters bleeds a little into his white body.

"Not my escort, Your Hi—Nerissa. My friends," Candy says.

"Says you," Sera grumbles.

"Lieutenant," Valiant reprimands.

"Sorry, sir."

Nerissa watches their exchange, her expression kind and never-changing. "Your friends are my friends. Come. Let me show you my home."

* * *

Nerissa leads us through Castle Solstice. Her pride is unmistakable, but never overbearing; never gloating. Fairies or sprites or pixies—who can really tell the difference—buzz about. There's so much going on in each room—if it's even fair to call them rooms—that I can't concentrate on what I'm seeing. I'm on sensory overload here.

"And through here," Nerissa is saying, "is the Augustus Sea." Sure enough, we find ourselves on a small beach looking out across a boundless body of water. "This is my favorite place…but look at me going on like this. You must all think me so rude."

"Of course not!" Candy says.

"You're sweet," the Queen says, "but I never once paused to let your friends introduce themselves. It was very uncouth. Would you all allow me to make amends? How does a picnic sound?"

None of us decline, not that Nerissa would have taken no for an answer, and it's not long before a few winged creatures have a picturesque picnic laid out before us.

Before seating herself, Nerissa introduces herself to each of us and we respond in kind. Once Nerissa has learned all our names Candy says, "Oops, I almost forgot. You have to meet Emma too!"

"Of course," Nerissa says. "Where is she?"

"She's…well she's in me. Her soul is, I mean. Say hello, Emma." Candy's voice lowers to Emma's register. "Um, hello."

"A pleasure to meet you," Nerissa says. "It must be nice sharing a body. You never have to be alone."

"Uh, well…I guess," Emma says.

Nerissa smiles. Like everything else she does, it's unobtrusive and gentle. "You're young. But someday you'll see."

"If," I interrupt, "if you don't mind me asking. Just, well, how old are you."

"I've not even lived a whole millennium yet, but often I feel older. I'm sure it shows in my face."

"Not even a little," Lily says.

"You're all so kind. I can't tell you how much it means to have your company. It's such a surprise. I thought all the passages between Candy Island and here were long closed."

"It wasn't a planned trip, Queen Nerissa," Valiant says. "Nor did we come from Candy Island."

"Candy Island is…is gone," Candy sniffles.

Nerrisa takes Candy's hand in her own, comforting her. "I'm so sorry to hear that. But however your visit came about, I'm delighted to have you here. I don't get many visitors these days. The Summerlands are made up of many kingdoms, but over the centuries most of the other monarchs have become reclusive. And now, now there's…oh but you don't need to hear all of that."

"Oh no, what's wrong!" Candy exclaims.

"It's nothing that need concern you. You're here as my guests. The Summerlands are my responsibility."

"With all due respect," Valiant says. "We are first and foremost *adventurers*. If there's a problem with your kingdom we would be remiss not to help."

Panik pops a grape in her mouth and I think swallows it whole, but at least she doesn't speak with her mouth full. "It's also worth noting that our problem and yours may very well intersect. There are no coincidences with Abstractions."

The Summer Queen looks from Panik to the rest of us. "I don't understand."

"I got this," I say. "Alright so like I've been unstuck from dimensional gravity and have this anti-gravity thingamabob surrounding me and always growing and junk. And somehow this has something to do with this other me who is a giant dick—"

"Victor!" Candy gasps.

"Sorry, he's a giant *penis*, and Panik thinks he's got this shard of Vicious Entitlement—"

"Enlightenment," Panik corrects.

"Whatever. The point is, apparently he feels entitled to be a, um, bad word." Candy smiles and nods, proud of my awesome fucking restraint. "Normally I wouldn't care, but I'm being dragged through all these places where stuff is always going wrong and everything wants to kill me, and that I do have a problem with. Oh, and if we don't stop whatever this is, time is going to overwrite us."

Nerissa stares at me. "I…still don't understand."

"Nobody does," I tell her. "Nobody does."

"What Victor is trying to say is that we'd love to help with whatever is troubling you," Valiant says.

"Well, love is a strong word," I say. Then I realize I inadvertently almost maybe sort of corrected Captain Valiant. Quick! Damage control! "And, uh…we are strong men. So what he said." Nailed it.

"Are you certain?" the Queen asks.

"Absolutely," Valiant says.

"What do you know of the Summerlands?" Nerissa asks.

"Well, according to this book," Jimmy says, flipping through the giant tome—he's even got a pen out to take notes with…what a nerd—and reciting from it, "it's a place of magic and endless summer."

"Seriously, Jimmy. You needed a book to tell you that?" I say.

"I haven't had a chance to get very far. That's just in the forward."

"That's enough for me to explain my worries," Nerissa says. "In the Summerlands, the sun shines upon my people and me for all but one hour a day. It's been that way for millennia. Yet that has all changed quite suddenly. Nights now last more than 3 hours. This is not without precedent, but it is a dark portent.

"Once upon a time the Summerlands were blanketed by a great darkness, for the heinous Ice Dragon, Haupuehuehu, ruled the kingdom--"

"Happywhowho?" I wonder aloud.

"Haupuehuehu," the Queen corrects, as if it sounded any different than the first time. "His very breath could summon a blizzard. His scales so cold they burned. The land was perpetually frozen. Nothing grew. People and creatures starved. It was only through sheer force of magic that anyone survived. It was a time of great turmoil and pain.

"The tale of how the terrible dragon was vanquished varies. Some legends says all the citizens of the Summerlands banded together to defeat him. The Minotaurs, of course, claim one of them slew the beast in single combat. But the most prevalent is that a small faction of the most powerful sorcerers and enchantresses put the monster to sleep in the Forbidden Caves, and that is where he's been ever since. The Summerlands have never had a single Winter's Day since. But now with the nights growing longer and colder, I fear that Haupuehuehu may be awakening and…and I don't know what to do."

"Well, I have a dragon slaying sword," I say.

"You've slain dragons?"

"My sword has."

"Victor can kill anything!" Candy Princess tells the Queen. "He's the greatest hero ever! He saved Candy Island from a terrible monster, and then saved Chalk and me from the destruction of Candy Island."

"For true?" Nerissa says.

"For true. Then he rescued Emma from Hell and saved Sera from…well, from me."

"From you, Candy Princess?"

Candy drops her gaze to the beach. "Yes. Before I met Victor I was something of a naughty girl. But he has saved us all sooo many times!"

"That's debatable," Sera says, but if Nerissa hears, she gives no indication.

Instead she turns to me. "And you'd be willing to brave the Forbidden Caves in search of the mighty Haupuehuehu?"

"I guess," I say.

"It would be an honor to aid your kingdom, my lady," Valiant says.

Then the Queen cries.

This time it is Candy who takes the Queens hands in hers.

"Don't cry, Queen Nerissa."

"I'm sorry," Nerissa says. "It's just that, while no one dares admit it, the age of heroes is long past. It used to be that great men and women from lands near and far would venture to The Summerlands, embarking on sensational quests to both save the kingdom and garner glory for themselves and their houses. But as those distant lands' faith in magic waned, so too did the doorways to and from them fade. And the Fair folk of the Summerlands became more interested in telling stories of great heroism than in creating new ones. It's been…so long."

"Hey, no worries," I say. "I always win."

"Again," Sera says. "Debatable."

"And you did always lose at Dungeons & Dragons," Lily says.

"You played Dungeons & Dragons?" Emma asks.

"No!" I say.

"Yes," Lily says.

"Okay, maybe like twice," I say.

"A week," Lily says.

"So what, I'm not allowed to have hobbies?"

"And you were terrible at it."

"Only because it's all based on rolling a dice, that's not what real adventuring is about."

"Unless you go up against the Galactic Gambler," Valiant says. "A dice game with him is harrowing."

My palm instinctively goes to my face, the clap from it must echo through the entire castle. That's how great my shame is right now. "I can't believe I forgot about the Galactic Gambler! That was one of the most compelling chapters in your autobiography."

"Indeed it was," Valiant agrees.

"Still, I do know how to stab things with swords and, Jimmy aside, everyone else is pretty efficient at killing things."

"Hey!" Jimmy objects.

"What?" I say. "All you do is bring stuff back to life. It's the literal antithesis of killing things."

"Oh, right."

I give my attention back to the Queen. "Don't worry, we've got this."

To my surprise, she's laughing. "You remind me of the last merry band of adventurers who visited me here. I certainly hope you don't end up like them." Then she laughs even harder. I'm…not sure how I should feel right now.

* * *

We're all anxious to get on our way or, in my case, anxious to get this all over with. Do I want people to write epic poems of my great heroism? Absolutely. But I'd prefer to do it with as little effort as possible. No effort would be preferable. However, I've learned that the life of a hero is filled with disappointment, and that disappointment usual starts with having to actually do heroic things. So I'm ready to do it. But Queen Nerissa insists that, with night rapidly approaching, we'd be wiser to spend those few hours resting in the comfort of the castle. She also assures us she will provide any assistance she can. Including a guide. He won't be back to the castle until later, though, so that's another reason we have to wait.

Not that I complain. I love hanging out in castles. It's maybe my favorite part about doing the whole hero thing. Big royal types treating me like a celebrity while I eat all their food and sleep in their cushy beds. Yep, that's the life. Granted it'd be a better life if my girlfriend wasn't currently trapped inside a body she hates. Because I've yet to get my bang on in a castle, and that's been on my list ever since I learned that some people make mental lists of weird sex stuff. Also, I don't like Emma being so depressed. Then again, knowing that there's a good chance Lily will be getting some while we're here, thus topping me once again makes *me* depressed.

I handle it, though.

Like a champ.

At least there's plenty to see and do around Castle Solstice. Panik finds some sort of magic laboratory and decides to get acquainted with it since it's the closest thing to science she's got. Lily hangs back with her. Valiant, Sera, and Jimmy are shown to the armory. I probably didn't need my new sword after all, but it was worth it to stick it to that Minotaur. Nerissa is happy to show off the rest of her castle to Chalk, Emma, Candy, and me, but it becomes increasingly clear that Emma and Candy aren't fully recovered from their drunken escapades. The Queen isn't oblivious to their weariness and offers them a room where they can rest.

"Thank you Nerissa, it's beautiful," Candy says.

"Just rest, Princess," Nerissa says before turning her attention back to Chalk and me. "Shall we continue our tour?"

"I think I might hold back here," I tell her.

"As you wish. What about you, little Heart, would you like to see more?"

YES PLEASE Chalk's face reads, and Queen Nerissa takes him by the hand.

"If you find yourself in need of anything at all, ring the bell by your bedside and one of the winged girls will attend to you." With that Nerissa and Chalk leave us, shutting the door behind them.

Emma and Candy settle themselves on a bed with rose petal sheets. "You should finish the tour."

I sit next to them. "I'd rather stay here with you, Em."

"I don't know what you expect to happen."

"I don't expect anything, but you shouldn't be alone."

"She's never alone!" Candy smiles and Emma groans. "Candy, could you just…I don't know, go hum one of your dumb songs quietly while I talk to Victor?"

"Okey-dokey! Anything for you, Emma!"

"At least she listens to you," I say.

Emma nods. Then she's crying. "I'm so tired."

"Then lie down and sleep."

"That's not what I mean. I'm tired of this. It's been what? A day? And I'm already so exhausted from fighting with Candy and being with her and—and—" The rest gets lost in a torrent of sobs. I scootch closer and put my arm around her. For a single breath she lets me. Then she pushes me away. "Can you—please can you," she motions towards the door, "stand over there somewhere."

I try to object. "But—"

"Please, you don't understand. When you're close…you smell so good. And when you're close she gets turned on an-and wants to eat you too. And I don't know where her urges end and mine begin anymore."

I get up and walk towards the door. "Is this far enough."

"For now," Emma sniffles. "Maybe you should go."

"I don't want to."

"I don't want him to either," Candy says.

"Damn it, Candy! I told you to give us privacy!" Emma yells.

"Sorry."

"Just go, Victor," Emma pleads.

"No," I tell her. "I need my rest too. Dragon slaying is hard work. Probably."

Emma sighs. "Fine. But stay over there."

"No problem. The ground is all grassy and soft. It'll be like camping."

Neither Emma or Candy say anything for a while after that. I think they've fallen asleep when Emma says, "I don't know if I'll ever be okay with…this."

"I'm not going anywhere," I say. This time there really is no response. I have no plans to sleep, but the room is spiked with a gentle concoction of lavender and junipers, and any plans I might have had are made irrelevant.

Interlude

"I can get it done for you," the thing lurking in his shadow says. He's already grown tired of this land of nearly endless sunshine. But the other is here now. He can resume his work. Finally. "I have something of a proclivity for the work you require."

"You don't look like much." He hates every second he has to spend talking to this creature. It is so beneath him. But no one claimed revenge would be easy.

"Which makes me all the better at such deeds."

"How did you even find me?"

"I keep my eyes open and my ears to the ground, so when I heard of a man at The Market looking for himself I got curious. And it's simple enough for me to follow others unnoticed. Then I figured, if a man is looking for himself, perhaps that other self might have similar inclinations. Or perhaps the very opposite. Either case seem rife with potential reward. And maybe a little mischief."

"This is no time for fun and games, it is a very serious matter. I expect my business taken care of properly."

"Taking care of business can be fun, though, can it not?" The thing grins a wicked grin. It disgusts him.

"And if you fail me?"

"Well then, I suppose you can chastise me over a hot cup of tea."

His shadow mimics him as he grunts. "Tea is a proper, serious drink."

"I couldn't agree more," it says.

It occurs to him that now would be the perfect time for a maniacal laugh. And he'd do it if only it wouldn't undermine the seriousness of the situation. These are the sacrifices of a true hero.

4.5

"Please, I've told you everything I know," a winged girl with fiery hair begs. She's duct taped to a piece of ply board.

"I think you're lying," a dark voice says from somewhere in the shadows. "I think you aren't taking me seriously enough." It's my voice. "Tell me how to get to them."

"It's forbidden..."

"Those are lovely wings you have," I say. "I'm wondering, do they grow back."

"No no, please don't..." her cries are replaced with screams as I...

...I wake up out of breath and nearly jump out of my skin when I see the fairy floating in front of my face. Her hair is a dull pink, though, not the burning red in my dream. "You scared me, fairy."

Her voice is a whisper. "I'm a pixie."

"Like there's a difference," I say.

"The Queen bid me wake you. The little lordling is back from the Market and he's able to guide you on your quest. Are you really going to slay the ice dragon?"

"Pixie-girl, you're cute, but I can't hear a word you're saying."

"You think I'm cute?" I stare at her for a while, waiting to find out if she'll ever speak at a volume humans can hear. When it's clear she won't I go to the bed to wake Emma and Candy. They don't respond to my voice, so I touch their shoulder with the intent of gently shaking them. I don't get that far. Instead Candy's hand darts out and grabs mine. She bites, drawing blood.

"Owwww, fuck!"

"Ohmygod, I'm so sorry," Emma apologizes. "Candy, you bitch!"

"What? I didn't do it," Candy says. "I have excellent self-control. Looks like you need to learn some, little Miss Eager Beaver."

"Well, if it wasn't for your stupid body—"

"My body is wonderful!"

"Uh, guys it's cool. It's only a little bite," I say.

"I'll get the salve." The pixie dashes off.

"Wait," Emma says. "What'd she say?"

I shrug and shake my head. A moment later the pixie returns and rubs something on my bite wound. It tickles. Emma continues apologizing over and over again, despite my assurance that I'm fine. She's still saying sorry as the pixie leads us out of the room and through the maze of Castle Solstice to wherever she might be taking us. The best part about the whole biting incident is that Emma has briefly forgotten the no touching policy she's instituted while sharing Candy's body. She caresses my hand with each sorry she utters. But all that ends when she dares to kiss my hand. She catches my scent—or maybe even tastes a little blood that lingered there—and drops my hand like the proverbial hot potato I used to hear so much about as a kid. I can't believe they made a game out of that, because when you find yourself as Mr. Hot PotatoHand, it hurts.

Emma mutters one final sorry and turns all her attention to following the pixie, who ends up leading us back to the meadow that that serves as the entry hall of the castle. Everyone else is there waiting. While I see Queen Nerissa and the entire Galley crew, I don't notice any extra bodies. "Where is this guide we were waiting for?"

"Down here, good sir" a voice says.

I look to the grass and find an impish fellow staring back at me. "What are you?"

"I'm an elf," he says with a sly smile.

"You got cookies?"

The elf looks confused for some reason. "I…do not."

"Not much of an elf then," I say.

I could be mistaken, but I believe anger briefly flashes across Mr. Elf's face. Then again, I'm not that interested so who really knows. "At any rate, as I was saying to your compatriots, my elfish name is too complex for the human tongue, so you all may call me Lord Vice."

"And you, my Lord, will be leading us to these Forbidden Caves?" Valiant asks.

"In due time," the elf replies. "First we may consider heading back to the Market. Castle Solstice has much and more in terms of supplies, but it is lacking in certain areas. Had I known of your arrival, I could have brought back what was needed, of course. But what's done is done."

"What do we need that's not here?" Sera wonders.

"Maps, for one," the little Lord says. "The maps of the Forbidden Caves are heavily outdated. Even those we will find at the Market aren't perfect—the caves are known to change as they please—but they are better than the ones in the castle. Besides, all the best pathways lead to and from the Market. It's a natural starting point."

"This is where we must part ways," the Queen says. "Take with you my blessing. And with courage and luck may you return to me."

"We won't fail you, Queen Nerissa," Valiant says. "Though please don't take it personally if we don't return. Our traveling schedule isn't quite in our control."

"I understand, Captain," Nerissa leans in and kisses Candy's cheek, "Fare thee well, Princess. And you too, my little Heart." She kisses Chalk's hand. If he has anything to say back to her, it gets lost when his whole body turns bright pink.

As we exit Castle Solstice with Lord Vice leading the way, I pull Chalk aside. "So what exactly went on between you and the Queen after you left us last night?"

A HEART NEVER KISSES AND TELLS his face reads.

"I understand," I say, though my disappointment is substantial.

Chalk senses it, though, and he's never one to disappoint. SHE LET ME TOUCH HER BOOBS

"Awesome," I say. And we punctuate it with an even awesomer high-five.

* * *

We don't take the same path back to the Market as we took getting to the castle, which is weird. Then again, apparently everything is weird when magic is involved. This path seems longer. But that could just be because I'm itching to stab something with my sword. While we walk, Panik goes on and on about whatever magic mumbo-jumbo she was up to last night. I thought her pseudo-science babble was confusing, but it's nothing compared to her magic-speak. Most of it, I'm fairly certain, isn't even in English. It's like ancient Sumerian or something. That language is dead for a reason. I'm not sure what that reason is, but my guess is that the sound of it offended people so much that they beat to death anyone who dared speak it. By today's standard, it probably would have been classified a hate crime. On the other hand, I hate when people don't speak English, so is that too not a hate crime?

I'm busy trying to conjure a proper legal defense that might be viable in making all offenses against me a crime when I realize Panik has finished speaking and it's safe for me to start paying attention to things outside my head again. I know everyone else gets mad at me when I don't listen to them, but there's enough other people around listening that not only is my attention irrelevant, it's kind of irresponsible. If we are all paying attention to the same thing, who knows what might be slipping past us. I'm doing a hero's work here. Someday they'll all understand. And if they don't, hopefully I'll be able to prosecute them successfully in a court of law for their lack of faith.

It's not long before we arrive at the Market. It's the same as yesterday. Teeming with life and chatter and magic. I see the Minotaur in his booth. He glares at me and I unsheathe my sword and make an obscene gesture or two in his direction.

"Would you stop that," Sera says.

"He started it," I tell her, pointing to the Minotaur.

"What, by looking at you?"

"No, Sera. By being born," I say, But I do re-sheathe my sword.

Little Lord Vice gestures for us to stop and hands us each a list of stalls to visit, along with a small pouch of gold. I'm not too keen on this whole operation. Mostly because I still haven't stabbed anything yet. Bartering is for Jimmy and people equally as lame as Jimmy. I'm a stabber and my blade demands blood! But Captain Valiant is here and he's not objecting, so I have to suck it up and do my duty. This distraction will only enhance my eventual swording of things. In fact, it'll enhance it so hard that swording will finally, officially be recognized as an actual word. It's long overdue.

My first stop is at Remy the Rabbit's produce booth. It's not on my list, but Remy's cool and I want to show him my blade so that we might mock Mr. Minotaur a little more. Because seriously and sincerely…fuck that guy!

"Hey, Remy," I offer my hand, he shakes it.

"Hey, Victor. Wait, you are the same guy I met yesterday, right?"

"Uh, yeah," I say. "Why wouldn't I be?"

"You could be that other you you talked about," Remy says.

"Good point."

"So let's see, how can we prove you're the right you. Oh, I know! Who's the biggest fur-biting, scum sucking creature in all the Summerlands?"

"That goddamn Minotaur."

Remy's ears twitch. "Well, welcome back, friend! So is it true that you met the Summer Queen?"

"Yep," I tell him. "We're actually embarking on a quest to save the land from eternal winter or dragons or something."

"No shit? You know I hear dragons hate lettuce. I can hook you up, no problem."

"Aw, sweet!" I hand him a couple of gold pieces and his ears stand straight up.

"That's way too much for a little lettuce."

"Don't sweat it; I got plenty of this stuff. And maybe you can rub it in the Minotaur's face."

"But this is more than I make in a whole fortnight."

I shrug. "If I run out I'll just get more from the little elf that's guiding us around."

"The Queen's little elf lord is your guide?"

"Yeah, why?"

Remy scratches behind his ear and lowers his voice. "Look, you didn't hear it from me, but word around the squirrel community is that elf is into some shady dealings. They say he came from one of the distant small kingdoms on the edge of the Summerlands and that he was on the run from something or other. So be careful."

"Don't worry, where I come from elves like him are supposed to make cookies. The fact that he doesn't already had me suspicious.

Anyway, I'm supposed to be getting stuff on this list, so I should probably get to that." I say goodbye to Remy. He wishes me luck with not dying and I finally get to work on my list. It's full of really mundane crap that I doubt will help with dragon slaying. But I've got gold to burn so I spend it liberally. I even stop by Groff's and Trilla's kiosks to give them a little gold for their help yesterday. Groff loses his ability to form a complete sentence and blurts out random noises that I take to be thanks. And I'm not even sure Trilla recognizes me, but she does offer to take me off into the woods to do things I've never even heard of. Then I give her the gold and I'm briefly worried the petals she's wearing will explode off her. Somehow they manage to stay in place, though. Instead she buzzes all around my head telling me that someday she'll return the favor. She then kisses my nose and flutters behind me, pinching my ass. Fairies are a cheeky sort.

After all that, I end up running into Jimmy and Sera. Jimmy has his usual goofy grin while Sera holds his hand. "Oh man, Vic, you'll never believe what I just got. It's…you know what, forget it. It's a surprise but it's awesome."

"So I don't get to see it?" I ask.

"Later," he says.

"Jimmy, have I told you lately that you suck?"

"Not in those exact words, no," Jimmy says, still sporting that dumb smile. "But you're gonna love this, man."

"Damn it, Jimmy."

"He's not wrong, you are going to love it," Sera says.

"Stop encouraging him, Sera," I say.

"Believe me, I try. But for some reason he won't stop talking to you."

"Well, I appreciate your effort," I tell her. She's good people. We all go back to the mouth of the forest to wait for everyone else to finish with their lists. Valiant and Panik are already there, and it's not long before Lord Vice and Chalk show up. I can see Candy and Emma over at Trilla's. They head our way once they've finished talking to her, leaving only Lily missing. We all stand around shuffling our feet. Well, I do anyway. It's so like Lily to hold everything up. Even if she's almost always punctual. But it's so rare that I get to blame her for stuff that I'm definitely going to be all smug about it when she finally shows up.

A half-hour must pass before the elf says, "Perhaps we should go find her. The days may be long, but they aren't endless and are growing shorter."

"I think I saw her at an Orc's store before we stopped by Trilla's," Candy says and points to one of the far ends of the Market. "It was over there!"

"Ah, I know just who you're talking about," Lord Vice says. We follow him to the Orc's stall. The thing about Orcs is, they're really ugly. I have no qualms with saying that. This Orc is no different. His or her store is directly under an overhanging oak tree. A couple of squirrels have seated themselves on a branch just above the Orc's head. Looks like the Orc sells secret maps or something. That's assuming the maps behind the Orc are any indication. Captain Valiant explains that we're looking for Lily and describes her in such vivid detail I can practically see her. Although I could have done without his meticulous description of her breasts, including his in-depth hypothesis—which Panik unnecessarily validates—of how her nipples must look. With such a nauseatingly comprehensive mental picture to work from, the Orc naturally shrugs.

"But I'm sure I saw her here," Candy frowns.

"You probably ate her," Sera says.

"I wouldn't have let that happen," Emma says.

"Oh right, sorry," Sera says, embarrassed.

"It's okay, I still kind of suspect her too."

"Hey!" Candy interrupts. "I'm not the one who tried to eat Victor this morning, am I, missy!"

Candy blushes with Emma's humiliation while Sera shoots silent accusations at me and Jimmy looks as confused as he always does.

"Now, now," Valiant says. "Whatever Victor, Emma, and the Princess choose to do in private is their business." Then looking at me and winking. "Though I do hope for a full report soon…but that's for later. Are you sure, sir Orc, that you haven't seen the maiden I've described?"

Again the Orc shrugs.

"You do know that Orc's only speak Orc, don't you?" Lord Vice says.

"Yeah," Sera says, "that's why the Captain wasted all that time not speaking Orc."

"Lieutenant, what do we say about sarcasm?" Valiant asks.

Sera's shoulders slump. "That it's the basest form of speech. Sorry, sir." Sera then addresses the elf. "But why would you send Lily here?"

"Everyone I know speaks Orc," Lord Vice smirks. His condescension is thick enough to spread on some toast and shove it down his throat. He really is kind of a giant dick. "I'll handle this." The elf approaches the Orc and speaks to it in a language just as ugly as the species it originates from. I'd be worried he was having a stroke if, you know, I cared. The two of them exchange some noises, and at one point the Orc points at me. Who knows why. Finally the elf turns back to us. "He says she left with you, Victor."

"Me? Well that doesn't make sense. I never even came close

to this side of the Market."

"Um, Vic," Jimmy interrupts.

Then Sera teaches him a lesson by interrupting him. "Shush. I want to see how long it takes him to figure it out."

I have no idea what they're talking about, so I just go on with what I was saying. "And furthermore, if she did leave with me, why isn't she currently here. You know what I think this is? I think this Orc is just another racist. Is that it, Orc, do you think all us humans look alike? That must be it because it's not like there are two of me walking around this Market, that's just…Oh." There's a whole hell of a lot of silence all over the place right now. "So, uh, anyone else want to talk, maybe?"

Captain Valiant comes to my rescue once again. "Would you ask the kind vendor which way the two of them went?"

"Of course," says Vice. There are more incomprehensible sounds and even some more pointing. "He says they went North, towards the Forbidden Caves."

"But he pointed West?" Sera says.

"Yes, well that's the direction your friend's double came from."

"Are you sure?"

"Can you suddenly speak Orc?" Sera shakes her head. "Then you'll have to trust me to do my job. Now we best go if we want to catch them."

Sera looks to Captain Valiant, who nods, and we all follow the elf. No matter how reluctantly. We only manage a few steps before Valiant grasps my shoulder, holding me back. "Pretend to admire the wares at this stall."

"Huh?" I say.

"Just do it," and of course I do, though it's kind of hard

considering the vendor is selling exotic insects. And not like butterflies, but giant non-buttered flies. Their faces look like any average fly if that fly had been in a horrible motorcycle accident and then had to have reconstructive facial surgery that went terribly wrong. "Victor, something feels fishy about this thing with Lord Vice, don't you agree?"

"I guess. I mean, my buddy Remy says the squirrels don't trust that elf." Without thinking about it, I glance back to where the squirrels were previously gathered on the oak tree, but they're gone now.

"That settles it. Gumdrop, it's time for Directive 3." Gumdrop mews before jumping from her perch on Valiant's shoulder.

"What's Directive 3?" I ask.

"A search and rescue mission. Gumdrop has been training extensively for just this scenario. She will head west while we head north. She and I will both leave nearly untraceable trails for the other to follow in order to find our way back to one another."

"What if the elf gets suspicious that Gumdrop is missing?"

"Simple," Valiant says. "A cat needs to hunt. That should suffice for a while, at least." Then the Captain gives his full attention to Gumdrop. "You know your mission. It could be that this Lord Vice is speaking true. But if not, you must find Lily and the other Victor's trail. Once you do—or if it becomes certain that they didn't go west—take the proper steps to return to me. Is that understood, soldier?"

Gumdrop mews again. Then she saunters off in the direction the Orc pointed.

"Aren't you worried we might jump again without her?" I ask.

Valiant smiles. "It's a price you pay for *adventure*. Quickly, we must rejoin the group before suspicion grows too great."

* * *

The next hour or so is spent walking. That's one thing you don't hear much about with regard to adventuring around; at least 95% of it is traveling. And as someone who has traveled by boat, space ship, jet-pack, a weird suped-up Lamborghini, a time machine, and a non-descript anti-gravitational field, I can say with complete confidence that walking is by far the worst way to travel. To make matters worse, our little elf guide isn't in any hurry. Which is strange considering one of our group has been kidnapped, and we're racing to slay a dragon that could bring eternal darkness to the Summerlands. But hey, it's not like this is my homeland.

"How much further, Lord Vice?" Captain Valiant asks.

"Not much, Captain," the elf replies.

"Mister Lord Vice, sir?" Candy says.

"Yes, Princess?"

"I was wondering, how did you come to serve Queen Nerissa?"

"It's not much of a tale, I'm afraid. Long ago I ran with a mischievous band of elves, but the monarchs of that little bit of the Summerlands grew tired of our exploits—and, if I'm being honest, so did I—so my merry little band, well…disbanded. And I set out to travel the lands.

"I spent years roaming the Summerlands perfecting a new art of…diplomacy. One day I happened upon Castle Solstice. I'd heard in my travels that there was great political unrest at the heart of the Summerlands. A revolution was brewing. So I took it upon myself to offer the Queen my services. Because the truth is, I'd tired of wandering. I was ready to have a home again.

"The would-be revolutionaries had been refusing to meet with the Queen. They believed her to be a great sorceress who would enchant the fight right out of them. I told Queen Nerissa to send me in her place. Elves are best known for causing a bit of trivial tomfoolery, which I admit might not make me the most trustworthy, but we're far from the most magical of the Fair Folk. And our small stature takes the edge off even the sharpest minds. I would talk the treason out of the hearts of these men and women, and in exchange I only asked for a roof over my head.

"The Queen agreed and a meeting was arranged. We had tea and honeyed biscuits, and at the end of it they were no longer a problem."

"That's quite impressive," Valiant says. "What did you say to convince them of their folly?"

"Oh, who can remember," Lord Vice says.

"You must be a very convincing orator," Panik says, though she seems more interested in studying the surroundings than anything anyone is saying. I can relate.

"I suppose I am," the elf says. "I also make a spectacular cup of tea. Speaking of which, there is a field of the most marvelous flowers just around the bend. The Fortuna. They're perfect for my patented tea."

"I don't think we have time to sit around and sip tea," Sera says.

"On the contrary, my dear. A good cup of tea can sharpen the senses and clear the mind. Just what's needed for a bit of heroism."

"But what about Lily?" I ask.

"Why, she's with you, is she not? Would you hurt her?"

"Me? No. But me? Maybe. That dude's messed up."

"Trust me, the tea won't take but a few moments. Besides, I've noticed the Captain's little pet has wandered off. We wouldn't want the little thing to get lost, would we?" Lord Vice leers at Captain

Valiant.

Captain Valiant betrays no emotion. “Gumdrop is a friend, not a pet. But you’re right, we should give her a few minutes to finish her hunt.”

“Very wise. Let me gather the Fortuna and we’ll be on our way before you know it.” With that, Lord Vice scampers off to pick flowers while the rest of us take a breather. Candy Princess and Emma spread out a blanket and sit themselves down. Jimmy sits too and pulls out a pen and the big Summerlands book. Poor guy can’t stop being dull as dirt. Sera and Valiant keep watch on the elf as he gathers his flowers. And Panik is kneeling near a tree, fingering the dirt around it. So I guess Jimmy is actually duller than dirt. I sit down next to him. I’d rather sit next to Emma and Candy, but I’m trying to respect Emma by keeping my distance. I look back at Panik, who is really going to town around that tree base. I consider asking her what she’s doing, but then I remember how I never understand anything she says, so instead I ask her about more important things: “Hey Panik.”

“Yes,” she says, still molesting the dirt.

“Don’t you have some crazy link with Lily, or something?”

“Lily and I are bonded, in a way.”

“So can’t you tell if we’re close to her or not?”

Panik slides her fingers from out the ground and wipes them on a fallen leaf. “The bond Lily and I share is sexual. Were she having orgasms or being sexual violated, I could track her easily.” I should have asked about the dirt instead. “As is, I can only hypothesize her current situation and location. I suspect she hasn’t come this way. In any sense of the word.”

“Gross,” I say.

Vice returns a minute or two later. He sparks a fire literally with the snap of his fingers. When he notices us all staring at him, he says, "That's about all the magic we elves can muster, I'm afraid."

As we wait for the water to boil I move a little closer to Emma. "How're you doing?"

"Pissed off at myself for letting Candy convince me that we should keep wearing this stupid dress."

"It's not stupid," Candy interrupts. "It's beautiful!"

"Well, it's going to be ruined after today," Emma says. "At least we can take these heels off for a little while. I really wish you'd at least agreed to wearing shoes more suitable for walking."

"Oh, Emma, wearing anything but heels with a dress? Now that is stupid!"

Emma groans. "Dying was less painful than this."

"I'm not that bad," Candy pouts.

"Not that bad!" Emma shouts. "How many times do we have to cover this? You murdered me! You gave me a big cup of poison and then, as I literally puked my guts out, you stood over me and gloated."

"So it's wrong to be proud of the things you do?" Candy wonders.

"When that thing happens to be killing your friends, yes!"

"We're friends?!"

"We *were* friends."

"Awww," Candy frowns.

"Or I thought we were. Until you killed me!"

As Emma and Candy continue on with another one of their internal cat fights, I turn to Jimmy. "Is this what it was like when I would talk to myself?"

"This is a little more coherent, but basically yeah," he says.

All the while, Emma is still reciting her pro/con list of sharing a body with Candy, which is essentially all cons. "And it's not bad enough that I have to share your body and your appetite—which is so gross, by the way—but my best friend can hardly stand to look me in the eye anymore, because they aren't my eyes, they're yours. And I can't even touch my boyfriend because that would mean he'd be touching you, and the thought of that makes my skin crawl. Except that it's your skin and it doesn't crawl at the thought of it. It tingles. Because you're not a proper princess, you slutbag!"

"Emma!" Candy gasps.

"Yeah, I know. Language. What the fuck ever," Emma trails off.

The little Lord Vice watches the whole display with a hint of amusement. "You know what might ease the tension? A nice cup of tea. It'll be ready in only minute."

"Tea does sound nice, doesn't it Candy?" Emma says. "Lord knows we could use a little tension release. But wait, you'd probably rather masturbate while thinking about eating my boyfriend!" Now technically none of our jaws drop, but Jimmy nearly drops his pen as he chokes a little on his own spit, Sera does an awkward grimace, Chalk hides behind his hands, and Valiant and Panik finally appear interested in the conversation. Mostly because where the fuck did that come from? "I, um…I kind of regret saying that last part out loud. It's just that she's so horny all the time and it's really confusing. I don't know how to handle it. I hate it so much in here."

"It's okay, Emma," Candy tells her. "Would you like me to hum you my favorite lullaby? It always makes me feel better when I'm sad."

Tears well in Candy's eyes as Emma sniffles and whispers, "Okay."

"Tea's ready," the elf says as he starts rummaging through one of our packs. "I know there are cups in here somewhere."

Jimmy, who is back to scribbling in that book again, jolts upright. "Uh, Captain, you need to see this."

Captain Valiant goes to Jimmy and peers over his shoulder. His eyes narrow. "A most *valiant* find, spaceboy."

"Um, what should we do about it?" Jimmy asks.

"That's up to you, spaceboy. Your find, your mission."

"But—" Jimmy starts, but Valiant simply holds up his hand. A clear sign he's not interested in Jimmy's protest. "Well, um, uh...Mr. Lord Vice, sir?"

The elf, at this point, has managed to pull out a number of cups from the sack he was digging through and is still in the process of pulling out another. "What is it?"

"Did, uh, did we ever tell you about our friend The Roboracle?"

"No," Vice says. I don't think he cares, but then that's pretty typical for anybody when Jimmy is talking.

"He was this robot—"

"I have no idea what that is," the elf says, giving a little more attention to Jimmy now.

"It's not really important. He was just this friend of ours who was kind of prophetic, which means—"

"I know what it means, boy," Vice snorts.

"Okay," Jimmy says, "but the thing about his prophecies is that they were always pretty vague. Mostly it was stuff about how we were all going to meet our doom. Like the last time we saw him, the last thing he said was...how did it go? Oh yeah, 'even the tiniest of bad habits can spell your doom'. Weird, right?"

The little elf cocks his head and studies Jimmy. "Very."

"And all this time I've been trying to figure out what it means when suddenly it hit me," Jimmy turns my way. "Hey, Vic, what's another word for bad habit?"

I freeze. No one told me there was going to be a pop quiz. Fuck you, Jimmy! Still, I think I see where he's going with this. "Uh…immorality?"

"Huh?" Jimmy says.

"You were just talking about The Roboracle. The Roboracle loved Donna. She was in the Immoral Many. I can follow your line of logic, Jimmy. What else could it be?" Everyone stares at me for a while—probably awed by my genius—when Chalk tugs at my sleeve.

His face reads BAD HABIT = VICE

"And also vice," I say. "A bad habit is a vice, which is something I knew this entire time. Oh hey, that's your name too, elf man!"

Lord Vice is busy pouring tea. "How about we all discuss this over a nice warm drink?"

"Of course," Jimmy says. "But after you."

The elf hesitates. "I'm not thirsty, myself."

Jimmy smiles. "There wouldn't be any other reason you don't want to drink. Like maybe that, let's see," Jimmy begins reciting from the big book of everything, "'the Fortuna derives its name from the bad fortune it cause anyone who consumes the flower. A fast acting poison with no known antidote the Fortuna…' etc. etc."

Vice doesn't say a word. He just drops the tea he was pouring and darts off. But Chalk scoops him up before he can take more than a few steps. Emma and Candy examine the pot of tea.

"Why does everyone try to poison me?" Emma sulks, dumping the tea onto the ground.

Captain Valiant claps Jimmy on the shoulder. "Well done, spaceboy." That should have been my shoulder clap.

"Thanks," Jimmy says. He blushes like a complete tool. What

kind of heroic adventurer blushes? "So what do we do with him now?"

I jump to my feet. "I got this, Jimbo." I'm going to get me one of those shoulder claps, damn it. "Chalk, outline that motherfucker!"

There is a collective "huh?" from everyone. Except Chalk. He just shrugs—the elf still firmly in his grasp—while a big question mark adorns his face.

"A chalk outline," I say. That should clear it up. It doesn't. "Okay, back on Earth, before the world ended, when there was a murder or whatever, cops would do a chalk outline of the body."

"I think they started using tape at some point," Emma says.

"I still don't get it," Sera says.

"I thought it was pretty good," Jimmy says. Which means it was terrible.

I mope. "Look, fine. I just meant to kill him."

Chalk's face transforms from a question mark to a giant YES!

Then to a I'VE GOT THIS!

Chalk squeezes and Lord Vice screams. Actually it's more like a yip. "Wait!" the elf manages. "You still need me."

Valiant gestures for Chalk to loosen the vise grip he's got on Vice. "Explain. Quickly."

"Obviously I know where your friend's double is, where he took the girl," Vice says. "I can take you there."

Captain Valiant chuckles. "Gumdrop already has that covered. She's been on their trail since we left the Market."

"Be that as it may, Captain, where is she now? The Summerlands has an ever shifting topography. Even if she managed to track your friend, without being born of the Fay she may never find her way back to you."

"And why should we trust you?" Sera asks. "You did just try to poison us."

"As difficult as it is to say," someone says. I have no idea who. "And it's even harder for me to admit," the new voice continues both to speak and baffle me with its origins, "Lord Vice speaks true." Seriously, who the fuck said that? Apparently I'm not the only one who's curious, because everyone searches our surroundings for the source of the voice. "Up here!" We all look up to see two squirrels. Perhaps the same two I saw in the tree above the Orc's kiosk. The squirrels scamper down from their branch.

"What is this to you, squirrels?" Vice wonders. He doesn't attempt to hide his annoyance. You'd think a guy on the precipice of being murdered most foul would be a little more contrite.

"Ah, but we aren't squirrels," the squirrel says, completely confusing me. "Don't you recognize the voices of your former compatriots?" The squirrels proceed to pull off their own heads, revealing the faces of two more elves. "Why it is I, Sir Plaught, and my brother in mischief, Master Dee!"

"Hello," the one called Dee waves to everyone. And Lord Vice groans.

"Does anyone else have any idea what's going on?" I ask.

"Our apologies," the elf who introduced himself as Sir Plaught says, "but we're old friends of Vice over there. We've been tracking him for more years than I wish to count."

"I'm flattered," Vice says.

The other elf, Dee, never takes his eyes off Vice. "Don't be. We've come for your head."

"And here I thought you two had no taste for murder," Vice laughs.

"Murder, no," Sir Plaught says, "but we do wish to make amends so that we might finally be allowed home again."

"Yeah, so I still don't know what's going on here," I say. Not that I ever do.

"And what has happened to Gumdrop?" Valiant asks.

"The kitten is fine, good sir," Dee reassures, "or she was when I left her. She's a capable tracker. We had a pleasant exchange and she continued her duty. We can help lead you back to her once we've dealt with Vice here."

"That's Lord Vice to you," Vice spits.

"You are lord over nothing but your name," Plaught says. "Your reckless treachery lost us our home and has kept us from making our gleeful brand of mischief for countless years."

"Nice to see you've grown a pair," Vice sneers. "I imagine that little knobsucking prince tasked you with bringing me to justice."

Dee causally approaches Chalk. "Could you lower him just a bit?" Chalk complies. "Thank you, Mr. Heart." Dee backhands Vice with surprising force. "That prince became king of our little borough, you know. He died years ago, but his bloodline lives on, and the story of your betrayal has blossomed into a flower as poisonous as those you would use to quiet anyone who crosses you."

"Oh, spare me your righteous indignation," Vice says. "That prince was an insufferable whelp and he deserved everything I gave to him."

"And did that girl deserve it too?" Plaught asks. "Did she deserve to be snatched up and murdered?"

"Wait, Lily's dead?!" I start to freak out.

"This was another girl, from long ago," Dee explains.

"There's always collateral damage in schemes of revenge," Vice says.

"Wait," Sera interrupts, "you've been involved with other kidnappings too?"

"Several," Vice says. "I'm quite good at it."

"Can we just kill him already?" Sera asks. "We clearly don't need him."

"Oh please do," Vice says. And as he continues to talk, Chalk gently sets him on the ground. "Because if I have to listen to one more minute of these two chastising me for actually making something of myself I'll kill myse—*" The elf's rant is cut short by Chalk's cartoonish foot squashing him. Elf guts aren't pretty.

Plaught and Dee approach the blob that used to be Vice, while Chalk wipes his foot on the ground. "Master Dee, I fear it's going to be hard to convince the young princess that that bit of goo is Lord Vice."

"And I fear you are correct, Sir Plaught."

Chalk's body slumps as his face reads SORRY

"Fret not, Mr. Heart," Dee says. "It's nothing less than he deserved. Perhaps we can petition the Summer Queen for a letter confirming Vice's demise?"

"Queen Nerissa is our friend," Candy tells them. "We'll ask her to help."

"Much obliged, my lady," Plaught says.

"Yes, but first we must help you all along your quest. It is the least we can do," says Master Dee. "Come. Time waits not even for heroes."

* * *

"So what about the Forbidden Caves?" Emma asks once we're back on the right path.

"I'm afraid that was just a ruse," says Dee.

"But it was Queen Nerissa who sent us to explore them," Candy says. "She wouldn't lie to us…would she?"

"My friend did not mean to insinuate the Summer Queen was

fraudulent," Plaught says. "Only that all the caves in the Summerlands are considered the Forbidden Caves. The current generation is quite the cowardly lot. Instead of going on adventures, they fabricate tales. Sadly, our journeys have shown that all of these Forbidden Caves are nothing but holes in mountains."

"But what about Hophopjoojoo?" I ask.

"Haupuehuehu?" Dee wonders. "Long dead. This is well known on the borders of the Summerlands, for that's where the poor ice dragon banished himself to."

"Banished himself?" Jimmy says.

"Indeed. While there are many tales of sorcery and wars to defeat the Breath of Winter—and they might be true enough—in the end the miserable creature took his own life. For he froze all those who came near. Loneliness was his downfall."

"How are you so certain of this?" Captain Valiant asks.

"Why he left a note, naturally," Plaught says.

"Very practical," Panik says. I'd forgotten she was still here, she's been so busy molesting the plant life she hasn't been very present. But I have more important things on my mind.

"You mean there won't be any dragon slaying?" I say.

"Most dragons are quite friendly," Dee says.

"My blade will not drink from the icy heart of hellfire?" I whisper.

"Sorry, sweetie," Emma tries to comfort me, but she still doesn't want to touch me, or even come too close, so it's kind of hollow. I do my sad walk for a while, which turns out is pretty similar to my regular walk because walking is soul crushing and stupid. I can't stress that enough, really. So I don't object when Plaught and Dee eventually jerk us to a halt.

"Shh," one of them says—though I can't tell which—and

points to a clearing. I'm not sure what the big deal is. All I can see is a white horse.

That's when Candy's eyes nearly burst out of her face. "HOLY FUCK A UNICORN!!!!" Before anyone can react, she races towards the thing.

"Did Candy just say fuck?" Jimmy asks.

"I think Emma must be a bad influence in her," I say.

"This could be bad," Dee says. Sir Plaught is already in a dead sprint after Candy. Considering his short legs, he moves shockingly fast. Dee starts running too. The rest of us share a befuddled look or two before deciding we should follow suit.

Ultimately it's a waste of time and energy. We catch up to Candy and the elves, and Candy is gushing some nonsense to the unicorn, who appears to bow slightly. Plaught keeps his distance while stammering an apology for some perceived transgression. "P-pardon our intrusion, Sir Unicorn."

The unicorn raises his head, making note of all the new visitors. "Fret not, elf, I have no business with you . And I would never dare steal from Confectionary royalty."

"You know who I am?" Candy says, awestruck.

"Naturally," the unicorn says. "Word of your arrival spread rapidly. I must say I'm jealous of all your…company."

Jimmy steps forward, though he almost falls doing so. "Um, Mr. Unicorn?"

"Yes, child?"

"This book I have, it says that your horn can heal all manners of illness and injury. Is that true?"

"Perhaps." Then the unicorn looks at Sera. "What might you be? You smell like creation. An evening with you must be divine." Sera blushes, which means her entire face—hair and eyes included—

burn bright pink. "And my envy for you, my sweet lady, grows evermore," the unicorn says to Candy.

"Okay," I say. "As fascinating as this is, I have a bone to pick with myself and this is getting us nowhere. So unless this unicorn is really me in disguise, we're wasting time."

"Victor, don't be rude!" Candy scolds.

"It's quite alright, I have business of my own to conduct," the unicorn says. "I bid you farewell." This time the unicorn definitely does bow, and Candy returns in kind with a curtsey.

"Yes, let's be on our way," Dee says. Both he and Plaught are pushing us to leave the unicorn alone—and I mean literally pushing us—which is about as effective as a light breeze. Once we've left the unicorn far behind Dee collapses to the ground. "That was too close."

"What's the big deal?" Emma asks.

"The big deal is that there is no more dangerous creature in all the Summerlands than the Unicorn."

"Nonsense," Candy says. "He was a perfect gentleman."

"I didn't like the way he flirted with me," Sera says.

"Trust me, dear lady, he wasn't flirting," Plaught tells her. "His tastes are much more literal than that."

"I once made love to a woman dressed as a unicorn," Panik says. The elves are the only ones that react at all—the rest of us are used to this stuff—and even they don't look too shocked. Probably because of the Fairies. They're pretty kinky. "She claimed she was an angel, but she was actually a clone genetically modeled after the second coming of the false goddess of beauty. She said the horn was from an actual unicorn and would heal whatever ailed me. What ailed me was a lack of tantric energies, and her use of the horn was expert in its precision. So perhaps she spoke true on that."

Captain Valiant applauds. "Another *valiant* tale, Miss Panik."

"Thank you, Captain."

Valiant then holds up one hand, a clear indicator to halt our tedious march. "Gumdrop has been here."

"Did you not believe we were leading you the right way?" Dee asks.

"Of course they didn't," Plaught says. "The only other elf they knew led them astray and attempted murder on their very persons."

"A fair point, Sir Plaught."

"I apologize for the doubt," Valiant says, "but you were true to your word, so I offer gratitude on behalf of us all. Our quest is not yours, however. No need to risk your lives further." The two elves huddle up, exchanging whispers and whatnot.

"As if any Victor could ever be competent enough to be a real threat," Sera says.

"Leiutenant?"

"Sorry, sir."

"Not to me, to Victor."

Sera sighs. "Sorry, Victor. Your recklessness has gotten us in plenty of trouble before. I have no problem perceiving you as a legitimate threat."

"Thanks," I say. That was one of the nicest thing anyone's ever said to me.

The elves finish up their conference and Plaught says, "Master Dee and I have decided to stay the course. The first time that scoundrel Vice kidnapped a girl, we abandoned the hunt prior to the climax and we've spent the remaining years trying to set it right. Never again."

"Besides, our petition to the Summer Queen will lack weight without the lot of you," Dee says.

Plaught nods. "Indeed."

* * *

After picking up Gumdrop's trail, Captain Valiant returns to his rightful place at the head of our search party. His tracking skills are so extraordinary that I have no idea what he's doing. At one point the action really picks up when something jumps on my back. "I'll kill you!" I scream and draw my sword. But as I twirl around I find nothing. So it's an invisible foe I face. "Show yourself, coward!"

Jimmy plucks something from my back and hands it to me. "Vic, it was just a leaf."

I examine the culprit, then drop it to the earth. "A worthy adversary, but no match for my sword." I stab the leaf heroically. "Your life force feeds my blade." It's not nearly as satisfying as I imagined dragon slaying would be.

"Was that really necessary?" Panik asks.

"Oh, I'm sorry," I say, picking the mangled leaf up and offering it to her. "Did you want to have sex with it?"

"Foliage makes for a poor sexual partner," Panik says, and I toss the leaf back to the ground.

"I thought the leaf had it coming," Jimmy says.

"Of course it did," I say. "Also, no one cares what you think."

With the leaf vanquished I try my best to stay focused on the task at hand. Even if that task is boring as fuck. This plan has a few fatal flaws, however. The first being that Captain Valiant's tracking skills are too incredible. I can't, hard as I try, follow how he's doing it. The second flaw is that I've made this trek before. Not this exact one, of course, but I've done the whole wandering-through-the-woods-in-search-of-a-kidnapped-girl thing. The first time it was Emma who had been nabbed by Jimmy as some sort of retribution for never calling him by his actual name. A bullshit excuse if I ever heard one. Emma doesn't mind that I never call her Gisela. She actually prefers it. Same with Chalk. Last time I called him George he threatened to kill me…okay that's a lie, but he did have a shotgun at the time and declared his name to be Chalk in epic action hero fashion. Jimmy's way too sensitive. Granted, we also killed his brother right in front of him and later let him drown in a flood that may or may not have been piss—and when I say may or may not, I mean it definitely was—but that's hardly a good excuse to have a hissy fit. In any case, this situation isn't that much different from that situation. We're off to rescue another kidnap victim, which I've done three times before, while marching through the forest. And if you count the Candy Jungle—and why not, it's just a slightly more exotic forest—this is at least my third time doing that too. And the thing is, they always end in death and fire. Believe it or not, that all gets kind of old after a while. That and we're running out of fodder. Sure, there's the elves. And they'll definitely be the first I throw to the wolves if I get the chance. But I can't count on that. I don't want the others to die. Not even Jimmy. If Emma ever gets free from Candy, I'll be spending a lot of time in Hell again. That place is bad enough with the Devil always demanding Star Wars cosplay and shoving fresh broccoli in my face. I don't need Jimmy tagging along too. I guess I wouldn't be too upset if Panik died, but Lily might be, so…

"Hey," Emma grabs me. "Is there a reason you were about to walk into that tree?"

I shake off the remnants of the daze that had hold of me only to find myself face to face with a redwood. Except it's not a redwood. It's just the closest approximation I can come up with for such a large tree. I'm not a fan of the slightly askew flora and fauna we keep running into. "Sorry, I was just thinking about whom here is most expendable."

"Why?" Emma does her best to sound exacerbated, but there's more than a hint of amusement in her voice.

I don't have a great answer, though. "The train of thought makes unexpected stops."

"Was is me?" Jimmy asks. I didn't notice him standing behind me.

"Don't flatter yourself," I say. "It's obviously the elves—"

"What was that?" one of the elves asks from up ahead. I can't really tell them apart when they aren't facing me.

"Oh, nothing," I shout back before lowering my voice to readdress Jimmy. "If anything, you're the least expendable. And it's not because you can build cool shit. That's nice and all, but Sera can do that too. It's because the idea of spending an eternity down in Hell with you is unbearable."

Jimmy's reaction is classic Jimmy. He grins like an idiot. "So what I'm hearing is I'm the least expendable. Thanks!"

"Did you just stop listening after that?"

"No, I also heard that I build cool stuff. Point is, you don't want me to die."

"Because you annoy me."

"I'll take it."

"You know, Jimmy, I'd hoped that having a girlfriend would give you more self-esteem and, more than that, I hoped it would lead you to telling me all the kinky stuff Sera's into in bed."

"Oh, well there is this one thing she does that—"

Sera whips around with such violent force I momentarily fear for the safety of my genitals. "Don't. You. DARE!" Her hair flows molten red, her eyes a fierce orange. I can almost feel the heat.

"Uh, sorry," is all Jimmy can manage. Once Sera settles down Jimmy whispers, "I'll tell you later."

"You better," I say.

Because anything that makes Sera that glowy must be pretty juicy.

* * *

Our journey continues, one boring step after another. But something shifts in the air. At first it's subtle. A slight breeze that soothes the beads of sweat on my brow. But a few minutes later the temperature plummets at least 15 degrees and, without warning, night falls across the Summerlands as if the sun were controlled by a light switch.

The elves come to a stop. Through the darkness I can only just make out their concern, but now I have an even more difficult time telling the two apart. "Night should not have come for several more hours," one of them says.

"Perhaps, Sir Plaught, we should make camp and continue on in the morning," Dee says.

"But when might that be, Master Dee?"

Captain Valiant cuts their exchange short. "You two may make camp if you wish, but we'll continue on the path. Gumdrop's trail is fresh now. I won't let it go cold."

"Understood," Plaught says. "But we must be careful. These woods hold many dangers in the dark."

We march for another half mile or so when Valiant silently commands us to stop. At first I don't understand why, but then I hear a soft rustling in the bushes up ahead. I unsheathe my sword. Captain Valiant motions me forward and the two of us creep up on the bush. Something howls in the distance. It's no animal I've ever heard before. I raise my sword, hilt just above my head, the blade pointed down ready to skewer anything that moves. Just as I'm about strike, the bush makes a familiar noise. It meows. Captain Valiant laughs and kneels as Gumdrop bursts from the bush and leaps onto his shoulder.

"Well done," Valiant says. Gumdrop purrs and drapes herself around his neck like a living scarf. "Are they nearby?" I don't expect Gumdrop to respond. Not so much because she's a cat, but because she looks to be sleeping already. Yet her tail twitches before pointing toward a barely visible break in the woods. Valiant turns back to the rest of the group. "You heard Gumdrop, *adventure* is at the end of that trail."

* * *

The new trail is much harder to follow than the last. Not just because it's dark, but because it's so overgrown that it is hardly a trail at all. I know Robert Frost was all about taking the road less traveled, but I'm starting to realize he must have been a real jackass because what's so character building about getting repeatedly smacked in the face by errant branches. Seriously, I don't know how many I run into. I could probably ask Candy, though, since every single one has led to a bout of cussing that's had her wagging her finger at me mouthing "language". To make matters worse, I could swear that the temperature drops a full degree with every dozen or so steps we take. It's not long before the air around us is rhythmically white with the steam of our individual breaths. None of us are dressed for this kind of weather, and we all instinctively hug ourselves, rubbing our arms for any friction we can get. Except for Sera, she doesn't seem bothered. Emma and Candy, however, practically shiver out of their dress. I wrap my arm around them, but Emma pulls away.

I try again. "You're freezing."

The results are the same. "I'll b-b-be f-f-fine."

"But he's so w-w-warm," Candy says. If Emma responds, it's not out loud. All she does is pick up their pace to get away from me.

"Sera," I say, "grab them." She looks confused at first, but I point to Candy and Emma and Sera snatches their wrist.

"Why am I doing this?" Sera wonders, but she figures it out quick enough. "Oh jeez, you're freezing." Sera drapes her arm around Candy and Emma. Her disdain for Candy is evident, but so is her love for Emma. Because as Emma tries to pull away, Sera's hold acts like a Chinese finger trap. The more Emma struggles the tighter it becomes until, finally, Emma and Candy melt into her warmth. And I know I shouldn't be, but I'm jealous that Emma won't allow me to be that close. I'm so caught up in my selfish woes that I don't even notice the dark browns and greens fading into dark whites until I feel a familiar crunch under my feet.

"Oh my," one of the elves says. "It hasn't snowed in the Summerlands since—"

"Since Haupuehuehu, Master Dee," Plaught says. I'm glad they insist on calling each other by name all the time.

"I thought Haupuehuehu was dead," Sera says, Emma and Candy still nuzzled against her.

"He is, I assure you," Plaught tells her.

"Although he wouldn't be the first thing to resurrect in the Summerlands," says Dee.

"So I might get to slay a dragon after all?" I ask. I don't bother waiting for an answer before drawing my sword. "Finally, some good news!"

Plaught looks at me, scratching his head. "Have you ever slain a dragon before?"

"No, but I've killed zombies and clowns and gross roadside monsters. It can't be that different. Unless…how big are dragons again?"

"The largest recorded dragon was about 200 cubits," Jimmy says. Everyone stares at him. "Uh, it was in the book."

"Well, what the fuck is a cubit?" Because what kind of stupid measurement is that?

"I think Noah's Arc was supposed to be 300 cubits," Jimmy informs me.

"So dragons are 2/3rds the size of something meant to be capable of housing two of every living creature," I say.

"At least the biggest one the book mentions."

"Although Haupuehuehu was likely bigger than that," Dee says.

"Huh," I say. "Well, I'm out!" I shove the sword at Jimmy.

"I don't want it," he protests.

"Come on, I'm sure that book says how to kill them."

"Just grow a pair, Victor," Sera says.

"A pair of what? Bazooka arms?!"

"Now, Victor," Captain Valiant interjects, "would you really want to miss out on this opportunity. Imagine the tales that will be told about you across these Summerlands."

"Tales? Hey elves, will minstrels write songs about my epic slaying of dragons?" The two elves look from me to each other back to me and then shrug. "Good enough for me. Let's get this done." I take the lead briefly before I realize something important. "I still don't know where we're going, so someone else better lead the way." And since chances are the first couple in line will be dragoned to death… "Preferably the elves."

I fall back to the middle of the pack and Panik pulls up beside me. "You realize the snow is just as likely a weather anomaly as it is the rebirth of an ancient ice dragon, don't you?"

"He'll claim he killed a dragon no matter what," Sera says. I nod. What can I say, she knows me pretty well.

* * *

The trail dead-ends at a cave. Of course it does. At least outside we have starlight and a moon to light our way. Inside that's unlikely. And that little asshole Lord Vice didn't pack any lanterns or candles. Nor did he have any of us buy some at the Market. Why would he? He didn't plan on actually taking us into any caves. On the plus side, still no sign of cruise-liner sized dragons, but there is a biting winter wind sprinkled with snowflakes emanating from the mouth of the cave. It must be like a wind tunnel in there, which makes me think the odds of this being a weather anomaly less likely. Unless there are big old storm clouds in that cave. I guess that's not entirely crazy considering Castle Solstice is a mountain with sunshine and meadows inside.

"Are we, uh, just going in there blind?" I ask.

Captain Valiant studies the surroundings, picking at random twigs and then tossing them aside. "I don't believe we have much choice. It's only getting colder and I fear for Lily's safety. Unfortunately all the kindling around is too damp from the snow for makeshift torches. Gumdrop has excellent night vision. We'll have to count on her."

"I also see much better in the dark," Panik says. "A side-effect from copulating with demi-gods."

"And, I mean," Sera starts, "I can glow a little. But it wears me out pretty fast if I glow too bright."

Suddenly a bright light streaks across my face. "An' I can 'elp too." It's Chessy, the mildly bitchy, fairy-hating sprite.

"Sup, Chessy!" I greet her with more enthusiasm than she

deserves.

“Remem’er my name do yeh? Too bad yeh dinna remem’er a light or two. Do yeh ever come prepared for anyt’ing?”

“Occasionally,” I say.

“What are you doing here?” Emma asks.

“Told yeh I’m ‘ere to ‘elp.”

“But I thought it was too dangerous for you to come with us?”

“Only to leave the forests, missus.”

“That cave isn’t the forest,” I say.

“No it ain’t. But I started t’inking ‘ow if I wanna know what ‘appened to Crim I couldna very well trust in you. An’ it looks like I was right. Now come on wit yeh, I’ll guide yeh where yeh need ta go.”

I assume everyone else managed to follow that, but I sure didn’t. All I can do is nod and go along with it as we follow Chessy into the mouth of Winter.

* * *

Even with Chessy’s and Sera’s glow in the dark abilities, and Panik’s weird sex vision, it’s still rough going. Cold too. Like my-fingers-might-fall-off cold. That’s not something conducive to handling a sword, so I walk up behind Sera and place my hands on her face.

She shrieks. “What the fuck are you doing? Your hands are freezing!”

“I know,” I say. “I’m warming them up.”

She shakes my hands off. “Well stop it.”

“But I need warm hands in case I have to stab things.”

“I don’t care.”

Captain Valiant backs me up, though. “Lieutenant, Victor is correct.”

Sera takes a deep breath and exhales slowly. “Fine.”

“Can I put my hands under your shirt?” I ask.

Sera says, “What?!” at the same time Emma says, “Excuse me?!”

“I won’t grab your boobs or anything. It’s just that it’s probably a lot warmer under your shirt.”

“No,” Sera says.

“Jimmy, can’t you talk some sense into your girlfriend?”

“Um, well,” Jimmy falls over his words as usual. “You are pretty warm and—”

Sera shoots Jimmy the most profoundly dirty look I’ve ever seen. And not sexy dirty, but more I’m going to bury you in the ground with actual dirt, dirty. You know, the looks she usually reserves for me.

Jimmy drops his gaze so far down I think he might be trying to do the job for Sera with only his eyes as a shovel. I’m rooting for him, for once. “Vic, you shouldn’t try to feel Sera up.”

Candy, who is still leaning against Sera, says, “You can put your hands under our dress to keep them warm.”

“He absolutely cannot,” Emma says.

“Oh, sorry Victor, Emma says no,” Candy pushes out her bottom lip in an embellished pout.

“It’s cool, Sera’s face is pretty nice,” I tell her, and Sera groans.

Besides keeping my hands warm, following Sera around like this offers another benefit. I don’t have to worry about running into most of the obstacles the cave throws at us. Like the giant icicles hanging from the ceiling. Some of them almost reach the ground. I do, however, have to worry about the patches of ice under our feet. Sera slips a few times, almost falling. At one point I manage to hold her up by her face. But does she thank me? Nope. Almost everyone is struggling to stay on their feet, causing the elves to give us all a wide berth so as not to be crushed should any of us tumble. Chalk has fallen on his backside so often that he's given up on standing and is now sliding around on his back. Even Captain Valiant's walk is less valiant than usual, though Gumdrop shows no sign of concern wrapped around his neck. Panik and Chessy are the only ones who have no difficulty navigating the terrain.

Occasionally we come across a place where the cave branches off into two or three directions, but it's never difficult to choose which way to go. It's simple. We follow the wind and the snow. I try to tell everyone that I, being me, am fairly certain that the other me is enough like me to not want to confront a dragon, but they don't listen. Because apparently we're determined to die. But hey, at least I won't have to die alone.

Making our way down one the cave branches the mini snowstorm grows to near blizzard levels. Then comes an ear piercing shriek. An echo that I'm afraid might never end. I remove my hands from Sera's face and draw my sword yet again. Not that holding it is all that easy when I can't stop shaking. The cold is so deep and penetrating that my bones ache from the violation. I'm probably not the only one feeling a little violated, either. Candy and Emma embrace Sera so tightly I'm convinced they're trying to push inside her body to escape the chill—in Emma's case that's probably more true than not—but I think I see even Sera tremble. I want to tell them to stay back, but the cold seems to have frozen my lungs in place during my last exhale. Breathing is now a luxury, I guess.

The end of our tunnel is in sight, and for a moment I think we might mercifully be headed back outside because there's so much light up ahead. We've probably been in here long enough for the sun to rise again over the Summerlands.

Except it's not light at all, only white. Our little tunnel opens into a massive cyclone of white, fluffy death. I can't see more than an inch in front of me and I'm worried my sword is about to shatter, so I do the only sensible thing. I charge into the flurry.

It's a decision I instantly regret. It feels like I've been punched in the stomach while every inch of my skin is being stung by wasps. Somehow I keep my footing and continue towards the source. There's another mind-melting scream. The only good thing about it is that it's close, so one way or the other this will end soon.

I don't know how far I've gone when something grasps my shoulder. My mind yells at my body to turn and kill whatever it is, but my body is too bogged down in what I can only assume is the onset of hypothermia. For once that works out for the best, though, otherwise Jimmy would have been sliced in two. Jimmy smiles through chattering teeth and, maybe for the first time ever, I'm glad to have him tag along.

Not that his presence makes the going any easier. Each step is more difficult than the last. Jimmy and I lose traction more than once. So much so that eventually I'm unable to force myself back to my feet. I can't even crawl and hold on to the sword at the same time. Jimmy notices and starts pushing me. The ice makes that easy enough, but even ice sliding becomes a chore as Jimmy loses his strength. Just when I think we're done for, Jimmy gives one final shove and we break through the blizzard.

Jimmy collapses. I'd do the same if I weren't already on the ground. Part of my thinks I must have died—or at least be on the verge of death—because the air is astonishingly warm. I'm content to let myself forget my mission, but another of those screeches shatters my contentment with ear-piercing authority. I blink a few times to regain my bearings. So far I don't see any dragon, but my eyes have only just begun adjusting to a world with color again and everything looks like a lot of earthy smudges. What I can make out is pretty phenomenal, though. We're actually inside a living dome of ice and snow. I follow it—attempting to regain some manner of focus as I do—from the wall we broke through, up to the ceiling, until I find its origin. A thin tornado that ends—or rather starts—in the mouth of a dragon.

I would be terrified, except this dragon isn't the size of an aircraft carrier. It's not even the size of a rowboat. It's not really nautical at all. It can't be any larger than a dog. And not even a big dog. Maybe it's as big as Lassie, but I'm not even sure about that. Looks like I finally caught a break. I push myself to my feet, raise the sword above my head, and resume my charge. I'm about to strike when the dragon stop breathing its winter tornado, taking note of me for the first time. It looks at me and then to my sword and does something I never expected. It starts to tremble. And the killer inside me melts just as Jimmy catches up.

"Here," I hand Jimmy the sword, "you do it."

Jimmy stares at the sword, unsure at first. But he takes it and readies for the death blow. As Jimmy puts the blade in motion, the dragon cowers away and I snatch Jimmy's arm.

"You were actually going to do it?" I ask.

"Well, yeah I guess," Jimmy says.

"But look, it's adorable."

"But—"

"But nothing, Jimmy! We don't go around killing cute little dragons." Then I hold out my hand to the dragon. "Come on, buddy, it's okay." The little guy cautiously approaches and sniffs the hand I've offered. His breath is chilly, but tolerable. I take a chance and pat his head. The dragon squeaks, flaps his little wings and lashes his tail back and forth. I think we're friends now.

"Hey, Vic," Jimmy says. "The blizzard is dying off."

"Obviously," I say. "Frosty isn't doing his blizzard breath thing."

"Frosty?"

"Yeah. He's a snow dragon. What else would his name be?"

Jimmy thinks about it for a minute, then shrugs. "Hey, Vic?"

"Jesus. What, Jimmy?!"

"Where's all the light in here coming from?"

"Um," I look all around the cavern again. "Huh, I have no idea." Frosty nudges my leg and claws the ground. "What's that, Frosty? The ground?" I cup my hands to my eyes before putting them flush to the floor, trying my best to block out any light. Sure enough, the ground is glowing. It's also a little too warm. Wonder what that's about?

As I pull myself back to my feet I'm attacked from behind. But it's just Emma and Candy. I guess they're happy I made it through the storm, but it's less than a minute before Emma pulls back again.

"Stop doing stuff like that!" she shoves me back to the ground. I'm seriously considering not bothering to get up again. I've expended entirely too much energy over the last several minutes trying to stand, and this ground is made of warm. I could use some warm. But Emma offers me Candy's hand, and she's been so stingy with physical contact that I'd hate to rebuke her.

"Sorry," I brush off my pants, more from habit than actual need. "But I probably won't."

She sighs. "I know."

Chalk claps his hands to get everyone's attention. DRAGON! his face reads.

"Oh yeah," I tell them. "This is Frosty. He's pretty cool."

Frosty hides behind me, peeking out from behind my legs periodically. "Don't worry, they won't hurt you." Frosty steps out from his hiding spot and bows, offering his head to anyone who wants to introduce themselves. Gumdrop is the first to make a move. She bounces off Captain Valiant's shoulder, landing right in Frosty's face. He jumps back slightly. The two size each other up for a second or two. Then Gumdrops nuzzles Frosty's snout. Frosty flaps his wings and does a little dance. He lowers his head to the ground and Gumdrop takes that as an invitation to jump on to Frosty's back. After that, the rest of the group take turns introducing themselves to the dragon.

"So this little guy was responsible for that huge blizzard?" Sera asks.

"Yeah," Jimmy says. "You should have seen him in action. It was something else."

Panik is busy acquainting herself to Frosty, scratching his chin. "A Storm Dragon, how fascinating." Frosty clearly loves all the new found attention, so when Panik loses interest and instead goes to caress the sky he deflates like an untied balloon. "The temperature is rising."

"Of course it is," Sera says. "We're no longer surrounded by snow."

Frosty goes back to clawing at the ground. This doesn't go unnoticed by Panik. She touches the tips of her finger to the dirt and drags them in a zigzag pattern. "We should leave now."

This is a realization that comes about 20 seconds too late. It begins with a soft rumble and grows to an earth shattering roar. And I mean literally earth shattering. The ground isn't just quaking, it's ripping itself apart. Chunks of rock fall from the sky causing us all to dive every which way to avoid a good skull crushing. We're all scattered throughout the cavern when a fissure opens, splitting the cave in half. Gumdrop almost falls in, but Frosty snatch her by the scruff of the neck. The shaking dies off. Jimmy, the elves, and I find ourselves on one side of the great divide, with everyone else on the other.

"What now?" I ask.

"Don't worry, Victor," Valiant says. "We'll find a way across. Just hold tight." Then he peers into the fracture. "On second thought, perhaps you should run." He dives out of the way as fire erupts from the fissure. Only it's not just fire. It's alive and it's not alone. One of the flame beasts lands nearly on top of Captain Valiant. Sera bulrushes it, shoving it back towards the pit. But the thing holds its ground and begins its attack anew. That's when Frosty flies into action—albeit it a clumsy flight—and breathes snowy death at the fire thing. It screams something fierce, but vanishes.

Then a couple of them notice Jimmy and me standing around like a couple of idiots who stand around like a couple of idiots. (Impressive word play.) I thought I told you to shut up back in Infinite City!

Jimmy is looking at me like he always looks at me. Obnoxiously. So I look back at him like I always do. Reluctantly. Your move, Jimmy. That's when I feel the heat and remember the fire monsters blazing towards us.

"Run!" The Captain commands.

"But—" Jimmy and I say together. Before I can let the shame of sharing a word with Jimmy snowball into a full blown sentence, Panik cuts us off.

"But nothing. We have a star child and Storm Dragon to protect us. Just go."

Sir Plaught tugs at my pants. "We would do well to listen to them."

"With haste!" Dee agrees, him pulling at Jimmy. With the flame monsters closing in, we don't have much of a choice. We dart for the only passageway we see.

"What are those things?" Jimmy asks.

"Who cares," I yell at him.

"I can't be curious?"

"Not when we're running for our lives."

"I think," Dee says. "Could I be correct, Sir Plaught, in thinking those are Feverencies?"

"Those are meant to be myths, Master Dee," Plaught explains.

"The heat I'm feeling is quite real, however."

"An astute observation, Dee."

"Thank you, Plaught."

"So wait, you guys believe in myths?" Jimmy asks. Because this is such a great time for casual conversation.

"Who cares!" I yell once again as the heat around me intensifies. Something scorches my back and instinctively I whirl around, slashing with my sword. I don't expect very impressive results, but I'm pleasantly surprised when the fever monster slices in half and turns to cinder.

"Whoa, that was sweet," Jimmy says. "Can I try?"

"You want me to give you my fire killing weapon?" Jimmy must be out of his mind. Then again, looking at the fire pouring down the tunnel… "You know what, buddy? Have a blast." I toss him the blade and go back to running for my life.

I turn back once to see Jimmy swing the sword with an insane sort of glee, extinguishing all the fire coming down our path. He's having the time of his life. I sigh. Why couldn't that be me? To make matters worse, as I'm checking on Jimmy, showing moderate concern for his safety, I trip and fall, sliding down a pitch black something into who the hell knows what. Thanks a lot, Jimmy.

I'm not going to lie; I'm pretty boned at this point. I have no idea where I am, and as much as I hated being chased by fire, it did provide a nice guiding light. Maybe I'll just lay here and rest my eyes. I'm sure everything will work out fine.

"What are yeh doin' yeh lazy sot!" My eyes snap open to find Chessy floating in front of me.

"Oh hey! How'd you get past the Frequencies?" I don't think Chessy understands, so I clarify. "Those fire things."

"They're Feverencies, not Frequencies—"

"I don't actually care."

"An' I'm tiny an' can fly an' I t'ought yeh migh' need a guide. What wit how useless yeh are."

"Good call."

"Should I lead yeh back to 'elp yer friend?"

"Is there still homicidal fire back there?"

"Yes."

"Jimmy can handle it. Let's go the other way. Because if I know myself, and I think I do, I probably went that way too."

"Yer a coward."

"I prefer the term 'pragmatist'."

"I don' care what yeh wanna call it, I jus' wanna find Crim."

"Great, stop bitching and start leading." Chessy offers me an honest-to-god harrumph, but she does start leading. She doesn't stop bitching, though. At least I think that's what she's doing. Her accent gets so thick that I can't really follow. Not that I was doing a great job before, so I keep nodding and saying "uh-huh" over and over again. I do such a good job of ignoring her, that I don't even notice when she stops talking. But I do notice when she smacks me in the face. She packs more punch than someone of her size should be able to.

"What was that for?" I ask.

"Shush!"

"I wasn't saying anything until you slapped me."

"Tha's cause yeh werenna lisnen ta me. I tol' yeh ta stop. There's a light up a'ead."

"I swear, you're accent is getting worse…"

"Would yeh lis'en ta me?"

"I'm trying!"

"Is that me I hear," my own voice echoes towards me.

Chessy buries her face in her hands. "Yeh're 'opeless."

"Hey, don't be so hard on yourself," I tell Chessy. "You got me where I need to go. I'm pretty sure I'm right at the end of this tunnel. Later!" I continue on towards my own voice.

"What abou' the rest o' yer group?" Chessy calls from behind.

"I have no idea what you're saying," I yell back without stopping.

* * *

The tunnel ends in another cavern, though it's not nearly as massive and impressive as Frosty's. This one is also well lit, but the source is much easier to decipher. There are dozens of candles and lanterns strewn about. And at the far end of the room is the other me, Victor3, holding some sort of contraption. His shadow paints the wall so ominously I'm almost certain that were I to throw a rock at it, the shadow would shatter into an unkindness of ravens that would peck my eyes out. And that's kind of awesome…if I could ignore my eyes being pecked out. Then again, there are two of me, so if they peck the right ones eyes out, I wouldn't mind. Oh yeah, and Lily is back there too, propped against the back wall looking as bored as I've ever seen.

I nod to her. "Sup."

"Took you long enough," she says.

"Yes," Victor3 says. "I too expected you sooner."

"Then why did you have that elf lead us in the opposite direction?" I ask. "Wait, no. I've got way more important questions to ask first."

"Ask away," I say.

"Did you set up the lighting to make that crazy menacing shadow, or what that just a happy accident?" That causes me to pause momentarily. "Wait…did I already ask that?"

Lily stands up. "No idea, but it's totally a set up. He made me spend, like, an hour getting it just right."

"You did a good job," I tell her.

"Thanks."

"That's what you wanted to ask? Again?" the other me wonders.

"Not the only thing, there's also the matter of—" But Jimmy chooses that moment to stumble into the cavern, running right into me. Plaught and Dee are right on his heels. He's covered in soot and dripping sweat.

"Sorry, Vic. Just dealing with the last," he stops as a final bout of flame explodes into the room, and Jimmy slashes it to ash. He takes a second to catch his breath. "Just dealing with the last Feverency."

"You interrupted a very important conversation, Jimmy."

"Yeah, my bad. I just…Vic watch out!" With my attention on Jimmy I don't notice Victor3 raise whatever he's holding and fire it. A swirling black ball emerges from its barrel, heading straight for me. Jimmy shoves me to the ground just as the blackness is about to hit me. It misses me, but Jimmy isn't so lucky. His eyes roll back into his head as he collapses beside me.

* * *

"Jimmy," I shake him lightly and his eye pop open.

"What happened?" he asks.

"Oh," I say, surprised that he's not dead. Let alone so easily roused. "Nothing, apparently. Except for you being a huge drama queen."

Victor3 is still in the same spot—probably doesn't want all of Lily's hard lighting work to go to waste—smacking the weapon he just fired. Then he tosses it aside. "That was disappointing. I was really hoping it would do…well, something. And I see you've brought more elves to our little gathering."

Plaught steps forward. "Allow me to introduce ourselves. I am Sir Plaught, and this is Master Dee." Dee waves at the mention of his name.

"At least you have manners," Victor3 says. "I've been saying for so long that in serious situations like these we must never lose our manners."

"It's true," Lily says. "He literally won't stop saying stuff like that. I have no idea what's wrong with him."

"Nothing's wrong with me!"

"They're in 'ere," Chessy says, zooming into the room. Everyone else is close behind, including Frosty.

"Why does this keep happening?" Victor3 mumbles, but the acoustics of the cave carry the sound well enough for me to hear.

"So what now?" Sera asks. "Can we just kill him."

Panik shakes her head. "We might need him to set dimensional gravity back to the status quo. Lily, are you alright?"

"I'm fine," Lily says. "I think he was trying to Stockholm's Syndrome me. But he's really bad at it."

"I'm not bad at it," Victor3 says. "You're a bad captive. And I didn't want you, I wanted Gisela. But that worthless elf failed me.

Or…maybe not. I don't see her here."

"I'm here," Emma says.

"And you are?"

"Em…uh, Gisela."

"No, you're not."

"Seriously," Lily interject, "who the fuck is Gisela?"

"Don't worry about it," I say. "We've got more important things to discuss."

"Finally!" Victor3 says. "Someone willing to take this serious situation seriously!"

"Absolutely. So let's get down to business. This is really important, and I've been thinking about this for a long time now. Do you still have our wallet?"

Victor3 loses his shit. "You can't be serious!"

"I'm very serious."

Victor3 reaches into his pocket. "This wallet?! Is this what you want? Take it!" He throws it at me.

Unsurprisingly, I catch it because I'm cool like that. "Dude, thanks!"

"Hey, is that the wallet I gave you when we were, like, fourteen?" Lily asks.

I nod.

"Okay, what's so great about that wallet," Sera wonders.

"What is a wallet?" Dee asks.

"Why won't anyone take this seriously?" Victor3 sulks in his corner.

"Whoa, one at a time," I tell them. "First, I'm not going to address the 'what is a wallet' question. That's stupid. As to what's so great about it, it's only the best present Lily ever gave me. It was our fourteenth birthday, we did this whole Gift of the Magi thing."

"No we didn't," Lily says.

"Sure we did. I spent all my money on that gift card for you, thus I had no money to put in my new wallet. And you shoplifted this wallet from that store the gift card was for and got banned for life, thus making the gift card worthless."

"That did not happen."

"Well, it's how I remember it so…"

"Would you all shut up and listen to me!" Victor3 interupts.

"Jeez, and here I thought you were all about manners," I say.

"All I want to do is layout my masterful scheme so that you can fully appreciate how hard I've worked and just how serious this serious situation is."

"Still, yelling is pretty rude."

Captain Valiant steps forward. "Now Victor, could it be that we are the ones being rude by once again not listening to…other Victor's thoughts and concerns?"

"I guess."

"Please do continue," Valiant instructs Victor3.

"Uh, thank you," Victor3 says. "So where was I…oh right, it was all your fault!" He points to me. I shrug. "You never took the serious situation as seriously as you should have, so after I escaped the burning shack I knew it was my duty to show you the error of your ways. I would find you and that other one of us again and I would teach you a lesson by killing you both."

"Seems excessive," I say, "but I'm with you so far."

"The problem was how to get to you. And then I remembered those stupid fairies."

Chessy spits. "We're sprites yeh daft dilly pickle." That's not actually what she says, but it might as well have been. She sounds so ridiculous.

Victor3 continues without acknowledging Chessy. "I knew that they could somehow travel between worlds, so after a fashion I returned to the site where the shack once stood and I waited. Waiting is all about patience and patience is a virtue, and I am nothing if not a virtuous man." Wow, I remember why we kept interrupting this guy. "Finally my virtue was rewarded when two of those winged beasts appeared."

"I ain't no beast!" Chessy protests.

"Just let him finish or we'll be here all night," Emma whispers.

"Thus I used all of my many charms," Victor3 goes on and on and on. "For a virtuous man is graced with a multitude of charms. And thus I captured one of those cloying insects."

"Wha' did yeh do wit' Crim!" Chessy blurts out.

"Was that her name? It's simple. I caged her and tortured her until she told me of the sacred ritual that would allow me to bleed through all the worlds. She called it the Hemoglobe Trotter. I call it my redemption!" I can't help but groan at that one. "It took some time to gather the proper materials, but eventually all was ready. And now here we are."

No one says anything for half a minute or so until Sera finally jumps in. "That's it? You did all of this just to kill yourself? What are you waiting for then?"

Victor3 considers this. "After watching the other of us die, I realized how empty it all was. This other me deserved much worse than death."

I stop him there. "Wait, then why did you try to shoot me a few minutes ago?"

"I got impatient."

"But I thought patience was a virtue…why don't you make more sense?!"

"May I finish?" he asks, and I nod. "Anyway, I wanted to take everything from him. So I set out to kidnap Gisela and turn her against him. I would charm her with my—"

"With your charming virtuous charms of seriousness. We get it," I say.

But Victor3 just keeps on keeping on. "And I would plant my seed inside her and—"

"Um, ew!" Emma says.

"You need to dial it back, dude," I tell him.

"An' I need ta know wha' 'appened to Crim?" Chessy says.

"The red headed insect? I sacrificed her to release the energy I needed to finish the ritual." Chessy starts to cry. "And then I ate her to absorb her essence like any true warrior."

"What" Jimmy starts.

"The fuck," I finish.

"I bet she tasted good," Candy says.

"Goddamn it, Candy," Emma says.

"Anyway, where was I…" Victor3 says.

"I think you're done," I say.

"Not, I'm not finished yet. My master plan is not fully revealed."

"Uh, yeah man, it is. And it's awful. I pissed you off and now you want revenge. That's exactly what happened with Jimmy when he went all villainous briefly. Except he did it better. And do you know how hard it is to be worse than Jimmy?"

"He's going to say 'very hard'," Jimmy says.

"No, Jimmy, it was rhetorical," I tell him. "But yes, very hard."

"But—" Victor3 tries to interrupt.

"No buts, it was a bad plan. So how about you just punch me

hard in the face, we shake hands, and then you'll help us fix this whole dimensional gravity nonsense before space/time collapses, or whatever."

"Wait, what?" Victor3 says.

"We need to undo your stupid ritual thingy before time rewrites itself. I think. I don't know, Panik can you explain it to him?"

"First give me the shard," Panik says.

"What's she talking about?" Victor3 asks.

"I never know," I tell him.

"She thinks you have something she needs," Lily says. "It's like really colorful obsidian."

"I know he has it," Panik says.

"But what's this about time being rewritten?" Victor3 says.

"I told you I don't really know," I say. Damn, I'm slow on the uptake.

Valiant claps my back. "I'll take it from here. We are on a grand *adventure* to save our current timestream from complete eradication. In order to do that, we need to know this ritual you performed and help you reverse it. Otherwise we may all cease to exist."

"What I'm hearing," Victor3 says, "is that I can completely destroy myself and everything he cares for, while simultaneously undoing all the chaos he failed to stop when he burned that cottage down. And all I have to do is run away?"

"Sure," I say. Sera slaps the palm of her hand to her forehead. "What?"

"Don't let him run away," Sera says.

"Oh, right." Valiant and I rush towards me, even Lily goes to stop him, but the air around him gets hazy. He transforms from a solid to a mirage in a matter of seconds, and we end up grasping air.

"Can he do that whenever he wants?" I ask nobody in particular. "Because I want to do that too. I'm gonna try." I concentrate as hard as I can on jumping, but I don't think anything is happening.

Then Sera yells, "Oh my god, Jimmy!" So maybe something is happening. But no, we're still in this stupid cave. Except Jimmy is back on the ground for some reason. He looks kind of pale, but I don't get why Sera is freaking out. "Are you okay?"

"Yeah," Jimmy tells her. "I've just felt a little weird since the other Victor shot me with that funny looking gun over there."

"You got shot?"

"Sort of. Victor was trying to shoot Victor, so I knocked him out of the way and got hit with this whirly black thing."

Captain Valiant picks up the gun Jimmy mentioned and studies it. His eyes grow wide. "Lieutenant."

"Yes, sir?"

Valiant motions her over to him and she complies. She reads something written on the weapon and her whole body drains of color. Tears trickles down her cheeks as she shakes her head.

Jimmy, meanwhile, has managed to push himself over to one of the cave walls and prop himself against it. He's even paler now. "What's, uh, what's going on?"

"Lieutenant, you have to compose yourself," Captain Valiant says. Sera only shakes her head harder. "Lieutenant…" Sera turns, trying to stumble her way out of the cave. Valiant grabs her by the wrist. "Twinkle Seraphim Cole, you must compose yourself this instant. For him." Hearing her full name like that shocks Sera back from whatever is going on in her head. "There will be time enough for tears later."

"Uh, guys…anyone care to tell me what the problem is?"

Jimmy says.

"I can tell him, if you'd like," Valiant says to Sera. She shakes her head and walks over to Jimmy. Kneeling beside him, she takes his hand in hers. "Hey babe." Her voice is calm, perfectly controlled. But she still can't control her tears.

"Why are you crying?" Jimmy's words shake and his eyes glisten. "Am I…am I dying?"

Sera leans in and brushes her lips against his. Their foreheads touch and Sera shows no sign of breaking that connection. She breathes a single word. "Yes."

"Oh is that all?" I say. "And here I was thinking it was something terrible." Sera doesn't move, but a little color returns to her. It's red. Red is usually bad. "Not that I want you dead. Like I said, I'm not looking forward to hanging out with you in Hell or anything, Jimmy, but you've died before. I'm sure you'll just come back again."

Jimmy smiles. "Hey, yeah. See you don't need to be sad, Sera. I'll get better." Sera raises her head, finally breaking her connection with Jimmy, and shakes her head. "No?"

"No," she almost whispers. "Th-that gun you were shot with, it was one of Soul Destroyer's. It's the same weapon that Lollipop was shot with." Candy and/or Emma gasps, while Valiant bows his head at the mention of Lollipop.

"Wait, I don't get it," Lily says. "What's wrong, exactly?"

Sera wipes her eyes. "His soul i-i-is…" But that's all she's able to choke out before she's overcome with hard sobs. Jimmy pulls her close and hugs her tight. "I-I'm the o-one who's supposed to be strong f-f-for you."

He whispers something to her and strokes her hair. Then he looks to Lily and says, "My soul is disintegrating." His look shifts to Valiant, searching for any sort of desperate hope. "That's what's happening, right Captain?"

Valiant offers him none. "Yes, Jimmy."

"Is it going to hurt?"

"Lollipop seemed peaceful in the end."

"That's good," Jimmy says as Chalk sits down beside him. His chest is blank. All he does is pat Jimmy's shoulder. "Thanks Chalk. So, um, how long until…you know?"

"Lollipop lasted nearly half an hour," Valiant tells him.

"Okay," Jimmy mouths, although no sound comes out. "Hey, Vic. Looks like I'm gonna die for you. Pretty awesome, right?" And he does the unthinkable. He smiles.

"Pretty awesome," I agree. But I don't mean it.

Finally, Sera lifts her head from Jimmy's shoulder and looks directly at me. "This is all your fault."

"Hey," Jimmy says, "Don't blame Vic. He would have done the same for me."

"Oh, Jimmy," I take a tentative step towards him, but then pull back. "I totally wouldn't have."

I see the fire around Sera a second before I feel the slap. She's screaming "How dare you" along with a lot of expletives as she continues to beat on me. I don't try to stop her. No one else does either. No one but Jimmy.

He forces himself to his feet and wraps his arms around her. Sera struggles at first, but eventually collapses into him. And they both collapse back to the floor.

"You've got to go easy on Vic, Sera," Jimmy explains. "That's just how we play off each other. He rags on me just like my brother used to. Only he's way nicer about it and never smacks me around."

"Wow, really?" I say.

"Yeah," Jimmy laughs. "My brother was a complete

motherfucker."

"But Jimmy I really don't think I would have—"

"You would have."

"No, Jimmy you aren't listening I—"

"Would you just leave," Sera says.

"Sera, he doesn't—"

"Yes, Jimmy, he does. Just go!"

Looking around the room, no one can meet my eyes. No one but Jimmy. Who, even though he looks like death himself, is still managing to smile up at me. And he shrugs. That's when I realize what I can do. The *only* thing I can do.

And I run.

Epilogue

The Unicorn waited in the clearing. The man arrived exactly as the Unicorn expected. There was no need to play games this time, and that suited the beast just fine. The man told no stories, gave no reasons, he only said, "I need your horn". The Unicorn laid out his terms. There was no bargaining, not even a moment's hesitation. The man agreed and the Unicorn shed his horn, making him appear as just another horse. Another would grow soon, but in the meantime the Unicorn would enjoy his anonymity. Perhaps visit a farmer's stable and take a filly for his own. The young ones were always wilder. When his horn regrew he'd have to kill her, of course. But then the younger ones also died more sweetly too. The Unicorn smiled his terrible smile.

The man didn't notice, however. He took the horn and ran back the same way from whence he came. Despite the rising sun, the Summerlands were still near freezing, but the man didn't notice. His lungs burned with each inhale and he wiped sweat from his brow. He didn't think he could run much longer, but he pushed on anyway. Time wasn't on his side. Time wasn't on anyone's side. But he wouldn't allow it to run out on him now. So he raced against Time. Perhaps he could have even won. But only Once Upon a Time.

THAT FALLING MOTION

Prologue

HEY,
THANKS FOR HOLDING MY HAIR BACK LAST NIGHT. I HOPE I DIDN'T PUKE ON YOU! I'LL MAKE IT UP TO YOU SOMEDAY. PROMISE!

HUH, I JUST REALIZED THE KID WHO OWNED THIS CRAYON MUST BE DEAD NOW :-/ OH WELL!

♥
EM

5

The days pass, and we wait.

By the time we emerged from the Winter Cave the sun was shining all across the Summerlands again. It was warm and pleasant and none of us really felt it. Except maybe Frosty. He joined us, and I don't think he'd ever been in the sun. He stared up at it. Tried to fly to it. But his wings weren't strong enough for him to get very far. Captain Valiant carried Jimmy's body in his arms. Sera insisted she be the one to carry him. She made it farther than I expected. But eventually her strength gave out. The weight was too much for her. Still, it took a long while for Valiant to convince her to let go. That he would take it from there.

Emma hugged Sera, but Sera gently pushed away and touched Jimmy's face one last time before joining Plaught and Dee at the head of our sorry little funeral procession. Emma and Candy wept. The rest of us just walked. I saw Panik take Lily's hand and I thought about taking Emma's, even if it wasn't really hers. But then I saw Sera up ahead, and Jimmy's lifeless arm hanging down from Valiant's embrace.

I kept on walking.

We didn't rush. I think we expected to jump again. Just like the other times. But we didn't. If anyone spoke, I didn't hear it. We had to pass through the Market to get back to Castle Solstice. There was a brief commotion when everyone spotted Frosty. Frosty cowered behind me until Chalk patted him on the head. Then they all saw Captain Valiant and Jimmy. Most of them bowed their heads or looked away. We passed Remy at one point, his ears that usually stood happy and tall hung low. And this time it was me who looked away.

At Castle Solstice, Queen Nerissa was waiting for us. Her bright smile vanished in an instant. Through damp eyes she asked what happened. Captain Valiant told her. I didn't listen. Although I could follow some of it by the Queen's reaction. She didn't even notice Frosty until Valiant mentioned him. I saw the fear in her eyes, but to her credit she kept her composure and beckoned Frosty forward. Chalk walked him over. Nerissa kissed Chalk before petting Frosty. Once she convinced herself the dragon wasn't a threat, she turned back to Valiant. He still held Jimmy in his arms, and the Queen bent down and lightly kissed Jimmy's forehead. And I guess that's where the story ended. After that Valiant laid Jimmy down. Sera sat down next to him while the rest of us were shown to rooms so that we might rest. I haven't really left mine since.

I'm still waiting to jump again.

And it still won't happen.

Today is Jimmy's funeral. Chalk comes to get me, but I tell him I'm not going. I'm staying here and I'm going to try to jump. And I want everyone as far away from me as they can get so they don't get dragged along.

* * *

It doesn't happen. I don't go anywhere. Why would I? I have no idea what I'm doing. I never do. That doesn't stop me from trying, and that's what I'm doing when I hear the knock at my door. When I don't answer, Lily lets herself in. Panik is with her.

"Thank god," Lily says. "I was worried I'd walk in on you…you know." I roll my eyes. "Too soon?"

"I would have warned you," Panik says.

"Huh?" Lily and I say together.

"If he'd been pleasuring himself, I would have known."

Lily sighs. "Of course you would." Then she looks at me and

says, "Sorry, she doesn't want to let me out of her sight since the whole kidnapping thing."

I shrug. "It's cool. I usually forget she's around anyway."

"That's because I'm well versed in the art of Cloaked Chronocience," Panik says, as if that explains anything. I guess our expressions betray our confusion because she continues. "When you travel through time the way I do, you need to leave as little a footprint as possible. I know how to be only as visible as I need to be." Then she looks at Lily and does something I don't think I've ever seen her do. She smiles. "With a few notable exceptions."

Lily blushes. "Right, well, um…you, uh, you weren't at the funeral."

"I don't think Sera wanted me there," I say.

"Oh," Lily says.

"Besides, I've been to a funeral for Jimmy before. My general rule is one funeral per person."

We sit in silence for too long. Lily fidgets with her fingers. I do nothing. Lily gets sick of the quiet before I do. "So I've been thinking…there were three of you, yeah?" I nod. "So there must have been three of me too, right? But, like, why am I the only me here? They must be dead. Or…or maybe I'm really *his* sister. You know, the other you."

"What difference does that make?" I say.

"Panik thinks since this whole gravity thing was started with some sort of blood ritual that that explains why I ended up involved in it."

"No, I mean why does it matter which world you came from?"

"I…he's a killer. I don't want to be related to that."

"Allegedly."

Lily sighs. "Are we going to have a real conversation or not?"

"About what? You aren't me. You aren't homicidal or genocidal or-or, I don't know, chornocidal? I don't see what the big deal is."

"Really? Then why are you hoarding up in here?"

I shrug.

"Shrug? I guess that means you wouldn't mind going outside for a bit?"

"For what? I've got all the sunshine I could need," I wave at the enchanted ceiling. "What more could I possibly need?"

"Social interaction?"

"And who should I interact with? My girlfriend who's trapped in the body of the woman who murdered her and doesn't want to come within two feet of me? Or how about you, my alledged sister, and her shadow lover? Oh wait, I know, I'll go hang out with Sera. Remind her all about her dead boyfriend."

"That wasn't your fault."

"It was entirely my fault," I take a deep breath. "Look, if I go out there it's all going to start again."

"What's going to start again?"

"The pain and the walking and the death. You haven't been here that long, but all this stuff that's happening has happened before. You got kidnapped by a crazy bastard just like Sera did by Candy Princess, or Emma did by that stupid pirate—"

"There was a pirate?" Lily asks, but I ignore her.

"—or like Emma did by Jimmy before that. All of those instances pretty much ended with someone dying. And then there's all the people who died inbetween. Jimmy, Entheus, The Roboracle, Ickby, a whole island of Candy people, Emma, Ickby again, RoboBot, Donna, and now Jimmy again. Except this time he's not coming back. And the only common denominator in all of this is me. I feel like I'm stuck in some infinite loop of violence and death."

"That's because you are," Panik says. I'd forgotten she was here. She really is good at going unnoticed.

"Could we not encourage his depression?" Lily says.

"But he is correct. Time is a cycle of violence and death. And of beauty and love and sex and sorrow. But mostly violence and death. And when Time gets infected by the meeting of two very powerful Abstractions, for instance, it closes in on itself as a sort of immune system reaction. Those cycles that are usually long and broad become increasingly narrow. More localized. It's Time's way of isolating the infection. The more serious the infection, the more specific and menial the loops become. As an Abstract infection approaches its terminal vector, thoughts may even repeat."

"Great, I'm doomed to walk around and watch everyone around me die until the end of time," I say.

"Only if we can't remove that final shard from your space/time. Of course, if we don't do that soon this space/time will be obliterated to destroy the infection, so you won't have to deal with it much longer."

"See," Lily smiles. "A bright side."

* * *

Since I continue to refuse to leave my room, Lily continues not leaving too. She can be pretty stubborn when she wants to be. We sit there not saying anything at all. I keep looking from her, to the door, and back to her in an exaggerated manner. She responds by lying down. This is the way of things for several minutes. Panik minds her own business as she sits in a corner reading something. I think it might be the little magic book Groff gave me.

I catch Lily making googly eyes at Panik, and when she notices me noticing her noticing Panik she breaks off her stare. She doesn't exactly blush, but it's obvious she's embarrassed for some reason. Not that I can figure out what it is. It's no secret what those two are up to, and Lily's never been modest when it comes to checking out other women.

"Hey, can I tell you something?" Lily asks, breaking the silence that I had so hoped would end with her departure.

"Whatever," I say.

"I, um," she pauses briefly. "I slept with Captain Valiant last night."

"Damn it, Lily! How am I supposed to react to that? I don't like hearing about what you do with people, but then I do love hearing about what Captain Valiant does to the ladies. Why would you tell me this?!" I look to Panik, but she hasn't raised her head from her book. I guess Lily sees where I'm looking.

"She was there too," Lily says.

"I don't want to hear about this," I decide.

"No, look, I'm not going to go into details or anything like that. It's just that, um, I'm totally gay." She sits up when she says it and looks at me.

I look back as seriously as I can manage. "Kay."

"That's it? Kay? You couldn't even bother with the O?"

"What's the big deal? We all know what you and Panik are up to. And then there was Callie. Plus, I grew up with you. We shared a computer. I know what you looked at?"

A crooked grin spreads across her face. "Oh yeah."

"I even tried to tell the Captain when he asked me to help seduce you."

"Wait, what?"

"He's Captain Valiant, Lily. Even lesbians don't say no to

him."

She cocks her head in some sort of half-nod. "That's true."

"And to my credit, the very first thing I told him when he asked what you're into was vaginas."

"That would explain the whole thing with the…uh, never mind." I hate myself for even considering asking her to elaborate. Why couldn't she just get her sex on with Jimmy instead? Oh right. Dead. Time to change the subject.

"So why the sudden revelation into the obvious?"

"I don't know," Lily shrugs. "Valiant was the first guy I've been with since, well, the first guy I'd ever been with and…"

"And if Captain Valiant can't do it for you, you must by gay?"

"Basically, yeah."

"He's one of the most technically proficient lovers I've ever encountered," Panik adds.

"I can't argue that," Lily says. "But it just didn't do it for me. Even if his body is amazing and—"

"And what about those eyes?" I say.

Lily eyes me crookedly. "You gay too, bro?"

I shove her off the bed, sending her tumbling to the mossy floor. Lily laughs, and for a few minutes I forget I'm supposed to be miserable.

* * *

I don't know if Panik reads something in that magic book or if she needs some sort of sex charge or whatever, but eventually she rises from her corner and insists Lily come with her. In any case, I'm happy to have my solitude back. I resume my fruitless attempts to jump away from here. I'm not getting any better at it. Not that my alone-time lasts very long. Panik and Lily can't have been gone more than fifteen minutes before there is a familiar scratch at my door.

I get up and let in Frosty. The room's temperature drops a good 5 degrees when he enters. The Queen has him in a sort of obedience school. The fairies or sprites or pixies or whatever are teaching him how to fly, and someone is training him to keep his Winter's breath under control. But occasionally he escapes and comes here to relax. The only problem with that, is it means I'll have more visitors soon. So I don't bother closing my door. I'll just have to get up again when whoever comes knocking. Here's hoping it's one of the pixies. They keep quiet while they guide him back to wherever he's supposed to be. No such luck, though. Captain Valiant is the one who shows up to retrieve him, Gumdrop right at his heel.

Frosty jumps to attention when he sees the Captain and heads straight for the door. Valiant nods his approval. "Gumdrop, see that Frosty gets where he needs to be." The two animals exit, but Valiant lingers. "You should come watch the dragon train. He's made much progress in the short time he's been here."

"Maybe some other time," I say.

"You haven't left this room in days."

"So I've been told. But who needs to leave when everyone comes to me."

Valiant shakes his head. "Victor, you know what I say about sarcasm."

"That it debases the very core of adventure," I say, not that I know how it does that. But if Captain Valiant says it, it must be true.

"You know, Victor, it's not uncommon for a man to falter in the face of death, but you must realize that eventually everyone runs out of time. It's one of life's simplest lessons, but also its cruelest. Those of us who choose this path of *adventure* face it more often than most, and we sometimes lose more than we can bear, but the only way to honor that loss—"

"Is to bear it anyway," I finish. "You know how I knew you were going to say that? Because you gave me that exact same speech when Emma died."

"Did I?" Valiant wonders to himself. "I'm sorry, Victor, I always try to keep my inspirational speeches fresh. This is very embarrassing."

"Don't worry about it. It's probably my fault. At least, I think that's the point Panik was making. I'm not really sure, though. Nothing she says ever makes much sense. But that's not important. Believe it or not, I've made peace with Jimmy being gone. It sucks, but I'm not moping about it."

"You could have fooled me," Valiant smirks.

"I'm trying to get back in the game, Captain. There has to be a way I can follow myself. Wherever I went. I just don't know how to do it."

"Panik has been doing similar research. Why not assist her like the rest of us."

"Because I don't want you to come along," I say. The hurt on Valiant's face is unmistakable. "Okay, it's not so much that I don't want you there. I just…no one else needs to die because of me. And I'm pretty sure all this adventure can bring is more pain. I've brought too much of that. Especially to Emma and Sera. And if I were to be responsible for Lily's death, then I better pray that my soul gets disintegrated too because I would have to spend an eternity hearing about that from my parents. I don't know. I'm fighting myself, here. Isn't that something people usually do alone?"

Valiant keep smiling his valiant smile. "Victor, that's a very selfish attitude. *Adventure* is my life. As my friend, I would expect you to respect that and never exclude me. And doesn't the Lieutenant deserve retribution? Certainly Panik needs to recover the artifact she's searching for. And while I know Emma is distant now, she'll always want to be by your side. As for Lily, are you aware that I made love to every inch of her body last night?"

I groan. "Captain, please don't…"

"Victor, I wish I didn't have to, but as you know our covenant of friendship dictates that I must. Jimmy was brave in the face of total annihilation, the Lieutenant has demonstrated great strength in that loss, Emma has risen to the challenge of living within the woman who killed her, and Lily rose to the challenge of battling the full force of my manhood. So you will steel yourself and you will listen. We all must face our fears, Victor. It is time to face yours."

* * *

I'm not sure how long Captain Valiant's tale of genital-jousting with lesbians lasts. I may or may not black out a few times. He's very graphic with his descriptions. I'm not going to be able to look Lily in the eye ever again. I'm not going to be able to look at her at all. When he's finished, Valiant heads back to his own room. For the first time in I don't know how many days, I need some fresh air. Without thinking about it, I sling my sword across my back and go explore the castle.

I have no idea where I'm going. Castle Solstice is too big and I paid too little attention during the tour. Not that it matters. I don't have any destination in mind. I follow a couple of pixies through a part of the castle I don't recognize and I almost step on Plaught or Dee. I thought those elves would have been on their way back to their homeland by now. But instead they're still here talking to me. At least the conversation is brief and I only have to pretend to listen. Before we part, the elf points toward something. I nod as if I've heard what he said. And for whatever reason I go that direction.

The thing about Castle Solstice is that the sun always shines within it, which is why I'm so surprised to walk through a door and find an open field blanketed by a moon and stars. There's an unsettled beauty when night falls on the Summerlands. I never noticed it before. Probably because I was too busy being pissed about all the walking I had to do. But it's peaceful in the dark. The field isn't as open as I first thought. There are stone markers all around. Even a few statues. It's Castle Solstice's very own cemetery.

Part of me wants to turn around and go back to my room. But even from here I can see the only fresh grave. Maybe I should stop pretending like I wasn't listening to what the elf said. Like I didn't ask him where to go. Like I wasn't headed here all along. It's why I brought the sword isn't it? Approaching Jimmy's grave, I wonder if this wasn't Captain Valiant's plan all along when telling me about his…adventures with Lily.

Standing in front of the plaque with Jimmy's name on it, I come to the sudden realization that I'm standing directly on top of him. I step awkwardly to the side muttering a pointless sorry. Then I take the sword from off my back and lay it over Jimmy.

"What are you doing?" a voice asks behind me. It's soft and void of any urgency.

I turn to face Sera. She's holding a package in her arms, with that stupid book of the Summerlands that Jimmy couldn't put down on top of it. "Oh, sorry I'll, uh, let you, um…" I try leave, but Sera steps in front of me.

"I didn't ask you to leave. I asked what you're doing."

"I thought the sword should stay with Jimmy. He got more use out of it than I did. And it'll make a cool marker, I guess." I try to look her in the eye when I say it. But I fail. "Anyway, I'll leave you to…you know."

"I'm not here for him," Sera says. "I saw you pass outside my room." She looks at the package she's carrying and shoves it at me. "Here."

All I do is stare at it. "What's this?"

"A present. From Jimmy. He said you had a birthday coming up, and he made me promise to give it to you along with your stupid book. So take it."

I do, but it doesn't alleviate my confusion. "Jimmy knew when my birthday is?"

"He listened to every damn thing you said." There is no anger hidden behind her words. She's quiet and calm and then she turns to leave. But she only takes a few steps before turning back, this time the moon reflecting off the tears welling in her eyes. "You could have lied to him."

"I—" is as far as I get.

"He was lying there dying—dying for you—and you couldn't even say 'of course I would have done the same for you, Jimmy'. No! You just had to be the same asshole you always are."

"I thought he deserved to know the truth."

"What he deserved was a better friend," she says, the tears now streaming down her face. She lets them do so uninterrupted. "What he deserved was to not know that the person he died for thought he was too worthless to do the same."

I want to explain that she's got it all wrong. That when I said I wouldn't have done the same for Jimmy it wasn't because I felt he was too worthless, but because I realized then that I didn't have the balls to do it. I don't get the chance, though, because Sera is already gone. And let's face it, if we're talking about who deserves what, then she probably deserves to hate me.

And me?

I don't deserve much of anything.

* * *

Working my way back to my room takes a while. I retrace my steps well enough, but I feel, I don't know, slow. The weight of the gift I'm carrying takes its toll. Not that it's heavy, just that it's too much. I want to get back to my bed and get my self-loathing on. But another surprise is waiting for me when I get there. I open the door to my room to find Emma and Candy sitting on my bed. It's the first time I've seen them since we got back.

"You left," Emma says, a master of stating the obvious.

Not wanting to be out done, I match her. "You're here."

They point to the package I'm carrying. "What's that?"

"Present from Jimmy," I say, but that doesn't seem to compute. "I ran into Sera. She said she promised to give me this stuff."

"What is it?"

I shrug. "Maybe he managed to build a bomb in his final moments. A little payback."

"Oh no!" Candy yelps.

"He's joking," Emma says, though she doesn't seem amused.

"So," I say.

"So," she says back. Then there's just silence.

"Well, this is fun."

A half smile creeps onto Candy's face, a smile that's all Emma. She pats the bed beside her. I hesitate. Every time I've tried to get near her since she got stuck in Candy, she's pulled away. But when she pats the bed a second time, cocking her head and raising her eyebrows as she does, I relent and sit. She takes my hand in hers and Candy does her little wiggle. Emma isn't too happy about that. "Candy, could you go to your private place while I talk to Victor?"

"Kay!"

"Her private place?" I say.

"You don't want to know." And before I can decide for myself if I do, Emma changes the subject. "So you saw Sera."

"Yeah."

"Did you tell her about the unicorn horn?" The surprise must show on my face, because she answers the question before I even ask it. "I saw you carrying it when you came back from your little run. Before you tucked it away."

"Oh. Sera doesn't need to hear about that."

"She'd probably like to hear that you didn't just run away. That you were trying to help Jimmy."

"But I failed so…I think she needs someone to aim her anger towards. Might as well be me."

"Why?"

"Because it's my fault."

"No it's—"

"Yes it is. And not just Jimmy. All of it."

"What are you talking about?"

"I'm talking about how I've spent so long touting myself as this big time hero, but I haven't done anything but fuck everything up. I failed to fix the world when that stupid cabin burned down. And that led directly to all this. Candy Island exploded on my watch too."

"That was a volcano, sweetie," Emma tries to reassure. "And fuck Candy Island anyway."

"Emma!" Candy exclaims.

"Stop listening to our private conversations, Candy!" Emma

orders.

"Sorry."

I wait for a few seconds to make sure they're done arguing. "Even if you ignore Candy Island, there are still things like the destruction of Infinite City. And, well, there's you. I didn't save you."

"You didn't?" she says like it's news to her. "I'm here, alive, because of you."

"Trapped in a body you can't stand," I remind her, because apparently she needs a reminder. But I didn't. I twist away from her so that maybe I can forget.

"Hey," she grabs my face, "look at me. I might hate the face I see when I look in the mirror, but the face I'm looking at right now... you are *not* him."

Maybe her words would mean more if every time I looked into her eyes it wasn't someone else's I was seeing. "That's the thing, though. I am him. He is me." Emma opens Candy's mouth, but I cut her off before she can start. "I know you're going to say he's different somehow, and maybe he is. But at some point he was probably exactly like me. I don't know what changed him. Maybe that stupid rock Panik wants. But I can feel his anger inside me. His violence. His bloodlust. And I kind of like it. I can feel myself falling apart all over again. I'm one little shove away from being that mess who talks to himself non-stop, and probably just a slightly bigger shove from murdering all my friends."

"Oh, Victor," Emma looks me dead in the eyes. "Don't be such a pussy." And she laughs, but she pulls out of it quickly. "Whoa, déjà vu. What's that about?"

I half shrug. "Time cycles or something."

I can tell Emma wants to ask what I mean by that, but she pushes it aside. "Look, I don't really care if you're some big hero or just a guy. I'm not after some ideal, it's you I love."

"Why?" I ask.

"What?"

"No, why?"

"Why do I what? Love you?"

"Yes. I mean, what sense does it make? I practically kidnapped you when we first met and was mostly completely out of my mind at the time. Then you got kidnapped at least twice more after that. Plus there's the whole murder thing. All-in-all I've done a pretty poor job protecting you."

"First off, I don't need protecting."

I roll my eyes. "All evidence to the contrary."

And then it's Emma's turn to roll her eyes. Or Candy's, at least. "Whatever. You're cherry picking all the moments that support your sulk-fest." I don't respond. "But why do I love you?" she pauses for a breath. "You remember that story I told at Donna's funeral?" I nod. "And do you remember what you said before I went out with Donna that night?"

"Please don't leave me with Jimmy and The Roboracle," I say.

"Well yeah, but you also said if I come home puking, I shouldn't expect you to hold my hair back. But I did come home puking. And you did hold my hair back. All night. I woke up in the morning on the bathroom floor with you passed out in the bathtub." I remember it, of course. She taped a note to my forehead that she wrote in crayon. She signed it with a heart. I've kept it ever since. "That's why I love you."

"Because I hold your hair back when you throw up?"

"Because you stand by me no matter what," she tells me. "I died, Victor. And you came to Hell for me. You *stayed* in Hell for me. And even now with this whole Candy thing, you still haven't run away.

I think it's time maybe I do the same."

"Huh?" I say.

"I'm not okay with my body situation and I can't promise that I'll ever be. But hey, who doesn't have body image issues? I can still be there for you when you need me." Emma pulls back the covers on the bed and takes off the pants she and Candy are wearing. "Get in."

"Um," I say.

She pats the space beside her. "Come on. We're not going to get frisky or anything, I'm still not okay with that. But I'm tired and I want to pretend like everything is normal. If only for tonight. So get under the covers and cuddle with me, bitch." How can a guy say no to that? I climb between the sheets, still wary of getting too close to Candy's body. But Emma takes my hand and wraps my arm around her.

"Yay!" Candy squeals.

Emma bolts to a sitting position and yells, "Shut your whore mouth, whore!" before slipping back into my arms.

Candy doesn't say anything else, but she does her little happy wiggle again and hums the same lullaby she hummed at Donna and RoboBot's wake. Emma doesn't object—at least not out loud—and it eventually trails off as Candy and Emma fall asleep. I lie there listening to their breathing, trying my best to imagine it is Emma's body I'm holding.

* * *

I don't sleep. I don't really want to. And not just because my dreams are lately filled with my other self's sadistic thoughts and memories. That doesn't faze me much anymore. No, I'm staying awake because this is the best I've felt in days and I want to hold on to it as long as possible, so I'm still wide awake when there's a gentle knock at my door. I don't want to answer it, but I don't want to wake Emma and Candy either. And I know if I choose the former that the knocking will insist upon the latter. Extricating my arm from the cuddling situation is tricky, but I'm sly enough to manage it and get to the door before the knocking gets any louder. Panik is waiting on the other side of the door.

"Where's Lily?" I ask.

"Sleeping," Panik says.

"I thought you didn't leave her unattended."

"I set Chalk to guard the door. And I wore her out so thoroughly she won't be waking anytime soon."

"I don't need to hear about it," I grumble.

Lucky for me Panik gets bored with conversations faster than I do. "Come with me."

I consider asking why, but I realize that will only lead to a speech I'll hardly understand and possibly a diagram of Lily's anatomy. So I shut up and follow. Where she takes me is to another room. Unlike on the Adventure Galley, I don't know whose room is whose, but I can assume it's not Panik's due to the lack of Chalk standing guard. "This isn't you trying to sex my body again, is it?"

Panik knocks on the door. "I thought I was clear about what I did with Lily, or should I elaborate?"

"Sorry," I say, and the door opens.

Sera stares out at us. She looks tired, but also like she was expecting us. "Make this quick," she says.

Panik walks through the open door, and when Sera shows no objection I follow. "What's this all about?"

"I'd like to know that too," Sera says.

"It's simple," Panik tells us. "I've been studying this land's arcane sciences for some time now. I think I've found a way to fix dimensional gravity."

Sera and I wait for Panik to go on, but she doesn't. Finally Sera gets sick of waiting. "And?"

Panik waits for a beat. "And you aren't going to like it." Brief. Cryptic. Typical.

* * *

Credit where it's due, though, I don't much like it. Sera, I'm sure, likes it even less. Maybe because she's better at following Panik speak than I am. I only grasped enough to know it's a sucky plan. On the plus side, Panik says it's a last resort sort of thing. If we can find Victor3 in time it might not be necessary. The problem being, of course, that we're stuck here until we're not stuck here. And who knows when that might be. Time really doesn't ever seem to want to be on our side.

When I arrive back to my room, Emma and Candy are still fast asleep. Part of me considers waking them and telling Emma what Panik just told me. But she looks so peaceful. Or that's the excuse I'm using.

More likely I'm just a coward. But that's not very flattering to me and I refuse to de-flatter myself in my own head. (since when?) Since I told you to shut up.

As I force the fissure in my mind closed again, my nose bleeds a little from the effort. But it's nothing to worry about. Probably. I glance over to Emma and Candy, worried I might have woken them. But they're still sound asleep.

Instead of going back to the bed I sit down at a desk in the corner of the room. It's always been there, but I never had any use for it so I didn't bother taking note of it until now. Actually, I think all my time working behind of desk pre-Apocalypse has given me a sort of Post Traumatic Stress Disorder, so I've developed a little mental block when it comes to desks. This one is a lot nicer than my old one though. It's sturdy and elegant. I want to say it's mahogany. Who knows why, I don't know wood from wood, but mahogany sounds like the kind of wood from which you make fancy desks. Whatever, it's a place to sit.

I take out my wallet. I considered tossing it after what happened to Jimmy, but then Jimmy would have died for nothing. This way he died for a wallet, and that's pretty cool. Or sad. I can't say which, for sure. I pull a folded piece of paper from where I'd normally keep money. It's the note Emma wrote me all those months ago. It's seen better days. But considering everything I've been through since then—the space slavery, an exploding island, time travel, dance parties, dimensional hopping, and so on—I'm not sure how I've managed to keep it intact.

I read it over and over. It's short and sweet and kind of goofy. In just a few sentences it captures everything I love about her. I don't understand how. It says almost nothing. But I've carried it with me ever since so…so I turn it over and write my own note. And it's not good enough. And I hate it. And I hope I never have to give it to her.

After way too much time spent on way too little, I fold the note up and put it back in my wallet. I'm still too awake to sleep. I start pacing. Then I notice the package Sera gave me earlier. The birthday present from Jimmy. It's still unopened, and my birthday is who the fuck knows when—seriously, I don't know how Jimmy was keeping track of time, because I kind of gave up on that when the world ended—but screw it. I grab it from off the floor. It's wrapped in plain brown paper and tied off with hemp string—or whatever they call hemp in the Summerlands—normally I'd expect something a bit fancier, but I'm going to give Jimmy a break due to being dead and all. I untie the string and rip at the paper and…and…goddamn it, Jimmy…

Sitting in my lap is the coolest leather jacket I've ever seen.

Interlude

He sits on the edge looking out across the pit. His shadow is somewhere behind him as he basks in the shining glory of the midday sun. And he reflects on the apropos nature of the moment. He sits on the edge because he knows he's on the precipice of victory. And the light of the sun is the universe sending its praise. He's finally done it. He is going to save the world.

No one will ever paint this scene. It's a bitter pill to swallow. Almost as bitter as all the metaphors forcing themselves upon him like a gang of would be rapists. But rape requires a lack of consent, and for now he's willing to allow it. Even if metaphors are for poets and daydreamers; people of inaction who never take the world seriously.

He vaguely registers a noise somewhere in the background. The air is electric with a hint of ozone burning his nostrils. And he smiles in his palace of ash and destruction and says to himself, "A storm must be coming."

5.5

I'm in my car.

Alone.

I'm running from something. Or to something. It's hard to tell. But I'm sure I've done this before.

I'm doing it now.

Again.

I know this road. It's where I live

where I used to live

I want to get home and forget everything I've seen.

What have I seen?

This is where it began.

when it began.

But it's not right, because I'm almost home and it's not burning. Then I see it. A streak across the sky. A boom that rattles my head. And my house ignites. This is how it happened.

This isn't how it happened.

I force my car to stop.

I'm standing outside screaming something at the flames. My comics are in there. Of all the things I've seen today that's the one I can't handle. It's been a bad morning.

Then my house explodes.

It never did.

Something flies toward me and a sharp burning rage pierces my leg. And I...

...wake in a cold sweat. I'm breathing hard and I'm...smiling.

Emma and Candy are by my side already. They must have been in the middle of getting dressed because they currently have only one leg in their pants. “You okay?”

“Sure,” I manage. Emma is on the verge of comforting me, but she pulls back. Again. Her brief respite from physical denial is over. The two of them finish dressing their shared body. Without another word they start to leave. It might be awkward if I were inclined to care, but that sounds like a waste of energy. “Hey, can you tell everyone to meet me for breakfast?”

That catches Emma off-guard. “So you’re done with your exile.”

“One of us has to be,” I say. It sounded less harsh inside my head. “I didn’t mean—” but Emma dismisses me with a simple hand wave.

“Yeah, I’ll tell everyone.” Then they’re both gone. I get out of bed in order to dress before realizing I’m still wearing all my clothes. That’s one less thing to do. This day is already looking up!

I’m halfway out the door when I remember my new jacket. I put it on for the first time, admiring myself in the mirror. Damn, I’m cool. With that, I’m off. Because I’m also fucking hungry.

* * *

Emma and Candy did as I asked. Everyone is waiting in the dining room. Even Queen Nerissa. Although now that I think about it, it is breakfast time so I probably didn’t even need to ask anyone to do anything. I’ve been the only one prone to the hermit way of life. Captain Valiant offers me a smile, as does Nerissa. Chalk, who is sitting next to the queen, waves and I give him a thumbs up.

I don’t say anything, I just sit down and start eating. Say what you want about royalty, but they do make the best meals. And the service? Impeccable. Pixies and sprites flutter all about delivering food and drink faster than I can devour it. And believe me I take that as a challenge. I'm shoveling food into my mouth so fast I'm worried I might choke. Not so worried that I slow down, of course. Because I live on the edge of adventure.

"I thought you had something to say," Sera interrupts my solo competitive eating challenge.

I look up from my plate, my mouth as full as it's ever been. I try to say something, but only food comes out. One of the winged girls near my head curses me as she flies off to clean up my mess. I'm not sure if I should be embarrassed. On the one hand, Captain Valiant holds proper table etiquette in high esteem, but at the same time he says shame is for the meek. I say "sorry" but it comes out more like "mmry".

To my great relief, Captain Valiant laughs. "I haven't seen such an appetite since I faced off against Emperor Oblisk in a pie-eating contest at the Intergalactic Fair. All for a kiss from Annabelle, the most beautiful Pie Girl the Fair had ever seen. Take your time, Victor. An empty stomach is friend to no man, but a full one may garner you a kiss. Or more."

I do my best to properly chew the rest of what is in my mouth. With that taken care of I say, "What's up?"

"Maybe you should tell us," Lily says. "You're the one who had something to say."

"Did I? Oh yeah, I guess so. I'm sure you've all noticed that we're all still here and not back on the Galley or in some other crazy place and I've been thinking…let's just leave."

Everyone stares at me like they expect me to continue, which I don't get because I think I laid out my case pretty well. Then again, it's possible we've started some sort of massive staring contest. But if so then where do I look? This may be the greatest challenge I've ever faced. I'm betting Panik is a master of staring. Emma and Lily both have a lot of practice. Captain Valiant is Captain Valiant. He doesn't lose. Chalk has no eyes. The Queen probably has some sort of royal staring etiquette that I can't beat, and Sera has spunk. Where the hell is Jimmy when I need him? He'd fold in seconds. Just like him to ruin things even in death.

"Holy crap!" Sera blurts out. "Are you ever going to tell us how you expect us to leave?"

"Huh? Oh that? I figure we just ask Chessy. She seems to be able to travel between here and our home easily enough."

"That…actually makes some sense," Sera says.

"The only problem is, I kind of killed and ate her friend. Sure it was the other me, but—"

"You also make fun of her accent a lot," Sera interrupts.

"It's really stupid."

"And she never did forgive you for burning down that cabin," Emma adds.

"That was really more The Roboracle than me. But yeah, she doesn't like me much."

"So all in favor of anyone but Victor asking for her help?" Lily says while raising her hand.

"I'll do it," Emma says. "She knows me, sort of."

"And I'll help!" Candy adds. Emma groans.

"We can guide you if you'd like," Master Dee says. I hadn't even noticed the elves were here until now.

"I'll accompany you as well," Captain Valiant says. "I'm sure the lot of us can convince the good lady Chessy to help. The rest of you should gather any belongings you may have here. Be ready to move out immediately." Valiant, Emma, and Candy excuse themselves from the table, but before leaving the room the Captain turns to me and says, “That is a most *valiant* jacket.” Then they’re gone, and I go back to shoving food in my face.

* * *

I ate too much. Now I feel ready to burst. So I just lay in bed. I know I’m meant to be packing up, but I only have three things of note worth taking: My jacket, the big old book from Groff that Jimmy insisted I keep, and the unicorn horn that was a complete waste of my time to acquire. I’m already wearing the jacket, and I immediately put the horn in my pocket when I got back to the room. Which leaves me plenty of time to be properly lazy. I thumb through the book while I’m sprawled out. Considering the short period of time Jimmy had it, it’s filled with an unbelievable amount of notes. Giving me back this book might have been Jimmy’s ultimate revenge. Because it might be the most boring thing I’ve ever experienced. And I once spent an entire evening with just Jimmy and The Roboracle. That’s why when I hear a knock on the door, I’m happy to jump out of bed and answer it.

Chalk is standing outside. I’m still not quite sure how Chalk sees stuff, but his face is turned towards the ground like he doesn’t want to look at me.

“Why so glum, chum?” I ask.

Chalk’s whole body slumps, but he turns his face upwards. It reads NERISSA WANTS ME 2 STAY

“Again I ask, why so glum? That’s great, buddy.”

In a blink his face reads I DON’T WANT 2 LEAVE U GUYS

I motion for Chalk to sit on the bed. “Listen, man, you’ve got a sexy queen who wants to cuddle your brains out for the foreseeable future. You can’t pass that up.”

BUT Chalk’s face tries to plead. There’s more after that, but I ignore it.

"Just let me finish. You and I, we've been through a lot, right? I rescued you from space. We outwitted a notorious space pirate. We fought living skyscrapers. We even won a dance contest together. That's a bond that can't be broken. Take it from a friend, you should stay."

Chalk's face remains blank.

"Let me put it this way: When a beautiful woman lets you touch her where other women would slap you for doing so, you don't walk away from that. At least not right away."

BUT HE KILLED JIMMY & DONNA

"Don't worry about that. We'll take care of things. You probably don't want to get in Sera's way when she finds me, anyway."

OK Chalk's face says as he hops off the bed and heads for the door. His body language hasn't changed.

"Hey, Chalk," I call after him. "Keep up that sad sack routine for a while, okay? Let Nerissa comfort you, if you know what I mean."

Chalk turns back to me, a little perkier than before and his face reads THAT'S THE PLAN!

What a roguish little son of a gun.

After Chalk leaves I go back to lying about and generally doing nothing. Chances are another round of walking-way-too-much is on the docket for today, so this might be my last opportunity to expend little to no effort. Unfortunately it doesn't last long. A pixie floats into the room to tell me it's time to go. Or I think that's what she's saying. But asking her to repeat herself will only lead to more whispers I can't hear, so I snatch up my book and follow her back to the meadow that serves as the greeting hall for Castle Solstice.

Sure enough, everyone is gathered there, including Chessy. Though she looks everywhere but at me. Even Frosty is waiting.

Actually, it looks like Panik and Lily are missing, which means, once again, I don't have to worry about Captain Valiant being disappointed in my lack of punctuality.

When Frosty sees me, he flaps his wings and flies over. He's gotten a lot better with the whole flying thing. He looks up at me with hopeful eyes.

"I think you have to stay here," I tell him.

"That's right, sweetling," Queen Nerissa says, walking over to the two of us and petting Frosty's head. "We have to continue your training." Frosty folds his wings and bows his head. I don't think he likes the answer.

"You'll take care of him," I say. It's not really a question, but the queen answers it anyway.

"Of course. He'll be a great asset to the kingdom. Even though the Fevrencies have once again vanished, they could return at any time. And if they don't, well, I think the Summerlands could do with a little winter now and again. I'm certain the children will love the snow as much as I'm coming to."

I bend down to scratch Frosty's chin. "See, Nerissa will take care of you."

"And Victor," Nerissa says. "Thank you for convincing my Heart to stay."

I shrug, not really sure what to say. Lily and Panik choose that moment to arrive, which saves me from having to continue not saying anything. I hate being speechless. If I'm not talking then someone else might start. And who wants to deal with that.

Lily and Panik stop to pet Frosty. They're both flushed and sweaty.

"Can't you keep it in your pants for ten minutes?" I wonder.

Lily doesn't look up, she's still busy nuzzling Frosty. But that doesn't mean I can't feel her smug smile. "Why would I want to do that?" Stupid Lily having a stupid girlfriend not currently trapped in a stupid body I'm not allowed to stupid touch.

"Can we just get on with this," I say. "Because I kind of want to kill myself right now, so..."

"He's right," Panik says. "We've wasted far too much Time waiting for another dimensional jump. That one hasn't happened suggests that the Uncertainty Clock is nearing critical mass. Soon things you're certain can't happen certainly will."

I make my very best ugh sound. "Are we going to stand around and listen to her blather on about nonsense, or are we going to dive head first into it?"

"Well put, Victor," Valiant smiles. "*Adventure* is just beyond the horizon."

* * *

Everyone says whatever goodbyes they might have to say. Candy Princess and Emma cry a little when talking to Chalk. It's probably mostly Candy's influence, but no one is really happy to leave Chalk behind. I overhear Plaught and Dee explaining to Valiant that they are staying behind to help with Frosty's training before they return to wherever their home is. Not that I expected them to come along. They are solid guides, but pretty useless otherwise. Mostly I worry I'm going to accidentally step on them.

On the way out of the castle I pass Chalk. We've said our farewells and what have you, so we don't say anything. Hell, we don't even look at each other, we just high five. And that's how I leave Castle Solstice behind.

Chessy guides us back through The Market. I see Groff and

wave. Then Remy hops up beside me, a tiny bouquet in one of his paws. “Off on another quest?”

I nod. “Suicide mission back home.”

Remy grimaces. “Ouch.”

“It’s less daunting when there’s two of you.”

“I’ll take your word for it. Just wanted to wish you luck, buddy.”

“Thanks. What’s with the flowers?”

“Holy haystacks! I almost forgot!” Remy hops over to Sera and clears his throat. “Excuse me, Miss.” Sera looks down at him. “My wife and I were very sorry to hear about your friend. She, uh, she wanted me to give you these.” He presents her with the flowers. “She made a new bouquet every day, just in case I saw you.”

Sera takes the flowers. “That’s, um…thanks.”

“Yeah, well. Give’em hell or something,” Remy says as he hops off, waving at us all as he goes. Sera takes off her pack to place the bouquet inside, and strapped to her back behind the pack is the sword I left on Jimmy’s grave.

“You stole from your dead boyfriend!” I blurt out.

Sera rolls her eyes. “Corpses can’t use swords. Usually.”

That’s a good point. “Uh, can I have it back?”

Sera turns her back to me, continuing to follow Chessy’s lead. “You gave it to Jimmy. He would have wanted me to have it.”

“This awesome jacket and book filled with boring notes says otherwise.”

“I’m better with a sword than you are,” Sera says. “And p.s. Fuck you.” Lily lets out a louder than necessary “ha!” at that. I think even Emma and Valiant might have snickered a bit. And I huff loudly. I’ve essentially transformed into the big bad wolf of indignance.

“Just let it go, bro,” Lily tells me. “If you think about it, the sword was always more hers than yours anyway."

"I demand support for that ludicrous postulation," I say.

"Sera and I essentially bought it by smacking you around." Damn it! That logic is sound.

"I could kick you in the balls again if you require further payment," Sera says. I can't see her face, but the way her hair is glowing all yellow and sunny I just know she's smiling.

"Oh yeah!" I say. "Well I'm just going to read this book and learn things! And when our lives are on the line I'm certain that your stupid sword will be useless, but me knowing that, um…" I flip through the book to a random page, "the second rarest tree in the Summerland is the Royal Poplar will totally save us. And also allow me to say 'I guess that tree isn't so *poplar* after all'. So let's just trade the book for the sword, maybe?"

"I'll take my chances," Sera says.

"Plus, all that seems pretty unlikely," Lily says.

"Bullshit! Panik was just saying how uncertainty will certainly become certainty. It's practically the most likely thing to ever happen ever." Panik shakes her head. I throw my hands in the air in frustration. "Fine! But I'm going to find something in this book so awesome that you're going to rue the day you refused my very generous trade offer."

"Whatever," Sera says.

"Whatever," I say back and get to reading, more determined than ever to prove myself right. Damn it, Jimmy, you better not let me down again.

I get so buried in searching for anything that's not remotely lame in this book that I don't notice when everyone else stops in front of me, and I end up walking right into Candy and Emma.

"Uh, sorry," I say.

“That’s okay,” Candy says. “You can bump into me anytime.”

I can see Emma grit Candy’s teeth. “In case any of you were wondering, the Princess here was alluding to her desire to bone my boyfriend.”

“Emma!” Candy gasps, her face burning. Who knows why, you think she’d be used to this by now.

“Oh, sorry was that a secret?” Emma says. “I couldn’t tell with how loudly—and vividly—you were screaming it in our head.”

“Awwww,” Candy says, which I think everyone would agree is a strange reaction. “You said *our* head.”

“Oh god, don’t make a thing out of it,” Emma says. But it’s too late. A river of pure joy is already cracking Emma’s dour expression defenses and leaking all over their face.

“We’re going to be the best friends ever!”

“Someone change the subject,” Emma pleads.

“Uh,” Sera starts, “so why are we stopping here, Chessy?”

“This issa way ta one a yer t’ree worl’s. Don’ know which is which, they all look mos’ly da same ta me. I kin take ye two atta time, but it’ll be slow werk, it will.”

“What are we waiting for,” Valiant says. “Onward to *adventure*.”

* * *

Chessy takes the Captain—gumdrop on his shoulder—and Emma/Candy over first. Since Sera has my sword now, Valiant tells her to stay behind in case something attacks us for some reason or another. Watching Chessy whisk them away is weird. One second they look normal then they flatten, narrow and vanish.

I use all the waiting time to continue my search for anything remotely interesting in the big book of the Summerlands. Most of it seems dedicated to flora and fauna with a bit of topography mixed in for good measure. Plants and hills don't appeal to me in the slightest, but I can't say the creature feature is much better. Like I need to know about squirrel and deer. There are plenty of those back home. I end up skipping straight to the dragon section. As I do, Chessy returns to take Lily and Panik. Panik says something to Sera and me, but I don't listen. Because I have finally found something worthwhile in this book. It's a note from Jimmy that starts "Vic, I figured the dragon section might be the only one the you'd care about, so hopefully you find this before anyone else. Don't have much time so here it goes…" I keep reading. And go it does.

"Bless you, Jimmy," I whisper.

"What?" Sera says.

I slam the book shut. "Nothing!"

"Why are you looking at me like that?"

"Like what?" I say. Am I looking at her like something? I try to stop looking at her altogether, but even as I turn my head away my eyes pivot like one of those freaky paintings or statues that seem to watch you wherever you go.

Thankfully that's when Chessy returns. "Yer turn."

I jump to my feet and Chessy takes my hand. Sera's a little slower. I can't believe she's been trusted with that sword. With those reflexes we'd both be dead if Chessy were a giant monster instead of an innocuous flying girl. Whatever Chessy does to lead us from the Summerlands to one of the three Earths feels a lot like dimension jumping. A tightness. A woozy feeling. A tiny pop. And that's it. Sort of like taking off on a plane while on allergy medicine.

Where we end up, I recognize quite well. A wooded clearing, slightly scorched where a cabin once stood. The frame is still there, actually.

"It's done," Chessy says. She's quiet for a few seconds before adding, "Kill 'im. Fer Crim." With that, she vanishes.

"Now what?" Lily asks.

"Depends on which Earth this is," I say.

"It looks like home," Emma says. "But I guess all three would look the same, right?"

Silence. Actual cricket chirping silence. Chessy might have been able to tell the difference on sight, but if she did she didn't offer that information up and now we can't ask her. Pretty rude of her. You'd think I'd killed her best friend, or something. I mean, yeah I did, but it wasn't me! Wait a second…best friends? Maybe…

I sprint over to the biggest pine tree on the edge of the clearing and I see it. "Yeah, we're home."

"How do you know that?" Lily says, she and everyone else already jogging my way.

Emma laughs. "It's that stupid carving you got pissed at Jimmy for making."

I nod. After Jimmy and I had that epic sword fight, and I'd helped burn down the cabin, Jimmy was trying anything to get back on my good side. And at the base of this tree he ended up carving "Emma+Victor+their #1 pal Jimmy". It almost makes me feel bad for all the names I called him afterwards. But only almost.

"Okay, so we're in our universe," Lily says. "How does that help us find the other you?"

"I think I know," Sera says. She rummages through her pack. "You said there was a cabin that used to be here. I assume you mean that burnt wreckage over there." Emma and I both nod, but Sera isn't looking. "And that cabin was a doorway or something until Victor did his usual fuck up and burned it down."

"It was The Roboracle," I say.

"Sure."

"Hey, I take credit for the fires I start. Like when I burned my own house down. Or the Candy Embassies."

"You burned my house down," Candy gasps.

"Um…of course not," I say while Candy glares at me something fierce. "Look why are we dwelling on the past?"

Sera stops rummaging and pulls out a small watch like device. The time machine she and Jimmy built. "Because the past is exactly what we need."

* * *

"Why do you always have that?" I ask.

"Huh?" Sera says.

"Shouldn't it be on the Galley?"

"Oh. Jimmy said The Roboracle told him that he should have it with him at all times."

Panik grabs the time machine from Sera and studies it for about half a second. "Cute toy."

"Time cycling, huh?" I say to her.

Panik studies me, squinting as she does. "No."

She sounds pretty certain so I squint right back at her. "I don't know, I think maybe our cycles are synching up."

"Tell me you did not just try to make a menstruation joke," Lily says.

"I didn't try, I did it."

"Can we just get on with this," Sera says, strapping the time machine to her wrist.

"The Lieutenant is right ," Valiant says. "Everyone join

hands." We do, and with the wooded setting and Lily by my side, I can't help but be reminded of all those summers spent at camp.

There was this one particularly eventful summer where a camper drowned and the rest of camp was an endless string of hijinks where that kid's mom went around trying to kill the rest of the campers. All the while, Lily was making crazy bets about which girl would lose her virginity first. (That's just the plots of Friday the 13th and Little Darlings.) Nobody asked you!

I notice everyone staring at me. It's annoying. "Like you all aren't used to this by now." No one argues. Sera even nods. And I stop being the center of attention. I think that's what I wanted. For some reason. Then Lily leans my way. At least someone is still paying attention to me.

"By the way," she whispers, "we never went to camp. We just spent the summers watching movies about camps."

"Close enough," I say.

"I worry about you, bro."

I shrug. Then I notice that we're all still standing here holding hands and definitely not traveling through time. "What's the hold up?"

"I need a date," Sera says.

"Don't look at me," I tell her. "Remembering shit is a big waste of my time." Emma gives her a date, though. It's one of the reasons we make such a great couple. She covers for all of my shortcomings, allowing me to focus all my time on being more awesome than ever.

Sera adjusts the time machine for whatever date Emma gives her—I still don't care enough to actually listen to what it is—and things go ZAAAAPP!!! and yep, there's the cabin all unburnt.

"Alright, let's go!" I say with as much excitement as I can muster. It's not much. It doesn't really deserve an exclamation point, but I'm going to imagine one anyway.

"Hold on, sweetie," Emma says. "What exactly is the plan?"

"Simple. We go in the cabin and then exit into Victor3's Earth. Then we travel back to the present and we find him."

"How?" Sera asks.

"And what if he's not on his Earth?" Lily asks.

I don't like when questions start to pile up, but they leave me no choice but to throw out my own. "Why do I have to think of everything? I'm going into the cabin. Anyone who wants to stay here is welcome to."

"I've got the time machine, though," Sera says.

"I've got one too. It's called my life. I'll catch up to me eventually."

"Except that you might actually need me if you blow it, which you will," Sera says.

"Need you for what?" Emma asks.

"Um," I say.

"Need her for what?" Emma asks again.

I'm not sure if I look guilty, but I feel like I probably definitely look guilty. "I'll tell you later." Emma's accusatory glare doesn't go away. "Could someone please change the subject?"

Valiant, as always, comes to my rescue. "Victor is right. We're wasting valuable *adventure* time. All other questions will be answered later. We will follow Victor's plan and then figure our next course of action from there. And we will do it together because we are a team. Is that understood?"

Sera says, "Yes sir" while the rest of give some form of assent. Me, I yell "Teamwork!" because I know the Captain loves enthusiasm. Everyone else looks sorry when compared to my gung-ho attitude, which I assume is why they're all shaking their heads at me.

But we hit a little snag as we approach the cabin door when a voice from just above my head says, “You can’t go in there.” I look up to find a familiar winged girl hovering there.

“Jaela?” I say.

“You’ve heard of me?” Wow, I got that right? That must be a first. “What am I saying, of course you have. I’m beautiful.”

“We kind of need to get in there,” I tell her. Not that she listens.

“Oh my, that jacket is fetching.” I turn to everyone, giving them my best I-told-you-so gesture regarding leather jackets, with the subliminal message that we probably could have avoided all this mess if they’d just let me get one when I first brought it up. There are a lot of eye rolls in return, except for Valiant who nods in agreement. And Panik, who really doesn’t care. “I bet you’d look even better with nothing on.” She winks at me.

“Obviously I do, but we have some really important work to do in the cabin.”

Jaele sighs. “Work? Guarding this stupid cabin is sprite work. But they tricked me into doing it.”

“That’s great but—”

“It wasn’t even a fair bet,” she still isn’t listening to me at all. “How could I go a whole day without showing off my body when those filthy sprites kept bringing strangers to the river to admire it? And do you know how long a day lasts in Faerie? Almost forever. Stupid, ugly sprites.” Huh, that’s gives me an idea.

“I bet you could *really* piss those sprites off by letting us into the cabin.”

“Oh yes.” Now we’re getting somewhere! “But I can’t.” Or maybe not. “Those uppity little bugs would probably think I went off to the river to wash my nubile body. Terrible things can happen if the doors inside are ever opened. If I let that happen I'd never hear the end of it. And I hear more from those sprites than I care to already."

Screw it. I'm just opening the door. I grab the knob and am hit with a massive shock. I think I might actually say "yowww!" as I yank my hand away.

Jaela giggles. "Can't open it as long as I'm here."

I'm still rubbing my hand when Emma says, "There's a river nearby?" Odd non sequitur, but I'm sure Emma has a plan. Or she just likes making small talk. Either one is fine with me.

"Mmm-hmm. Just at the bottom of the little cliff back that way," Jaela points behind the cabin.

"A soak in the river sounds awfully nice," Emma continues. "I mean, if we can't get into the cabin, might as well relax for a while. I don't suppose you'd like to join us?"

Jaela perks up immediately. "Would you scrub my back and tell me how pert my breast are?"

"Absolutely," Lily says.

Jaela floats off in the direction of the river. "Well come on then. My breasts won't compliment themselves."

"Oh, uh," Emma stutters, "we...we'll meet you there. We need to, um, make sure our breasts are perky enough?"

"Naturally," Jaela says, shedding petals as she flutters away.

Once she's out of sight Emma says, "Okay let's go."

Then a frown spreads across Candy's face. "We're still not going to go play with the fairy?"

"No, of course not," Emma says.

Both Candy and Lily let out a sizable "Awwww".

"Hurry, before she figures it out," Emma says.

"I'm not touching that door again," I say.

Sera shoves me out of the way. "Man up," she says and opens

the door.

* * *

I take the lead back from Sera once we're inside. I remember this hallway quite well. It's long and hall like. Classic hallway. I get to the door at end of the hall and am about to open it when Emma stops me. "Are you sure we should do this?"

"I don't think I ever had a choice," I tell her, and open the door. As it swings in, I'm just able to see the other three doors inside the main room slam open before I'm hit hard by some invisible force, throwing me to the ground. I'm not alone in that, either. Everyone else is laid flat too. And then…

Nothing.

"What was that all about?" Lily wonders.

I shrug after getting to my feet. "End of the world."

I enter the room and head straight for the door to our left.

"How do you know which door?" Lily asks, but I don't answer. I just know.

The door to the left unsurprisingly leads to an identical hallway, which of course leads right outside to an identical forest. We all hold hands again and ZAAAAPP!!! the forest transforms into a wasteland of ash.

"What happened here?" Lily says, her voice hushed.

"Guess the fire got out of hand," I say just as softly for no reason.

"The shard is close," Panik says. "I can feel it."

"*Adventure* is close," Valiant says. "I can feel it."

"That's nice. But seriously, now what?" Sera asks.

"I—" I start and stop. Because out in the distance I can see the cliff Jaela was talking about. And there is someone sitting at the cliff's edge. "No way." I almost laugh. Then everyone else notices too.

"I refuse to believe it," Sera says But I shush her.

I motion for everyone to follow me and they do. We aren't exactly the quietest group, trampling through a bunch of charred forest, but the figure at the cliff must be lost in their own thoughts because they don't make a single move. As we close in, I very clearly hear my own voice say, "A storm must be coming."

I stop a few feet short of Victor3 and say, "I hope that means everyone is going to start calling me The Hurricane."

Victor3 springs to his feet, turning to face me, his back now against the cliff. He stares at me long and hard, as if he's searching for something to say. Then he finally speaks. "Both of you need to buckle down."

I look around, my confusion nearly to the point of palpability. "Both?"

But it's like he doesn't even hear me. "This is a very serious situation and we don't have time for games! Games are for kids and we are adults so we don't play games!"

Then it gets even weirder as Lily walks to my left and yells, "It's not a game!" That alone doesn't make much sense, but she follows it with, "I think...I think I'm possessed by some sort of sex demon...wait what the fuck did I just say?"

She's looking at me, and I actually think I might kind of sort of know what's going on. But when I go to explain all I say is, "What hot piece of ass?"

"Emma," Lily says.

"What?" Emma says.

"Fascinating," Panik says. "These woods appear to be haunted by a particularly potent piece of code from this time cycle."

"What?" Everyone but Lily and I say.

"Time is trying to isolate the foreign Abstraction. It's locked on to this code. I've never seen anything like it. Embrace it, Lily."

I can tell it's the last thing Lily wants to do, but she listens to Panik. "She got impaled by a tree branch a-and it made me do things to her."

Emma moans. "Oh god, so that did happen."

Lily's voice turns raspy and vicious. "Give it a rest pussy! A hole's a hole's a hole's a hole, if you know..." Lily trails off and shakes her head, "Nope, not doing this anymore," and she bolts from our little Victor triangle. "What is wrong with you, bro?"

"It wasn't me," I manage to say. "I mean, it was, but...you know what I mean?"

"I don't know what any of that means," says Victor3, "but it is not at all suitable to this very serious situation. I'm serious guys, let's get serious or I'll have to do to you like I did to the others."

"You did something to the others too?" I say against my will. I know very well what he did, but he's going to explain it again anyway.

"They kept falling asleep. I told them not to sleep..." and blah blah blah. I stop listening. If I have to relive this, I refuse to give it any of my attention. Especially considering how much Victor3 loves the sound of his own voice.

Eventually I say, "Um." Then there is silence.

"What's happened?" Valiant asks.

"I think they're waiting for the absent 3rd Victor," Panik says, looking to Lily.

Lily shakes her head. "I'm not going back in there."

I want to tell them to just attack Victor3. For the life of me I can't figure why they haven't. Instead all that happens is Candy raising her hand squealing, "Ooo, I want to play!" Before Emma can object, she runs to the spot formally occupied by Lily. "Yeah," she says. Tears forming in her eyes just so she can wipe them away, "Even with me being possessed by a sex demon my Roboracle didn't get stabbed." Candy's voice lowers closer to Emma's octave and there's a bite to it. "Oh I'll stab him! I'll stab you all! With my—Shut up!—I mean to say I'll violate you all!—SHUT UP!—Sexually!" That breaks whatever trance Candy was in as she gasps. "Victor!"

I'd protest, but I can't seem to break out of whatever this is. The longer it goes on the more stuck I become. I guess I'm going to be forced to relive this exactly as it played out. Except…something is off. Candy and Emma are to my left and Victor3 is right in front of me, but when this first happened it was Victor3 who was to my left. I feel the moment's hold on me loosen. And I see Victor3 inches away from the cliff's edge. Jaela did say it was a little cliff, right? Fuck it, no time to think about it. I bulrush myself before the time cycle can take hold again and send us both over the edge.

* * *

And then we fall.

And fall.

And fall some more.

Little cliff my ass! And where's this river? All I see is pavement, which seems pretty out of place. Ah, what's it matter, I'm only seconds away from splatting all over the place. At least I'm taking me with me. I close my eyes and wait for the end to come, realizing I've blown it once again. That's when I stop falling. Death is a lot less painful than I imagined. I open my eyes to a familiar face. "Entheus?" What the ^*%$?

"It's nice to see you again, my friend, but you really must stop falling from the sky like this," Entheus says. I look to my left and see Lucky with Victor3 in her arms. We're all floating above the Steel Canyon of Anexia. At least that explains the pavement. I probably should have noticed all the buildings earlier, but when you're staring death in the face some details elude you.

Lucky smiles when she catches me staring. She looks a lot better now that she's not dead. "It's a good thing The Roboracle told us to do a flyby or you two would have been street art," she says.

Victor3 looks up at the girl who saved his life and tells her, "Your costume is ridiculous. No one will ever take you seriously."

"You're one rude fella, aren't you?" Lucky says as she and Entheus make a smooth landing, giving us our feet back. "Hey, I'm not sure which one of you is which, but could one of you tell that Jimmy guy thanks. I hear he was a real pal while I was sick—" But I don't get to hear the rest of what she says, because Victor3 breaks into a sprint the first chance he gets. I dive to grab him, catching his ankle. And we fall…into a pile of metal and debris. I search for Entheus or Lucky, but they're gone. Anexia is gone. Replaced by some sort of elephant graveyard. Except instead of elephant bones it's a pile of robot parts. The only movement I see is one lone robot sweeping at the mountain of wreckage. Trying to regain my footing, Victor3 tackles me and we…splash? The debris has been replaced by a picturesque lake and I'm struggling to tread water, having inhaled far too much of it. When I finally gather myself, there's a multitude of tiny naked girls buzzing about my face. Catching my breath I say, "Ladies." That's all I can manage before I see Victor3 swimming away from me. I chase after him, dragging us both under as I catch him. He's fighting for the surface when something grabs us both a pull us from the lake. Only the lake is gone. It's a river now. And the something that grabbed us is a grinning Captain Valiant.

"Where the hell did you go?" Emma is almost yelling.

"No…idea," I say through heavy breaths. "But I caught him."

Victor3 is sitting in the middle of the river. Staring up at the sky, he laughs. "You're too late."

We all look up. It's the middle of the day, but the moon is out. Except it's not the moon at all. It's another Earth.

"We're nearing terminal Uncertainty," Panik says.

Then something even more unlikely happens. Someone says, "Looks like we're just in time for *adventure.*" And it's not Captain Valiant.

It's his shadow.

And it's not alone.

* * *

So here we are all are, everyone face to face with their newly corporeal shadow. Except… "Hey, where's my shadow," I complain. "Seriously, why don't I get one?" Then I look to Victor3 who is smiling like a complete douchebag and I get it. "Oh, that's disappointing."

That's when all hell breaks loose. Shadow vs. self. This is probably some psychologist's wet dream. I overhear Captain Valiant's shadow gloating. "Defeating the great Captain Valiant, this will make a *valiant* story for my next book."

"Remind me to look for it," Valiant responds. "In the fiction section." He punctuates it with a mean left hook. Man, he's cool.

I'm so distracted admiring the Captain that I almost get the drop on me. But I know myself pretty well and manage to dodge Victor3's charge. Looks like it's time we had a proper fight.

Being that we're the same person, I expect us to struggle to land a single punch, I mean we should know what the other is planning on doing, right? It's the complete opposite, as we both nail each other with right hooks. The shadow chaos vanishes and it replaced with a new kind of crazy. A stadium of cheering pandas.

"WELCOME TO PANDAMONIUM!" a voice booms. "WHERE TWO PANDAS ENTER BUT ONLY ONE MAY LEAVE!" The cheers build to a roar. And then one of the pandas points at us. Followed by another. And another.

The booming voice returns. "IT SEEMS WE HAVE VISITORS!" I smile and wave. "A BONUS WARM UP! THE FIRST PANDA TO DELIVER ME THEIR HEARTS WILL BE GRANTED THEIR VERY OWN BAMBOO TREE!"

"Oh shit," I say. Victor3's attention is still occupied by the horde of murderous pandas closing in on us. It's a good opening. I sure hope this works. I tackle myself and punch me.

The pandas disappear and we're in a desert.

Boring!

I punch again.

We're floating on a cloud. A man sitting on a throne stands and bellows, "Who dares disturb the mighty Zeus?"

"Awesome," I say, but it's still not where I need to be so another punch it is.

I see a school of…octosharks?

Punch!

A giant statue of Donna?

"I AM THE ROBORACLE."

No!

Punch!

Dino-pirates.

Punch!

A teenage girl writhes on a lawn tearing at her skin screaming "Run!"

Can do.

Punch!

A world where everything is inside out.

Gross.

Punch!

I don't know how many times I punch myself before we finally find ourselves back at the river. Everyone is still battling their shadows. The second Earth looks a little bigger, but I don't think we were gone long.

I push away from Victor3. "Anyone want to switch? Every time we hit each other we end up somewhere weird."

Emma and Candy kick Shadow Candy. "Sure thing, sweetie. Just keep this bitch occupied."

"Emma, language!" Candy and her shadow say together.

"Got it," I say, and Emma and I switch places, putting me face to face with Shadow Candy.

She shuffles her feet, bites her lip and says, "Hi, Victor."

"Uh, hey. I guess we have to fight now."

"Yeah," she pouts. "Or…we could make out?"

"Um," I say. "Maybe…maybe if you help fight the other shadows?"

"Really?! Kay!" Without another word, Candy's shadow skips off, viciously attacking Lily's shadow, tearing at its throat.

"Hey, I could use some help over here," Sera yells. She's a little way down the river, her shadow on top of her as she struggles beneath. It's one of the top 3 most erotic things I've ever seen. "Hello!"

"Oh, sorry," I say rushing over to her. "I was imagining you naked." Sera and her shadow give me the finger. "What do you want me to do?"

"Get her off me!"

"But you're half star?"

"So?"

"So, I've seen you do crazy light shows. Shadows don't like light, right?"

"Good point," Sera start to glow. "Everyone might want to cover their eyes!" I turn away from Sera, noticing for the first time that we're in a little canyon of sorts, all of us between Sera and the canyon walls. Something occurs to me then, but it's too late. The world goes white momentarily. Behind me Sera is saying, "Hey, it worked!" Only I can't celebrate because I'm still looking at the canyon walls, where everyone's shadows—except for Sera's and mine—are now a whole hell of a lot bigger.

* * *

"Nice going, Sera!" I yell.

"It was your idea!" she yells back. Her sword drawn as we both dodge attacks from Shadow Valiant.

"Since when do you listen to my ideas?"

"Shut up!"

Things aren't looking good for our merry band of adventurers, that's for sure. Candy's shadow continues to fight on our side until Panik's shadow starts kissing all over her. Their PDA quickly gets out of hand. It's distracting. I have no idea how Emma, Candy, Lily, and Panik are faring because Sera, Valiant, and I are cornered by Valiant's giant shadow. I attempt to dodge him again, but this time I'm too slow. He scoops me up and chuckles. Yep, I'm doomed. But in a series of seriously unlikely events, maybe I should have expect another, because that's just what I get as, out of nowhere, Frosty swoops down off the cliff with Chalk on his back. Nothing about any of this makes sense, but I'll take it. Frosty freezes the shadow's face and I tumble to the ground.

Frosty lands next to me and I pat his head. "What are you doing here?"

SAVING YOUR ASS Chalk's face reads.

"But—"

NERISSA KNEW I WANTED 2 HELP

"But—"

"An' she asked me ta 'elp 'im 'elp you," Chessy flutters down from the cliff top. "An' when da queen calls on yeh, yeh answer."

"Whatever," I say. "Thanks."

Unfortunately things don't get easier. Because why would they. No, instead Chalk and Frosty's shadows come to life. Of course they do. I see the shadow dragon gear up to unleash his dragon breath all over the place. He inhales so deeply I can feel the air shift. A warm wind pushed at my back, getting hotter by the seconds. I don't think this guy breathes pretty little snowflakes like Frosty. He opens his mouth and proves me right as the air ignites in a ferocious torrent. I just have time enough to get out of the way. Sera isn't so lucky. The fire doesn't hurt her, but it does destroy a good portion of her clothes.

"Seriously," Sera says. She swipes at the dragon with the sword and the dragon takes flight. Frosty follows. The battle between the dragons stops everyone, and their shadows, in their tracks. The air fills with fire and ice. The resulting steam drifts to the canyon floor, blanketing us in fog. The shadows fade as the fog thickens. Before too long the fog is so dense I can hardly see more than a foot in front of me. Sera is by my side, but I can't see anyone else.

"Give me your jacket," Sera says.

"What?"

"Come on, I'm half naked here. Don't be an asshole about this. It's not like you even liked Jimmy."

"But I do like this jacket," I say, handing it to her. Sera doesn't have to say anything for me to know she's pissed. "Come on, you served that one up so nicely."

"Such a dick," she mutters and heads deeper into the fog.

I do my best to follow. "When are you going to let this go?"

She ignores me.

"So I ragged on the guy. Someone had to."

"Really? Someone had to treat him like crap even though he idolized him for some stupid reason?!"

"Well, yeah."

"You're unbelievable."

"Thanks, but back to Jimmy. You do realize that he could build incredibly cool shit, raise his own personal army of the dead, and he had a super-hot girlfriend, right? Do you know what he would have been like without someone to keep his ego in check?"

"You, probably," Sera says without looking at me.

"Yeah, me. Exactly. And I think these last few weeks have shown us what happens when there's too many of me?"

Sera shakes her head. "You're still an asshole, you know, but—" I never get to find out what that but might be because Victor3 appears out of the mist and snatches Sera. She drops her sword, but the fog is so dense I can't find it.

"Looks like you get to watch another friend die before it all ends," he says while giving Sera a one-handed pat down. "And what's this?" He reaches into my jacket pocket and retrieves the unicorn horn. "Unconventional, but it'll do."

I don't have time to do anything other than run straight at him.

In retrospect, it's a terrible plan. Hell, in current-o-spect, it's pretty bad. But I'm not exactly known for my planning skills. I feel a brief pressure on my chest as the unicorn horn pierces my heart. And that's it. I'm dead. It's such a simple thing. Doesn't even hurt. I wait for my life to flash before my eyes, or something equally cliché. I wait for my body to drop to the ground. I wait for anything to happen. But the only thing I see before my eyes is a unicorn horn jutting out of my chest. And I'm still standing. I'm still breathing. I touch the horn tentatively. Victor3 and Sera haven't moved a muscle. Then I pull it out and drop to my knees. Victor3 smiles.

But just like our first sexual encounter, that smile is premature. I feel my heart repair itself. "Huh, I guess unicorn horns do heal anything." And I jam the horn into Victor3's foot, anchoring him to the ground like a tent. He screams and drops to one knee. Sera pushes away and somehow finds the sword, holding the point to Victor3's throat.

"Go ahead," he tells her. "You're already too late. I'll never help you stop it." And almost as an after-thought. "I finally did it. I'm going to save everyone."

Panik emerges from the fog, seemingly unscathed from the battle. "Luckily we don't need your cooperation. Just your blood. Lots of it. Now hand over the shard."

He looks to me for some reason. "What's she talking about?"

"I know you have it." Panik gives him as thorough a frisking as she can. "Where is it?"

Victor3's only response is to laugh in her face. And I'm hit with a sudden, searing pain in my left leg. It's so intense I lose my balance again.

"What's wrong?" Panik asks.

"I, um," I try to clear my thoughts. "Try his left leg."

Panik gives me a curious glance before pulling out another one of her shards and slicing open Victor3's pants to reveal a nasty scar. She doesn't hesitate. She plunges her rock deep into Victor3's scar. His screams are even worse than when I tethered him to the ground. Panik shoves her hand into the new wound and comes out with a new shard.

"Let's prepare for the ritual," Panik tells us.

"Victor!" Emma calls out from somewhere in the mist. "Please tell me all that screaming is the other you?"

"He's fine," Sera calls back. Then she turns to me. "The unicorn horn…that's where you ran off to when Jimmy…that's where you went?"

"I thought maybe…I don't know. Doesn't matter. I was too late."

"Oh," Sera says. "Um, I'm gonna go find the others, lead them over here."

I nod as she goes and then sit down in front of Victor3. He grabs my arm. "Don't do this. We failed to save the world once. But we have a chance to reset everything. We can be heroes."

I don't say anything. Maybe because part of me thinks he's right, but I could never tell him that. He's fucking crazy. I see a couple of figures approaching in the fog. I think one is Captain Valiant.

"Over here, Captain," I say.

"Ah, Victor, there you are." But that's not Captain Valiant's voice. "Time to die." The Dredd Space Pirate Robots emerges from the mist and shoots me right in the face. Well, he shoots Victor3 in the face, anyway.

"I want to kill him too," says the other figure with him.

Son of a bitch. "Ickby?" I wonder. "How many times am I

gonna have to kill you?"

He doesn't pay me any mind, however, as he pulls out some weapon and zaps Victor3's corpse. Completely incinerating it.

* * *

"What the fuck, Ickby!" I'm insanely pissed off right now and kind of freaking the fuck out.

"Two for one? Excellent," Ickby says, pointing his stupid vaporizer at me and pulling the trigger. Nothing happens. "Dratsticks! Only one charge. Of course there was only one charge. Don't know why I designed it that way. Maybe to give me something to fix later. Yes, that's make sense. Always thinking ahead. Kill the other one, Robots, so that I can dance on his corpse."

I sit there completely helpless. "What are you waiting for?"

"I only owed you a single death," the pirate says. "That debt is paid. A pleasure to see you, by the way."

Sera chooses that moment to return with everyone else. "Where'd they come from? And where's the other Victor?"

"I have no idea to the first question," I say, "but Ickby incinerated the other me."

Sera goes jet-black. "What the fuck, Ickby?"

"The what of the fuck is simple," Ickby says and points to me. "Hate him."

"Well, yeah but…" Sera runs out of words and leg strength as she plops down beside me. "…fuck."

"As to the where we came from," Robots says, "I can answer that."

"Sure, why not," I mumble. "It's not like space/time is about to implode or anything."

Robots doesn't hear me, though. "As you all must know, I owed Victor a bit of revenge after our last meeting. I was content playing the slow game, but imagine my surprise when one of my robot's tracking signals was suddenly activated." Robots reaches around his back and produces the recognizably mowhawked head of The Robot With No Name.

"Hello sirs," No Name's detached head says.

"Naturally, I thought it a trap. Why would a long deactivated signal suddenly burst into life again?"

"Is this Jimmy's fault?" I ask no one in particular.

No Name answers anyway. "No, sir, I believe it was The Roboracle who reactivated my signal when he was dismantling me."

That bastard set me up…I hate robots so much.

"But eventually I had to investigate," the pirate continues. "When it became clear that your ship had been abandoned, I went to retrieve my old friend to see if he knew of your whereabouts."

"I did not know," No Name says, as if we all didn't know that.

"But it was my lucky day," Robots says, "because lo and behold, Dr. Ickby and the Colossal Unity appeared."

"But we're not even in the same universe," I say, completely exacerbated with this story.

"The Colossal Unity goes where it needs to go," Ickby says. "I've told you that. You never learn. Listen better. Hate you."

Sera stands back up. "Dr. Ickby, how many of those clone bodies do you have?"

"Enough. Always enough. Don't be stupid."

"Do you think your mind can download across universes?"

"Interesting postulation. Never tried."

"Try now," Sera says. And in one swift motion she cuts his head off.

Ickby's head half-bounces towards the Dread Space Pirate Robots. He kicks it aside. "My business here is complete," he says. "Best of luck with whatever your little escapade here is about. Until we meet again." With a smile he heads back towards wherever he came. No one bothers to stop him. What's the point. After a few yards he tosses No Name's head over his shoulder.

"Goodbye Mr. Pirate," No Name says. "It was a pleasure to see you again."

Sera looks back to the sky. Then she offers me her hand. "Looks like we're up."

* * *

"What are you talking about?" Emma asks.

"Panik can explain it better than I can," Sera says.

Panik doesn't waste a second. "The ritual that unglued the Victors and Lily from dimensional gravity was a blood ritual. It can be fixed with another. Blood for blood. Simple and effective. But the ritual also requires a certain amount of energy. The amount of which is exponentially inverse to the amount of blood available. We had planned to bleed the other Victor dry, thus requiring only the tiniest sources of energy. A fire may have sufficed. But that's no longer an option.

"I approached Victor and Sera with a secondary course of action. Should we fail to catch the other Victor in time, or should his blood be unavailable for whatever reason, we could use Victor's blood. The conundrum arises in that the amount of blood he can offer without dying requires a much larger energy source."

"That'd be me," Sera says. "Like always."

"I blame the time cycles," I say.

"Okay," Emma says, "that sounds reasonable. It's not like it'll kill them." Emma looks at me, but I can't meet her eyes. And that's when she knows it's not that simple.

"Hopefully," Panik says, "but in any case, Victor and Sera will be forced to enter the dimensional bleed. Assuming they survive, there's no telling where they might end up."

Emma and Candy shake their head. "No."

"We're kind of out of options, Em," Sera says.

"Wait," Lily says. "Maybe I can go. Sera would probably prefer hanging out with me anyway."

"Lily, what are you talking about?" I ask.

"It's a blood thing. Our blood has to be similar. That's why I got dragged into this, right? Because we're twins."

"Allegedly, Lily," I say.

"Victor, you know as well as I do that's bullshit."

I grab my sister's shoulders and look her square in the eye. "That's just not a chance I'm willing to take."

For a second or two, I'm sure Lily is about to cry, but she only smiles and nods instead. I turn to Emma. She's refusing to look at me.

"Em," I try.

"Don't," is all she says.

I look to the sky now that the fog has started to clear. The other Earth, our Earth, is larger than ever. It's clear we don't have much time. But I won't leave things like this. "Em, I know this is a crappy thing. Especially after last night and what you said, but I have to do this. I wish I could…" I stop. Nothing else I say is going to make a difference. "I just have to." I take out my wallet and the note inside it. I give it to Emma.

Emma looks at it in disbelief. "This…this is the note I…why do you still have this?"

"Who could say. Keep it safe for me, okay?"

And then Chalk is hugging my leg. His face says I'LL COME 2.

"And risk the wrath of a queen? Not a chance little buddy. You get back to her. Both of you." I give Frosty a pat.

Valiant salutes me. "It's been a hell of an *adventure* hasn't it." I nod. "You two take care of each other."

"You too, sir," I say.

"We should get on with this," Sera says.

"Wait," it's Candy who stops us. "Victor…I'm gonna miss you. I'd give you a kiss for good luck but—"

Emma cuts her short. "Fuck it." And the two of them kiss the holy bejesus out of me.

Sera pulls me away. "Let's go, Casanova, before the princess rips your clothes off."

"Don't you want to say goodbye to anyone?" I ask.

Sera turns back to the group. "Later, guys." Then she looks me dead in the face and says, "That's how a man does it." And she continues leading me away from the group. But she turns back one more time and pauses before finally breaking away from me to go embrace Emma. They don't say anything, they just hug. Then she shakes everyone else's hand, pets Frosty, high fives Chalk, and stops right in front of Captain Valiant. He salutes her as he did me. She doesn't return it, though. She hugs him instead. She gives Gumdrop a final nuzzle before coming back to me.

"Don't say a word," she says. And I don't. I just keep looking at Emma and Candy.

I'm still looking when Emma cries out, "I'll find you. Both of you."

I can hear the hurt in her voice. And the hope. So I do the only thing I can for her right now. I lie. "I know."

I look away and let Sera lead me as far away as she needs to. She's already sporting a soft glow that deepens with each step. I'm not paying much attention to where I'm walking. Mostly I'm doing my best not to look back. I just keep my gaze forward. And I end up tripping on No Name's head. Stupid robot ruined my heroic walk. I kick No Name out of the way and he says, "Excuse me, Lieutenant and sir, but I couldn't help overhearing of your impending and possibly fatal quest. Would it be a bother if I joined you? I could be quite useful if you manage not to survive."

I want to object, but Sera's already picking him up and saying, "If we manage to survive, it would be nice to have someone I can actually talk to."

I sigh. No point in fighting her on this. "And I guess if there's a chance we might all die, it'd be nice to know I took you with me."

"Oh joy! You won't even know I'm here." But that's a lie. I already do know.

"Can you hold him?" Sera asks.

"No," I say.

"Then take the sword for a minute," she says. That seems fine, so I reach for it and Sera quickly slices my hand open.

"What the hell was that for?!"

"Lots of things. But we need your blood."

"You could have just told me that."

"You would have been a pussy about it. Don't clot to fast or I'll have to do it again.

I want to look back to Emma and everyone for some support on this outrage, but I know I can't. I know if I do I'll never take another step forward.

Instead I concentrate on Sera. And the way she glows. And

the way my hand throbs. And not the way my heart aches. “Being a hero blows,” is all I say.

Sera looks at me with the hint of something that might almost be a smile. “Tell me about it.” The light of her intensifies, building a nearly unbearable coolness around us. My body relaxes.

“Hey Sera?”

“Yeah?”

“You know how Jimmy liked to take notes in that book?”

“Sure,” she says. Her body illuminating to make the day even brighter. I can feel my pulse pounding through my hand. I feel it mix with Sera’s. There’s no pain anymore. “He kept on doing it even at the end.” She smiles at the memory. And her light gets sharper.

“And you know that thing you didn’t want him to tell me?”

“What thing?”

“You know.”

“No I…” She pauses and shakes her head. “No. There’s no way he spent some of his last moments writing that to you.”

My only answer is an ever widening smile.

The world starts to vibrate, Sera’s glow singing a silent melody. Her light making us light. We’re almost floating.

She looks at me one last time, shining so forcefully it’s impossible to look away. I’m sure all she sees is my grin.

“Goddamn it, Jimmy,” she whispers.

And everything explodes.

Epilogue

In a series of increasingly unfathomable events, you are the only thing that's made sense

I love you

Always.

www.ingramcontent.com/pod-product-compliance
Lightning Source LLC
Chambersburg PA
CBHW051543250626
47157CB00001B/158

* 9 7 8 0 9 8 2 7 9 3 0 2 2 *